DOCTOR REYNARD'S EXPERIMENT

Robert Black

First published in Great Britain in 1998 by
Idol
an imprint of Virgin Publishing Ltd
332 Ladbroke Grove
London W10 5AH

ISBN 0 352 33252 2

Cover photograph by Colin Clarke Photography

Typeset by SetSystems Ltd, Saffron Walden, Essex
Printed and bound in Great Britain by
Cox & Wyman Ltd, Reading, Berks

Thanks to the Victoria and Albert Museum,
South Kensington, and to Clone Zone,
Old Compton Street, for their invaluable assistance.

Special thanks to Nicholas Holdsworth, Bryan O'Byrne
and Marcus Burrows.

SAFER SEX GUIDELINES

These books are sexual fantasies – in real life, everyone needs to think about safe sex.

While there have been major advances in the drug treatments for people with HIV and AIDS, there is still no cure for AIDS or a vaccine against HIV. Safe sex is still the only way of being sure of avoiding HIV sexually.

HIV can only be transmitted through blood, come and vaginal fluids (but no other body fluids) – passing from one person (with HIV) into another person's bloodstream. It cannot get through healthy, undamaged skin. The only real risk of HIV is through anal sex without a condom – this accounts for almost all HIV transmissions between men.

Being Safe:
Even if you don't come inside someone, there is still a risk to both partners from blood (tiny cuts in the arse) and pre-come. Using strong condoms and water-based lubricant greatly reduces the risk of HIV. However, condoms can break or slip off, so:

* Make sure that condoms are stored away from hot or damp places.
* Check the expiry date – condoms have a limited life.
* Gently squeeze the air out of the tip.
* Check the condom is put on the right way up and unroll it down the erect cock.
* Use plenty of water-based lubricant (lube), up the arse and on the condom.
* While fucking, check occasionally to see the condom is still in one piece (you could also add more lube).
* When you withdraw, hold the condom tight to your cock as you pull out.

* Never re-use a condom or use the same condom with more than one person.
* If you're not used to condoms you might practise putting them on.
* Sex toys like dildos and plugs are safe. But if you're sharing them use a new condom each time or wash the toys well.

For the safest sex, make sure you use the strongest condoms, such as Durex Ultra Strong, Mates Super Strong, HT Specials and Rubberstuffers packs. Condoms are free in many STD (Sexually Transmitted Disease) clinics (sometimes called GUM clinics) and from many gay bars. It's also essential to use lots of water-based lube such as KY, Wet Stuff, Slik or Liquid Silk. Never use come as a lubricant.

Oral Sex:
Compared with fucking, sucking someone's cock is far safer. Swallowing come does not necessarily mean that HIV gets absorbed into the bloodstream. While a tiny fraction of cases of HIV infection have been linked to sucking, we know the risk is minimal. But certain factors increase the risk:
* Letting someone come in your mouth
* Throat infections such as gonorrhoea
* If you have cuts, sores or infections in your mouth and throat

So what is safe?
There are so many things you can do which are absolutely safe: wanking each other; rubbing your cocks against one another; kissing, sucking and licking all over the body; rimming – to name but a few.

If you're finding safe sex difficult, call a helpline or speak to someone you feel you can trust for support. The Terrence Higgins Trust Helpline, which is open from noon to 10pm every day, can be reached on 0171 242 1010.

Or, if you're in the United States, you can ring the Center for Disease Control toll free on 1 800 458 5231.

Book One

9th September, 1884

It really is remarkable: Spearman has opened up a whole new world for me. I feel as if a blindfold has been lifted from my eyes. He took me, as he has been threatening to do for some months now, to one of his molly-houses, somewhere on the northern edge of Bloomsbury. The exterior of the building was deceptively small and unassuming, and in need of some repair; one might have taken it for the dwelling of a professional man of no more than average means with wife and children and perhaps two servants – no more than two, assuredly.

Spearman knocked, and a spy-hole slid open, startling me somewhat. A moment later I could hear bolts being drawn back, and we were admitted. A servant – a little negro lad of perhaps seven or eight years – took our coats and led us along a narrow passage into a very large, comfortable room, lit only very dimly. A small, elegant woman in late middle age, dressed as if for the opera, stood at the entrance to the room. She shook my hand, introducing herself as Mrs Warren. She addressed Spearman as 'Baron', although he does not in point of fact hold that rank, and he introduced me as 'Mister Fox', which no doubt appealed to his devious sense of humour. We were invited to sit and make ourselves comfortable. The house was much larger on the inside than the impression it gave from the street. The room, which seemed to serve as a central atrium, with many doors and passages leading from it, was decorated in a deep blood red.

As my eyes grew accustomed to the dim light, I confess I stepped back in some confusion: a sight greeted my eyes that I'm sure hasn't been seen since the days of Sodom and Gomorrah. Darkly, redly, forms swam out of the shadows. Human bodies, young, male and lithe, reclined on the many divans which littered the room; some clothed, some only partly so, some unashamedly naked as if in the Garden of Eden.

Twice in the above passage I have resorted to biblical metaphor. I find this strange, given my atheistic instincts. I can only infer that I am trying to cloak my own sense of guilt and impropriety in a facade of holy respectability. And yet this secret world, both wonderful and terrible, does indeed seem almost biblical in its excesses. And in accompanying Spearman, it was my intention to witness, not judge.

But I must for the moment resist further digression. It is a hard thing to do, but my task is to lay out the facts of last night's encounter as fully and plainly as I may. Spearman led me into a side room, similarly furnished, and immediately a young man entered. He was wearing the uniform – well, the jacket – of a young hotel porter: pale blue with military cross-braiding down the front, like a little hussar. Apart from this jacket, open at the front to reveal a pale, slender chest, he was naked. He was tumescent, and his engorged glans penis danced between the jacket's stiff folds. I should say his prick, for I am resolved, whilst never abandoning my scientific objectivity, to make my report in a manner which accurately reflects my thoughts and sensations of the time, and thus I must not cloak this memoir in the cold, prim language of the surgery. In truth, glans penis bore no resemblance to the phrase which entered my mind at the time.

The lower edges of the jacket brushed and flapped around the lad's long, slightly curved prick. His foreskin was tight and drawn back and, as the jacket's hard braid grazed against the swollen purple head, the whole prick twitched and danced.

I confess, to my shame, I found myself quite unaroused, and, sitting myself in an armchair, I studied the boy with something very close to my usual doctor's composure and detachment. I meticulously noted in my mind the pale smoothness of his skin and the sheaves of golden hair that hung, too long to be respectable, around his neck and face. His eyes were green, his nose slightly retroussé. Apart from his teeth, of which several were missing (something all too common at his age among this city's poor), he looked to be robust and in good health. I took him to be about eighteen.

He clamped his mouth against Spearman's and pressed his hard prick against his leg. Spearman reclined across the divan and the boy blindly but deftly began opening his fly-buttons.

A second, smaller young man entered and sat on the other side of Spearman. Dark haired with pale skin, he had a bewitching smile and twinkling black eyes. He was quite naked. His prick grew large as I watched.

Spearman sprawled on the couch, his shirt open and his legs apart. The two naked young men writhed and rubbed themselves against him, gently tugging his clothes away, piece by piece. It was like watching fish effortlessly and gracefully stripping a bone of meat. His shirt, his trousers, his undergarments. I watched entranced until Spearman too was quite naked. Then I felt a hot breath on my neck, and from behind me a hand slid across my thigh. It lingered for a moment before moving upward, its fingers probing the underside of my bollocks. I felt my jacket being peeled from my shoulders, and altered my position to allow its removal. A second hand was moving down my shirt front, opening the buttons. I craned my neck to see the fellow at my back. He was tall and muscular, about the same age as his fellows, with cropped brown hair, a handsome, somewhat square face and large brown eyes.

I noticed Spearman staring at me intently as the two lads ran their lips and tongues across his hard, swarthy body, and I flinched and attempted to draw my shirt about me. Seemingly aware of my sudden discomfort, my lad drew me by the hand to my feet and led me through a door into an adjoining room dominated by a large bed. He moved to close the door behind us, but an abrupt 'No!' from Spearman stopped him. Gently but firmly – for he was strong – he propelled me down on to the bed. I offered no further resistance as he removed my clothes, his thickly engorged prick nudging against me as he did so. I felt myself becoming erect as my clothes fell to the floor. I lay naked upon my back staring up at him, my cock dancing above my belly. He came down on top of me and his lips engaged mine before he drove his salty tongue forward between my teeth. The realisation struck me that, for all my surgical experience and for all my intimate knowledge of the human body, both externally and internally, to this situation I was a complete neophyte. I had never before seen a man in a state of sexual arousal, nor had I ever tasted another man's mouth.

He withdrew his tongue and moved his face down my body, nipping at my skin with his teeth, biting hard on my nipples, tugging with his teeth at the hair of my chest, his torso rubbing against my prick. Somewhat self-consciously I began bucking upward with my hips, pushing my cock against his hard abdominal muscles.

Through the open door my eye caught Spearman's. He was on all fours on the floor, covering the blond boy as a dog mounts a bitch, pumping his long cock in and out of the boy's anus. The dark-haired boy was on his knees behind Spearman, his face pressed to my friend's buttock crack, his tongue doubtless seeking the sphincter within. Spearman was staring, and smiling.

It took me some time to spend myself, the unfamiliar sensation of a stranger bringing me to orgasm being utterly arousing and yet confusing for my prick. I saw Spearman's face tighten, his lips drawn back over his teeth, and the thrusting of his pelvis become faster and harder as he approached orgasm. The slap of his thighs against the boy's buttocks were loud. His cock slipped from the boy's arse and thrust forward up his buttock crease and on to his back, where it began pumping its pearly fluid over the boy's pale skin.

When I eventually came, it was an experience more

intense than any other I can recall, exhilarating and exhausting. The boy continued to caress me, moving again towards my prick, but I gently moved his hand away. After a while he rose from the bed and crossed to the open door. Spearman was fucking the dark-haired boy, who lay on his back with his legs spread over Spearman's shoulders. My boy beckoned to his blond colleague. The two kissed and sank to the floor, where they lay in the doorway and began slowly, sensuously, sucking on one another's cocks, fingers – first one, then two, then three – probing deep into one another's arseholes, squirming with pleasure.

My cock was hard again, my mind awash with conflicting emotions. I masturbated as I watched, coming more quickly the second time under the familiar rhythm of my own hand.

Spearman had to support me as we left Mrs Warren's house. Some years ago, I took a little laudanum with Spearman. I felt now as I had felt then, my senses overwhelmed so that I behaved as a drunken man. I had perhaps been a timid initiate – for I had seen more than I had done – but even before we arrived back at the house I had determined to elicit from Spearman the promise of more night-time expeditions. I wanted to know all of the sensations – the tastes, the smells – of male bodies in the most intimate congress.

One

———

Autumn had descended early on London, the trees that lined the broad avenue outside the front door already shedding their leaves. They stood stark and skeletal in the early-morning mist, ghost fingers vanishing into the damp grey of the early dawn. The railings which separated the house from the street became a barrier of mist as they receded up the street.

Squatting on the broad front step, Walter shivered and hugged his arms to his chest. The Sunday morning was still and bitter. The rains of the last few days had washed the air clear and cold. Gone was the cloying smog which had sat over Kensington – and, for all Walter knew, over the entire world – for days, fuelled by sea-coal and the seasonal burnings of dead vegetation which were taking place in parks and private gardens every day now. The fires, and the smog, would be back almost immediately, Walter knew, but for the moment, in spite of the cold, he was enjoying the freshness of this quiet, lonely time when the city still slept.

He had polished the brass plate beside the door – *Dr Richard Reynard, LSA, MRCS* – and swept the step clean of leaves. Now he took his hard brush from the wooden brush box and, bracing himself against the wall, began work on the foot scraper. The bristles skated back and forth over the metal blade. Mud and leaf mulch bounced off Walter's leather apron and finely showered the step. Walter tutted. He'd have to see to that.

On his hands and knees on cold, damp stone, the morning's chill seemed to crawl up through his limbs. The brush slipped from his numb fingers and clattered to the concrete. He muttered the mildest of oaths, then raised his eyes guiltily heavenward for a moment.

As he reached for the brush he became aware of footsteps behind him. The metal tip of a cane flashed into view, knocking the brush over the edge of the steps and at the same time catching Walter hard on the knuckles. He pulled his stinging hand back with a cry and his eyes again shot upward. A man – a gentleman, perhaps foreign, dressed for the evening – towered over him, tall, gaunt and tanned, with an unruly shock of black hair worn too long over his collar. Beyond that single, contemptuous flick of the cane, the man seemed not to have acknowledged Walter's existence: he was talking to Walter's master, his voice the languid drawl of one who knows that, by his very station in life, he is not required to make any effort at all to be either personable or useful. The master now slipped past him and pushed his key into the heavy front door of the house, acknowledging the servant with the faintest drawing back of the lips before passing inside, his aristocratic friend in tow.

'. . . And you should reflect on the words of Mr and Mrs Adams in their inestimable work *The Complete Servant*. For the better dispatch of his own particular business, *it is indispensably necessary that the footman should rise early!*'

In the big kitchen, Philip was being lectured by Mr Brakes again. Through the door, Walter could see the white-haired old butler pacing around the long wooden table. Philip, the footman, reclined cheekily in a chair, his legs stretched out and crossed under the long wooden table, and yawned.

Old Brakes tutted in exasperation. 'It's a very poor example to be setting your junior, too. Walter shows a great deal more diligence and enterprise than you, Philip.' The butler's voice, tempered by years in service, registered disappointment and weariness rather than anger.

Tom, Dr Reynard's valet, was more acerbic. 'The Lord sees thy idleness,' he spat in a broad Yorkshire brogue. Tom was, if anything, even older than the butler, stooped and bald, and rarely left his chamber nowadays except to attend to the master in his rooms. He had been in the household longer than anybody – Mr Brakes included – and was held in a kind of awe by the community of servants. Most of Tom's below-stairs duties were divided between Walter and Philip. Walter didn't mind. In a way, he was relieved by Tom's customary absence: there was a scowling severity about the old man which unnerved him. 'The Lord sees into thy heart, Philip,' growled Tom, 'and he's keeping score of what he sees there.'

Philip ignored him. 'Walter's new,' he said to the butler. 'That's why he's so keen. You wait till Christmas. See if he's still up at five and not complaining after all that palaver.'

In the boot room Walter smiled. Through the open door he briefly caught Brakes's disapproving stare, and immediately attempted a more sombre expression as he turned back to the row of shoes he was cleaning. He felt warm again; the warmth of the kitchen permeated everywhere below stairs. The smell of baking bread filled the room, and he could hear Mrs Donaldson, the cook, over by the ovens, fussing loudly as Brakes scolded softly.

'I did not suggest that the master appoint an under-footman so that you might lie in bed until whatever time takes your fancy, Philip,' the old butler continued. He shook his head in his sharp, disapproving manner. 'But enough of this. It is nearly six o'clock. The master will be rising in an hour and practically nothing has been done. Philip, for heaven's sake will you go and prepare the breakfast parlour? Walter, leave the rest of the shoes for now. You go up, too. Prepare the fires and clean the lamps.'

And with another quick shake of his head the old butler turned his attention elsewhere.

'So there I am, my nightshirt pulled up . . . I've my eye to the peep-hole and Meg's down to her bloomers on the other side of it . . . So I'm flogging away at my old feller and who should walk in, bold as brass, but Mrs bleeding Donaldson.'

Walter blushed. Walter always blushed when Philip was in full flow. His one topic of conversation – outside the company of Mr Brakes – was sex, and his one pastime was trying to get it, or at least to see others having it. He had discovered a spy-hole between the cramped quarters he shared with Walter and the adjacent room, shared by Meg and Ruby, the two young Irish housemaids.

'Well, you can imagine . . .' He put down the cloth with which he was idly chasing dust around the breakfast-parlour table and smiled at the memory of the previous night. 'I sort of collapses into a heap on the bed, trying to cover myself up, and starts flannelling some rubbish or other, but of course the old dear hasn't even noticed nothing. She's flapping about a missing skillet and have I seen it and how she needs it first thing . . . And by the time she slings her hook Meg's all undressed and in bed and next thing you come through the door. Where did you go last night, anyways?'

'Bible class,' Walter said quietly, tipping coal into the empty fireplace which he'd just cleaned and lined with paper and wood. 'And then I stayed behind to straighten chairs and tidy up for Pastor Meek.'

'By . . . You're a little devil, Walter, I'll say that for you.' Philip turned back to his polishing. 'Bleeding waste of a night off . . .' he muttered.

They worked on in silence for a while, Walter moving about the walls of the room, stretching on tiptoe, taking down the glass lampshades, trimming the wicks, then polishing the brass fittings until they shone dully, Philip pretending to polish the huge, ornately framed mirror which hung opposite the window, catching the light and drenching the room with it. Philip basked in his own reflection. He was a good-looking lad and knew it, with dark-brown hair, straight and slightly too long, parted in the centre so that it fell and flopped about his face, and a look of permanent bedevilment about his quick mouth and narrow, shapely eyes. There was something keen and rodent-like about him, Walter always thought.

'The master was late getting in this morning,' Walter eventually said. 'I was already up.'

'Ah, he'll have been at the casual ward all night,' replied Philip. 'He does that sometimes.'

'He was dressed for dinner. He had someone with him.'

Philip raised his eyebrows. 'Not like the master,' he said. 'He hardly ever goes out socially when he can help it. Many's the time I've heard him complaining to Tom while he was getting dressed to go to some function or other. Always says he'd rather spend a lifetime in the company of the sick than an hour in that of the merely idle. Course, he gets plenty of invitations, though what sort of an invitation would keep him out till dawn?'

Walter moved out into the hall, carrying before him the wooden box containing the jar of polish and clean and dirty rags. One by one he took down and wiped the shades, trimmed the wicks and polished the lamps which lined the passageway.

The door next to where Walter was standing on tiptoe opened suddenly with a loud click and a figure emerged – that same tall, haughty aristocrat who had earlier accompanied the master into the house. Startled, Walter momentarily lost his balance and pressed on the brass fitting of the lamp he was polishing for support. He had put too much polish in the rag. A fat, dirty droplet squeezed out from its folds, ran down the lamp and plunged downward towards the ground. The man stepped forward. Walter's mouth opened in horror as the elongated droplet bounced off his shoe.

'I ... I ...' He attempted to mumble some sort of apology. The man's face was cruelly drawn back into a snarl of fury.

'You clumsy little –' One hand gripped Walter's shoulder hard, the other raised his cane to strike him across the face. For one frozen moment the two men stood paralysed, one by rage, the other by fear. In that time the man's appearance branded itself on Walter's memory. He was tall, his face long and hawklike, deeply tanned and curiously pock-marked. His eyes burned black beneath heavy, black brows. He might have been handsome, Walter thought, had it not been for a wildness of expression that hung about his features. It transcended his mask of anger and reminded Walter of an animal.

'No ...' the aristocratic stranger suddenly purred. 'No, no, no.' The fury in his face seemed to melt into something altogether less readable. His hand relaxed its grip on Walter's shoulder and moved gently up his neck to his face. Slowly the stranger stroked the servant's cheek. 'Such beauty ... should not be marred in mere anger. To despoil something so perfect should be a sublime act. Sublime . . .'

Walter shot a glance at his master, who now stood in the doorway of the room, silent and observant, his eyes darting between the two men but not attempting to intervene.

The stranger seemed to wake from his reverie. 'You've kept me in the dark about this one, Reynard. Where have you been hiding him?' He turned back to Walter. 'What's your name, boy?'

Stammering, Walter answered him. 'Starling, sir. Walter Starling.'

'And what is your position in this fine house?'

'Under-footman, sir.'

'Yes . . . perhaps that explains why you were under foot. I shall ignore the brass polish on my shoe in tribute to your startling beauty.'

The master stepped forward, smiling. 'All right, Walter,' he said, not unkindly, 'be about your business. Spearman, you have servants enough of your own to abuse.'

The stranger began to laugh, a loveless, haughty smile stretching his mouth. The sound was deep and hoarse and malevolent.

Gathering up his cleaning materials, Walter fled.

All through chapel that morning, Walter couldn't get the stranger's face out of his mind. He could still feel the wild, burning intensity of that gaze. Pastor Meek was roaring from the pulpit about the seven deadly sins, sins which could transform the face of man to that of a beast, which could drive mad the higher mind, extinguish the light of reason, cast off the angelic and summon in its place the demonic. Sins which could twist and scar their way deep into the soul.

What poisonous compound of sins, Walter could not help but wonder, had etched their way across the face of his assailant of this morning? Wrath? Undoubtedly. Lust?

The organ was striking up 'Oh What A Friend We Have In Jesus'. Walter joined in the singing with fervour.

His morning fury assuaged, Pastor Meek clasped each member of the congregation warmly by the hand as they filed past him and out of the little chapel. Walter queued impatiently. It was a long way back to St Mary-le-bone, and the inevitable slow procession from the building always threatened to make Walter late for his duties around the house. While Mr Brakes had scarcely been able to criticise Walter's insistence on attending worship every Sunday, Walter had been pressed to choose a house of God nearer to the house of his earthly master. But he had been adamant – this was where his father and mother had worshipped, and where he had worshipped as a child. Philip had called him a 'bleeding heretic'. What was wrong with the good old C of E? the footman, who had probably never set foot in a church in his life, had demanded.

It distressed Walter slightly, the level of godlessness among the staff of the household (except for old Tom, and everybody either ignored or mocked him). It seemed that the master, Dr Reynard, didn't encourage religious worship. Walter was resolved not to be deflected from his faith and never to take his salvation for granted.

'Walter!'

Someone was calling him from down the street. The mist had lifted while the faithful had been at prayer, and he could see a tall figure swathed in a heavy overcoat. The figure began to walk towards him, gathering speed.

Walter opened his mouth to call back, then stopped. It was the master. What could he be doing in this part of the city?

'The workhouse is close by,' he said, as if reading his servant's thoughts. 'I tend the casual ward there.' He paused, recovering his breath. 'So, you're a Christian.'

'Yes, sir,' Walter replied.

'Interesting . . . I'm sorry we haven't had a chance to talk before now. How long have you been with the household?'

'Nearly a week, sir.'

'And are you settling in?'

'Yes, sir, I – I'm very grateful to be in your employment, sir.'

The master smiled a little awkwardly. His face was open and handsome; always kindly, always curious. Grey eyes shone palely from a smooth complexion. He had luxuriant brown hair and a strong chest and arms.

His mouth undulated somewhere between speech and smile. He seemed to be trying to say something.

'Walter . . .' He seemed to hesitate. 'I wanted to apologise for my friend's conduct this morning.'

Walter was silent and confused. Why should he apologise to a servant in this manner?

'Lord Spearman can be . . . brutal, sometimes. It's his way, and you must try not to mind it. None the less, it was ill mannered of him, and I must take responsibility, as your employer, as his host and as his friend.' He coughed awkwardly. 'I suppose you might have been wondering at my very late return home this morning.'

Walter lowered his eyes, shocked and embarrassed by this strange display of forthrightness. Walter would never have dreamed of wondering such a thing of his employer.

'Philip said you'd probably been at the casual ward all night,' he mumbled.

'Indeed. Well . . . I have detained you long enough. I daresay I shall have to answer to Mr Brakes for it. Here.' He reached into his pocket and took out a sovereign. 'Take a cab back to the house.'

'Really, sir, there's no need.'

The master pressed the coin into his hand. 'I have made you late,' he said. 'I insist.' He extended an arm into the road. 'Cab!' he called.

For the rest of the day, Walter's mind dwelled on the morning's twin encounters. The two men – his master, Dr Reynard, and the stranger he had called Lord Spearman – could scarcely have been more different, and yet Reynard had called Spearman his friend. He couldn't decide which of the two meetings he found more strange – the wrath of the stranger or the curious breach of social protocol from his master.

He had been told that Dr Richard Reynard was an unusual man, renowned for his keen intelligence and mastery of the surgeon's knife, looked at askance and adored for what was perceived as his youthful vigour and unorthodox approach to life. Eccentric, Philip had said dismissively. Judging by his behaviour today, perhaps the footman was right.

He found it difficult to concentrate on his work, and this was made no easier by Ruby, who constantly fluttered around him. She had been doing this since he arrived in the house.

'She's set her cap at you,' said Philip. 'Lucky bleeder. You want to get in there, boy.'

Walter flushed with embarrassment and anger, dismissing his suggestion with a wave.

'You're mad,' said Philip. 'I'd run a mile over broken glass to be up our Ruby.'

Tom, the valet, scowled and snarled. 'Thou'll be in hell, Philip, mark my words.'

Philip nudged Walter. 'That's what you'll turn into if you keep up this God stuff. A miserable old bastard.'

'Eh, what?' muttered Tom deafly.

'I said you're a miserable old bastard,' Philip shouted. 'A . . . Miserable . . .'

'Tha'll be in hell, mark me,' the old man repeated and stomped from the room.

'Bleeding old hypocrite,' Philip said to Walter. He leant in close to him. 'There was a groom here a few years back, told me a thing or two about our Tom. Apparently, in his young days, when he was valet to old Hugo, Reynard's dad, he were a right bad 'un. All kinds of malarkey, I heard. It was only when he got old and got the wind up him a bit that he turned all religious. Have you seen inside his room?'

Walter shook his head.

'Crosses and pages from the Bible all over the walls. It's like he's scared Old Nick's going to come round one night and drag him to hell. Gives me the flaming creeps.'

Mr Brakes's voice cut in from the next room. 'More work and less idle gossip if you please, Philip. Walter, come here, please.'

'Well, *he* sure as heck ain't deaf,' said Philip.

Ruby winked at Walter as he left the room. He tried to ignore her.

Mr Brakes was sitting in his little parlour. 'Now, Walter,' he said, as the under-footman entered, 'you know that the master is entertaining in a few days. You will be required to wear full livery and wait at the table. As this is the first time since being engaged

17

here you have been called upon to perform these duties, I should like to go over exactly what will be required of you.'

Walter climbed the narrow stairs to bed, exhausted and distracted. The low-ceilinged servants' floor at the top of the house was quiet, but he heard muffled voices and girlish giggles coming from the room shared by Meg and Ruby as he padded past it and turned into his own room.

'Sssh! Quiet!' Philip hissed as the door creaked open. Walter stopped. Philip was standing in front of him, his eye pressed to the spy-hole he had found. He was stooping slightly to bring his eye level with the aperture, and presenting Walter with his profile. He was dressed only in his vest and long johns.

Walter immediately and automatically cast his eyes modestly downward. Seeking the floor, they didn't get past the bulge that stood out at the front of Philip's underwear. The thick white cotton was stretched over what was a rapidly tumefying member.

'They've both got their titties out,' Philip whispered.

Quite unconsciously, it seemed to Walter, the young footman's hand tugged at the cotton of the tight garment, loosening the constriction about his manhood and allowing it to stand upright. Walter caught a glimpse of a dark-pink, fleshy bulb, its end poking out of a ruff of surrounding skin, before Philip allowed the elastic to snap back.

'Ruby's at the wash stand . . . Oh my gawd . . .'

Turning away from his voyeuristic roommate, Walter stripped to the waist and slipped into his long, heavy nightshirt before removing the rest of his clothes. He climbed into the double bed he shared with Philip, and turned on to his side, facing the wall. Huddled under the blankets, he silently said his nightly prayers (he had given up kneeling to pray because Philip would immediately try to ruin his concentration), eyes closed, pretending to be asleep. While still at prayer he heard Philip undress and climb into bed.

'You ever had a woman?' the footman asked.

Walter didn't reply.

'You could have a good time, pretty boy like you,' he continued. 'That Ruby . . .'

He snuffed out the candle.

Walter tried to concentrate on his prayers, but the images of the day intruded. He found it strange and disturbing to be an object of attraction to another human being. He often sneaked glances at himself in the mirror when Philip wasn't around, and always rebuked himself afterwards for his vanity, but deep down he knew his dark-blond hair, blue-grey eyes and pale skin were passable.

Certainly, Ruby seemed rudely appreciative. The master's companion, too, had passed comment on his apparent beauty. He thought about Pastor Meek's words: about how the evil within could twist and deform the features. Yet as an injunction against straying from the righteous path, it was not without its problems. Was it not vain to value, and to seek to preserve, one's own physical beauty? And was not vanity also a sin?

He tried to meditate on the meaning of the day's events but began to feel confused and frightened. As he so often did when feeling alone or ill at ease, he recited to himself the twenty-third psalm. *The Lord is my shepherd; I shall not want.*

Philip shifted, thumped his pillow a few times and appeared to settle.

He maketh me to lie down in green pastures: he leadeth me beside the still waters.

The minutest sound at Walter's back interrupted his holy meditation. A tiny, shuffling, rubbing sound. He sensed Philip shifting again in the bed, and heard a small sigh.

The rubbing sound became louder and acquired a wetness; a slick, slight, squelching. There was no doubt about it: inches behind Walter, Philip was masturbating.

He restoreth my soul: he leadeth me in the paths of righteousness for his name's sake.

In spite of his prayers, Walter's manhood was growing large and hard. He tried to ignore it and to concentrate on the liturgy.

Philip's breathing was faster and shallower now. The rubbing sound was speeding up. The bed was creaking very slightly.

Yea, though I walk through the valley of the shadow of death, I will fear no evil: for thou art with me; thy rod and thy staff they comfort me . . .

In spite of himself, Walter's hand found its way to where his hardness jutted against the folds of his nightshirt, and closed the thick white linen about the rigid pole. He began slowly squeezing through the cloth. His buttocks clenched involuntarily; his inner thighs tightened about his testes.

He tried to get a grip on his thoughts. Behind him, Philip rubbed and twitched and panted. Slowly, Walter turned on to his stomach, pressing his hardness, still in his hand, into the mattress. He turned his head until he could see Philip's silhouette in the darkness. He was on his back with his knees raised and his legs apart. His head was thrust back against the pillow, his dark fringe not quite covering his eyes. His arm, pivoting from the elbow, vanished beneath the blankets, which moved like a turbulent sea.

Walter crushed his rigid penis in his fist, tightening and relaxing his grip and squeezing the hard, pliant bulb. Ever so slowly, his hand still tight on his erect member, Walter drew his foreskin back and then forward again. He paused, relishing the sensation but anxious not to be heard.

Philip emitted a small choking sound. His breathing was agitated now. The heaving blankets slid down the bed, drawing themselves up his thighs and over his knees. Walter felt them slip down his own back and over his buttocks. He lay, exposed, next to his masturbating companion. His first instinct was to claw them back, but that would entail moving and letting Philip know he was not asleep. He felt a surge of panic. His hard penis, enclosed in his fist, poked slightly out from underneath him. If Philip turned his head . . .

Philip didn't seem to have noticed anything. Walter could see the silhouette of the footman's genitals now, his hand flying up and down his long, thick pole with its swollen head. Philip gasped. He drew his knees up, lifting his feet from the bed. His back and neck arched and his buttocks heaved. He ejaculated a great wave of white fluid over his stomach and chest. Spots splashed his face.

Philip slumped back on to the bed and lay still for a moment. His eyes turned to Walter. Walter could feel his gaze lingering on his bare legs and buttocks and eased his hand away from his penis and out of sight. After a moment, Philip gathered the blankets to himself and roughly rubbed the glistening trails from his skin. He turned in the bed, wrapped the blankets snugly around him, and closed his eyes.

Utterly uncovered now, Walter watched Philip sink into sleep and listened to his breathing roughen into its usual abrasive snore.

Normally after a day's work, Walter slept swiftly, soundly and heavily. Tonight, sleep eluded him. His body longed to sleep but his mind was racing.

Two

The evening of Dr Reynard's dinner party arrived. The table in the dining room was decorated with flowers, with places set and cutlery laid out. The kitchen steamed and bubbled with activity. By 9.30 Walter, in his best livery, was standing next to Philip behind a row of chairs, watching the backs of Dr Reynard's guests.

For the last few days, Walter had given no thought to this evening. Only when the diners were arriving had it occurred to him to wonder whether or not the man his master had called Spearman would be among their number. The thought troubled Walter until the party filed into dinner and he could see for himself that this was not the case.

Four of the guests were women: a rich old dowager called Mrs Maitland and her two unmarried daughters, and a distant cousin of the doctor's, middle-aged and stern-faced. The three male guests were all colleagues from the Royal College of Physicians. It seemed an eclectic and not very successful social mix. Miss Reynard sat at the opposite end of the table to the host, silent and grim, eating primly and with no real air of enjoyment. To the doctor's right was Mrs Maitland, who talked incessantly about her daughters' many accomplishments, while down the table from her the daughters themselves giggled and fawned in the direction of their host. The three guest doctors, who seemed to have drunk a considerable amount before they arrived, sat opposite the Maitland ladies, loudly debating some abstruse medical point between themselves and ignoring the rest of the company. Frequently, their heated exchanges skirted subjects entirely inappropriate to the dinner table, drawing sour, tight-lipped glances from Miss Reynard.

Dr Reynard himself, at the head of the table, seemed barely to be there at all. He appeared to be listening politely to Mrs Maitland's effusions, but was invariably found wanting when a response was sought from him. Only occasionally did he cast his eyes briefly in the direction of his arguing colleagues, generally when the vigour of their brawl became intrusive. He seemed unaware of, or unconcerned about, the content of their debate, and never once sought to temper their enthusiasm. For the most part he stared vacantly into the floral display in the middle of the table, his head cocked slightly in the direction of the proud mother. Walter had been told that, at the age of thirty-four and still unmarried, the master was considered one of the most eligible bachelors in London. He constantly found himself prey to mothers seeking an illustrious match for their daughters. That he had little time for the elaborate mating rituals into which his station in society periodically forced him was a source of gossip and speculation among the junior servants ('He's mad! If I was in his boots,' Philip was apt to drool). This perhaps explained the doctor's diffidence towards the Maitland family, but he seemed no more interested in his colleagues' debate. He looked politely bored, his mind far from the table, and as the evening went on his boredom turned to restlessness. Pressed for a reaction to a statement at his ear, he responded sharply and dismissively. Mrs Maitland seemed not to notice, and enthused on.

It must have been approaching eleven o'clock when, to everyone's surprise, the doorbell rang. 'Walter,' said Mr Brakes quietly, and Walter slipped from the room.

'Message for Dr Reynard,' said the telegraph boy at the door, handing Walter a piece of paper. Walter returned to the party and handed the note to his master, who read it closely. Walter was sure that he was trying to suppress a smile of relief when he rose from his seat and said, 'Friends, transported though I have been by this exquisite evening, I must, alas, leave you. My attendance is urgently required at the casual ward. Pray, continue to enjoy yourselves. My home is your home.'

And with that he strode from the room, leaving Mrs Maitland in raptures. 'Such a Christian soul. So dedicated, so compassionate!'

Dinner was finished in due course, the ladies largely silent now but the men louder and more drunk. Hopes of Dr Reynard's early return began to melt and the Maitland daughters began to bicker among themselves. Their mother snapped at them. Eventually, Miss Reynard, at the foot of the table, sprang to her feet, declaring, 'Well, it is already past the hour when Christian souls should be in their beds. Permit me to take my leave of you. This really is too bad of my cousin.'

The Misses Maitland, too, were openly canvassing departure to their mama. Bowing to the inevitable, she acquiesced, casting a final wistful glance at their host's empty chair. Carriages were summoned, and the ladies departed.

The young doctors insisted – in accordance, they asserted, with the spirit of Dr Reynard's parting words – on retiring to smoke, and Walter was instructed to wait on them.

Even before the ladies had left, their conversation was lurching alarmingly in the direction of disorders of the mind engendered by obsessive self-abuse. Walter had blushed furiously; Philip had smirked openly. Now, over brandy and cigars in the smoking room, the conversation burst its banks.

'It is an indisputable fact,' one of their number ranted, 'that masturbation causes a light-headedness upon orgasm which, whilst a not unpleasing sensation in itself –'

'Hear, hear!' another cut in, banging his glass on the arm of his chair.

'– can nevertheless lead, over time, to a softening of the brain, particularly in obsessive cases.'

'Which perhaps explains the amount of drivel you've been coming out with tonight, Garrick. You've been overdoing it, old man. Your brain has gone soft!'

Garrick, a tall, well-built man with a somewhat ruddy complexion, smiled beneath a heavy, pitch-black moustache. 'Jimmy,

Jimmy,' he said, 'you stoop to insult because you have no argument. Besides, the appetites of youth decline . . . decline . . .'

'Rot, Garrick! You're barely thirty. The same age as me and Charles here. Don't tell me you never indulge in the greatest and most secret of all vices.'

'I think the whole thing is a colossal overreaction,' the third said. 'I have parents coming to me regularly now, asking for protection for their adolescent sons.'

'Those damned girdle things!' Jimmy reddened with indignation. 'Forcing young men into chastity belts so that they can't interfere with themselves. It will make them into women! It's abominable!'

'I hand them out like sugared almonds,' said Garrick, shrugging.

Walter tried not to listen. He had always found doctors to have an unnerving frankness. At times, such as now, they seemed to actively court heavenly disapprobation.

'You there!' Walter started. One of the doctors – the one called Jimmy – was hailing him.

'How old are you, boy?'

'N-nineteen, sir,' Walter stammered.

'There you are,' Doctor Jimmy said to his companions. 'Nineteen. At the height of his sexual awareness.' He turned back to Walter. 'Tell me, boy, how often do you masturbate?'

Walter's jaw dropped. He thought of his nights next to Philip. He thought of his all-too-frequent struggle against the urge to self-abuse. 'Onanism is a temptation of the devil', he had heard Pastor Meek growl on many occasions. 'It must be fought for the sake of the soul.' And how hard Walter fought. And how unjust of the doctor, in his drunkenness and ignorance, to place him in this position.

The other doctors were howling with delighted disbelief. 'Really, Jimmy,' the one called Charles cried, 'you're embarrassing the boy terribly.'

'How often?' Jimmy persisted. 'Once a day? More?'

'I . . . try to resist the urge, sir.'

'You try, but you don't succeed. So come along, how often?'

'Perhaps once or twice . . . a month, sir. Sometimes I weaken . . .'

'Weaken, damn it?' Jimmy roared. 'What do you mean, weaken? It is not harmful to you in any way. It won't –' he spat the words out '– soften your brain.'

'Jimmy . . .' Charles tugged at his colleague's sleeve. 'Send the boy away. You really are mortifying him. Boy, leave us. We shall ring when we need you. Oh, and bring some more brandy.'

'Anyway,' he said, returning to the subject, 'none of this is relevant, provided a chap doesn't overspend his semen. Semen production, it is now widely acknowledged, is regulated by the amount and nature of food one consumes. Finer foods are, of course, more potent. Chocolate in particular.'

'Then why are the working classes so damned rampant, Charles?' Garrick shrieked. 'Widely acknowledged, indeed? Your theory is preposterous. Why, on the strength of it, given the fine foods we have eaten here tonight, including chocolate, we should all be struggling against an irresistible urge to –'

Walter was glad to close the door on the conversation. He returned below stairs and removed a bottle of brandy from the cellar. The kitchens were quiet now; the rest of the staff had gone to bed. He pictured Philip at the top of the house, face against his spy-hole, turning his brain to suet.

He climbed the stairs and stood uncertainly in the hallway. His instructions were confusing: wait until called and bring more brandy. He decided to slip unobtrusively back into the room, leave the bottle and go until summoned.

The conversation in the room appeared to have died down. Walter opened the door of the room as quietly as he could and stole around the back of the armchairs. At first he couldn't see the three young doctors – the lamplight was dim in the room and they were partially screened by chair backs. A small grunting sound made him step closer to the cluster of chairs. He froze, almost dropping the brandy bottle.

The three chairs were set in a tight semi-circle, facing the fire. The doctors sat in thick silence, each low in his chair. Garrick was almost facing Walter, his clothes dishevelled, staring into his lap. His long legs were splayed out across the carpet; his trousers were bunched around his thighs and the bottom of his shirt was open. His tumescent pole, short and fat, jutted upward from a thick, dark patch of hair. The other two doctors – Jimmy and Charles – were similarly deported across their chairs. Their clothes, too, were undone and hanging loosely about their bellies. Their penises were hard. Each was masturbating himself intently.

Walter stepped back into an alcove. He didn't know what to do. To effect an escape and move back across the room to the door, would mean he would almost certainly be seen. Trapped, he watched the three young doctors with horrified fascination.

Garrick was pushing upward with his pelvis, thrusting into his motionless hand.

'That's a great, fat prick you have there, Garrick,' said Jimmy. 'Rather short . . .'

'It's the width that counts when it comes to the ladies,' said Garrick. 'Now that feeble cock of yours . . .'

Jimmy was slighter than Garrick. He was tugging on a thin, curving penis that was longer than his friend's. His other hand cupped his testicles, squeezing and pulling.

'No, if anything makes a difference, it's having a good set of balls,' said Jimmy. His voice sounded a little strained.

Charles said nothing. His head was cocked at a strange angle, his tongue protruding slightly between his lips. Of the three, he had the largest prick and was pumping it with both hands.

From nowhere, a memory of long ago descended on Walter. A memory from his school days. His cock grew hard beneath his uniform.

Gradually, the doctors lapsed into silence. Garrick's face was screwed up tight beneath his thick, dark side-whiskers and his eyes were shut. Next to him, Jimmy stared from lap to lap, still pumping and pulling.

Walter was struck by an awful realisation. Just as he could not leave without being seen, if any of the three moved towards the door he would certainly be discovered. Either way, he could not escape.

He stared at the doctors. The advancing urgency of the situation was driving him to desperation. He decided, finally, to try to move while they were distracted. He began edging towards the door.

Garrick let out a strangled groan and arched his pelvis upward.

His cock was livid and spasming, pumping its load in thick globs over his belly and shirt. He opened his eyes and stared directly into Walter's. Both men froze. Garrick's mouth moved wordlessly, a look of horror on his face. Beside him, the other men were also coming.

Walter's nerve broke. He fled from the room, up the narrow servants' stairs to the top of the house. He reached the room, panting, undressed quickly and crawled into bed next to Philip, who was mercifully asleep.

13th September, 1884

I must confess, my overwhelming feeling last night when summoned from my own ghastly dinner party was one of relief. I felt like a shipwrecked man, suddenly rescued. I gathered up my bag of instruments and, not wishing to raise the coachman at this hour, hailed a hansom.

I entered the casual ward to find it silent and still. All of the patients seemed to be slumbering. I looked about for one of the night staff to direct me to whatever patient was in crisis, and instead spotted Spearman, standing in the shadows, regarding me without speaking.

'Spearman!' I cried, but he stepped forward, pressing his finger to my lips.

'I guessed that you might need rescuing from your engagement,' he said to me, smiling. I attempted some show of annoyance – for indeed I did feel that I ought to be annoyed – but I fear my effort was feebly inadequate, for Spearman merely smiled more broadly.

'Come,' he said, and drew me back on to the street.

His carriage was waiting close by, and we boarded it and clattered into the foggy night. He was quiet, lost in some meditation and quite unstimulated by my attempts at conversation.

At length he picked up a package that was lying on the seat and presented it to me. He wouldn't let me open it there and then, but rather counselled me to keep it for when quite alone and in private. It was something rare and valuable, he told me.

Our destination was once more Mrs Warren's house. We were admitted as before, and shown to the same little suite.

The young men were back: the same three naked, brilliant, mythic creatures who had attended us on our previous visit. There was the slim, pale, green-eyed one, his hair like collapsing sheaves of corn; his small companion, dark-haired and puckishly featured; and the one who had pleasured me, tall, crop-headed and muscular, something of the young soldier about his manner. James, Joe and Arthur – or so they had introduced themselves at the close of our last meeting. Do they use false names, I wonder?

Ignoring Spearman, the boys immediately set about me, the muscular Arthur pushing me back across the bed and pinning me there while his friends kissed about my face and neck, slowly removing my clothes and tracing my advancing nakedness with tongues and teeth.

I saw Spearman move to a chair at the foot of the bed and sit there, leaning forward slightly and watching as my clothes were slowly drawn from me. His gaze made me feel a little uneasy, but my cock was hard, and even now twitching with pleasure as James's blond head danced about it, his teeth nipping and testing the taut underside of the shaft, sending deliciously sharp twinges down to my balls and up my stomach. I was seized of a great desire to take the initiative. I gripped James's blond head and forced it down on to my prick. He made a slight gagging sound, then began a steady, slow, cool, wet rhythm up and down its length.

Arthur leaned over me and lifted my arms from James's head. He vaulted on to the bed and straddled me, pinning my arms with his knees. His semi-hard cock dangled in front of my mouth. I extended a tentative tongue and balanced the end of Arthur's cock on its tip, testing its weight. It rose and fattened as I watched, bumping its way up my face. Arthur began drawing his tight foreskin over the distended globe beneath. He masturbated himself fully hard, then bent his cock downward and drove it into my mouth. At first I felt I was choking – I couldn't breathe! As he thrust forward and withdrew, thrust and withdrew, his cock battered the back of my throat and threatened to make me gag. It took a considerable effort of concentration to master my gag reflex, but I managed it, and began to enjoy the musky effusion which filled my nose and mouth.

I sensed a change of pace on my own cock: the strokes were shorter now, and sharper, the head of my cock feeling the occasional graze of teeth. It must have been the mouth of small, dark Joe, for the next moment I saw James appear above my head and embrace Arthur, their tongues intertwining above me and their chests – one coarse and muscular, the other slender and elegant – slapping and grinding together. Arthur continued to fuck my mouth while James's long prick bounced against my forehead and the bridge of my nose.

Arthur began to grunt and his strokes became faster and shorter. His cock swelled in my mouth, and then spurted. For the first time, I felt the hot cascade of a man's semen sluicing tartly down my throat.

He fell away from me with a groan, tearing his cock from inside me and rolling across the bed. I could now see Joe's black curls bobbing up and down on my cock. He raised his eyes and caught mine. Smiling eyes. I let my head loll backward, letting James's balls sit across my eyes. I felt the grizzle of pubic hair on my eyelids. Suddenly, I decided I wanted this boy. I drew myself up on the bed, pulling my cock from Joe's mouth. I clumsily dragged James down on top of me and rolled him on to his stomach. I parted his buttock cheeks and peered at the dark sphincter within. In the course of my medical career, I have had occasion to do this, but now, departing from all the accepted medical texts, I pressed my face forward and touched the exquisite hole with the tip of my tongue.

I plastered the crack with my saliva and drove my tongue wetly inside the boy. Then I crawled up his back and, taking my cock in my hand, positioned it in the slippery crevice and pushed forward. I felt the sphincter yield and the muscles relax and close around my shaft. I began a rocking motion, pushing my prick slowly forward and feeling James's passage open around me, then pulling back, forward, back. It did not take me long to come. I thrust my face into James's golden hair as my climax came upon me. I bit down hard on his neck as it burst through my cock, high inside the boy's hole. I held, and I bit, as I shuddered to stillness.

I fucked each of the lads in turn that night. Spearman, who remained fully clothed and had hitherto done nothing but watch, then disappeared into the adjoining room with the three, closing the door behind them – the cad – and detaining them for nearly an hour. I dozed on the bed, listening to the sounds from next door.

When they returned to my room it was without Spearman. They stood in a semi-circle beside the bed, each naked, erect and silent. They smiled smiles of anticipation, occasionally catching one another's eye.

There was something irresistible in their expectation. I tumbled from the bed to my knees and sank my mouth around each cock in turn, moving from lad to lad with a fervent hunger. James's pale, slender pole, Joe's small, pert, lively prick and Arthur's great battering ram: I swallowed them all, drank their fluids and let them spend themselves inside me.

I wasted no time upon my return, but set to the parcel which Spearman had given me at the commencement of our night's adventure. It was flat and rectangular, wrapped in plain brown paper. The wrapping came away easily to reveal a slim book. It consists of a narrative – somewhat rambling, I should say, at first glance – interspersed with fine watercolours. Pornographic watercolours, indeed, each depicting numbers of males, naked and engaged in all manner of copulations. Does Spearman know that I have for nearly a year been amassing such works in my library? Certainly I have never discussed it with him, or with anyone else.

The book declares itself to be the memoir of a French nobleman of the sixteenth century called the Duc du Guerrand. Stopping at random at any page in the book reveals the nature of the man all too plainly. He was a libertine of the most singular kind. A Uranian, as we might say today.

Then again, I suppose I too might be described as such. What has Spearman done to me? There was a card enclosed with the book – a plain white card embossed with the Spearman crest. On it he had written a single word. 'Wisdom'.

Three

It was another bitter morning and Walter was once more on his hands and knees, taking a hard-bristled brush to the foot scraper outside Dr Richard Reynard's front door. His fingers were numb and his head was aching. He had hardly had any sleep. He was working to drive away the images which kept stealing into his mind: images of three grown men, his social betters, deporting themselves like beasts and revelling in carnality.

After a short while, a hansom cab clattered along the road and stopped behind him. He turned to see the master disembarking and handing a coin to the cabman. The hat the master had been wearing when he left last night was missing, Walter noted. His luxuriant brown hair was untidy, his strong, chiselled face rough with stubble and his eyes bloodshot and wide.

'Very generous, I'm sure, sir. Thank you kindly,' the cabman chirped, before cajoling his horse into a slow trot and disappearing back into the damp morning mist.

Walter drew to one side on the step to allow his employer to pass him. The doctor stopped and looked down, catching Walter's eye for a second. Once again, as outside chapel the previous Sunday, he seemed to be struggling to find words to say something. Instead he looked away, mumbling something Walter couldn't catch, and then pushed past into the house, closing the door hard behind him.

Walter turned his attention back to his work. A good servant is concerned, but never curious, Mr Brakes always said. Walter had seen a great deal to pique his curiosity in his short time in Dr Reynard's service. He must exercise more mental discipline.

Richard Reynard wrote furiously. He hadn't even paused to remove his coat. He had rushed through the house to the wing which contained his practice rooms, pulling the key from his pocket, thrusting it into the lock and opening the door, barely breaking his stride. He had closed the door and locked it behind him, drawing in a deep breath.

To his left was the plush consulting room where he saw his paying clients, a far cry from the St Luke's parish casual ward. Beyond that lay what he sometimes referred to as 'the cutting room', and some of his more boisterous colleagues generally called 'the butcher's shop': his huge surgical theatre-cum-laboratory. Now that so much of his work was among London's poor, he rarely used either room.

To his right was his small study, and it was to this that he had retired, again locking the door behind him. Sitting at his desk, still in his overcoat, he had taken from his pocket the package which Spearman had given him and ripped it open, his fingers fumbling with the contents, clumsily leafing from page to page, his eyes darting about like an animal's.

Attempting to collect himself, he had laid the book aside, taken a journal from the desk drawer and written for twenty minutes without pause.

Now he put down his pen and took up the book again.

'I learned early on in life,' the narrative began, 'how easy it was to turn power into pleasure. I can have been but fourteen years old the first time I terrorised a servant into having sex with me. There was a stable boy called Benoit, several years older than myself, dark-haired with deep, brooding eyes and a moody, resentful expression. He was tanned and muscular, in the way of the countryfolk in this part of France, and I thought him desperately attractive. In particular, his unconcealed resentment in the face of authority – and his contemptuous treatment of me – stoked up my desires. I hung about the stables watching him work, the sweat glistening on his bare, muscular back, only to be told in the most insolent terms to take myself off. I even hid where I could observe him in his little garret above the stables undressing for bed. My hiding place was not a good one, and I fear I made a little noise as his mighty prick came into view, for, quite naked, he turned and discovered me. His response was a sharp blow across my jaw, which sent me sprawling to the floor.

'My father had been for some years trying to induce me to overcome my aversion to horses and learn to ride. I decided to stop fighting him, on condition that Benoit should be my instructor. The lad was unhappy at the prospect, and said nothing as we rode our beasts slowly to the lower paddock.

'"Take me to the ridge," I said suddenly.

'"No," he grunted.

'"I know you go riding there," I persisted. "I know you take my father's horses up there without permission. Take me, or I shall tell!"

'With a scowl and an oath he spurred his horse hard in the direction of the ridge. I struggled to keep up. We soon reached the belt of fields, rising at an alarming angle and stopping dead, it seemed, in a blade which sliced the sky. In fact, there was a narrow plateau running the length of the escarpment, and fields falling away on the other side. From the top it was possible to see for miles. I had secretly watched him in the past gallop the length of the ridge, effortlessly jumping gates and fences. Now he did it for me, unbidden, showing off, still scowling. When he drew up to me on his breathless horse I immediately spurred my mount at the nearest fence.

'"No!" he called after me. I did not listen. I dug my boots into the horse's flank and we sailed over a wooden gate.

'My feet left the stirrups, my legs lost their grip on the animal, and he and I parted company. I had expected no less. I hit the ground hard and rolled. Benoit was galloping up to me.

'"You little fool!" he shouted. "Are you hurt?"

'"I think I have broken my leg," I lied, for in truth I was at worst bruised, and my breeches torn. Theatrically, holding on to a fence post, I struggled to my feet. Benoit looked anxious. He extended an ineffectual hand, wanting to touch me, to help me, but suddenly afraid.

'"Look,' he said. "Please do not tell your father I brought you up here. Say it happened in the lower paddock. I shall lose my position . . ."

'I merely watched him, smiling slightly.

'"Why do you stare?" he demanded. "What is it you want?"

'I reached forward and placed my hand upon the front of his breeches. Instantly, he stepped back beyond my reach. My face must have registered its displeasure, for he instantly said, "What? You want this?" and pulled down his breeches to reveal a heavy, lolling prick surrounded with thick black hair. I stepped forward – abandoning any pretence of injury – and placed my hand around it, squeezing. It began to harden as I did so.

'When Benoit was fully erect I ordered him to strip himself naked. Meekly, he did so. Then I ordered him on to his hands and knees. You must remember that, whilst I desired the lad, I owed him several dozen humiliations.

'"This is supposed to be a riding lesson," I said. "That was my father's wish. So let us commence."

'I vaulted on to the back of the surprised Benoit and dug my boots hard into his flank. Surprised, defeated, he began to crawl forward.

'"Faster!" I shouted, and gave him a crack across the buttocks with my crop.

'As we galloped, I leaned forward, pressing my hard cock, through the stiff padding of my riding breeches, into Benoit's back, and grinding it back and forth. When we reached the fence I straightened up and gave my horse another crack of the whip. Benoit stopped abruptly, his face close to the fence, and I slid backwards off him, undoing my breeches as I did so. My cock was small and hairless in those days, but seemed forever hard and eager. I plunged it now between the buttocks of my steed, hearing Benoit gasp as I pushed through the doors of his anus, but he said nothing more, and feeling his underside revealed that his cock was hard. I pumped at it as I pumped at his buttocks, but stopped when my seed began to erupt inside him. Pulling away from him, I collapsed back on the grass.

'"What now?" he asked after a moment. He was still hard.

'"You may continue," I said. "I shall watch."

'"What? Oh, no . . ." It took him a moment to realise what I was driving at.

'"What might I tell my father now?" I goaded.

'Reluctantly at first, he began to masturbate himself under my disdainful gaze. Every so often I would order a particular elaboration on the routine, such as "Put some fingers up you arse" or "Rub your prick against the fence".

'All of my commands were obeyed with increasing alacrity before I finally allowed him to come, lying on his back, splashing his belly with his own juices. Even then I had not a mind to release him from his humiliations.

'"Remain on your back," I ordered. "Piss over yourself."

'Without a word, without even a sullen glance, my slave did as he was bid. His half-hard cock lolled up his belly. It rolled slightly under pressure from within, and then a hot yellow stream jetted out, mingling with the white mess on his belly, and splashing his chest.

'"Open your mouth," I ordered. "Drink it."

'He took hold of his pissing cock. His golden jet splashed about his lips and plunged into the gorge of his mouth until it overflowed.

'I had good mileage out of Benoit, for the more guilty we made ourselves, the more bound together we became. Thus I learned a central lesson of my life.'

Reynard was beginning to wish the embers of the previous night would burn themselves out and free his mind for matters more suited to the hour.

He flicked forward through the book. It was a curious work, combining outright pornography with a sort of angry ethical polemic. The Duc uses his position, his natural magnetism and a great deal of cunning to indulge in acts of often brutal physical gratification with the boys and young men of the region. The local townspeople – very much the villains of the piece, mean-spirited and hypocritical – ultimately take violent action against the Duc's excesses; they imprison him in a medieval fortress and burn it to the ground. Several of his young conquests insist on sharing their master's fate, and burn with him.

He found himself thinking of Walter. It had struck him on the doorstep how nearly he resembled James, Mrs Warren's boy. The same slim build, the same fine blond hair, the slight upward lilt of the nose and fullness of the lips. Only their demeanour differed. James had had a knowing self-confidence about him. Walter looked self-conscious and scared all the time. Guilty, even. Reynard smiled. What had that timid creature to feel guilty about? Such a strange beast, conscience.

It happened the following day that Mr Brakes instructed Walter to dust the shelves and books in the master's library. The room looked as if it had not been used in some time. It was locked when Walter first sought entry and the curtains were half drawn. A heavy layer of dust covered everything. Walter moved from shelf to shelf, pushing the ornately carved ladder-on-wheels in front of him, ascending and descending, straightening, dusting.

The books seemed to be in no apparent order on the shelves: medical treatises stood sandwiched between novels and books of woodcut illustration. Walter swatted at cobwebs, blew the dust into a mini-storm that made him cough and choke, and wiped and wiped again. One corner-shelf stood out as different from the others. The books in this section were clean of dust, as was the shelf itself. Moreover, there seemed to be some order about them. The Bible was there, Walter was pleased to note, along with Bunyan's *Pilgrim's Progress* and St Augustine's *City of God*. There was a work he knew well from Pastor Meek's thunderous sermons – *The Broad Way to Destruction* – and other retributive tomes.

Further along the shelf the books thinned out – there were spaces now, as if some texts had been removed – and things began to get mixed up. The Reverend Thomas Malthus's celebrated treatise *On the Principles of Population* – a worthy book, written as a dire warning (according to Pastor Meek) about how unchecked lust can cause a population to expand beyond its ability to sustain itself – was there in a new edition. The great man had argued against the procreation of too many offspring: nowadays he was increasingly interpreted as justifying unnatural practices in preventing issue. Next to it stood Francis Place's later, infamous publication on the same topic.

Finally, there were a series of truly scandalous writings: the Marquis de Sade's *120 Days in Sodom* and perhaps seven or eight similar, unspeakable texts. Walter was shocked to see them so close to the holy books. He snatched an unfamiliar tome from the midst of this literary Gomorrah. *The Saved and the Sinning* by John Birkett. He flicked it open at the introduction. 'Many roads lead to Hell', he read, 'but none is more sure and direct, nor more lined with temptations, than the road of carnality, the road of lust.'

He closed the book thoughtfully, about to place it next to Bunyan, but instead slipped it inside his fustian house-coat. At the earliest opportunity he stole up to his room at the top of the house and hid the book under the mattress of the bed, before returning to his duties. He hadn't read anything – not even his Bible – since joining the household: he had simply been too exhausted at the end of the day. Now he felt in need of moral sustenance.

That night, Philip was in bed before him, knees up and grinning like a Cheshire cat. Walter undressed with his usual modesty and, nightshirt on, got into bed beside him. He said his prayers silently, then fished under the mattress for the furtive volume.

''Night then,' murmured Philip. He turned away from Walter, and almost immediately began snoring his sawtooth snore.

'Good night,' mouthed Walter silently, reaching over Philip for the candle and setting it beside the bed.

He leafed through the pages by the flickering light. 'Readers,' the preface began, 'this book must serve as a dire warning for those who would indulge their lusts at the expense of their souls. It tells the awful story of a woman who yielded to every stirring of her basest instincts, who sated every craving of her body, and who gave no thought to the eyes of the Almighty, watching her, waiting.

'It is a harrowing tale, and a true one. See how the woman's infamies taint those around her, sucking them down the whirlpool of fire that leads to eternal damnation.

'In imitation of his Maker, the writer has looked unflinchingly upon the wretched woman's debauches, insofar as it is possible to gaze steadily upon horrors which would curl the beard of Lucifer himself. With a heart steadfast in faith, "Onward Christian Soldiers" on my lips, let me lead you now into the Valley of the Shadow.'

A cautionary tale seemed to be just what Walter needed at the moment.

The book concerned a woman called Fanny, poor but intelligent, who used her feminine charms to procure the love, or at least the lust, of a rich man. Attracting his attention, she set out to gain power over him by leading him down the shameful road of lustful practices and unnatural vices. He in turn corrupted others, and by the end of the tale concupiscence had spread like a virus. As for the woman, she fell from the glittering heights which she had so briefly reached and ended up a whore; a worthless, abused drab, used by men, broken and finally abandoned.

The book was indeed unflinching, though, reading it, Walter flinched continually. The language was, to say the least, immediate: *his great hard cock thrust upward . . . her heaving bosoms . . . sponging his balls with her tongue . . .*

He turned a few pages more.

His legs clenched hard together as he spent, his prick spasming, sending a fountain of cream splashing up his belly.

Walter's eyes darted from page to page like frogs hopping on a bakestone, the pages too hot to linger for more than an instant. He barely noticed his penis hardening and jutting out in front of him. He barely noticed as his hand brushed the shaft and curled around under his balls, feeling the sparse, coarse hair springing back against the weight of his palm.

His eyes settled, at last, somewhere in chapter eleven. 'The Three Wise Men'. It told of three intellectuals, each of whom had had their lives corrupted by the woman Fanny. They considered themselves enlightened thinkers, and openly began questioning the moral restraints imposed by society and the church. This led them inevitably to experimenting with that most forbidden of sins, the vice of Sodom.

The incident happened in a London club, late at night. It arrested Walter's attention because it was similar in its beginning to his encounter with his master's three medical colleagues. It began – as most of the chapters seemed to – with a perverse argument between the parties, which led inevitably to a series of appalling dares and challenges.

A young servant, Samuel, was watching them from a hiding place. Like Walter, he had accidentally stumbled upon the scene and become trapped.

Walter's heart was beating fast. His cock was hard. Behind him, Philip snored on. He began slowly wanking – he loved that word – as he read.

'The colonel held Samuel with his hellish, burning stare. The boy seemed paralysed as the appalling apparition closed on him. Like his friends, the colonel was naked, his cock standing shamefully out from his body. He stepped up to the boy and gripped the collar of his uniform. He pulled his hands apart, tearing the boy's uniform open. He pushed the boy brutally backwards until he was pressed hard against the billiard table. He gave him a final hard shove, forcing the boy back across the table, sending balls flying.'

Walter's hand was running up and down his shaft now, pulling his foreskin out beyond the end of his knob, then plunging back down towards his balls.

'As one of his friends pinned the terrified boy to the table, the colonel ripped the boy's trousers down his legs and over his shoes. The boy struggled and cried, but his cries were silenced as one of his torturers jammed a fist down into his mouth. Soon he was shamefully naked. He felt a sharp pain as the colonel's lust burned into him, parting his buttocks, invading into his innermost sanctum.'

Walter was enthralled and terrified. Almost unwillingly, he extended his free hand down between his legs and under his balls, seeking his own arsehole. In imitation of the lurid scene unfolding on the candlelit page, he slipped a finger into the tight hole. It hurt slightly – his muscles were clenched tight around the invading digit – but he pushed it in further, moved it around a little, clenched even tighter, then relaxed and clenched again.

He began thrusting forward with his hips, ramming his cock, still clamped in his fist, into the mattress and shooting his seed into the bed-sheet, gasping quietly.

Slowly he turned in the bed, moving away from the dampness soaking through the sheet.

There was silence. Walter froze, his hand still holding on to the deflating head of his cock. The snoring had stopped.

'You dirty sod,' said Philip.

Four

————

Philip was unusually chirpy the next morning. He lay on his back in the bed, his hands behind his head, whistling tunelessly. With his back to the bed, blushing furiously, Walter stood by the wash stand, naked. Walter sincerely thanked God for Philip's tardiness in the mornings and for the fact that his bedmate was usually still asleep when Walter rose, washed and dressed. He hated washing in front of Philip. Even facing the wash stand, the big mirror on the wall reflected Walter's nakedness back into the room.

On his first morning of work, Philip had been awake and had lain there, commenting on Walter's naked body. 'Ain't got much hair, have you? On your chest, I mean.'

Philip's chest was liberally salted with dark hairs, thick at the nipples, thinning as they descended to his belly.

'Plenty round the old pecker,' Philip continued, without shame. 'Looks quite big, too, your chopper. Far as I can tell, on the soft.' Mortifyingly, Walter's 'chopper' had lengthened and swelled slightly. Philip had chortled slightly then turned over and gone back to sleep.

This morning, Philip was wide awake. He watched without embarrassment as Walter self-consciously wetted his body, then soaped his chest and arms and back. When he moved his soapy hands down over his buttocks and up into his crack, Philip let out

43

a low whistle. Walter was becoming hard. He soaped his balls and his lengthening, thickening cock as quickly and as lightly as he could.

'Bit sore, is it?' Philip asked nonchalantly.

Walter dried and dressed clumsily, tripping and hopping about the room as he tried to modestly don his undergarments, his part-hardened cock flapping in front of him. He was being mortified for his transgression.

All through the morning, wherever in the house his duties took him, he could sense Philip smirking. He tried without success to ignore the sensation, dismissing it as fanciful. When his path actually crossed Philip's, the footman was indeed smirking.

'You're a dark horse,' Philip teased. 'I come across the book under the bed when you was still below stairs. I had a quick hand-shank myself, so I shouldn't feel so bad about it. I tell you, there's good stuff in that book, ain't there? I mean, I don't read so good myself, but even I could tell it was the real thing. What's old Reynard doing with stuff like that, I wonder? Has he got any more like it?'

Just before eleven o'clock, Mr Brakes summoned Walter below stairs.

'Walter,' said the butler, 'the master appears to have mislaid a book from the library. Given that you were cleaning in there yesterday, I thought perhaps you might be able to shed some light upon the matter.'

'N-no,' stammered Walter. He could almost feel the colour draining from his face. 'No, I haven't seen it.'

'But I haven't told you which book it is yet.' Mr Brakes's eyes narrowed perceptibly. 'It is called *The Saved and the Sinning*.'

'No, Mr Brakes. I . . . There are a lot of books in there. Perhaps it's just lost among them.'

'The master was quite specific as to its location on the shelves, and nobody but he uses the library. As you know, it is kept locked most of the time.'

'No, I . . . I'm sorry. I can't help you.'

'Very well, Walter.' With his customary sharp, quick shake of the head, the butler turned his mind back to the business of the day. 'Now, I want you to carry this note to Mr Kilby the chemist and bring back some preparations for the master,' he said, and handed Walter a piece of paper. Walter took the note mutely and stuffed it into his pocket. 'Chop chop, now,' said Brakes. 'It is most important that this be done before midday.'

All the way to the chemist's and all the way back Walter shook and sweated. Brakes had given him no opportunity to recover the book before despatching him on his errand.

Mr Kilby was even older than Brakes, and moved with what seemed like infinite slowness. The wait while he prepared the ordered compounds was endless.

Walter re-entered the house with dread in his heart. The hallways were quiet, and Walter made silently for the little door which opened on the narrow staircase leading up to the servants' floor.

'Walter.'

His stomach lurched and he froze, halfway through the door. Brakes's voice was quiet and stern.

'Unable to locate the book, I examined your room while you were out. I found the volume in question under your mattress. Now I know Philip is no reader, and given that you alone have been into the library of late, I can only assume that you are the culprit. I have reported my findings to the master and he would like to see you in his study immediately.'

Walter had never before passed through the heavy door that led to the doctor's consulting rooms. Normally, this wing was off-limits to the staff; even to Mr Brakes. Now Walter crept through the door and stood at the end of the corridor, awaiting his fate.

'Come in, Walter.' The master's voice came from a door to Walter's right. He stepped through it, into a smallish room dominated by a desk and untidy shelves teetering with books and papers.

The master was sitting behind the desk. The book lay in front of him.

'Mr Brakes has told me that this was found in your room. Did you take it?'

'Yes, sir,' Walter whispered.

His master regarded him, saying nothing. At last he blandly declared, 'Well, that's that, then.'

'Sir . . .?'

The master sighed wearily. 'Quite honestly, Walter, I find this situation absurd. I went to fetch the book last night, but couldn't locate it. I only mentioned the fact to Brakes in the hope that he might be able to shed light upon its whereabouts. Unfortunately, my butler is most solicitous in his duties, and seems to think that this is a breach of trust, and that I deal with it in some way. In fact, I have no objection to your borrowing books, provided you return them. It's good that you read, although I find your choice of subject matter a little surprising.'

Walter stood with his head bowed.

'Then again, perhaps not. The overtones of the book are decidedly Christian. Your God has always taken an interest in the private lives of his children which manages to be both utterly self-righteous and wholly salacious.'

The master leaned forward and took a key from his desk drawer.

'Here,' he said.

Puzzled, Walter took the key.

'It's a spare key to the library. Feel free to make use of it whenever you wish. I don't see why you should have to sneak around, scrumping apples from the tree of knowledge. Feed to your heart's content.'

'I . . . Thank you, sir,' said Walter, more for his master's clemency than his offer.

'Just don't tell Brakes,' said Dr Reynard. 'He would think it a dreadful breach of form.'

'I do not know what the master said to you, but I hope he was firm,' the old butler lectured. 'Although of course I did not presume to examine its contents, I gather from the title that the book in question was religious in nature. I suppose that fact counted in your favour in some small way, but I would counsel you not to let your religious zeal cloud your judgement or your sense of duty again. The master has been lenient this once, but it would be entirely too much to expect him to show the same clemency for a second offence. Now go about your duties. We have wasted quite enough time on this matter.'

The incident diverted Reynard's thoughts for much of the day. It amused him to think of his under-footman's discomfort. How recently would he, too, have been mortified by any association with such a book. *The Saved and the Sinning*, indeed! Nowadays his only discomfort would have come from the crudeness of its execution: the looseness of the grammar, the unchanging monotony of the style and the preposterous nature of the book's attempted moral stance. The Duc du Guerrand's memoir was a far superior volume.

He passed Tom in his dressing room that evening, laying out his wardrobe for the next day, carefully covering each garment – coat, trousers – in a brown Holland wrap to protect it from the dust. How strange, he thought, that he, an atheist, should have two practising Christians in his staff.

Tom had been in service to the family for ever, or so it seemed to Reynard. He certainly pre-dated Brakes's appointment as butler. He had been Reynard's valet for ten years, and valet to his ailing father for seven years before that, and previous to that he had been a footman below stairs. Reynard himself had chosen Tom to be his father's valet when, on coming of age, he had been required to take charge of the household due to his father's incapacity. He was sure Tom had not been religious in inclination at the time.

He watched as the servant carefully straightened the portrait of his father which hung above the fireplace. Like all of the portraits of his father which littered the house, it showed a man of strong mind and noble purpose. How different from the old man he had watched sliding ever deeper into feeble-mindedness as his life drew to its wretched and premature close.

Tom had cared for Sir Hugo Reynard during those final years with a combination of discreet loyalty and quiet diligence. It was a rare and precious combination in a servant.

Young Walter had something of the same manner, Reynard thought. That was perhaps what amused him about the book incident. It seemed to sit so incongruously on the young under-footman's shoulders. He could never have imagined Tom putting even a foot from the path of righteousness.

Perhaps his father had been wrong. Perhaps Christians did make the best servants.

Philip was sitting up in bed when Walter retired for the night.

'Jammy bugger,' he said. 'Reynard could have dismissed you without a reference.' Walter didn't reply. 'Don't say much, do you?' Philip persisted. He rubbed his hands together excitedly. 'Nice of him to let us use his library, though.'

'What?'

'I was listening outside the door. I heard the lot. Now, here's me thinking, I could learn a lot from them books. If you was to help me.'

'W-what?' Walter stammered a second time.

'Well, the way I see it, if you scratch my back, I'll scratch yours, if you get my meaning.'

Walter didn't.

'I mean, if you get me some of them books and help me to read 'em, I'll keep my mouth shut below stairs about just what kind of book it was you nicked. Brakesy seems to think it was some kind of prayer book. I don't think the truth'd go down too well, whatever the master thinks.'

'You want me to teach you to read . . .' Walter's voice was breathless with relief.

'No, dimwit, I want you to bring up some more books like the last one and . . . well . . .'

'Well . . .'

'Well, I don't read so good, like I said. So you can read 'em for me. Now I know you got a key to the library, so look smart.'

'You want to do this now . . .'

'The house is quiet. Nobody'll see you. And like old Brakesy says, today's occupation is tomorrow's burden.'

Not knowing what else to do, Walter did as he was told. The library was pitch-dark. By candlelight, and almost at random, Walter selected a book from the shelf. It was called *The Seduction of an Upright Man*.

'Get in,' said Philip when Walter returned to the room. He was lying in bed as Walter had seen him before – on his back with his legs apart and his knees drawn up. He was naked beneath the covers.

Walter undressed and climbed into the bed.

'Now,' said Philip. 'Read.'

Walter opened the book at random. None of the passages appealed to Walter: the upright man's doom came in exclusively female form. Philip, however, seemed more than content. He lay back, one arm slung across his eyes, the other under the blankets, working on his cock.

Walter's eyes flickered from the page to Philip, wanking intently. Awkwardly, propping the book against the headboard, he lifted his nightshirt, took hold of his own cock and massaged it quietly beneath the covers.

Philip was going at it strongly. He looked over at Walter and caught his eye, before staring directly into his covered lap. Self-consciously, Walter masturbated himself beneath the gaze of his fellow servant.

The book toppled forward, unheeded.

Philip reached across the bed and pulled Walter's hand from his cock. Walter flinched as Philip's knuckles brushed his hard shaft. Philip pulled him across the bed and clamped his hand on his own cock.

Walter felt a horrified thrill as he felt the thick, gristly pole with its fat, hard bulge. He slid his hand down the shaft, his fingers buffeting against Philip's balls, running through the coarse mat of hair which clung to them and curled away up Philip's taut stomach. He tugged at the hair, then tested the tight foreskin, drawing it slightly back, pulling it forward, squeezing the bulb beneath. Closing his eyes, Philip groaned with pleasure.

Philip kicked the blankets away, affording Walter his first full view of his cock, long and thick and veiny. Walter slid closer to Philip, gripping his own cock with his spare hand, somewhat clumsily manipulating both members.

'Faster . . .' whispered Philip. 'Harder . . .'

Walter tightened his grip and increased the pace. Philip was rubbing his balls hard. He raised his buttocks from the bed, pushing his cock up into Walter's pistoning hand. With a groan he turned on to his side and rolled on top of Walter, thrusting forward with his buttocks, jamming his cock into the crease of Walter's groin and running it up and down, ploughing through Walter's golden cock-hair, colliding with his hard prick.

Philip, his eyes screwed shut, was muttering something under his breath. It sounded to Walter like 'Ruby'. His cock began to spurt its hot liquid out on to Walter's stomach. He gripped Walter's shoulders, his face contorted and he bit down on his lower lip. With a final spasm he rolled away and lay silent and smiling. Philip's seed pooled and cooled in Walter's belly button. Walter raised his pungent hand to his face and sniffed deeply, closing his eyes.

Silently, barely moving, Walter began to wank himself again with tight, minute strokes. He pressed his musky, slimy palm against his lips, his nose, his tongue, filling himself with Philip's tang as his buttocks clenched and his silent, furtive orgasm hit him.

18th September, 1884

Spearman called again last night. I must confess, although I never admitted it to myself at the time, I had been restless since our last outing, and had been awaiting our next with a sort of anxious anticipation.

My mind seems to be on little else. At first I tried unsuccessfully to drive these thoughts away by increased application to my medical duties, which have, I fear, become somewhat neglected of late. They say, after all, that the devil makes work for idle hands. (Am I now starting to believe in the devil?) My best efforts failed to set my fevered mind in order, and by the end of the week I had cancelled a lecture and several of my patients. I am determined, however, not to neglect the casual ward.

Spearman's carriage arrived at ten, whilst I was finishing dinner. He burst in abruptly, abused Brakes shamefully, and demanded my immediate presence at an undisclosed destination across town, declaring that we had an appointment with danger. I should have thrown him out: he is a cur, I own, lord or no lord. But of course I did not. I bolted down my pudding and left with my demon.

Young Walter gave me a curious and lingering look when I departed with Spearman. I wonder whether he suspects anything. He is obviously highly intelligent, yet fights all the time against knowledge which he already possesses. I shall have to keep an eye on him and make sure he loses the fight.

Spearman would say nothing of our destination. It was already dark, but I had a pretty fair notion of the direction in which we were heading, and it was one which occasioned some alarm. My fears were soon confirmed. There could be no doubt that we were heading for the notorious rookery known as the Seven Dials.

We stopped outside a small, dilapidated theatre, whose name was obscured by grime and pigeon ordure. A single poster advertised the attraction within: The Infernal Cabaret. The show appeared to be over, as a small, chattering crowd was leaving. We waited for them to depart, then entered the barely lit building. In response to my curiosity, Spearman merely placed a finger across my lips, smiling darkly.

We passed the tiny, empty auditorium and made our way backstage. As we crept in almost total darkness through a shadowy paraphernalia of props and devices – which, as far as I could make out, suggested some sort of exotic magic show – I stumbled and fell. Immediately, my arms and legs were gripped by unseen hands and I was carried in a second on to the stage and deposited on some sort of long, exotic couch. The lights suddenly came on, and I was dazzled for a moment. A figure I struggled to make out was standing in front of me. He was tall, dark skinned and foreign looking, dressed all in black, his head entirely bald. He appeared every inch the stage magician. There were others around him, some dressed all in black, some in white: diaphanous shifts through which their bodies – all youthful, all male – could clearly be seen. The same material covered their heads and faces, blurring their features beyond recognition.

They closed in around me, reaching for my clothes and stripping them from me as expertly as the boys at Mrs Warren's house had done. I felt my shoes come away and my trousers slide down my legs. My jacket and shirt came off, then I felt my undergarments being pulled from me, momentarily snagging around my hard prick.

The couch was made of a material so sheer it offered no resistance as my clothes were dragged away. Once I was naked, the men turned me on to my back. They ran their hands all over me, pinching, weighing and testing, every inch of my flesh. My nipples were pulled gently, my balls hefted and squeezed, my anus probed by inquisitive, anonymous fingers. Only my prick was left untouched.

Groups of men, moving like dancers at the ballet, twined around each other, their muscles bulging beneath their tissue-thin clothing, chests pressing together, erect penises, clearly defined by thin, stretched cloth, bumping and dancing.

The lights slowly dimmed to a dull, smoky red. There was a perfume in the air that I didn't recognise, but it made my head spin thrillingly. A shower of fine, warm rain – some theatrical artifice, no doubt – began descending from above. It rendered the gossamer garments of the players even more sheer, causing them to cling like skin to their wet bodies. I watched a trio – two black-clad, one white – sink to the floor of the stage in front of me. The vision in white was laid on his back and his legs raised and parted by one of his fellows, who wrapped them around his waist. The thin, white trousers were lowered to expose the young man's wet buttocks, and his friend placed himself between his parted thighs and ripped his own trousers down. A long, straight penis, circumcised in the manner of the Hebrews, stood out from a thick cluster of black hairs which clung wetly about the base of the shaft. He parted the other's buttock cheeks, placed the circumcised head against the crack and pushed forward.

As he was being fucked, the young man in white arched his head back and lifted his mask away from his mouth, revealing a smooth, brown chin and a full, dark pair of lips. The third member of the trio was kneeling at his head, his thick, pale cock exposed and seeking the eager mouth.

I watched as the lad was fucked, arse and face, on the wet boards. All around I was witnessing similar scenes. There – two lads, one executing a handstand, the other kneeling, holding his friend's feet high, performing a vertical sixty-nine. There – a ring of men fucking each other in a circle.

The tall, bald, magisterial figure in black walked among the revellers, watching and smiling. Of Spearman, I could catch no sight.

The treatment I was receiving from a dozen inquiring hands was becoming rougher. Palms had given way to nails; lips to teeth. My nipples and my balls came under painful attack, as if by a shoal of piranha fish. My arms and legs were held, gently but immovably.

At last, the bald man clapped his hands, and all sound and movement ceased. A single youth, dressed in white (I got the impression that white was, as it were, the passive colour), mounted my divan and stood over me. He lowered himself until his arsehole was nested upon the head of my prick, and then, without using his hands, took it inside himself, his sphincter opening to accommodate me and tightening with a quiver. His hands caressed his own wet body through the shift as he rose and fell on my prick, filling me with the most marvellous sensations. The entire company was gathered, motionless, watching from behind their masks.

The young man's neat, erect cock seemed to be dancing a dance of its own, flexing and twitching as he sunk himself again and again on to my manhood. With a low sigh, and entirely unaided by hand, he shot a great gulp of semen over my chest and face. The stimulation was too great and I, too, began coming, pumping my seed inside the boy.

I spent myself, breathless.

The youth was again standing over me, his prick limp and hanging now. He looked down at me and – I am sure – smiled through his mask, then to my horror began urinating over me. I struggled to move, but now found my arms and legs held immovably. Hot piss gushed about my face, splashing my eyes and drenching my hair. I tried to cry out, but the piss entered my mouth, its iodine tang stinging the back of my throat.

Somebody gripped my head and I felt a thick black cloth bag being lowered over it. Everything went black and a cord was pulled tight around my throat. I could still feel the warm patter of the boy's piss, soaking into the mask.

I felt myself being pulled down the divan by the legs until my buttocks hung over the edge, then my legs were parted and my arms raised, and I felt the snap of manacles around my wrists and ankles. I was completely immobile now, and painfully so. My excitement turned to alarm.

It was then that I felt the terrible straining, burning sensation of a penis entering me. I struggled, but the cock forced its way forward, prising apart my tightly clenched muscles. I concentrated on relaxing about the invading member, but almost instantly received another shock. My head was forced backward. There was an opening in my mask at the level of my mouth, and through this two fingers burst, forcing themselves between my teeth and prising my mouth open. The fingers were followed by a cock. I felt the weight of a man pressing down on my face, his balls banging against my chin and his musky-tasting prick filling my throat.

I struggled to remain the master of my overwhelmed senses as, like the fellow I had watched, I was taken by two men at once. The stench of piss filled my mask and, with my mouth full to choking, breathing was difficult and painful. My arse was spasming with exquisite pain – clenching and unclenching – entirely outside my conscious control.

I was not to be freed from my shackles, nor have the mask lifted from my eyes, for two full hours. In that time I was taken constantly so that I could feel nothing of my arse bar the dribbles of cold semen finding their way out and down my legs. My throat stung with the zinc taste of jissom; the mask was soaked with it.

At last, I sensed a general withdrawal, and the mask was snatched from my eyes.

I was alone on stage with Spearman. He was nodding and smiling. 'Oh, yes,' he muttered with relish. 'Oh, yes.'

He would reveal little to me during the journey home, save that The Infernal Cabaret was quite unique in his experience (and in mine, too, I had to add!), and entirely the creation of an Italian individual named Sabbato. It was he, it seemed, who had been the black-clad maestro of the night's festivities.

As for the question of who had fucked me, and where, Spearman would only say, 'Certain of the company were chosen. You should view it as a sort of initiation rite. In a sense, we all had you.'

I looked in horror at Spearman. 'You?' I squeaked.

He merely smiled.

I still carry in my pocket the card which Spearman placed inside the Duc's memoir, on the reverse of which he wrote 'Wisdom'. Now safely home and locked inside my study, I do not feel wise. As an educated and civilised man, I ought to be able to bring my rational faculties to bear on the night's events that have just gone; to analyse what my recent experiences have to tell me about good and evil, about intent and appetite, about morality and abandon.

And yet still my mind is in confusion. The shadows cast by the firelight dance like the boys of Sabbato's troupe, threatening to fly at me. I feel no rational presence in this room.

Five

To Mr Brakes's irritation, Walter had received no fewer than nine summonses from the master that week, sending him off on special errands. He had been to Mr Kilby's three times, each time returning with a box heavy with jereboams full of coloured powders. He had accompanied the master to several patients' prosperous houses and once to the St Luke's parish casual ward. The contrast could not have been more stark. Two long, broad wings of drab grey stone led from a high, bare central hall. These were the wards, crowded with narrow beds, heavy with the smell of sickness. The building sat in the shadow of the much larger edifice of the parish workhouse.

On some of these trips, Walter was sent back to the house, following the master's diagnosis, with a list of substances to be brought from the laboratory.

'Here,' the master had said, handing him two keys. 'The large one opens the outer door and the other opens the door to the laboratory itself. All of the jars are labelled; you should have no trouble finding anything.'

Walter had entered the forbidden wing of the house with trepidation. The laboratory was a large, open space with high windows which looked out on to the garden.

The room was surprisingly bare of equipment. Apart from the surgeon's table, standing starkly in the centre of the floor, there was none of the paraphernalia of surgery to be seen. Walter recalled hearing that his master had moved most of his equipment to a room at the casual ward. Apparently, with the exception of those he performed at the hospital, he was conducting almost all of his surgical operations there, to the disapproval of his medical colleagues and – judging by the tone of the gossip in the kitchen – his own domestic staff.

The walls were lined with shelves, and the shelves heavy with vats and bottles. Walter began searching for the required substances. It was a harder task than he had anticipated. All of the vessels were labelled, certainly, but most of the labels were faded, or stained curious colours. Translating the labels and decanting their contents into smaller jars took Walter over an hour.

He had returned to his master, mumbling apologies, but Dr Reynard had seemed pleased. 'I'll get you a set of keys cut,' he had said.

Thenceforward, Walter had found himself relieved of many of his duties, much to the displeasure of Philip, who was required to perform them in his stead and grumbled loudly about it to anyone who cared to listen.

Formal occasions, however, saw Walter back in his proper role, and presently he found himself once again in livery, standing behind the dining chair of one of his master's guests. The guest of honour this evening was Sir Godfrey Saddler-Lyon, dean of surgery at St Mary's Hospital, to which his master was attached. Dr Reynard was attentive and conversational, and the evening went well until shortly before ten o'clock, when a messenger came to the door with a note for him. His manner immediately changed. He was wanted at the casual ward urgently. He was almost rude in the abruptness of his apology to his guests and out of the door before they had a chance to reply.

Nor did the guests themselves take their time. By the time the master's hansom was disappearing into the darkness, they were putting on their coats. The dean of surgery was openly complaining about the abominable manners of young doctors nowadays.

They were just about to leave when the doorbell rang. A servant of one of the master's most illustrious patients, the member of parliament Sir Archibald Ince, was on the step, in a highly agitated state. His master had collapsed after dinner and was now barely conscious and breathing with difficulty.

Mr Brakes was adamant. 'You must go and fetch the master at once. Take him directly to Sir Archibald's house. Number thirteen, isn't it?' The messenger nodded. 'Number thirteen, Grosvenor Square.' Walter was pushed into the night, still scrambling into his overcoat, with two sovereigns clutched in his hand.

Few lights burned in the long, low shadow-buildings of the St Luke's casual ward at that time of night. The entrance was lit but deserted as Walter walked through it. To his left and to his right the wards stretched out in darkness, rows of beds jutting out from the side walls like teeth. There were no nurses or porters to be seen; the diseased lay alone in their ordered ranks. He could hear, like the murmur of the countryside at night, the sleepers in their beds, breathing, snoring, some dredging painful air, some twisting and turning in their sick sleep. He felt like a lone intruder in some strange landscape; there was something about this verdant hush that made Walter desperate not to break it. It seemed as if any noise would have clanged and jarred and reverberated. Like a sneak-thief he stole silently down the long central aisle between the bed rows.

Another ward lay beyond this one, separated from it by a thick wall and a tall archway. As he approached it, he saw a pale light. Still he didn't call out. He reached the partition wall and stopped. Someone was speaking.

'Yes . . . Yes, I thought I recognised you.' Spearman's voice. 'It's . . .'

'John, my lord.' Another voice, one that Walter didn't recognise.

'John, yes. Now, where have I seen you before?'

'I used to be at Mrs Warren's, my lord.'

'Mrs Warren's, of course. My . . . what a small world we live in.' Spearman spoke in a low, soothing voice that discomfited Walter. 'You say you *used* to be there.'

'She . . . I left, sir.'

'I see. And you've been living rough since then, I suppose?'

'Yes, sir. I've been renting on the streets, but it's hard, sir.'

'And now you're here.'

What could Spearman possibly be doing here among society's unfortunates? Walter peered around the arch into the ward. Spearman stood facing the end bed, a lantern in his hand. On the bed was a young man of eighteen or nineteen, a mop of loose blond curls framing a delicate, narrow face which peered up from the pillow at the towering aristocrat.

'Yes, sir,' the boy on the bed croaked. 'It's pleurisy, sir. The doctor cut me open the day before yesterday and drained the fluids off my chest.'

'Really? Let me see.'

The youth allowed Spearman to lower the bedclothes to his waist. He had a pale, thin body. A bandage, padded at the front, criss-crossed his chest.

Gently Spearman hooked his fingertips under the edge of the bandage and eased it upward and back. The boy winced.

'I shouldn't do that, sir,' he whispered. 'The doctor'll –'

'Do you want to earn some money, John?' cooed Spearman. 'I can be generous. You know I'm always generous, John.'

'I suppose so, but –'

Spearman laid a hand over John's mouth and the rest of the words never came. He peeled the bandage back further, exposing the wound and causing the boy to cry out slightly and grip the sides of the bed in pain. Putting the lantern on the window-sill, Spearman bent over the lad until his face was inches from his chest. He stared hungrily at the wound, licking his lips. His hand reached under the bedclothes which lay rumpled around the lad's waist.

He tossed the sheets to one side and climbed up the bed, unbuttoning his trousers as he did so. He pulled out a long, slim, heavily veined prick with a loose foreskin and, wanking it to full hardness, raised the boy's buttocks and plunged it between them.

He grunted as he sodomised the boy, his immaculate boots digging into the bed and pushing him forward as he rammed the boy's head against the wall with a sickening, quickening rhythm.

'Did you know that restriction of the oxygen supply to the lungs during moments of sexual arousal can heighten or even induce orgasm?' Spearman whispered to the boy. 'This is something I have experienced myself.' He sighed. 'I envy you.'

He moved his arms towards the boy's head. Walter inched forward to see what he was doing. His hands were around the boy's throat, squeezing off his airway. The boy gagged. His eyes were wide, his face becoming livid. Spearman stared down at him with a look of savage abandon. The bed was rocking beneath the force of his thrustings.

The boy's arms flapped ineffectually, his fists clenching and relaxing. Walter feared he was going to die. With horror, he realised he would have to intervene. It was his duty as a Christian.

At that moment, Spearman reached his growling climax. His hands relaxed about the boy's neck and he slumped forward. Then he climbed from the bed, smoothing his shirt front and doing up his trousers.

Footsteps echoed down the stone floor. Walter crouched back in the shadows as Dr Reynard swept past him. He was out of breath.

'Spearman!' he panted. 'I've been looking all over for you. We passed an accident. Had to stop.'

'Ah, well,' said Spearman, straightening his neck-tie. 'Better late than never.'

There was a wheezing, coughing sound from the bed. Reynard stooped by the patient.

'John,' he said quietly. 'It's Dr Reynard. Are you all right?'

'Yes, sir,' croaked the figure on the bed, then coughed again.

'Let me examine you,' said Dr Reynard, leaning closer.

'No, really, sir, I'm all right. I'm –'

'Oh, for heaven's sake, Reynard,' said Spearman petulantly. 'Leave the boy be. You're not playing the good Samaritan tonight. You're with me. You're inexcusably late as it is, and the entertainment I have planned will not wait for ever.'

Dr Reynard wasn't listening. He reached for Spearman's lamp and held it close to the boy's face.

'What are these marks around your neck, John?' he asked.

'Nothing, sir,' the boy answered hoarsely. He shot a quick glance at Spearman, who was standing over them, staring hard at the boy on the bed.

Reynard's face clouded. He stood up.

'John, has anything . . . happened here tonight?' he asked levelly.

The boy cast his eyes downward, saying nothing. Reynard leaned forward and raised the blankets. The boy's nightshirt was still rucked up around his chest. The bandage was twisted so that its bulk was now under the boy's arm. His chest wound was exposed and weeping.

Reynard replaced the blanket gently, then turned to face Spearman and raised the lamp.

'What is the meaning of this?' he asked, his voice low and even.

'You were late,' said Spearman sulkily. 'I was tired of waiting for you. Besides, he's one of Mrs Warren's brats. I paid him a whole bloody sovereign for barely ten minutes.'

'I don't care if you paid him a hundred pounds!' Reynard hissed. 'This is an appalling state of affairs. I performed a cannulation on this boy only two days ago. His health is extremely fragile.'

'He'll live,' Spearman said, shrugging. 'If this place doesn't kill him. You know, I've never been inside one of these places before.'

'Let me tell you something about this place, Spearman.' Reynard's eyes flashed with barely restrained fury. 'Most of the casual wards in London are little more than places for people to die. Keep the dying off the street, pretend they don't exist. Thanks to my efforts and those of a few dedicated others, the St Luke's ward actually offers its patients some hope of recovery. I make a point of treating all of them like decent human beings, and to afford them the best medical care that lies within my limited powers. I have even set up a small operating theatre here. I will not have you behaving like an animal in here, Spearman. It's abominable, man!'

Spearman took a slim silver flask from his pocket, raised it to his lips and took a quick draught. 'Calm yourself, Reynard,' he said. 'You're hysterical.'

'Get out,' said Reynard. 'Never come here again. You have appalled me, tonight. The very sight of you offends me.'

'A shame,' Spearman replied. 'You would have enjoyed tonight's show. Lots of pretty boys, just like John here, being degraded for your entertainment. Still, the curtain rises, and I must be gone. Another time, perhaps.'

He turned nonchalantly on his cane and sauntered away down the dark passageway.

'I think not,' said Reynard coldly to his friend's disappearing silhouette. He returned his attention to John. 'Did he hurt you?' he asked.

'Not really, sir,' he said. 'Nothing I ain't used to, leastways. No need to make a fuss.'

Reynard gently set the bandage back in its proper place on his chest.

'You are one of Mrs Warren's boys, John?' he asked.

'Yes, sir,' John replied. 'At least, I was. I left six months ago. I didn't want to rent no more.'

'And I suppose you've been homeless since then?'

'Yes, sir,' said John.

'I see . . .' mused Reynard. 'Very well, try to get some sleep, and I shall visit you in the morning.' He turned to leave, then turned back. 'I really cannot apologise enough for the behaviour of my . . . friend.'

'I'm used to his lordship,' said John. 'He ain't so bad. Anyways, I'm not doing that no more. Not when I get out of here. I'm going to get myself a decent job.' He smiled, then coughed weakly.

Reynard smiled back. 'Sleep,' he whispered, then turned and left.

Walter waited for his master's lamp to vanish. The shadows and sounds of the casual ward closed once again around him. He could hear John, breathing raggedly, trying to make himself comfortable in the bed.

As he picked his way down the aisle, feeling his way clumsily from bedpost to bedpost, he thought of the way Spearman had walked away into the dark with perfect confidence. He doubted he'd even find a cab at this time of the night.

The obituaries appeared in the newspapers the next day. Sir Archibald Ince had died suddenly the previous night. At first light, the dean of surgery of St Mary's paid an informal call on Dr Reynard.

They sat in the drawing room, Reynard impatiently glancing at the clock every few moments. Walter served tea.

'Terrible news about Ince,' the dean said.

'Ince, yes,' answered Reynard absently. He had other things on his mind.

'Dead when you got there, was he?'

'I beg your pardon?'

'Last night.'

'I . . . didn't see Ince last night.'

'Didn't see him? But . . . Didn't you get the message?'

'I don't know what you're talking about,' said Reynard impatiently.

'This . . . boy –' the dean gestured towards Walter '– was sent to that damned poor ward of yours to fetch you. Ince had collapsed.'

'I . . .' Reynard's eyes flashed in sudden panic. 'I received no such message.'

Both men turned to Walter.

'I . . . I got lost, sir,' he spluttered. 'In the fog the cabman dropped me at the wrong place.'

'Wrong place?' the dean exploded. 'Do you realise that a man died last night?'

'I'm sorry, sir,' Walter whispered.

'Sorry indeed –'

'Yes, all right, Sir Godfrey, you've made your point quite clear,' Reynard suddenly snapped. 'Now unless there is anything else you wish to discuss with me, I shan't detain you any longer.'

He rose to his feet. Clearly slightly shocked, the dean did likewise.

'I'll show you to the door,' said Reynard.

Walter struggled to clear away the tea things before Reynard returned. It was as much as he could do to keep from dropping the crockery to the floor, so badly was he shaking.

Too late. His master re-entered the room.

Dr Reynard looked pale and shocked. He slumped down in a chair and let his head sink into his hands. Walter tried to carry on with his work as silently as possible, but the cups rattled and banged against one another in his trembling grip.

Presently Reynard looked up, directly at Walter, questioningly, penetratingly, perhaps a little fearfully.

'Walter . . .' he said.

'Sir?'

Reynard studied him for another long moment. 'Nothing,' he said at last. 'Carry on with your work.'

And he got up and left the room.

Reynard went directly to his study and locked himself in. He slumped behind his desk, deep in thought. This only affirmed his resolve of last night. A man had died . . .

He thought about Walter. Why had he got the impression that the boy was lying to the dean? What was he concealing? How much did he know about last night? Had he in fact been to the casual ward?

One thing was clear. His excursions with Spearman were over.

He reached into his desk drawer and pulled out the Duc du Guerrand. He envied the old fiend's breathtaking lack of conscience. He stormed through life, not giving a damn what anyone thought of him and not caring about the human wreckage he left in his wake. Spearman was like that; Reynard was not. Spearman used people as he pleased. He courted open scandal in his pursuit of sensual pleasure.

What was it that made Spearman behave as he did? Fear of discovery had certainly added a frisson to Reynard's own experience of their adventures, but to Spearman it barely seemed to be a consideration. Was this what freed his conscience so alarmingly? Was it only fear of detection which moderated Reynard's own behaviour; which gave him any sense of responsibility? Was that all he really felt over Ince, he wondered. A sick fear of so nearly getting caught. A foreknowledge of how his peers and colleagues would brand him, allowing a patient to die while indulging in abominable vices.

What held him in check? What called him back to sanity, conscience and reason when Spearman – or the Duc du Guerrand – would just have charged forward?

64

He turned a page of the Duc.

'I was always a generous landlord,' the old reprobate wrote. 'When came the season in which the rents were to be collected, I had evolved a fair and just system of payment, whereby those whose harvests had been poor might render me service in kind rather than a money payment. On the appointed day, every year, those who could afford the rent gathered in the great hall; those who could not sent their sons.

'It was my custom to deal with the financial aspects of the day as swiftly as I might, then send those good, solvent tenants back to their holdings without ceremony, dismiss my steward and lock the doors of the great hall. Then, alone with my pretty payments-in-kind, I would indulge my annual duties. This year I had conceived of a wrestling match as an amusing way of whittling down the size of my rather daunting task (for the harvest was bad this year, and half of the county seemed to have sent their strapping offspring). A wrestling match – nude, of course, in true Olympian fashion – would show off these farm-lads to perfection. I bid them pair up and strip off, which they did without complaint, then I bid them wrestle.

'I walked among their straining bodies, admiring the flexing of backs, the bracing of legs, strong arms, locked, trembling with exertion. I demonstrated my fine swordsmanship by taking out my épée and inserting it deftly into the midst of a tangled couple, playing its point around the two dangling penises it found there.

'One of the two lads, strawberry blond, muscular and freckled, was clearly losing to the other, but what interested me was the way his cock, feeling the tickle of cold steel, lengthened and hardened. He would be the first. Conveniently, his opponent propelled him across the room and pinned him to the high table, where he lay, staring at the ceiling, his legs floundering, his conqueror pinned across his chest, the remains of the banquet spilled and scattered.

'Without hesitation I removed my clothes and advanced upon him. He began to cry out as he discerned my intention, and I ordered a third boy – a heavy lad – to mount the table and place his anus over the boy's face to silence him. This was done, and I entered him hard, for in truth I was aroused almost to bursting.

Even through the bulk of the heavy lad's buttocks I could hear his cries, which served to push me even more swiftly towards my climax.

'The other boys had stopped wrestling and had gathered in a great circle around the table. All were hard, now, and all were masturbating as they watched me take their neighbour. One buckled and climaxed, splashing the side of my face.

'When I came I rested but briefly before having another boy hauled up to take his place. Six boys I fucked in total that afternoon as the spunk from the wanking circle showered down on my back, and several more I gobbled.

'I fornicated until I was exhausted. Those lads I had fucked, I dismissed. Those I had not I ordered to perform for me while I watched their copulations. Those who failed to please me in this I kept to the last, and my servants and I got drunk together and threw knives at them.'

It was no good: Reynard had looked at the end of the book. He knew what lay in wait for the Duc, and with that lucky perspective he could only see how everything the Duc did led him deeper into a fatal trap.

Six

——————

For the whole of the next fortnight, Reynard applied himself diligently to his duties, both social and professional. He spent his days at the hospital, or in private consultation, and his nights – several of them, at least – at the casual ward. He delivered a lecture, went to the opera (Covent Garden *and* Her Majesty's) and accepted invitations to two dinner parties. He caught up on his overdue correspondence and issued some invitations of his own. He even sent one to the dean of surgery, doubting that he would come.

He attended John as he had promised, and every day thenceforward. The boy would survive Lord Spearman's visit, but he was weak and would never, Reynard feared, be otherwise.

He also paid a visit to Mrs Warren.

'My Johnny in the poor ward?' she gasped. 'Oh, the poor mite. What's the matter with him, sir?'

'Pleurisy,' Reynard replied. 'I performed an operation, and he will live, but he will never be strong. I understand he was no longer . . . working here.'

'Oh, Doctor, it broke my heart to turn him out,' the woman wailed. 'But he left me no choice. He hadn't been happy here for a while. Said he didn't want to do renting no more.'

'Mrs Warren, John will have to be discharged from the casual ward in a week's time. There is great pressure for the beds. Living on the streets, he wouldn't last two months. Now ... I fear he will never again be fit enough to be a renter again, but I would like you to consider taking him back, perhaps in some less demanding role.'

'I don't know, sir. I'm not a rich woman. I have a dozen other boys to think of. If he couldn't earn his keep –'

'I would be prepared to pay for his board here.'

'Well in that case, Doctor . . .'

'You decide how much it will cost you to keep him here, and communicate the sum to me. I shall meet whatever sum you think appropriate.'

Mrs Warren clapped her hands around Reynard's. 'Bless you, Doctor,' she said. 'You're a good man.'

'Naturally, this arrangement must remain highly confidential.' He placed his hat upon his head and left.

He was vaguely aware of a side door opening slowly behind him, and a young voice saying, 'Thank you, sir.' He didn't turn to see which of his peers had been pleasuring himself behind the door; rather he accelerated his pace, and was glad to be back on the pavement, the front door closed behind him.

Walter and Philip's late-night reading sessions continued, albeit sporadically. Walter found Philip's interest capricious and unpredictable. Frequently the footman would badger a tired Walter into selecting a new book and reading while he masturbated, but other times, when Walter somewhat timidly took the initiative, Philip didn't seem at all interested.

'What's up with you?' he would mock. 'Randy *again*?' Walter sensed that Philip enjoyed making him squirm; making him do all the work, accept all the responsibility. Usually, with however much feigned indifference in the beginning, Philip would end up flogging himself as Walter read. Sometimes he would pull Walter's hand unceremoniously on to his hard cock, expecting him to take over while he lay back on the bed, hands clasped behind his head, enjoying the sensation.

The precise sexual nature of their reading matter was a bone of contention between the young servants. Philip wanted to hear about women. Woman alone; women with men; women with women. Walter found himself curiously ill at ease with the presence of women in the sexual passages he read. To Walter there was something alien and unsettling about women and sex. He felt much more at home with those books which spoke of the classical Greek ideal. As a boy he had read – in secret – the myths and legends of Ancient Greece. They had inspired him with their tales of bravery and manly comradeship. Now he was discovering, in the pages of Dr Reynard's library, the principles of Platonic and Socratic love, which the authors evoked with eloquence and passion before launching into vivid descriptions of male-on-male debaucheries. To his surprise and alarm, he found himself wondering if he would ever find a mentor, wise and compassionate; someone at whose feet he could sit and learn and love.

The nearest thing he had had was Pastor Meek. The pastor, in the little school he had run for ten years, had taught him to read and write. The texts had been exclusively Christian, however. Greek thought had been roundly condemned so Walter had hidden his few Greek books. The pastor was a harsh disciplinarian and most transgressions of his exacting code of conduct had resulted in thrashings. Masturbation, and all other manifestations of the sexual urge, had been particularly frowned upon, and vigorously discouraged.

He thought of Lord Spearman and the boy, John, in the casual ward. Their coupling had been cruel, and anything but uplifting and enlightening. Perhaps, he thought sadly, that was all that remained in the modern age of the Greek conception – a shameful, brutal physical remnant of a once noble ideal. And yet, as he read aloud to Philip, his eyes flicking constantly to the footman's engorged cock and pumping hand, the memory of what he had seen in the casual ward endlessly intruded on his thoughts, adding a disturbing piquancy to his own arousal.

In the mornings following their sessions, Walter would usually find it impossible to meet Philip's eyes, blushing with an unsettling mix of shame and further arousal. He would wash at the bowl, naked, a prickly awareness of Philip's presence in the room causing him to blush with mortification at the way his cock would, quite unbidden, swell and harden. Philip seemed completely unaffected by their night-time activities. He would either ignore Walter's manly embarrassment entirely or fire crude quips at him from the bed. He never referred to their strange couplings, and behaved by day as if the nights had never occurred.

On each of these mornings, Walter would slip into the library and replace the last night's tome, afraid to leave the books in the room, in case of discovery by Mr Brakes. Then, at the end of the day when the staff had retired to bed, he would steal back in, select a volume and creep to the top of the house to the fecund bed he and Philip shared.

Emerging at the top of the narrow stairs late one night he was startled to collide with Tom, carrying his full piss-pot. The book he was holding slipped from his hands to the floor. The chamber-pot slooshed and some of its contents splashed over the edge, showering down on the book. Mumbling an apology to the old man, Walter stooped to pick it up. He saw that Tom was staring down at the volume, his face white. He gripped Walter's arm with a weak hand. 'That infernal book,' he said. 'Beware, boy. Beware its poisoned pages. I know the seductions of the master's library. They can only lead to hell, boy! Remember your Bible!'

He continued to cling to Walter's arm. Walter was struck by how frail, how old, how pale his hand was; the skin so thin as to be almost transparent, the veins twisting like old twigs beneath. Tom released his grip and shuffled on, wheezing as he walked.

Walter wiped the old man's water off the book. He examined the volume. It was one of his favourites, a collection of mock-Greek texts and verses which were beautiful, sensual and highly erotic. It was entitled *Ganymede*.

It had probably been in the library in the master's father's day. He turned for the first time to the fly-sheet. On it there was an inscription, handwritten in ink. It said, *For true Thomas, my Ganymede, my master, my pupil, my angel, my doom.* It was signed Hugo Reynard, and dated 1820.

Philip was already in bed when Walter entered the room. He undressed, his member already beginning to swell, donned his nightshirt and climbed into bed next to the footman.

He let the book fall open where it would, and began to read.

'Not that Greek thing again,' Philip complained. 'It's full of buggers.' With a resigned sigh, he lowered the sheets, hitched up his nightshirt and began a slow, weary wank.

Next to him, Walter's cock stood upright beneath his night-clothing, making the linen stand like a proud, Olympian peak.

Walter chose a poem about a man and a beautiful youth and their couplings by a river. It was subtly infused with a vibrancy and a tenderness that Walter found both moving and arousing.

Philip's hand slowed, and after a moment stopped altogether.

'Fuck this,' he said, and swiped the book from Walter's hands. 'Come 'ere.' He scrambled across the bed and swiftly mounted Walter, as was his habit. 'Fucking rubbish book,' he muttered as he ground his cock into Walter's flank.

Walter's head banged against the wall. Philip stopped for a moment and dragged him down the bed. He straddled his chest and began masturbating himself once more, pressing his cock-head hard into Walter's face. His hand struck Walter's cheek painfully as it pumped the livid, swollen organ.

At length he raised his buttocks slightly from Walter's chest and grasped a great sheaf of golden hair on Walter's head, pulling it forward. Walter's eyes widened. He tried to struggle. Philip forced the tip of his knob between Walter's lips. Walter clenched his jaw; Philip responded with a hard blow to the side of Walter's head, sending it cracking into the wall. Walter surrendered to his fate and relaxed his mouth. Philip pushed his thick knob past Walter's teeth and back along his tongue until Walter felt he would choke. He pulled back, then thrust forward, driving Walter's head into the mattress again and again. His balls smacked against Walter's chin; the smell and the taste of Philip's groin overwhelmed Walter.

'Dirty . . . little . . . bitch!' Philip muttered as he thrust. Walter guessed he was thinking of Ruby. He was no more to the young footman than what Philip himself called a 'posh wank'. In his very disillusionment, Walter found solace. He was enjoying the feeling of being utterly used.

Philip grunted his way to orgasm. As he started to discharge his load, his cock slipped from between Walter's lips, firing a white, warm cannonade point blank into his face.

Philip retreated across the bed as his cock, dark red at the head, oozed its final droplets. He gave Walter an odd look: sheepish, guilty, like nothing Walter had ever seen in the footman's face before. Walter read the look. Philip had just crossed a line. He had penetrated – albeit orally – another man. His lust had brought him hard against the boundaries of his own manhood. He turned over and went to sleep in silence, as he usually did, but for once it was not a silence born of contempt and disdain.

The next morning Walter rose early, as was his wont, in order to replace the book in the library. He listened to old Tom shuffling along the passageway outside his door, coughing weakly. He turned again to the inscription at the front of the book. What did it mean?

Tom descended the stairway creakily. Only when he heard the door at the foot of the stairs open and close again did Walter emerge from the room, the book clutched in his hands. Instead of following the valet down the stairs, he turned along the passage and stopped outside the old man's door. He remembered Philip's description of the room with a shudder. Gingerly he opened the door and stepped inside.

It was not yet light outside. The curtains were drawn and the room was bathed in gloom. There was no furniture save for a narrow bed, a wash stand (but no mirror), a wardrobe and a small table.

The walls were alive. Crosses and crucifixes – dozens of them, all sizes, wood, metal, carved stone – covered the walls. The space in between the holy symbols were patched with small, finely printed pages from the Bible. The inside of the door was also covered in the holy word, so that only the doorknob was visible.

Walter had always disliked crucifixes. He had been brought up to dislike them. 'Idolatry', Pastor Meek called them. 'Blasphemous graven images.' They were pornographic, he would rant. They turned the saviour of mankind into a whore.

Tom's walls were studded with holy pornography. Naked, nailed bodies stretched in bony agony, rags hanging limply from their genitals. Christ figures screamed mutely at him from all sides. They crowded in on him. The packed torture walls seemed about to crush him.

Dropping the book, he ran from the room.

Seven

Dr Richard Reynard's days of conscientious abstinence ended at about 5.30 one afternoon with a commotion from the passageway. A voice he didn't recognise – a child's voice – was demanding to see him.

'You can't go in there!' Brakes's voice was shouting hoarsely. 'Even the staff are not allowed . . .'

Reynard rose from his desk and opened the door. A black boy was dodging around the old butler, who swayed and teetered in the hallway, trying to catch him.

'All right, Brakes,' said Reynard, suppressing a smile. He reached out and caught the boy, who stopped, breathless, and looked up at him with a wide-eyed, urgent stare.

'I'm sorry, sir,' wheezed the old butler. 'He slipped past me. I've chased him all over the house.'

'Doctor, sir!' the boy suddenly cried. 'You've got to come now.'

'What?' laughed Reynard.

'Come now,' the boy repeated. 'Come now to Mrs Warren's, sir.'

Reynard felt himself turn cold. Suddenly he recognised his little captive – the black boy from the brothel. He glanced anxiously at Brakes, but the old man was still too out of breath to be listening.

'It John, sir,' the boy said. 'He real sick. Mrs Warren think he gonna die.'

The butler was becoming his old self again. Reynard had no time to hesitate. 'I'm going out for a while,' he announced, grasping an overcoat and reaching for his doctor's bag.

'Yes, sir,' wheezed the butler.

The boy was pulling him by the hand towards the door.

'And for God's sake, sit down, man. Have a rest. Get your breath back.'

They travelled by hansom and stopped several streets from Mrs Warren's house. He could get little information out of the boy beyond his name – coincidentally, Richard – and the fact that John was curled up and screaming in agony, clutching his stomach and vomiting.

When they arrived they were ushered in by the ever-elegant mother of the house. From the sound of things, it was business as usual.

Reynard and young Richard followed Mrs Warren into a small side room where John was lying curled on a bed. But for his disordered blankets, which now lay tangled around his legs and trailing the floor, he was naked. The three stood and regarded the slim body in front of them. The scar on his chest was still red and angry. His penis was curled snail-like against his body.

'Hello, John,' said Reynard.

'Doctor,' the figure on the bed said feebly.

Reynard stooped at the boy's bedside and began his examination. Temperature high, stomach tender to the touch, spasms of vomiting – he examined the collected vomit carefully – and copious shivering.

'Poisoning,' Reynard declared. 'Probably from something he ate. Has anybody else been ill?'

Mrs Warren shook her head firmly. 'Not one soul, doctor,' she said.

'Normally this wouldn't be dangerous,' Reynard said, 'but in John's condition we must be very careful.' He opened his little black bag and rummaged through the contents. 'Damn and blast!' he exclaimed. In his haste to get young Richard out of the house he had neglected to check on the contents of the bag. He took out a pen and some paper and scribbled a note, which he handed to Richard.

'Take this note to my house,' he instructed. 'Give it to my servant, Walter, and bring him back here with the compounds I have listed.'

Richard took the note. Reynard gripped his arm.

'Be certain that it is Walter who brings the compounds. No-one else from my household is to come here.'

Richard nodded and left. Reynard continued to examine the patient. 'Mrs Warren,' he said. 'Boil a kettle. There is something we can do before my servant arrives.'

Forty minutes later he returned to the large central room. Mrs Warren had slipped away and the room was empty. A door opened and a young man entered: an exotic creature, tall, lithe and athletically muscular. His hair was long and black and cascaded down his bare back and shoulders, almost to his waist. His body was olive coloured and his legs and chest were downed with fine black hair which thickened at the nipples. He was wearing nothing but a native loincloth of white linen. His erection made the front of his loincloth stand out in a point. He was carrying a silver tray of sweetmeats and quails' eggs.

He stood in front of Reynard, his swollen groin level with Reynard's face, and held the tray against his upper thighs.

'I'm Soojay,' he said. 'Eat.'

Reynard reached uncertainly for an egg. The boy's long erection, straining at its covering, protruded tantalisingly over the top of the feast. Reynard brushed it lightly with the back of his hand.

The boy withdrew the tray and stood facing Reynard.

'Eat,' he repeated.

Dropping to his knees, Reynard fell on the boy's cock like a starving man. His teeth closed on the loincloth and clamped together over the covered bulb of the boy's cock. He sunk his face on to the cloth-covered pole, feeling it fill his mouth. He drew back and nipped at the cloth with his teeth. Soojay winced and smiled as Reynard worked his way down the tall shaft beneath to the tight, full globes of his bollocks. Each one in turn he took in his mouth, tugging first lightly at them then harder.

All this was accomplished quickly. Reynard tore the loincloth away from the boy and buried his face in the tight black curls of pubic fuzz which gathered above the bollocks and spidered away up to his belly button. He breathed deeply of the boy's heavy scent, then wrapped his lips around the base of his brown cock, slurping and sucking his way back up its length and tasting his musky cock-flesh until he arrived at the circumcised head and plunged on it like a diving bird. He played with it in his mouth, traced the ridge of the helmet with his tongue, caught the sensitive frenulum with his teeth and finally drew it deep into his throat. His hands clutching and clawing at the boy's buttocks and his fingers finding the damp warmth of his arsehole, Reynard sucked like a baby at the nipple.

When the lad came, Reynard drank his essence greedily. His hands were already loosening the front of his own trousers and unbuttoning his undergarments. Reynard freed his throbbing cock and sought the boy's supple arsehole, pushing him back against the wall. Soojay leaned back and spread his legs. Reynard stepped between them, pushing his cock upward and feeling his taut young flesh yielding. The boy drew in a long breath as Reynard penetrated him. His cock seeped the last of its juice over Reynard's suit. He dragged his unshaven jaw roughly across the boy's smooth cheeks. He bit his ears and his lips hard, and all the time he drove his cock high into him. His hands clawed up and down the boy's arse and back. He dug his nails in deep as he came, letting out a great sob of relief.

Walter enjoyed the break from his household chores which his special errands for Dr Reynard occasioned. He had scrutinised the doctor's list and moved artfully about the laboratory, hefting large jereboams. He had selected the three specified substances and decanted their powders into smaller earthenware pots, then set off with the anxious young black boy.

They travelled up through Bloomsbury to the fringes of Somers Town and entered an unassuming house. The passageways inside were dark, the atmosphere thick and perfumed. It made Walter cough as he stumbled blindly forward. He saw his master ahead of him stand suddenly from the sofa where he had been reclining.

Walter stopped dead. Still draped across the sofa was a man, as naked as a savage, with nothing but a flimsy wrap of white cloth covering his shame.

'Ah, Walter. Of course, Walter . . . Good of you to get here so soon. That is . . .' He sounded flustered. 'Come with me.'

Walter accompanied the master into a side room where a young lad – the boy he had seen in the casual ward – lay motionless on the bed. He watched as the master mixed the recently arrived compounds with others from his bag. He decanted the mixture into a glass and held it to the boy's lips. As the boy sipped, he stroked Reynard's arm.

'Dr Reynard,' he whispered between mouthfuls. 'Nice Dr Reynard. I was tickled to find out you were one of Mrs W's gentlemen.'

'Sssh,' said the doctor softly. 'Drink it up.'

The boy swallowed the draught gingerly. His hand, Walter was shocked to see, was no longer on Dr Reynard's but clamped on his master's inner thigh, rubbing gently back and forth. The patient must be delirious.

Dr Reynard moved his leg out of reach of the boy's hand. Walter felt a pressure on his shoulder. The long-haired savage snaked past him, allowing a languid hand to trail his neck and cheek. Walter flinched but the boy didn't seem to notice. He passed on, stopping beside Reynard and placing a hand on his shoulder.

Reynard lurched awkwardly to his feet.

'I think we have done all that we can do here, Walter,' he said in a voice of strained cheeriness. 'Come. John, I shall return to see you tomorrow.'

Casting an awkward glance at Walter, Reynard stepped from the room. Walter gathered the earthenware pots together and left the room. For the first time he noticed sounds coming from other parts of the house. Giggles from behind doors; whispers; the faint, rhythmic creak of furniture. For the first time he noticed the decor in the dimly lit central room. Tall, pale panels framed with painted vines of Greek soldiers – hoplights – fighting, wrestling or reclining, many of them naked bar the odd shield, belt or helmet. Until recently it would have seemed purely noble to Walter.

Through a chink in the open door, Lord Spearman watched his friend depart with his pretty servant boy. He lay back on the bed and smiled broadly. A good evening's work. Casually he began unbuttoning his trousers. Reaching across to the table beside the bed, he tinkled a little bell and waited.

Five hours later, Reynard returned to Mrs Warren's, alone and by hansom. Young Richard ushered him into a side room and bade him sit down. Reynard smiled. It was almost as if he were expected. The servant boy left the room and was replaced after a few moments by Soojay, the dark youth of the morning.

He was dressed like an Indian prince, in a tiny white silk tunic, not quite covering his chest, and a pair of white silk pantaloons which fell loosely to his knees. He was barefoot. His long black hair cascaded over his shoulders and down his back. His hips swayed, catlike, as he walked into the room. He draped himself on the couch and rested his head on Reynard's shoulder. Reynard could see the boy's cock swelling beneath his thin wrap. Soojay ran his hand down Reynard's chest and let it fall languidly into his lap. Reynard's cock was growing large, rising up beneath the fine worsted of his trousers. Soojay gripped the hard shaft through the cloth and massaged it slowly and firmly.

Another young man, dressed identically to Soojay, entered the room. They were practically a matching pair: brown skinned with long, silky hair, sleek musculature and peppered with black body hair.

The newcomer stood in front of Reynard, smiled and removed his pantaloons. His cock lengthened and rose, long and straight and circumcised. He sank nimbly into a chair, bent forward at the neck and back and wrapped his legs around the back of his neck. His hair swept in a great black fan across the seat. Curled thus into a ball he opened his mouth and – to Reynard's astonishment – wrapped his lips around his own cock. His head bobbed slightly as he massaged the dark, swollen bulb.

He rolled on to his back, still sucking himself, his arsehole now exposed between stretched cheeks.

Soojay rose from the couch, his cock straining against the front of his white silk pantaloons. He sank gracefully to his haunches and speared his friend's wide-open arsehole with his cock. His knees braced on the edge of the chair; he then pivoted backward, pulling his tightly curled, sucking friend with him, off the chair and on to his belly. Soojay lay flat on the carpet, his hands supporting his friend's buttocks, and jerked upward with his hips, bouncing his friend – a human ball – on his long prick. Reynard watched, enthralled.

The auto-fellator came first, drinking deeply of his own juices and dribbling them happily down his chin. Soojay came immediately afterwards, arching his back and thrusting his prick upward. For a moment he released his arms and the boy, curled into a ball, sat balanced on Soojay's spurting member.

The acrobats, naked but for their tiny white tunics, sat one on either side of Reynard. Soojay leaned forward and nibbled his ear. His friend did the same. In near-perfect synchronicity, their lips danced over the sides of Reynard's head, cheeks and eyes. Their long hair brushed and tickled him. They peeled away his clothing as they worked, tooth and tongue, down his neck to his chest, sharp on his nipples in their bed of fine, rich hair, taking it in turns at the belly-button. His trousers and underpants were eased off and away and he reclined, naked and erect, allowing these youths to wander where they would with their mouths.

Soojay's friend climbed on to Reynard's bare lap and sat facing him. He curved forward once again, arching his remarkable back. His fist clamped his long cock against Reynard's slightly shorter, thicker one. Pressing the twin helmets together he closed his lips around them, his teeth grazing lightly on the taut, engorged skin.

The twin cocks squirmed together in the warm, dark cavity of the lad's mouth. Reynard felt his muscles beginning to tense and tingle in sympathy with the exquisite anguish of his enraged cock.

He could bear it no longer. He turned beneath the lad and rolled him on to his back. He flowed up between his legs and over him, biting and kissing his black-furred balls, his cock and his olive-brown, hair-dappled chest. He kissed him deeply, at the same time feeling for his rich arsehole with his prick. His arse was already wet and sticky with Soojay's come. He entered him frantically and clumsily, his toes digging into the couch, spurring his prick deeper into the lad's slippery arse.

He felt a pressure on his back, the swish of a luxuriant mane and a cock probing at his own arsehole. Soojay was behind him, practically on top of him. His hair billowed about Reynard's cock, tangling itself around it and disappearing into the other boy's dark crack.

Supporting himself on his hands, grazing Reynard's back with the slightest pressure of his chest and stomach, Soojay began to expertly fuck him, moving his body only minimally and using the rise and fall of Reynard's own buttocks as he fucked the lad beneath to propel him on to his cock.

The slightest tension from the statuesque Soojay indicated to Reynard that the lad was registering the first pangs of approaching orgasm. He could feel the youth's hot breath quickening on his neck. Soojay bit down hard with his teeth, sucking like a leech as Reynard's arse rose and fell beneath his cock, and came hotly in his burning hole. Reynard's own climax was bearing down on him fast. It took him forcibly; he shuddered against the lad's buttocks, clutched at his shoulders and spasmed and burst inside him.

The three collapsed in a sticky heap, the two youths' acrobatic grace gone and their Eastern poise giving way to easy laughter.

Reynard gazed at the pair with admiration. 'You're astonishing,' he said.

'We are a special present,' said Soojay. 'We come from far away. A special present from a friend.'

The door to the room swung open, as if propelled by an invisible hand. In front of Reynard, across the atrium, slouched in a tall armchair, was Spearman. He raised a glass to his friend.

'Reynard!' he called. 'What a delightful surprise. Do join me for some champagne.'

Eight

'I tell you,' said Philip, half-heartedly polishing the table in the breakfast room, 'he sneaked out again last night, after we'd all gone off to bed. Hailed a hansom. Ruby told me. Didn't get back till near dawn again.'

Walter tipped coal on to the fire and said nothing. Mr Brakes's voice drifted in from the hallway. 'A good servant should be concerned but never curious, Philip. It is no concern whatever of ours how the master chooses to spend his evenings.'

'Yes, Mr Brakes,' said Philip automatically. He waited until the butler's footsteps receded down the hall. 'Then there was that business this afternoon,' he continued. 'Didn't look right to me. That little pickaninny sprat, he weren't no servant. And he weren't nobody's son. So who was he? Where did you say you went again?'

Again Walter remained silent. He could sense Philip's mounting irritation.

'What is it with you, anyway?' he whined. 'Master's pet, running round after him. Us servants ain't got no secrets, Walter, mate.'

'It was a patient of the master's from the casual ward,' Walter said finally. 'He was taken sick at home. The master feared he might die, so he paid him a return visit. The boy was just a friend . . .'

The words tailed away to nothing. The master was standing in the doorway, staring directly at him. He was wearing the same garments as he had been wearing the previous night. He looked tired. He smiled awkwardly and shuffled on down the passageway. Walter turned back to the coal scuttle, resolving to avoid the master for the rest of the day.

Shortly afterwards, Dr Reynard appeared below stairs, inquiring after the whereabouts of his valet. Apparently, Tom had not appeared to attend the master that morning. None of the other staff had seen him either.

'I bet he's dead,' Philip whispered to Walter. 'I bet Old Nick come to carry him off in the night.'

In point of fact, the old man had not been carried off in the night, but was nevertheless discovered by Dr Reynard to be seriously ill. He lay on his bed, his face grey and his breathing ragged and shallow. When Reynard spoke to him, his only response was a minute, voiceless movement of his cracked, mucus-flecked lips.

Reynard felt his temperature and his pulse. His skin was cold; his pulse weak. He leaned forward and gently pulled the old man's eyelids apart with his fingertips. A cloudy film covered both eyes.

'Make sure that he is properly and regularly fed,' said Reynard to the hovering Brakes. 'Lots of Mrs Donaldson's hot, thick broths. The odd tot of hot whisky would not go amiss either.'

'Oh, Tom doesn't drink, sir,' the butler responded. 'May I ask what ails him, sir?'

Reynard looked the butler in the eye and shook his head almost imperceptibly. He tucked the old man's blankets tight around him and said, 'Get some rest, Tom. You've been working too hard.'

The butler turned and left the room. Reynard looked around with distaste at the icon-crowded walls. There had always been something penitential in the way Tom conducted himself, but it had been many years before Reynard had entered this room and come to learn just how desperately penitential Tom actually was.

The whole thing was depressing, not so much for its serious – or rather, fanatical – tone but for the tawdriness and appalling vulgarity of it all. The clutter of religious paraphernalia put him in mind of some sort of cheap market stall. He smiled grimly.

Salvation off a barrow. Was this what the old man was clinging to in his extremity?

With a parting glance at the dying old man, Reynard made to follow his butler. His foot kicked something lying beside the wardrobe. It was a book. He bent to pick it up. *Ganymede.* He recognised it from his library. He let it fall open at the inscription on the fly-page. He had read the oblique inscription before – many years before, for it was not a volume he had perused recently – but had never given too much thought to what it meant. Certainly he had never associated the Tom to whom the book was dedicated with the old man who lay dying before him on the bed.

He knew so little about his father. If the words implied . . . Were there echoes here of the poems and passages within the book? Ganymede was the mortal cup-bearer to Zeus, and beloved of the god for his great beauty. Had Tom once been beautiful? Had his father . . .

Truly, Sir Hugo Reynard had been an Olympian figure, a giant in the medical profession of his day, both sought after and feared by the great and the good, and adored from afar. It was he who had set his son Richard on the path of dedicated enquiry. As a schoolboy, far away from his family, the father had both inspired and in some way terrorised the son. Reynard's atheism was rooted in his father's militant aversion to religion ('grotesque superstition' – Hugo Reynard would not let any priest set foot inside his house), and his belief in man as a rational rather than an emotional being had been driven into the son by lengthy, well-crafted letters almost from infancy. But love? Reynard had admired and respected his father, and worked hard to be worthy of his approbation, but could he, upon reflection, say with total honesty that he had loved him? He had seen so little of him. Certainly his father had never demonstrated any overt love either to his son or, insofar as Reynard could tell, to his wife. Had he then loved his young servant? Or at least lusted after him? But the inscription seemed to suggest more than mere lust. It implied an already deep familiarity and warmth.

Something slipped from between the pages of the book and fluttered to the floor. Reynard stooped to pick it up. It was a narrow strip torn from the top of a sheet of notepaper, quite new-looking, which had presumably been serving as a bookmark. Printed along its edge were the words 'Featherstone Street Congregationalist Church', and then, underneath, in smaller letters, 'Pastor Nathaniel Meek'.

Walter. Of course.

Thoughtfully tapping the book against his chin, Reynard cast a final glance back at the slumbering Tom. Placing the book on the man-servant's table, he left the room.

Reynard caught Walter cleaning some portraits late that afternoon.

'I . . . wanted to thank you for not revealing where we went yesterday,' the master said to his servant.

Walter was coming to dread these frank exchanges: they hardly befitted their relationship.

'It would be awkward explaining it to the staff,' Reynard continued. He ran his finger along the edge of one of the portraits – a shepherd boy calling to his flock. 'I can scarcely explain it to myself.'

Walter mumbled something under his breath.

'Were you shocked?' Reynard asked.

'It's not my business to be shocked, sir. Mr Brakes says a good servant is concerned but –'

'Never curious, I know. It's a good maxim, Walter. I . . . promised I would pay a return visit to that place today, to check on the young man's condition. Should an emergency arise you may come and get me, but only you. And make sure none of the other staff know where I am.' He turned to go. 'I appreciate this, Walter,' he said.

Over the next three days, whenever the opportunity presented itself, Dr Reynard climbed to the top of the house to Tom's room. Tom drifted between periods of frail lucidity, rambling incoherence and deathlike slumber. Frequently finding him asleep, Reynard would sit at the side of the bed and read to himself passages from *Ganymede*, trying to imagine the old man as young and perhaps handsome, his eyes bright and his complexion rosy with youthful sexual allure. He found it difficult to reconcile such a picture with the parchment-white, brittle body before him.

Once only Tom awoke when Reynard was thus occupied. Absorbed in the book, Reynard at first did not notice that his valet was awake, until a slight noise from the bed arrested his attention. Tom's palsied eyes focused slowly on the book, then widened into an expression Reynard could only interpret as one of mortal fear. He began mumbling something to himself, low at first, then getting louder, fast and breathless. It sounded to Reynard like a prayer, or a passage from the Bible. The old man drew his blankets up to his chin, his veiny, skeletal hands clutching at their folds with all their meagre strength and shaking horribly. Reynard removed the book from the old man's sight and gradually his voice faded and he sunk back into restless sleep. Reynard slipped from the room, taking the book with him.

In order that the master should not be unattended during Tom's incapacity, Mr Brakes had hastily instructed Philip in the duties of a valet. The demands upon his time and energy which these extra labours imposed upon him were a source of much complaint for the young footman. He was required to rise a full half-hour earlier in order to prepare his master's dressing room before commencing his duties below stairs. Even the extra money promised did nothing to soothe his black humour.

'Can't a man bath himself?' he moaned. 'I tell you, toffs is like children. I can't do all this. It'll drive me mad.'

He and Walter were in the dining room, polishing the silver. Philip threw the sugar salver he was carelessly buffing down on to the table's sheen surface.

'Bugger this,' he said to Walter. 'I've got to sort his togs out for this evening. You'll have to finish here.' He slouched towards the door. 'And then there's the glassware. And don't say nothing about this to old Brakes.'

Walter worked hard. He didn't know why and he was aware that Philip was taking unfair advantage of what he supposed was a too-compliant nature, but he did it anyway. In a strange way, he felt comfortable with the casual abuses showered upon him by Philip.

'The blacking round the grates needs doing,' Philip would say, or, 'The luncheon table needs setting,' and he would toss down a pile of linen napkins and leave the room.

Somehow, Walter felt this treatment complemented their surreptitious night-time activities, with Walter reading and Philip lying back like a sultan, stroking himself or rubbing his engorged penis against Walter's legs or belly until it erupted over him.

Surely some of the domestic duties he was now undertaking should normally have fallen to Ruby. Perhaps that explained why she was no longer mooning about him, smiling and fluttering and playing the coquette. She and Philip seemed quite thick now. Whatever the reason for her sudden cessation of interest in him, Walter was relieved to be free of it.

On the third day of Tom's illness, just before midday, Walter was interrupted in his work by Mr Brakes. 'The master wishes to see you in his study,' the butler said.

There was something about the formality of the announcement which unnerved Walter. Normally, when the master wanted him to run an errand he would summon him to the laboratory or merely accost him at whatever task he was about.

He knocked nervously at the door of the master's study and waited to be admitted. The master was seated behind his desk.

'Sit down,' he said to Walter.

'Sir . . .'

'Sit down, please.'

Awkwardly, Walter sat. He blanched. On the desk between them was the copy of *Ganymede* he had dropped in Tom's room and not dared collect. He realised that to have neglected the book in such a way was an abuse of the privilege the master had granted him. He would at the very least be admonished.

The master was silent and thoughtful, looking down at the book.

'Walter,' he said eventually, 'you know of course that Tom has been sick for several days now. I have been tending him in his room, and it's quite serious. Philip has been undertaking some of Tom's duties, but . . .' He shrugged his shoulders slightly. 'Walter,' said Reynard again, seeming to reach a decision. 'How would you like to become my valet?'

Walter was taken aback. 'I . . .'

'It is entirely up to you, of course. But poor Tom will not work again. Of course, if you would rather decline the offer then I can get Brakes to advertise the position.'

'No. No,' said Walter hastily. The words tumbled out of him. 'I'll do it.'

The master was bathing and dressing for dinner. Walter stood in attendance. The master chatted easily and unselfconsciously as Walter poured hot water down his back. So accustomed to being surrounded by servants even at one's most intimate moments, he seemed almost wholly unaware of their presence and completely unaffected by it.

Walter was surprised, therefore, by Reynard's sudden question. 'Where were you before you came into my service, Walter?' he asked.

'I was in service at another house, sir,' he replied. 'A much smaller house than this, in Cheapside. There was only myself and a maid-of-all-work.'

'And how long were you there?' Reynard asked.

'A little over a year, sir.'

'I see . . . And before that?'

'I . . .' Walter hesitated, always reluctant to discuss or even think about his earlier employment. 'I was a fish-porter, sir. I worked at Billingsgate Market.'

'A fish-porter. Good lord.' Reynard seemed wryly amused by this.

'My father was a fish-porter before me, sir. He died quite suddenly when I was twelve years of age, and I had to go out to work to keep my mother, so I followed him into the same line. It was never the way things were intended to be.'

'Mmm.' Reynard smiled to himself. 'I too followed my father into his profession,' he said, 'but there was never any question of my doing anything else. Strange . . . My father was a passionate advocate of the free will of man, and yet in this matter I exercised no will at all, even after he had died.'

Walter glanced at the portrait of Sir Hugo Reynard which hung over the fireplace. A large picture in a heavy frame, it dominated the room, not only on account of its size but of the visage of the man it depicted. He was a large, striking man with a stern mouth and a look in his eyes which reminded Walter of no-one so much as Pastor Meek. He was clearly a fierce, uncompromising, intelligent man. He looked somewhat like his son, but Dr Richard Reynard's visage was softened by compassionate eyes (though still keen and bright) and a more forgiving, more generous mouth.

'I saw little of my parents when I was growing up,' said Reynard, 'for I was schooled in Geneva. My mother died when I was young. She is remembered by her contemporaries as artistic – though I never found her to be so – and quite beautiful, as her portraits show.' Walter could not recall having seen any portraits of Lady Reynard. 'I remember her only very dimly. After she died my father devoted himself to his work and to his philosophy, and I suppose in a strange way – and from a great distance – to me. He was determined that my life should emulate his; that I should follow in his footsteps.'

'And you did, sir.'

'Yes . . .' said Reynard thoughtfully. 'As the years pass I find that that is true in many more ways than I ever suspected.' He seemed lost in thought for a moment. 'And what of your mother?' he asked.

'She is also with God, sir. She passed on shortly after I went into service.'

Reynard nodded slowly. 'So we are both foundlings, Walter,' he mused. 'Orphans, adrift on the vast and turbulent sea of life.'

He began to soap himself. Walter watched as he ran his hands over his broad back and soaped his light-brown chest hair, his full armpits and his sinewy arms. He raised himself out of the water, crablike, balancing on one arm while the other soaped his buttocks, the dark, hairy cleft between them and his thick, heavy cock and lolling balls. Walter raised his eyes to see his master staring at him. He blushed, and his master plunged himself back into the water before standing upright in the bath. Walter raised the jug and poured, washing the remaining soap-suds away and watching the water sluicing down his master's chest, across the taut lattice of his stomach and down into his brown bush, jetting out off the head of his cock.

★   ★   ★

Tom was noisy that night. A stream of gibberish, non-words and heavy Yorkshire dialect spilled along the passage and through Walter and Philip's door.

'D'ya hear that?' Philip said. 'He's lost it. Gone in the head. Meg was telling me as how he's gone mortal scared of the dark. Has to have a lamp burning all night in his room.'

Philip leaned from the bed and blew out the candle.

'G'night,' he said.

Walter had brought no book to the room tonight. Nevertheless, his cock was hard, throbbing beneath his nightshirt in anticipation, but without the pretence of the book . . .

Walter lay motionless in the dark, his body rigid. With painful slowness he moved a hand towards Philip's leg until he could feel the heat of the footman's body through his fingertips. But still his fingers hovered within a fraction of an inch of Philip's skin. He could not break the final barrier. He could not touch him.

He snatched his hand back and lay rigid, fists clenched, trembling slightly.

He felt something graze the outside of his nightshirt, his chest, his stomach, his hard cock.

'Chicken,' Philip whispered, squeezing Walter's penis through the white linen.

This was the first time Philip had sought Walter's cock with his hand. Shocked and delighted, Walter laid back and tried to relax into the surprising sensation. Philip was a little rough, but Walter sensed a genuine tenderness underlying his coarse caresses.

He pulled Walter's nightshirt up and, smiling with something like embarrassment, lowered his head over his cock, nipping at the foreskin, drawing it taut then letting it spring back, pushing it down over his engorged cock-head with his teeth and engulfing Walter's whole cock with his hot, wet mouth.

Walter closed his eyes and concentrated on the strange new sensation. He felt warm and secure and wanted. Philip's chin slapped against his balls. Walter ran his fingers through Philip's dark fringe, down his neck and on to his wiry shoulders. Philip gripped Walter's buttocks hard as he sucked, tightening his grip as Walter came in a great surge, filling his mouth.

They lay for a while, motionless.

Then for some reason, Walter said, 'The master asked me to be his valet.'

Philip seemed to tense. He spat out Walter's softening prick.

'Valet!?' he shrieked indignantly. 'If anyone should be his valet, it ought to be me! I'm the fucking footman.'

Swearing to himself, he turned away and would not face Walter or speak to him.

20th October, 1884

I truly believed I would never set my pen to this journal again: that my explorations with Spearman were over. I now see that it was a weakness of spirit on my part which led me to abandon our quest. I was frightened for my social position and perhaps for something else. My soul?

My back is scourged; my mind is alight. The pain makes me perceive things much more clearly than usual. I have slept not a wink, yet my reflexes are sharp, my senses almost painfully alert.

Spearman sent a note yesterday afternoon, demanding that I keep myself free in the evening. I returned a message conveying my apologies, and explaining that I was entertaining the dean of surgery to dinner and tried to deny to myself my disappointment. Had it been anybody else I would have cancelled the engagement, but I felt I had some ground to make up with the dean.

We sat to dinner at eight. Within ten minutes, Spearman's servant had arrived with a note demanding my presence at the casual ward. Once again I abandoned the dean to a solitary supper attended only by my staff.

Spearman's carriage was waiting at the casual ward. We passed close to Mrs Warren's house, but did not stop there. In response to my enquiries as to our destination Spearman would merely say, 'Somewhere special.'

We alighted near to Regent's Park, outside the Albany Barracks. Spearman led me around the large, low buildings to a small gate in a back wall. I stopped. 'Surely you are not serious?' I demanded, for I well knew the sort of penalties exacted in the military for our manner of pursuit.

Spearman pushed some money into the hand of a guard, who saluted him in a slovenly manner. The guard appeared drunk. We crossed a broad, cobbled courtyard and entered a long barrack room, empty and in good order. From somewhere beyond the block came the low sound of chanting, male voices.

'He's bound to be guilty or he wouldn't be here ... Starboard gun ... FIRE! Shooting's too good for him. Kick the louse out ... Port gun ... FIRE!'

The shanty was endlessly repeated, always climaxing in that great shout of 'FIRE!' This was punctuated by a sharp, rending crack which cut through the tumult of voices.

Spearman led me to a door at the far end of the room and into a smaller yard surrounded by high, largely windowless walls. Around twenty young soldiers stood about in various states of undress, some stripped to their vests. There were perhaps half that number of civilians present: gentlemen, by their appearance, of all ages. In the middle of a courtyard was a cannon, and across the great barrel of the gun was draped a soldier. He was naked to the waist, and clinging hard to the gun. Another soldier was standing close by, a cat-o'-nine-tails hanging from his clenched fist. As I watched he ran at the cannon, drawing his arm back and swinging the lash into the bound man's bare back. 'FIRE!'

'Enough,' the man on the cannon croaked. He rose and was helped away. The chanting was replaced by earnest conversation. Money changed hands. Another soldier stepped up to the cannon and bared his back, to cheers from his comrades.

A small, neatly dressed civilian of about fifty stepped forward and, in exchange for a sovereign, was handed the whip.

'You were never flogged at school, were you, Reynard?' said Spearman. 'I myself rarely felt the lash. We were fortunate to be educated beyond these shores. The English ruling class is obsessed with flagellation. It is literally beaten into them at school. You know on the Continent they refer to this as the Englishman's vice?'

'But these soldiers . . .' I protested.

'The officers bring this with them from school and inflict it upon the men,' said Spearman. 'It has been thus for centuries. Besides, a foot soldier's pay is poor. Few can survive on it. Mrs Warren herself employs a few soldier boys. This . . . occasion . . . is a source of extra income for them, plus a chance to prove their manhood across the gun.'

We watched as the soldier was subjected to rather a feeble whipping by the man, to jeers from his comrades. The man had an erection beneath his trousers throughout.

The crowd looked on and drank rum. Some masturbated themselves openly. I noticed how, every so often, a man would slip through the door and into the barrack room with one or more soldiers in tow.

Some of the civilians had come to flog; others to be flogged. One man took such a lashing at the hands of one of the soldiers that he had to be carried from the gun, barely conscious. At no point did he call 'Enough'.

The crowd thinned as more and more men left with soldiers or were carried away. I began to wonder what, if anything, would be required of Spearman and myself. 'It's up to you,' said Spearman. 'I am merely opening doors for you.'

With that he strode up to the soldier currently wielding the cat and took it from him. He took a swig at that damned flask he carries everywhere, then lashed the man on the gun mercilessly. The crowd chanted and cheered.

I felt a strong hand cupping my neck and squeezing hard, drawing me around and pushing me back against a water-butt which stood by the wall. A soldier stood over me. He was strong, well over six feet tall and in his late twenties, with dark hair, a heavy moustache and a coarsely unshaven face. With a harsh smile, he leaned me back over the barrel until I thought I should fall. He came down on top of me, pushing his bristly face against mine. I gripped the sides of the butt for support. He bit my cheek hard and stabbed his tongue between my teeth. His mouth tasted strongly of rum; his body smelt of stale sweat. He ripped the front of my shirt open and gouged about my chest and stomach with powerful, blunt, dirty fingers. Slightly drunk myself by this time, I reached for the distended cock which pushed at the front of his trousers, squeezing it as it continued to grow. He pressed it forward, forcing my legs apart and crushing his groin against my own swollen member.

Someone handed him a jug brimming over with rum. He raised his face from mine, clamped a hand upon my chin and, forcing my mouth open, placed the jug to my lips and poured. Rum filled my mouth so that I coughed and choked. It ran across my cheeks and up my nose. It sluiced down my throat, burning all the way to my stomach. I struggled but he was far stronger than I had realised. My head began to swim.

'Six at most.' A man was brandishing a £5 note at my tormentor. He grunted and hauled me from the water-butt and across the yard. With drunken horror, I realised what the man's words meant. Seeing my sudden apprehension, my tormentor gave my cock a rough tweak. It was still hard.

He pulled my jacket and shirt from my back and pulled my combinations down to my waist, where they hung limply. Then, taking up the lash, he pushed me forward across the gun. I saw two of his comrades move forward as if to restrain me. Bowing to the inevitable, I took hold of the giant gun and braced myself.

'FIRE!'

The first stroke was the worst. It knocked the breath from me and sent jagged spikes of pain searing up my back. I thought I should lose consciousness with the pain. I recalled in panic the blows and lacerations I had treated over the years. The second stroke I felt less, and the third less still. A warmth seemed to infuse me, growing from my balls and spreading across my back, mingling with the sheet of pain which was already masking the bite of the cat. Sweat dripped from me. My vision blurred and my head spun. My hard cock was jammed against the gun-carriage. In truth, I felt its insistent throbbing more than the pain across my back.

At the sixth stroke, an appalling silence fell. I looked behind me. My torturer was stripped to the waist and facing away from me. I could see that his sinewy back was criss-crossed with ancient, irregular scars – the tongues of the cat. He spat an oath and, turning, ran at me, swinging the lash as he did so. I closed my eyes and gritted my teeth. The force of his blow knocked me from the gun to the ground, and a great cheer went up.

The soldier picked me up and slung me effortlessly over his shoulder. 'You have just cost me five pounds,' he growled at me. 'We shall have to see about that.'

He carried me through the door and into the barrack room, where he tossed me unceremoniously on to a rough horse-hair mattress whose course fibres raked my back. He pulled my trousers and combinations down in a single movement, causing my still-hard cock to bend painfully before springing free. He swiped it contemptuously with the back of his hands and parted my legs, as he had done outside over the butt.

On other beds, I could see men fucking and being fucked by soldiers. I could hear their gasps and cries.

He loosened the front of his trousers and lowered them. He had a long, thick prick, somewhat dark in colour, which bent to one side as if under its own weight. A dense weave of brown hair clung to his balls and climbed all the way to his broad, deep chest. His face was muscular and handsome although his eyes were narrow, set and hard. His broad mouth was open.

He felt roughly for my arsehole with his fingers, inserting several and prising my sphincter apart. His cock poked up and down my crack until it found the open hole. The fingers did not withdraw, instead I felt his cock-head forcing its way in alongside them. He pushed it deep inside me, then thrust forward hard with his hips, propelling me inches up the bed. The mattress tore at my back. The pain was acute now –

more so than it had been on the gun. It mingled with the hot burning of my anus as he plunged it mercilessly. Every few strokes he pulled me agonisingly back down the bed and continued fucking me.

He pulled the fingers out from inside me and thrust them into my mouth. The taste of my own shit, of dirt and sweat, filled my mouth. He was fucking me hard now, his face a rictus of fury. He let out a scream of the sort soldiers are taught to use when bayoneting an enemy. He was coming inside me. I was delirious with burning pain.

I lay insensible on the mattress for many moments. He had my trousers in his hand, going through the pockets. He extracted a £5 note and, tossing the trousers at me, left the room.

Hallowe'en is approaching, and Spearman well knows what that means. He wants my leave to construct an entertainment in my laboratory. Something furtive; invisible. While my guests drink champagne and dance elegantly behind their masks, Spearman wants us to perform some secret rite under their noses. Sex magic, he calls it. It is a term I have heard ascribed to the occult groups that seem to be everywhere nowadays – the Theosophists, the Rosicrucians, that Blavatsky woman, Mr Yeats, the poet. Perhaps Sabbato's group is one such.

Of course, I do not believe in magic, and yet it seems so much more in keeping with the traditions of All Hallows' Eve than the glittering, decadent charade which the rest of my guests will be acting out. If I am honest with myself, it is some years since these Hallowe'en events have engaged my interest. I host them because my father did, and because it is expected of me. Spearman's plan appeals to that sense of mischief which used to accompany the Hallowe'en parties of my youth, and so I have given him leave to carry out his plan. He called around this morning in the company of Sabbato, that singular man from The Infernal Cabaret. They took measurements and whispered and conspired together continuously. I was not permitted to be privy to their consultations: it seems I am not to find out their intentions until the night of the spirits is actually upon us.

Already I am restless with anticipation.

Nine

'Walter,' the master called from his bathroom. 'More hot water, if you please.'

Walter entered the room and crossed to the fire, where a large metal pitcher steamed on a hot-plate over the coals. Wrapping a linen cloth around the handle, Walter heaved the heavy vessel from the heat and carried it to the bath in which Reynard sat, quite naked, knees raised above the water. His eyes fell on his master's manhood, thick and heavy and flaccid, floating just below the surface of the water. Averting his eyes, Walter began pouring the pitcher's contents into the tub behind the doctor.

Reynard called out in involuntary pain and Walter stopped pouring. For the first time he noticed his master's back. Red weals covered the flesh: livid, swollen stripes of pain.

'Carry on,' said Reynard in a strained voice.

Gently, Walter did so.

'Tell me,' said Reynard, 'what does your religion teach you about good and evil?'

Walter was taken aback by the sudden question. What should he say?

'That ... That God is the repository of all goodness,' he stammered, 'and that to dwell with him we must aspire to follow his good example.'

'And of evil?'

'The opposite, sir. Evil comes from Satan, and can only lead back to him.'

'I see. So when God tortured Job for no apparent reason other than, perhaps, he was bored, that was good.'

'No . . . I . . . The mind of God is unknowable. It is not always possible for us to see the goodness in God's works.'

'And in our own? You Christians say we can barely tell good from evil in God's own peerless example, and yet you presume to be able to root out the evil in the life of man, that pale, confused imitation of the creator.'

'I suppose –'

'You see, if you remove the personalities from good and evil, what do you get? How do we explain a man's actions without these two opposing beacons to guide us? What is goodness without God?'

'There is no goodness without God,' Walter retorted.

'No . . .' mused Reynard. 'No . . . there I agree with you.'

Hallowe'en, it seemed, was the social highlight of the year in Dr Reynard's house. Every year for as long as anyone could remember, the evening was marked by a masked ball.

Mr Brakes cracked open the door to the so-little-used ballroom and he, Walter and Philip entered.

'I was a footman here in his father's day,' said old Brakes, his soft voice echoing around the room.

'Oh, Christ, 'ere we go. More of his "I was at bleeding Waterloo" routine,' muttered Philip. His words reverberated loudly. The rhapsodic Brakes ignored him.

'Oh, the parties we had then . . .'

In the days leading up to the event, the old butler's mood fluctuated between nostalgia and worry. He had been dismayed that at this most important period in the household's social calendar he should have lost Walter to the master's rooms, and so Dr Reynard had agreed to Walter temporarily resuming certain duties of the under-footman. This did nothing to mollify Philip, who still had to undertake the remainder of Walter's former tasks, nor Mr Brakes, who muttered anxiously and incessantly to himself while Mrs Donaldson flapped her arms and shouted.

The situation was not eased by the fact that, several days before the event, the master insisted on removing Walter once again from his household duties.

'Walter, this is Lord Spearman,' said Dr Reynard. They were standing in the laboratory. Reynard had locked the door which led to the rest of the house. 'He will be preparing an . . . entertainment in here. For my guests. For the party. He has requested your assistance. As this is to be a surprise, I shall require your absolute discretion. I do not wish anybody else to know about this, and particularly not the staff. Can I rely upon you?'

'Yes, sir,' Walter answered. He looked warily at Lord Spearman, who smiled his loveless smile.

'I am sure we shall enjoy working together,' Spearman purred.

'Spearman . . .'

There was a note of warning in his master's tone.

'Yes, yes, Reynard,' Spearman said airily. 'Your pretty little servant will come to no harm, I assure you. Now you must leave us, Reynard. But before you go, please make it clear to your servant that the gag on his tongue applies to you, also. After all, this surprise is for you most of all.'

After a second's hesitation, Reynard nodded. 'Yes, Walter,' he said. 'You're not even to tell *me* what his lordship has in mind.'

Even if he had wanted to, Walter could have told nobody anything of the preparations of the next three days. He struggled to make sense of them: they merely baffled him. The door from the laboratory to the house remained locked and Lord Spearman came and went by the rear entrance, creaky from disuse, which led through the garden and out past the stables on to a back street. Each day he was accompanied by a man called Sabbato. If anything, he frightened Walter more than Spearman did. There was a strange complicity between the two men. Often they seemed to be communicating without talking, some unseen current passing between their dark eyes.

Sabbato was even darker skinned than Spearman. His features were more handsomely fixed than those of the lord, though no hair whatsoever seemed to grow about his head. His dark eyes were deeply hooded by his great brow bone, but he had no eyebrows, just a bony ridge. His curious lack of hair made his age extremely difficult to discern. In certain lights he looked ancient and severe; in other lights he didn't seem too much older than Walter.

He was handsome, certainly, but there was something terribly cold about Sabbato's presence, Walter thought. It brought him out in goosebumps.

He spoke little. His voice was quiet and somewhat sibilant, with a thick accent that Walter took to be Italian. He seemed to speak very little English and issued whispered orders in his native tongue to two silent workmen, who hauled wooden boxes, larger than a man, into the laboratory.

Spearman, meanwhile, laid out heavy black drapes on Dr Reynard's operating table, now moved by Walter and one of the workmen to the side of the room.

He continually drank from the slim silver flask which he kept in his inside pocket. Every draught he took made him wince; his brow would cloud and he would frequently snap at one or other of the workmen. To Walter, though, he was the soul of grace and good manners. He directed the servant to hang the heavy cloth drapes over all of the walls, windows and doors, and to cover the floor in them. They were not all black, but patterned with a variety of odd symbols and words in stark white and blood red. The writing looked to Walter to be Arabic, or perhaps Hebrew. Other far less obscure images, such as huge phalluses, made Walter blush.

The laboratory had been turned into a cave of black velvet.

On the day, Mr Brakes was still muttering and Mrs Donaldson was still shouting. In spite of their worries, everything went smoothly and even Philip had the good sense to keep his mouth shut and his hands active.

The guests began to arrive at about 7.30. Fully liveried, Walter, Mr Brakes and Philip were all required to wait on the lords, ladies and gentlemen, elegant behind sequinned face masks and many in full fancy dress. An Eastern grand vizier – in reality the Bishop of London – danced in turban, silk pantaloons and curly slippers with Queen Marie-Antoinette, wife of the MP for Finchley. Two witches and numerous spectres and fetches danced around tables groaning under the food Mrs Donaldson had prepared. Pumpkin lanterns hung about the walls. In the corner of the ballroom, a string quartet played minuets as the resplendent company danced.

'And shall we see you in church for All Saints' Day tomorrow, Dr Reynard?' the Bishop of London asked Reynard.

Reynard smiled evasively. Walter suspected his master was a little drunk. 'All Saints' Day,' he said. 'You know, I'd quite forgotten tomorrow was All Saints' Day.'

'But this is why we are here, is it not?' said the bishop. 'To celebrate All Hallows' Eve.'

'I think when my father began these gatherings he had something a little older in mind. Tonight was the pagan festival of the dead long before your God took it over, Bishop.'

The bishop laughed, a little uncertainly. Further discussion was cut short by the florid arrival of Mrs Maitland and daughters, who glided around Dr Reynard like a family of swans.

Walter went on serving.

Reynard's three young colleagues from St Mary's were all present (although the dean of surgery was not), and all drunk. They did not dance, nor did they mingle with the other guests, but argued long and loud just as at their last visit, while continuously drinking champagne. Walter did his best to avoid them until they wandered from the ballroom in search of brandy and a setting more congenial to their discussions.

Lord Spearman was not among the crowd. Walter spied him standing, alone and unnoticed, in the gallery overlooking the ballroom, silently watching the revellers below.

Sabbato, however, was there. Never speaking a word, he moved silently through the gathering, his cold presence turning masked heads wherever he went. He was clad from head to foot in a flowing monk's habit of a deep, blood-red colour. Its cowl was pulled low over his face, which occasionally revealed itself beneath the red folds to be a grinning skull. His hands, too, which clutched a tall ebony staff, were skeleton hands. He moved about the big room, killing conversations. Spearman watched him intently.

At 11.30 Walter felt His Lordship's hand on his shoulder. He hadn't noticed him coming down from the gallery. Wordlessly, Spearman led him from the room and through the house. It got quieter and darker and eerily still as the bright hubbub of the ballroom receded.

As the darkness closed in, Spearman lit a lamp and held it out in front of them. It shed an unsettling pool of light which turned furniture and hangings into lancing shadow-beasts as they picked their way through the silent rooms.

Even the laboratory was in darkness. Spearman stopped as they passed through the door and held the lamp up to his face. He looked deathly and stark in its glow. He raised the edge of one of the hanging black drapes beside the door.

'Stand behind here,' he whispered to Walter. 'Don't move and don't make a sound. Just watch.'

Walter's eyes adjusted slowly to the darkness. Before him the laboratory lay, bathed in moonlight. But what a transformation had been affected. The giant crates were gone and in their place stood machines: great machines of polished wood and brass, levers, pivots and frames, ratchets and sockets and great hinges, standing in a broad circle, cutting the moonlight into long shards, looming over the centre of the room. Some of them Walter recognised as classic devices of torture: a rack, an iron maiden, its door open, and a thick, black rubber penis – a godemiche – jutting forward from the back wall. There was a bed of nails of the sort which the fakirs of the Indus were supposed to use during their devotions. At the room's focus, suspended from the ceiling by twin chains, was a metal bar, from which six lengths of chain hung down, each ending in a sharp hook.

Spearman vanished and the room remained silent and empty for perhaps twenty minutes. Then Sabbato, still in his death mask, glided silently into the room. He stood beneath the line of hooks and turned in a slow circle. Quietly, eerily, he began to sing a high, warbling soprano; no language Walter had ever heard. Young men filed into the room, wearing black or white shifts which hung loosely from their shoulders and ended unevenly about their ankles, each carrying a candle on a long stick. They set down their candles in a broad ring and stood, facing Sabbato.

Spearman reappeared, leading Dr Reynard by the arm. They stood outside the circle, watching. Leaning on his walking cane, Spearman glanced across at Walter and smiled.

The incense rising from the ring of candles was intense and heady. It caught the nose sharply, and made Walter feel unsteady on his feet.

Sabbato was silent now, and the singing was taken up by his attendant minions, low and dronelike. A figure – a man clad entirely in a red shift, his head and face covered by a hood of the same deep scarlet – was led by two of the acolytes into the centre of the circle. They stripped him naked, leaving only the hood in place. He appeared to be young: his body was slim and hairless save for the curly, reddish-blond crown which sat around his cock, which was long, slim, smooth and hard.

Noiselessly, the metal frame was lowered from the ceiling until it was just above the man's head. His arms were raised to form a cross. One by one, Sabbato took the hooks and, pinching the man's flesh, drove them through it. Walter winced. To his surprise, there was no blood. One hook went through either shoulder, and one through either arm, just above the crook of the elbow. The other two Sabbato pushed through the man's chest so that they pulled his nipples far out. When he had done this, Sabbato took a circlet of vicious-looking needles and jammed it down hard over the red hood. A crown of pins.

Two of the attendants pulled slowly at a rope and the whole structure rose into the air, hauling the blindfolded victim from his feet until he hung, crucified, in the centre of the room. He made no sound beneath the mask.

Sabbato took up a long pole with a small loop of wire at one end and hooked it over the man's erect cock and balls, drawing the noose tight. He passed the end of the pole to one of his circle of attendants, who passed it to his neighbour, then he to his. Faster and faster – their chanting also gathering speed and urgency – they passed the pole from hand to hand. Faster and faster the frame turned and the hanging man spun. His cock and balls were purple with the constriction of the wire.

Eventually, Sabbato once more seized the pole. As he did so the wire noose detached itself. The man continued to spin, under his own momentum now, the wire still tight. One of the machines was wheeled into place beneath him: two interlocking rectangular wooden frames, each larger than a man, with buckled straps set at the corners. The frames were joined by a great hinge so that they seemed to form two giant, joined Xs. Further struts and beams within the frames came together and supported a candle which was over a foot long, pointed at the top but rapidly becoming as thick as a man's forearm. Sabbato lit the candle.

Gradually the man's spinning slowed, then stopped, and he was lowered towards the machine. Two of the attendants took hold of his bare legs and pulled them apart, then strapped the ankles to one of the machine's twin frames. His wrists were shackled to the opposite frame. The lengths of chain fell away from the supporting metal bar and clanked to the floor, still hanging by the hooks from his flesh. Sabbato pulled on a lever set at one end of the machine, and the frames began to flatten, stretching and lowering the prisoner. At the same time the candle rose until the flame licked his buttocks. He writhed and squirmed, but still made no sound. The candle rose further. The flame snuffled out as the hot wax phallus began to force his cheeks apart and bury itself inside him.

The circle of acolytes was masturbating as one now. Each had pulled up his robe to reveal a hard cock beneath. Manacled hand and foot, the captive began to gyrate his stretched body. He seemed not so much to be trying to free himself as to heighten the sensation he was feeling. His buttocks clenched and unclenched around the candle and, quite suddenly, his cock, still held by the wire noose, twitched and disgorged a jet of semen, which showered back down on to his stomach and pubes.

He was unstrapped and allowed to fall from the machine. When, after a few moments, he picked himself up, his cock was still hard. He was immediately seized and thrown on to the bed of nails, his chains dragging after him. Sabbato removed his blood-red habit. He was quite naked underneath, and quite hairless. A long, thick, slightly curving prick stood proud from a baby-smooth belly. He still wore the skull mask. With a fluid motion he mounted the man, fucking him with violent energy and coming swiftly. As he climaxed, the needle crown fell from the man's head and clattered to the floor.

'He is ours now,' whispered Spearman to Reynard.

Sabbato climbed from the man's back and his acolytes closed in. The man was flung to the floor, where one of them immediately took him on all fours, plunging his cock into the boy's anus. Another pulled the mask from his head and plunged his cock into his mouth. The boy was little older than Walter. He had a pale, delicate face – too small, it seemed, to accommodate the mammoth prick which now disappeared inside him – and a head of ginger-blond hair.

Others of the company fell upon one another, tearing at their robes, biting and kissing, pinching, pulling, cocks invading mouths and arseholes. Light-headed to a point where he had to lean against the wall for support, Walter's eyes danced in the candlelit perfume chamber. Within moments, an orgy was in progress.

The young man – the sacrificial lamb – crawled about the floor, sucking with relish and being fucked, beaten and kicked, his face frozen in an ecstatic grimace.

Spearman stepped forward and grabbed him by the hair. He dragged him to a metal box, curved at its edges and covered in sharp ridges and bolt-heads, and pushed him over it. Taking up his ebony walking cane, he placed the brass bulb handle against the boy's buttock crack and pushed it hard inside him, driving his naked torso against the box's metal contours.

He handed the cane, buried in the lad, to Reynard.

'Now, healer of the sick,' said Spearman, 'let us see how you inflict pain.'

He moved around to the young man's head, unbuttoning his own trousers as he did so. Licking his lips, Reynard began working the cane in and out of the lad's arsehole. Kneeling, Spearman pulled his prick from his trousers and thrust it into the lad's open mouth. The twin phalluses, one metal and ebony, one flesh, hammered at the boy. Walter could see the distracted look on his master's face and the urgent bulge in his trousers. Reynard tore the cane from the young man's arse and, freeing his thick, long cock, plunged it into him. The two friends fucked him from either end, Spearman holding Reynard's gaze. They came together.

The orgy lasted several hours. Walter watched his master fucking and being fucked. When the company silently departed, his heart was still rolling and hammering in his chest. His head was spinning and his senses tingled and fired brightly. All sorts of morbid fears were beginning to come upon him.

He tried not to breathe, tremble, or make a sound as the master and Lord Spearman left the laboratory, breathless and exhilarated. They were leaning against one another for support. He listened to their footsteps and their excited gasps recede into the darkness before daring to emerge from behind the hanging.

His overwhelming instinct was to flee this awful place, but he didn't. He stepped shakily into the centre of the room and extended a trembling hand to the nearest of the machines. He flinched as he touched it. 'An engine of Satan,' Pastor Meek thundered in the back of his mind.

His cock was hard.

He ran his hands slowly, gingerly, along the contraption's side-struts. He gripped the horse-leather straps, gently at first, then with more force, tugging against them. He turned his attention to the lever, then tested his weight against it and pushed it. The manacle frame descended; the candle rose to meet it. Walter pulled the lever back. The candle withdrew from its phantom penetration.

He reached out and touched it, pressing a fingerprint into its waxy ridges. He withdrew his hand and put it gently to his lips.

A tiny noise from outside made him leap back in fright. Turning to the one exposed window, he peered out.

There was a man standing in the garden. The moonlight flashed off a bald head. For a moment, Walter thought it was Tom; that the ancient had somehow wandered down to the garden in his near-death delirium and now couldn't get back to his room. Certainly, he was looking up at the top floor, towards the pale light that burned in Tom's window.

The figure turned out of the moonlight and Walter saw his mistake. It was Sabbato. He looked more handsome than Walter had ever before thought him.

Sabbato was staring directly at him. He began making his way across the garden towards Walter, staring and unblinking.

Walter's nerve finally gave out. He turned and hurried from the laboratory.

The dark house was treacherous. Walter groped his way unsteadily through rooms which should have been familiar, even in the dark, but were not. Somehow everything seemed to be in the wrong place. He collided with furniture, missed doors and reduced himself to a state of nervous sobbing.

He ascended the stairs to the top floor and froze. Behind his penitential door, old Tom was praying, loud and fast, breathless and hysterical, over and over again. Praying for the forgiveness of his sins. Walter stumbled to the door of his own room. A noise from within made him stop. It was Philip, laughing, low and wicked. And Ruby's unmistakable giggle. The bed creaked rhythmically beneath them.

He retreated to the shadowy stair-top. He was trapped between the gratification and the mortification of the flesh. He had nowhere to go.

3rd November, 1884

My mind is in confusion. No, I think it not inappropriate to say turmoil at what we have done. I have lain awake nights meditating on it, and even now cannot sleep. Nor, after days, can I yet begin to put into words the experience, and yet I feel that in the academic interest I must at least try to record some of the sensations I felt.

It is as Spearman says: pain has always been the enemy. I have dedicated my life to combatting it. Now I am beginning to see it in an entirely new light. I myself have experienced its transcendental nature. It seems disconcertingly fitting that I should dedicate this, my other life, to the experience and the infliction of pain. How better to understand its mysteries? Can it but make me a better physician?

Spearman might see this as magic, but I see no reason to abandon my scientific objectivity. And so it is in the sincere spirit of experimentation and enquiry that I continue with these activities.

My senses are still raw and tingling. The days pass as if in a dream.

Though I force myself to live my daily life with the same

diligence which I now seem to be showing in my nightly one, yet I find little enthusiasm for either my friends or my practice. I feel my presence in the world – the brightly lit world of modern society – becoming less, somehow. On All Hallows' Eve I felt real.

Ten

***

Hallowe'en seemed to have cast a spell upon the denizens below stairs. The atmosphere changed overnight and grief and suspicion crept among them.

It began with the news that Tom had died in the night. The master himself went to the servants' dining hall to make the sad, brief announcement.

Walter shuddered with the memory of the night. Ruby burst into tears.

That was the next obvious sign of change: the immediate cooling of relations between Ruby and Philip. He had stood, quite inappropriately, with his arm around her during the master's announcement. Within an hour they had begun avoiding each other. When forced into one another's presence, the aura of muted hostility emanating from Philip towards the maid and the looks of sullen rebuke she returned filled the room.

Mrs Donaldson was all concern.

'I don't know what's come over that girl,' she said. 'Jumping at shadows . . .'

Philip sulked and waited for her to bustle off to the ovens. Silently, roughly, he gripped Walter by the arm.

'Have you been saying anything to Ruby?' he hissed.

'What?' Walter spluttered. 'No!'

'None of that religious crap?'

'No!' Walter repeated.

Philip relaxed his grip. 'No . . .' he muttered. 'I reckon it was that old bastard Tom, putting the fear of God in her. And now he's dead she won't touch me.'

He stopped. Ruby was standing in the doorway, staring her silent, solemn stare.

'You Irish girls, I don't know,' Mrs Donaldson scolded across the room. 'With your fetches and fancies and silly superstitions. Do you not think that old man has anything better to do in the great hereafter but run around after a silly Irish girl with nothing between her ears bar fresh air?'

Philip put it more succinctly. 'Frigid, Bible-punching bitch.'

Walter was once more accompanying Dr Reynard on his medical rounds. Even the master's mood seemed to have changed. He was distracted, and remained so as day followed day. They rode in silence from house to house and to the hospital and casual ward. The doctor worked diligently and ceaselessly, it seemed, but, to all of his patients, colleagues and attendants, he displayed the same intense, distracted quietness. It made their trips painfully awkward to Walter.

Only once during their travails did Dr Reynard break his silence.

'Where did you learn to read, Walter?' he asked quite suddenly one morning in the carriage.

'Church school, sir,' he replied. 'Pastor Meek. It was thought I might become some sort of clerk . . . or even a preacher.' His voice saddened in tone. 'I had to leave when my father passed on so suddenly.'

'I see. Of course.' Reynard nodded sympathetically. 'Parents religious, were they? Brought you up to believe, and all that?'

'Yes, sir. Although I believe I should have come upon the Word in any event.'

'Oh? Why?'

Walter was taken aback by the bluntness of his master's question. 'Wh . . .' he stammered. 'The . . . Surely the truth is self-evident. It comes unbidden to those of open mind and pure heart.'

'And do I then not have an open mind and pure heart? For I do not see your truth.'

'As to your mind, sir,' Walter replied, 'there can be little doubt of its openness.'

'And my heart?'

Walter was silent. What could he say? What could he even say about his own heart?

'No,' mused Reynard. 'I suppose you may have a point. But let me tell you, Walter, this impure heart of mine has led me of late to other truths, less neat and less comforting than your credo; self-contradictory truths; truths which tear at one another; truths which might tear at your very soul.'

That had been the day after they buried Tom. A tiny huddle of men: Dr Reynard and the male servants of his household, the officiating priest and a loitering gravedigger in the yard of the little church where the old man had worshipped.

It had rained throughout.

Walter's thoughts were still dominated by what he had seen in the laboratory. The memory kept him awake at nights. Philip was barely speaking to him: the footman bore with ill grace the twin blows of his rejection by Ruby and Walter's appointment over him as valet. By night they lay, side by side, in silence, a cold six-inch strip of bed between them. They both lay wide awake for hours, Philip doubtless brooding on the slings and arrows of outrageous fortune and Walter entertaining much darker thoughts. Several nights he heard muted voices from the benighted garden – Spearman's and others – and the characteristic creak of the laboratory door. He rolled in the memory of Hallowe'en night and his body tingled and his cock became hard. He reached out for Philip, his hand trembling so close he could feel the heat of the footman's body. Always he withdrew his hand and bit down on his thoughts.

Some days after they had buried Tom, Mr Brakes called Walter into his little office.

'Walter,' he said, 'the master has suggested that you move into Tom's room. Decency forbade us from using it until now, of course, but the master feels a sufficient period of mourning has now elapsed. The room has been prepared.'

'No!' exclaimed Walter, shocked. 'I mean . . . I am very grateful for the thought, Mr Brakes, but I am quite happy where I am.'

'Come, boy,' the butler cajoled. 'The room is very pleasantly situated, and quite as large as the one you now share with Philip. And it is yours alone, Walter.'

'Yes, but . . . not that room, please, Mr Brakes.'

'Walter,' said the old butler. 'Surely you are not frightened of a room just because somebody died in it? A good Christian like you, believing in ghosts!' He leaned forward, smiling slyly. 'Just think about it, Walter. Your own room.'

'Really, Mr Brakes,' Walter pleaded. 'I beg you –'

'It would be proper,' the butler interrupted. His tone had cooled. 'You are, after all, acting as the master's valet in what seems to be settling into a permanent arrangement. Do you realise how lucky you are, Walter? That is a quite unprecedented promotion from under-footman. If the master were a less generous – and less unorthodox – man, you would be cleaning the grates for many a year. And now you are offered a room of your own. Really, I am surprised at your ingratitude, Walter. Come, prepare yourself.'

To Walter's relief, the room had been cleared of Tom's effects. The spiky crucifixes and pages from the Bible had been removed from the walls. But he could still see the impression they had made over the years and the result was a sort of creeping, invisible half-presence. The seat was still warm, the cushion dented and his cigarette smoke lingered faintly in the air, but the Lord God had departed this place.

He remembered Tom's incessant, petrified prayers. Was this the end that awaited Walter? A life of devotion and piety and struggling against the ever-present pit, only to reach the end of his life and find himself staring into its infernal maw? A God-fearing life ending in terror?

He dreaded the onset of night. When at last he retired for bed he felt feverish with anticipation. Perhaps he was sickening for something.

His thoughts were wandering wildly. The tumbling, fevered images frightened and – somewhere down there – fascinated him.

He lay awake, listening to the house shrugging off its day: Mrs

Donaldson shouting good night to Mr Croup, the gardener; the hourly chiming of the big grandfather clock on the master staircase. Gradually the house settled into silence.

For hours, Walter hovered uneasily on the threshold between waking and sleep, unaware where the former state ended and the latter began. He was sweating profusely. He became persistently troubled by the notion that somebody was standing in the garden, looking up at him. Three times (he thought) he rose from the bed, crossed to the window and stared down into the moonlit wilderness below. But each time the garden was empty.

He was dimly aware of far-off voices raised in anger. Philip shouting; Ruby crying.

The voices rattled around inside his head, getting louder. Other voices joined them, talking over the top of one another; everyone shouting and no-one listening. The Tower of Babel.

The voices were above him. Lamentations for the dead. For poor, dead Tom.

He lay on Tom's deathbed.

This wasn't sweat that soaked through his sheets. This was blood, bile, saliva, semen, all of the fluids of life being carried away on a deluge of water. His body fluids were being washed from him. He felt old. Close to death.

The sudden silence was slowly being invaded by new sounds. Moaning, wailing sounds. Lamentations. The crucifixes were back. Nailed to the walls all around him the Christ-figures hung and suffered as the sky turned hot and black and desert women wept.

Somewhere a door slammed. Calamitous footsteps hammered up the corridor. The door opened and a figure stood facing Walter. For a petrified second he thought it was the old man, back to reclaim his bed. The figure moved from shadow into moonlight. Sabbato stood over Walter, naked, younger and more infernally beautiful than he had ever seemed before. Then he wasn't even sure about that. The face seemed to blur.

Walter attempted to rise up and cry out. A hand gripped his shoulder and propelled it back down to the bed. Another covered his mouth.

'Bitch.'

Walter tried to focus his eyes and his mind on the figure. It

114

flung itself on top of him and clamped its mouth into Walter's neck, sucking at him. Teeth bit down hard.

Walter winced and tried to pull himself away. He felt his shoulders being gripped hard.

'Fucking bitch,' the voice said again.

Philip . . . Walter blinked in surprise. The footman gazed with fury into his eyes, then heaved him over in the bed, so that he was lying on his stomach.

'Philip, what –'

Hands clutched at the hem of Walter's nightshirt, pulling it up until it was bunched around his shoulders. Philip was breathing hard. He crushed Walter's face down into the pillow. Walter let out a muffled shout as he felt the swollen tip of Philip's penis pushing its way between his buttocks, seeking his hole. His sphincter was prised open by the invading rod, wrenching and burning its way in. Philip pumped him with short, frantic thrusts, gasping and swearing under his breath. His teeth sunk themselves painfully into Walter's neck; his hot saliva drenching the skin.

He came within moments, then rose from the bed, wiping his cock on Walter's discarded shirt, before tossing the garment contemptuously across Walter's face and leaving as swiftly as he had arrived.

Walter listened to Philip's footsteps recede down the passage. He lay, half out of his nightshirt. He pulled it from his body and let it fall. It was still hot in the room and he was still sweating. His sphincter burned. His cock was hard.

He rose from the bed and crossed to the window. The room was well situated to furnish a view of the laboratory. There was light within.

The house was silent. Taking up the keys his master had given him, he dressed again and exited the room and descended through the house, ghostly in his nightshirt. He unlocked the door to the consulting wing and crept to the little staircase leading up on to the laboratory's viewing gallery.

Dreading the creak of the wooden boards, he mounted the stairs. Below, he could hear voices – Spearman's, his master's, and others – and the clank of the machines. His cock throbbing in anticipation, he crawled towards the edge of the platform.

Below him, naked, stood Reynard and Spearman, one broad and muscular, his handsome brow creased and troubled and a pale, thick cock standing out from his belly, and the other dark and sinewy, his hawklike face and untidy black curls drenched in sweat.

A young man, also naked, was kneeling in front of Spearman, his cropped bullet-head rising and falling on the peer's long cock. Spearman ignored him. He was at the controls of the great X-frame machine. Another young man was strapped to the crossed wooden frames. He was Oriental: small, with sleek, dark hair, bronze skin and a cock which stood upright, quivering slightly, from a small, dark patch of hair.

His body was painfully stretched by the flattening wooden frames. The huge candle rose and butted against his tight, round buttocks.

'Spearman, for pity's sake,' said Reynard. 'He's too small. You'll never –'

'Be quiet, Reynard,' snapped Spearman. 'Here.'

Roughly he pushed the boy from his cock, shoving him across the floor. 'Fuck my whore,' he said. 'I'm trying to concentrate.'

The boy prostrated himself before Reynard, arse in the air. His arms were covered in crudely executed tattoos. He looked to Walter like a convict. Reynard took him from behind, fucking him hastily and pushing him along the floor with the force of his thrusts.

The Oriental boy was jabbering in high, hysterical Chinese, thrashing his head back and forth as the huge candle forced his cheeks apart and began to disappear inside him. The hooks and chains, which again dangled from above, clanked about his face. His babble gave way to long, deeply drawn sighs. He opened his mouth and took one of the hooks inside it, sucking hard.

Walter, up in the gallery, resisted the urge to masturbate. He watched his master come inside the crop-headed youth with a low cry. He watched Spearman unstrap the Oriental lad and let him fall to the ground in a heap, then pounce upon him, rubbing his rampant cock against any part of the lad he could reach, finally fucking his armpit and drenching the trim clump of black hair in white glutin.

Walter waited patiently, his cock throbbing, for the participants to leave before descending into the pit.

Slowly, he leaned forward into the machine and brought his face level with the candle. The wax was warm and flecked with excrement. Walter let his lips graze the candle, forming a seal and kissing it. He opened his mouth and ran his tongue up its slick length. Naked, he pumped his cock hard, letting the smell of shit and wax fill his nostrils. He came within seconds.

Eleven

Pastor Meek was on painfully good form. Walter could not look at him. Instead, he kept his eyes fixed upon the simple cross which stood on the otherwise-unadorned wooden altar. Even in that plain, wholesome emblem he could find no comfort. In his mind's eye he saw the Lord, crucified for our sins, transfixed there, as on the walls of Tom's room. Then that image itself became displaced by the vision of the man in the laboratory, hanging from his hooks, crowned with the vicious ring of pins. Under the unforgiving scrutiny of the pastor, and of the Almighty, Walter found himself growing hard.

'The beast in men can take many manifestations,' Pastor Meek growled. 'Some become pigs, unable to raise heads from the trough, unable on account of their own gluttony to raise their eyes to God. Others become dogs in season, panting and scampering after their doglike lusts. Others become as drunken apes, half-men, parodies of civilisation and rational thought. But perhaps the most insidious of all are those men who become scavenger beasts. Outwardly, they might appear as you and I but their hearts are black and full of sin. They sin in secret. They sin with their thoughts and with their eyes. They sin at second-hand; they feed off the sins of others. They become spies and carrion-sniffers. Jackals!'

After the performance, Walter joined the line of the faithful,

118

shuffling past the stern pastor, shaking hands and moving on. He hoped the pastor wouldn't want to say much to him.

'So, how are you getting on in that great house?'

'Uhh ... Quite well, I think, Pastor. I'm valet to Dr Reynard now.'

'Valet, you say.' Pastor Meek's brow clouded. His voice was low. 'You missed church these past few weeks.'

'Yes, Pastor.' Walter had almost not gone today. He had feared something like this.

'Be sure not to let the example of the idle rich lure you away from God, Walter.' There was a note of warning in his voice. 'Remember the words of our Lord: it is easier for a camel to pass through the eye of a needle than for a rich man to enter the Kingdom of Heaven.'

'Yes, Pastor,' Walter replied with automatic deference.

'You do not mix much with your fellow congregationists, do you, Walter?' said the pastor. 'This is not good, for we fortify one another in faith and in righteousness. When is your next day off?'

'Uh ... Thursday, sir.'

'Thursday. Come to tea on Thursday, then. Four o'clock.'

'Yes, Pastor,' said Walter again, knowing he would not go.

Without further discussion, the pastor turned and clasped the hand of the man standing patiently at Walter's rear. Walter shuffled along the line to freedom.

And so Walter's days turned. He attended his master at his morning toilette – studiously ignoring the marks left by his master's night-time exertions – and many times rode with him about his medical calls. Always his master maintained the edgy silence, which barely concealed his distraction and repressed restlessness.

Twice Walter journeyed alone to Mrs Warren's house, each time handing her a small envelope. There was no accompanying message.

Philip barely spoke to him by day, but held him in long, smouldering, mocking glances which Walter tried but – to Philip's evident satisfaction – failed to hold.

Two things punctuated Walter's nights: the first was the footman's quick, brutal visits and silent departures. Once, when he should have been going about his duties below stairs, Philip came upon him at mid-morning when he was setting his master's dressing room in order, pushing him over his master's dressing-table. Another time, in the afternoon, Walter was on his hands and knees in the boot room when Philip took him, kicking the door shut and pushing Walter's face down among the shoes. Without a word, he tore down Walter's trousers and long johns. Hawking a great gob of phlegm from the back of his throat, he pulled Walter's cheeks apart and spat into the crevice, splattering Walter's hole. He mounted him like a dog, swiftly locating the moistened hole with his prick.

Outside the glass-windowed door Walter could hear the other servants passing. He could see the shadows they cast. In spite of his fear of discovery, his cock was hard. He masturbated himself as Philip crushed his face into the master's boot. The smell of leather and polish overwhelmed him. His arsehole burned with the now-familiar sensation of Philip's distended cock rutting its way inside him. He was learning to relax before the assault. As ever, Philip spent himself without ceremony and walked away, leaving Walter lying among the boots and brushes, semen dripping down his inner thighs.

Walter bore these violations in silence. A part of him dreaded them, but a part always looked forward to the next.

There was a second defining feature of Walter's nights, and one he conscientiously concealed from Philip: his lonely, nocturnal trips to the laboratory. Three, sometimes four times a week he would see Spearman slipping past the stables in the dead of the night and crossing the garden to the laboratory.

His cock aching beneath his nightshirt, he would watch his master and Spearman and the array of young men Spearman always brought with him enacting their passion play below, then descend from the gallery to the laboratory floor, shedding the loose garment and prostrating himself before his new altar.

His temple, restored, just as the Lord had promised in the gospel. Scarcely a temple but a great Gothic cathedral of mahogany buttresses and brass gargoyles; a cathedral of moonlight.

He learned to mount the great central frame unaided, his feet balancing on a crossbar, his hands clinging to the hooks which once more dangled from above. Often they cut ragged, shallow stigmata into his palms.

He learned how to lower himself on to the candle's great, greasy girth. At first he felt it was pulling him apart – he doubted that any man could take such a violation – but gradually, working to relax his muscles, he could take it deep into himself. One night, quite unexpectedly, as the pole settled up inside him, he came spontaneously, without ever having touched his penis, shooting high in the air, his seed raining down on the laboratory floor.

Whatever god dwelt in here, he felt his presence then.

Only once more did his master raise the veil of silence on their days together. He was dressing for breakfast. The huge picture of his father was missing from its place above the fire. Walter pretended not to notice.

'You are doubtless wondering about the picture,' Reynard said to him.

'A good servant –'

'– is concerned but never curious,' sang Reynard impatiently. 'The virtuous Brakes.'

He sat before his mirror and began to lather his face.

'My father was a virtuous man,' said Reynard. 'A giant in his field. His advice was sought by royalty. He went mad, Walter. He ended his life as an imbecile, confined to this house.'

Walter moved forward to shave his master.

'No,' said Reynard. 'Today I shall do it.'

He opened the slick blade and drew it flatly down his face.

'Do you think I resemble him, Walter? The portrait, I mean.'

'Sir . . .' Walter, as ever, was floored by his master's sudden familiarity.

'I could see it in his eyes,' said Reynard. 'The madness, growing. It's odd, but my only memory of how my father looked when I was a child comes from his portraits, I saw so little of him. And there is something in them – that one in particular – which disturbs me deeply; which doesn't fit with the image I always had of him. It is something I have come to notice more and more.'

'Sir . . .'

'Oh, damn it, Walter, can't you say anything else but –'

The master didn't finish his sentence, but flinched as the blade nicked his skin. A drop of blood clung to the edge of the razor. Walter rushed to get a cloth but Reynard waved him to stillness and carried on shaving.

'Walter,' he said, 'I know I have given you leave to enter the laboratory when need dictates, but from now on you are to consider it out of bounds, as does the rest of the household. You are only to attend there with my express instructions.'

He seemed to sense Walter's guilty shock.

'Do not think me displeased with you,' he continued. 'I take this measure for your own safety. I . . . am conducting a delicate experiment in there. I have installed some dangerous equipment and –'

Reynard cried out as the razor blade cut a thin slash in his cheek. He held his hand out in front of him. It shook uncontrollably. The bloody razor clattered through his fingers.

'This happened to me when I was operating yesterday,' he said quietly. 'I nearly killed a patient.'

He began hastily wiping the scarlet suds from his face.

'It's my . . . work,' he said. 'It's . . . taking too much out of me. Too much.'

He rose from his seat. For almost a minute he stared out of the window, saying nothing.

'I have done some things which men might consider abominable,' he said in a low voice. 'You would find them so –' Then he spun around to face Walter, his eyes wide. 'If only you could know my motives, Walter,' he said in sudden excitement. 'Experience what I am experiencing. Learn what I am learning . . . about myself! About men's minds and about men's hearts!'

'And about men's souls?' asked Walter, looking up suddenly with involuntary vehemence. He immediately lowered his head, ashamed at his own presumption.

'Do you really believe in the soul, Walter?' Reynard asked quietly.

Walter wasn't sure what he believed any more. All he was sure of was that he no longer *wanted* to believe in it.

That night, Walter waited at his window for Lord Spearman's arrival. He saw his shadowy arrival and heard the creak of the laboratory door, and then voices. His master's, Spearman's, low but insistent, then growing angry. The door creaked shut again, and Spearman strode away past the stables to the street.

The light from the laboratory died and Walter rose from his bed. Ensuring by habit now that nobody was watching him, he slipped downstairs to the laboratory and stood there, gazing at the strange, moonlit, sexual instruments. Sometimes he thought of the giant, ancient skeletons the scientists had recently found and assembled in London. Dead beasts of another age. God-beasts, waiting to feed.

He removed his nightshirt and stepped through the door, quite naked, his cock growing before him.

He stopped, frozen in a moonlit moment. At the centre of the ring of holy machines stood Dr Reynard, also naked, his back to Walter. He turned in a broad arc, surveying the machines, his mouth slightly open, his cock, like Walter's, hard. Were there tears in his eyes?

Walter ducked back as Reynard's gaze skimmed past him. He got the feeling that his master would not have seen him standing there even in broad daylight. Nevertheless, he retreated from the doorway and beat a path back through the house to his bed, feeling at the same time tantalised by what he had seen and resentful that, once again, he was reduced to spying from the shadows while his master communed with the infinite.

21st November, 1884

I cannot continue in this manner. The strain is becoming unbearable. By day I work myself like an Israelite slave, as if to atone for what is to come. By night I debase myself on Spearman's infernal machines, and I feel free. Free until the dawn wakes me and condemns me to another blasted day.

I feel as if I am living two lives: one by day, spreading light, and the other by night, drowning in darkness. Can a man be split this way? Already I feel a growing imbalance between these two halves of my nature. All through the day

I feel the pressure of my night-self, clawing its way up from within. I am becoming by day a physical wreck.

Am I indeed losing my mind?

I find Walter's presence particularly distressing, and yet I find his absence more so. He has a way of looking at me – something of respect, something of fear. Something, I am sure, of an understanding he does not wish to have.

Does he know of my activities? I fear he knows something. I sense a question always on his lips, never voiced.

How I should love to know what is going on in his mind.

Tonight I turned Spearman away. He was less than pleased. He complained about the expense of equipping the laboratory, of acquiring willing men. He accused me of moral cowardice. He evoked my father.

Always my father.

Twelve

Reynard read the letter again. 'Dear Doctor,' it said. 'I know what you are about in your laboratory with your machines and your nob friends and if you don't want this to be a public scandal and jail too as I shouldn't wonder you had better come up with some money and quick. Let us say four thousand pounds, which should be easy blunt for a man of your standing. I will write again with directions where to leave the money. Signed A Friend.'

Reynard crumpled the letter in his hand and applied his boot to the door in front of him. After a few hard kicks, it collapsed inward on its rusty hinges.

'Sabbato!' Reynard called, stepping inside. 'Show yourself, man!'

This was where Spearman had brought him that night – it seemed long ago now, although little more than a month had passed since their fateful visit – to The Infernal Cabaret. Now it just looked like an old, disused theatre. Dust and pigeon ordure lay over everything. The only response to Reynard's call was a sustained billing and flapping from the rafters.

The place looked as if it had been deserted for years. Reynard approached the little stage. The curtain was down; torn and stained. Stepping behind it, he found himself picking his way between stage weights, lines and pulleys and huge, broken flats which littered the bare boards.

There was no indication that Sabbato and his infernal crew had ever been here.

Discarded in the wings lay a single play-bill, crimson and black. Sabbato stared malevolently from its crumpled surface, while naked bodies writhed around him against a field of dark flames.

Apart from the play-bill it was as if The Infernal Cabaret had never been there.

Lord Spearman's face was grave. 'This is a serious business, Reynard,' he said.

They were in the morning room of Spearman's sprawling town house. The lord sipped at his coffee.

'Damn it, do you think I don't know that?' Reynard snapped. 'Ruin, social disgrace . . . jail, more than likely! What am I to do, Spearman?'

'Well, there is nothing that can be done until you receive the next communication.'

Reynard slapped a second letter on to the table. 'It came this morning,' he said.

Spearman scrutinised the new missive. 'Limehouse,' he said. 'I know it slightly. A less than salubrious quarter, and practically off-limits to the police.'

'We cannot possibly involve the police,' Reynard countered.

'I know,' said Spearman.

'Well?' Reynard was becoming impatient.

'Pay them,' said Spearman blandly.

'It's four thousand pounds, Spearman! It might be little to you, but I don't have that sort of money.'

'You waste too much on that damned poor ward of yours.'

Reynard threw Spearman an angry glance.

'Who do you think might be behind this?' Spearman asked.

'I thought that cur Sabbato,' Reynard replied. 'I found my way back to that theatre of his, but it was quite deserted.'

Spearman laughed an abrupt, contemptuous laugh. 'My dear Reynard,' he said, 'you may take it from me that this is not the work of our friend Sabbato. Believe me, he has no interest in your money. Besides, as you say, The Infernal Cabaret has departed. Sabbato has left these shores for France.'

'Then it must be one or more of the boys you always manage to procure.'

'I can assure you, Reynard, that none of them would hazard such an adventure,' Spearman replied. 'They are all consummate professionals and well paid for their . . . pains.'

'I should never have let you lead me into all this,' Reynard said sulkily. 'I should have listened to my better judgement at the beginning.'

'Confound it, Reynard,' Spearman countered. 'Do you want to live your whole life sniffing after the approbation of the idlers, fools and hypocrites we laughingly call the English upper classes? Give me some hungry working fellows any day. I've freed you, man. Think of the Duc du Guerrand.'

'Fiction! A man cannot really live like that.'

'Think of your father, then,' said Spearman quietly. 'He never lived his life according to anyone's lights but his own. In many ways he reminds me of the Duc.'

'We're talking about prison, man!' Reynard thumped the table. His coffee cup jumped, splashing its contents on the polished mahogany surface.

'Leave this to me,' the peer said thoughtfully. 'Put it quite out of your mind, Reynard. I shall attend to it.'

Reynard smiled a pinched smile. For all Spearman's defects, he was adept at managing scandal. He was far more used to soiling his hands with such matters than anyone else Reynard knew. Reynard finished his cup of coffee and rose to leave.

'My thanks, Spearman,' he said, hearing the relief in his voice.

'Don't mention it, old man,' Spearman replied airily as Reynard was leaving. 'Oh, and keep Thursday night free, will you?'

Reynard heard nothing from Spearman in the intervening days. The spectre of ruin haunted him and he could concentrate neither on his patients nor on his social engagements. To the extent that he acknowledged the presence of other people at all, it was through the narrow, jaundiced eye of acute suspicion. Could one of these persons – some impoverished unfortunate from the casual ward or one of his private clients, unexpectedly come up against hard times – be the blackmailer?

He was silent except when addressed, and frequently his

responses, even to the servants, were short and surly. Attending him while he bathed, Walter barely dared open his mouth.

Late on the Thursday afternoon, Reynard was shut in his study, slouched in his chair, in the company of his friend the Duc du Guerrand, as was generally his habit when troubled in his mind. The Duc had such a clear, honest, fearless view of the world. It was what Reynard's father had had. It was what Reynard himself had always aspired to.

The Duc's broad, winding road had merely led Reynard to doubt and confusion.

His reverie was interrupted by a soft knocking at his study door.

'Lady Horsnail and party have arrived, sir,' the butler announced upon entry.

'What?' said Reynard, snapped from his thoughts.

'Lady Horsnail, sir —'

'My aunt? What the deuce does she want?'

'She —' The butler looked taken aback. 'She . . . is expected, sir. You informed me some time ago that she was due on this date. She is staying until beyond Christmas, sir.'

'The devil take her, I'd forgotten,' Reynard spat. 'And party — did you say party?'

'Yes, sir,' Brakes replied. 'They too were expected, though they will not be staying beyond dinner, sir.'

'All right,' said Reynard, 'show them into the drawing room. I will join you shortly.'

Reynard drummed his desk with his fingers in irritation. His aunt was the last person he wanted to see at the moment. She had a temperament similar to his own — and his father, her brother's. She was clear thinking, independent minded and all too knowing. Her perceptions about her nephew had always had a tendency to be unnervingly accurate. For this — the mental games of hide and seek they had played with one another since his childhood — he usually looked forward to her visits. He had invited her shortly after his adventures with Spearman had begun. Flushed with exhilaration, he had conceived with relish the challenge of carrying on his new secret life while living under the same roof as his perspicacious aunt. Now, with the prospect of exposure and ruin a mere breath away, her visit had taken on a decidedly threatening air.

Dinner that night was a tense affair. Lady Horsnail's two young companions were 'students of political economy'. During her visits she often brought along such morsels for her nephew's amusement. One, a Mr Puddephatt, was, it seemed, a radical. A democrat, no less. The other, a Mr Carnforth, was an enthusiastic Malthusian. Both had loud, penetrating voices. Both, it seemed, regarded the good Dr Reynard as an ally.

'Your much-celebrated work is a living example of what I am advocating, Dr Reynard,' said thin, pale, earnest Puddephatt. 'Your work at the St Luke's casual ward, sir, provides a more powerful argument in favour of what can be achieved by social change than I ever could.'

'Damn it, Puddy,' mumbled the corpulent Carnforth around a mouthful of venison, 'Dr Reynard is a man of breeding, of culture and education. He is no radical: he doesn't need some absurd political credo to drive his work at the poor ward. And the same can be said for virtually all of the men and women – *and women*, mark you – who go into those rookeries every day to aid the moral and physical well-being of the poor.'

'A handful of idle aristocratic men and women have deemed philanthropy fashionable. That is no long-term solution to the problems of poverty found in every so-called civilised country of the world.'

'What do you think of that, Richard?' His aunt smiled mischievously. 'Are you simply a follower of fashion?'

'That is, no, I ... did not mean to imply ...' stammered Puddephatt, a blush serving to bring some small life to his pallid complexion.

'Oh, well done, Puddy,' said Carnforth, thumping the table with glee. 'Insult our host. I apologise for my friend, Doctor. He is a revolutionary. He would like to see you stood up against a wall and shot.' He thumped the table again.

'Now, now, Carnforth,' said Lady Horsnail. 'Don't be naughty.'

'I take no offence at your words, Mr Puddephatt,' Reynard said absently, smiling an unfelt smile. Had he even been in the mood for such discourse, these were disappointing specimens. Aunt Julia had not done well tonight.

'No, you're anything but a follower of fashion, Richard,' she said. 'I know that. If anything, it is the rebel in you that sends you out there.'

The debate continued but Reynard was only half-listening. When he spoke he was addressing himself as much as anyone else; the venom in his voice was – initially, at least – inwardly directed.

'I shall tell you why I spend so much of my time at the casual ward,' he said. 'It is not out of any missionary zeal, or any burning desire to change the fabric of society . . .'

'There!' exclaimed Carnforth, banging the table again.

'Naturally, I despair much of the time of the conditions in which these people live. Disease and early death is the lot of most of them, and this often angers me, but as a doctor I cannot let these considerations affect my professional objectivity. I am, first and foremost, a doctor, and it is on that capacity that I can best serve these people.'

'Well said, sir,' shouted Carnforth. 'Let each man keep to his appointed task. And if he perform it well, we shall all be the better for it.'

'No, if I am honest, what drives me out there is a deep dissatisfaction with my own class, the shallowness and timidness of society, the hypocrisy, the pointless, wasteful ritual. I find among the poor a vibrancy and a vitality, a tenacity for life and yet at the same time an acknowledgement of its many perils and of the imminence of disaster which gives them a clearer, sharper, simpler moral perspective than we can ever hope to achieve. They can afford to waste nothing, and that includes the few narrow avenues of pleasure which life affords them. This means recognising that which is important and discarding the rest. In short, I would say, the poor at large possess a raw intelligence born of life on the edge of the abyss. I find it infinitely more rewarding than the pale pleasures, the endless, pointless and posturing dining-room chatter of the educated classes.'

The gentlemen were silenced. Lady Horsnail tried to suppress a wry smile. The rest of the meal was taken in silence.

At last the gentlemen left and the master and his aunt retired to the drawing room.

'You were not pleased with my offering tonight, Richard,' Reynard's aunt said to him as they entered the drawing room.

'I'm tired,' said Reynard. 'My work . . .'

'Really,' his aunt replied. 'You seem quite agitated to me, although you try to conceal it. You know you can never keep anything from me, nephew.'

'No, really, Aunt,' Reynard replied. 'Now if you will excuse me, I feel I should retire for the night.'

She looked at him long and hard. 'More than ever you reminded me of your father tonight,' she said. 'That declaration you made, that so easily squashed those two minnows. That could have been your poor father speaking. Towards the end, before he . . .'

There was concern and a carefully placed warning in her words.

'Don't worry, Aunt,' he said, forcing a smile. 'I'm not going mad. But, really, you must excuse me. I am tired.'

'Yes, yes. You go,' his aunt said. 'I shall stay up a while. You know the trouble I have sleeping. My late husband used to call me a nightbird. You may dismiss the servants. I shan't require anything tonight.'

Walter and Philip, in full livery, had been waiting on the assembly all night. The evening had been an uncomfortable one for Walter. He had sensed, perhaps more than anyone else in the house, the change in his master's bearing. By night he had waited in vain for Spearman to come creeping through the garden. He had an intuition that his temple would once more be stripped, and so he had continued to visit it at night, in defiance of his master's prohibition.

Last night, naked, he had lain on the bed of nails, moon bathing and masturbating. The sharp, even patina of tiny spikes had felt good against his back: he had pressed down with his shoulders, his hips, his buttocks. Running one tight hand up and down the length of his shaft, he had stretched his ball-sac down with the other and pressed it hard into the lattice of nails, savouring the sharp bite of the metal teeth. Grinding himself into the iron bed he had come high in the air, soaking his own chest and face.

When he had woken up the following morning, his bedsheet had been flecked with blood. His uniform had chafed him painfully all evening. Now he just wanted to clear the table and go to bed.

'Christ,' said Philip when the party had withdrawn and he and Walter stood alone in the dining room. 'I'm glad that's over. I don't know what was more boring, listening to them rabbiting on and on or none of them talking at all. I was thinking of Ruby all night. Give me a raging hard-on, it did, and the old girl could see it, for one. I caught her staring straight at it a few times. And she knew I'd rumbled her, but she just kept on staring, all the same. Dirty old strumpet.'

Suddenly he turned and pushed Walter back on to the table, ripping open the front of his jacket as he did so. Brass buttons clacked on to the table. Others hung by a thread. Plates were tipped, and a bottle knocked to the floor. Philip tore at Walter's vest and trousers.

'No,' Walter whispered urgently. They were taking a terrible risk, here in the dining room. He tried to push Philip off. Philip rolled him on to his front and twisted his arm viciously.

'Don't be difficult, Walter, mate,' he hissed. 'Let Uncle Philip get your pants off.'

Walter struggled, but couldn't move. Philip groped underneath him, slipping his fly-buttons open. Walter was hard beneath. Philip pinched his cock roughly.

'There now,' said Philip. 'You wants it after all.'

He bared Walter's buttocks and ran his fingers up and down the crack, then pushed his fingers deep into Walter's sphincter.

'You know,' he said, 'I swear you're getting looser.'

He pulled his cock from the front of his uniform, spat on his hand and, pulling back his foreskin, rubbed the spit into the dancing purple head.

'Not much need of this,' he said, angling the erection downward, nudging it against Walter's buttocks and running it wetly down his crack.

He found Walter's hole and pushed inside it. In truth, though Philip was not small, Walter barely felt any discomfort nowadays: he was as nothing compared to the candle in the laboratory.

The voice of Lady Horsnail echoed through the door, then stopped.

'Is anything wrong, milady?'

Brakes. Both Walter and, inside him, Philip froze. The old man had usually retired by now.

'No . . . I thought I heard . . . It doesn't matter.'

The two of them walked on, their voices fading to nothing.

'Now,' said Philip, 'where was we? Oh, yes.'

With a grunt he thrust forward again. Walter raised his arse slightly and clenched his buttocks around the footman's pole. He shocked himself with the realisation that he was learning where the most sensitive parts of his tunnel were, and how best to stimulate them. He ground Philip's throbbing cock between his cheeks as the footman pushed and pulled.

'Oh . . . Jesus . . .' Philip reached around Walter's waist and gripped his cock, drawing his foreskin clumsily down the shaft, then back again. He ran his hands up Walter's back, pushing his uniform high. His hands played roughly across the pattern of tiny wounds, which covered Walter's back, and his fingernails clawed at them, prising them open. Walter stifled a cry of pain and half-twisted around beneath Philip. Philip's cock slipped from Walter's arse and skimmed up his buttock crack, shedding its load over his lower back.

There was a noise from the window, which caused both Walter and Philip to turn their heads. The dining room faced the back of the house, its large windows overlooking the garden. It was a clear night. Silhouetted in the moonlight was the figure of Lord Spearman, his face close to the glass, staring in at them. Their sudden awareness of his presence didn't seem to bother the lord at all. He continued to hold them in a long, cool and unblinking gaze before slowly turning and walking away.

Philip sprang from the table, shoving his still-disgorging cock back into his trousers. 'There's that bloke again,' he said. 'Lord Whassisname.'

A puddle of light spilled on to the path as the laboratory door opened. Another figure, young and tall, with close-cut blond hair, joined Spearman in the doorway. Before they could step through into the laboratory the figure of Reynard emerged. He seemed to anxiously address the lord who, with a word and a gesture of his hand, ushered them inside.

'What do they get up to in there?' Philip asked. 'Who's the boy? Looked like a bleeding Margery to me.'

Walter was silent.

'Come on, Walter. I know you see more than you let on. I see you watching all the time. You're a bigger peeping Tom than me. And I know you got a key to the lab. What are you hiding, Walter?' Another thought seemed to occur to him. 'How did you get them nicks on your back?' he asked suspiciously.

Walter didn't reply. Philip's hand shot out and hit Walter sharply on the penis, now half-hard.

'Come on,' he said, a note of coercion in his voice. He hit Walter a second time on the cock. He lowered his hand and brought it up sharply under Walter's balls.

He winced, but his cock grew hard again.

Why not tell Philip? So much of the ceremonial of his temple was denied him by having no henchman and having to be celebrant *and* sacrifice. Yes, why not tell Philip?'

'All right,' he said. 'Come with me. But you've got to be deadly quiet, and you must swear not to breathe a word of what you see to a living soul.'

He remembered Lord Spearman issuing him with similar instructions prior to preparing the laboratory – the temple – for that first Hallowe'en night's ritual. Suddenly he felt in command. He was the initiator now: Philip was merely the acolyte.

Fishing his keys from his pocket, he led the footman quietly from the room.

Reynard had been waiting in the laboratory for Spearman since eleven o'clock. The lord – and his boy – arrived half an hour later.

Reynard rushed forward to greet him. 'Well, Spearman,' he said hurriedly, 'what news do you have for me?'

Spearman strolled past him and into the centre of the room, where he stood, turning in a slow circle, regarding the silent, attendant machines like an engineer surveying his works. He extracted his silver flask from his pocket and took a long, slow draught.

'Spearman, damn it!' snapped Reynard.

'The unfortunate matter is resolved to the satisfaction of all,' interrupted the peer, 'and you may give it no further thought.'

'What did you —'

Spearman held up his hand. 'Not another thought,' he repeated. 'Let us just say that you will never again hear from the other parties in this . . . exchange.'

'But who were they?'

'They were quite unknown to me,' Spearman replied. He lit a large cigar and offered one to Reynard, who absently took it. 'Low-born persons of the sort to whom you devote so much of your time and energy. How they came by the information I have not the faintest idea, but it is of no consequence. Simply accept my assurance that the matter is at an end.'

A wave of relief flooded over Reynard, and he clasped Spearman by the hand, shaking it vigorously.

Spearman pulled back and beckoned the boy forward. He was tall and white-blond, with porcelain-pale skin and bright blue eyes.

'Hans will soothe your troubled brow,' whispered the lord. 'And then we shall torment his flawless one.'

Hans took the cigar from Reynard's hand and put it in the doctor's mouth. He struck a Lucifer and held it to its tip. Reynard sucked dutifully on the cheroot. Hans ran a smooth hand down Reynard's cheek and neck, loosening the front of his shirt, tracing patterns with his lips, grazing on the fine mat of brown hair that sat around Reynard's nipples and tapered away down his stomach to his belly button, then thickened as it disappeared beneath his belt.

Hans loosened the belt and eased Reynard's trousers down. His cock stood to attention beneath the white cloth of his underwear. Hans freed it and licked it with a long tongue, pasting it in saliva, then slipped his full, flawless lips over the swollen head, easing back the foreskin with his teeth. He sucked with expertise, teasing the frenulum and the ridge around the helmet and engulfing the rigid member in a delicious, warm wetness. Cigar clamped between his lips, Reynard placed his hands on the boy's head, feeling it ride and bob on his cock, while the white-gold hair sprung through his fingers. As his climax drew close, his fingers tightened into fists, pulling the hair taut and at the same time crushing the boy's head with the heels of his palms. He thrust Hans's head down as he came, feeling his cock slam against the back of the boy's throat, and then the sublime recoil of his own sluicing jissom.

Silently, Spearman drew Hans to his feet and swiftly undressed him. The boy was elegantly muscular; his skin was white and flawless and, apart from a thin white down around his long, slim cock and under his arms, quite hairless. Spearman led him to the rack, a low wooden bench with manacles at one end and a series of weights and ropes and a great ratcheted roller at the other. Hans said something in quiet, eager German and then laid himself on his back on the device, his arms above his head. Spearman spread his legs wide and manacled them to the outer edges of the platform, then roped his wrists.

'Now, Reynard,' he said. 'What shall we make him confess?'

He released a brake and the weights dropped and the roller turned. The boy let out a low hiss as his body was stretched. Reynard could see his muscles tensing as he tried in vain to resist the pull of the ropes. His cock remained hard, rising sometimes in involuntary convulsion.

'Hans likes playing with fire,' said Spearman. 'Don't you, Hans?'

He took the cigar from his mouth and held the glowing nub of ash next to one of the boy's nipples. The boy let out a low groan. Spearman trailed the hot cherry just above the boy's chest to the other nipple.

'At home in Germany they call him the human ashtray,' said Spearman. 'Do use him as such, Reynard.'

He ratcheted the rack still tighter. Reynard's hand was shaking as he took the cigar from his lips and held it above the boy's stomach. Beneath it, there developed a faint circular red weal. Gingerly, Reynard did it again.

He felt Spearman's hand clamp itself around his wrist, driving it down towards Hans's hard cock, towards the base just where it met his wrinkled ball-sac. The boy's cock spasmed with the sensation. Spearman took his own cigar and, peeling the boy's foreskin back, held its tip above the purple bulb beneath. This time the boy did cry out in high, rapid German.

'For God's sake, Spearman,' Reynard said. 'What if someone hears him?'

Spearman threw his cigar to the floor. 'No-one will hear him,' he said.

He moved to the head of the rack and undid his trousers. Advancing the roller by another vicious ratchet, Spearman bared his long, veiny cock and climbed on to the rack. He kneeled over Hans, his knees upon the boy's shoulders and his cock bouncing off his face. Spearman leaned forward, resting his arms on the awful ratchet mechanism, and thrust his cock down into Hans's mouth.

Reynard moved his cigar down towards the boy's balls, holding it above first one then the other before moving it back along his taut perineum. Then he pushed the cigar high into the boy's anus, where it finally extinguished itself.

Spearman was grunting and spitting in time to the rise and fall of his hollow buttocks, his balls slapping against Hans's chin, his cock drilling into his face. Reynard looked down at the circular trail of faint brands which now dotted the boy's body. Under different circumstances, in this very room, he might be conducting a medical examination of the boy. The thought sent a glad shudder through Reynard. He lowered his head – as a doctor never would – and licked at the burn he had made on the boy's belly, tickling it with his tongue and wetting it with his saliva. He moved from brand to brand with his wet tongue, from ball to full, tight ball and back along the cord of muscle between his open legs. He pushed his tongue into the dark crack between Hans's cheeks, searching for the brown ring of his anus, licking and penetrating and tasting. Finally he dragged his tongue forward again, up the slim, straight shaft of Hans's hard cock to the knob at the end, which he licked like a child's lollipop.

He heard Spearman groan and raised his eyes to see his friend's red cock, clutched in his fist, spurting its hot ballast into Hans's smooth, pale face.

For nearly two hours, Reynard and Spearman tortured and tantalised the youth. For nearly two hours, Walter and Philip crouched on the balcony above and watched until at last Spearman and his captive vanished into the night and Reynard dressed, smoothed his hair and walked from the laboratory, locking it behind him.

Walter had never seen Philip so quiet. He was pale, and his eyes were wide. He was trembling slightly. He crouched, motionless, for long minutes after the laboratory below had been deserted.

'Jesus,' he whispered eventually.

'Are you ready?' Walter asked him.

'Ready?' Philip replied nervously. 'Ready for what?'

'To go down,' said Walter.

'Down there . . .' Philip swallowed dryly. 'Jesus . . .'

'Come along,' whispered Walter, gently prising loose the footman's grip on the gallery's wooden balustrade and drawing him to his feet.

'Righto,' croaked Philip, and allowed himself to be led away.

He walked among the machines as if in a trance. Walter watched him, smiling, then began to remove his own uniform.

'Well . . .' he said to Philip.

'What . . . Uh . . . yeah.' Philip took a deep breath and followed suit.

When both were naked, Walter led Philip by the hand from machine to machine. Philip moved like a sleepwalker.

He paused at the iron maiden and touched its black internal phallus with his hand.

'Turn around,' said Walter.

Philip obeyed. His eyes widened and his mouth opened to shout as Walter slammed the sarcophagus door on him. The shout became a scream of panic.

'Get me off this thing! Walter . . . get it out of me!'

Many times Walter had examined the maiden's internal mechanism (although he had never dared try it for fear of being unable to open it from the inside). As the door closed, twin metal wedges on its inner side forced the occupant backward and downward. The only place to go was on to the phallus.

It was now buried inside Philip. Walter began stroking his cock at the thought, massaging his balls with his free hand.

'Put your John Thomas through the hole in the door,' said Walter. 'I'll suck you.'

Philip didn't reply. He was screaming.

Walter moved to the back of the cabinet, grasped a small metal plate and pulled, drawing the phallus out of the device and out of Philip's arse. He licked it slowly and carefully.

'Jesus . . .' croaked Philip, inside the machine.

Walter placed his cock in line with the hole where the plate had been. Once, following their wanking sessions, back when they had still shared a room together and before Philip had taken to having Walter more or less at will, Walter had lain behind the sleeping footman and placed his hard cock against his puckered sphincter, pushing lightly. He had wanted, even then, to penetrate Philip, but had not dared. He doubted he would ever be able to actually thrust his penis inside someone. Now, with Philip caged and invisible, he felt no compunction. He pushed his cock slowly forward, feeling Philip's hole against his tip, and forced it open, feeling his walls close about the sensitive head of his cock and cover his shaft.

'Walter!' Philip shouted. 'What are you doing? What are you –'

Walter's buttocks rolled and his belly slapped against the cold metal casing as he pumped his cock in and out of the footman's arse. Philip had stopped shouting: Walter could hear the gasps with which he punctuated his thrusts. Walter pumped faster. He felt his balls tightening and a great wave pass upward from them, flushing through his body. His cock clenched and exploded, deep inside Philip.

He stood, breathless for a moment, then slowly dressed.

'Walter . . .' Philip's voice was tearful. 'Walter, where are you? Don't leave me here . . .'

Walter replaced and straightened his uniform as well as he could, given that most of the buttons were now missing, and strolled slowly about the laboratory, gazing in admiration at the machines.

Eventually he stepped up to the iron maiden. Philip was sobbing within. Silently, Walter lifted the latch on the machine and walked from the laboratory.

Thirteen

A warm glow suffused Walter all through the following morning's work. He even found himself whistling (a hymn, admittedly – Pastor Meek's dirges were about all he knew) as he went about his duties.

For once Philip was keeping his eyes down, avoiding Walter's gaze. Walter tried, whenever he caught the footman's eye, to effect a smirk. He wasn't much good at it, but he suspected he was making his point.

He thought little of it when the master summoned him to his study at mid-morning.

Walter stood for several moments before Reynard's desk. The doctor was rigid and silent, staring at the mahogany desktop.

At last he spoke.

'Why, Walter?' was all he said. His voice was flat, but Walter could discern some deep disappointment in the meaningless question.

'Sir?'

'Why did you betray me?'

'I don't . . . I . . .'

'You were in the laboratory last night.'

Walter was silent. His stomach lurched and a numbing chill crawled like a spider up his body to his head. He felt suddenly unsteady on his feet.

'My aunt saw you entering that wing of the house at approximately eleven-thirty, in the company of Philip,' Reynard continued. 'She also saw you leave, much later. I granted you special dispensation to come and go from that wing as necessity dictated. That dispensation did not permit you to take in any guests with you, nor did it include night-time excursions.'

'Sir . . .' Walter's voice was barely a whisper.

Reynard tossed a brass button on to the desk. It was from the household livery.

'I discovered this in the viewing gallery. There was another in the laboratory itself.'

What excuse could Walter offer? He was guilty, he knew, of the most dreadful indiscretion; of the basest betrayal of trust.

'I'm sorry, sir,' was the best he could do.

'I take it you saw what was going on there.' It was more a statement than a question.

'Sir . . .'

'And I take it that this is not the first time you have witnessed these events.'

'No, sir.'

'I have already spoken to Philip and he assures me that it was you who dragged him in there, and that he had no idea what he was going to see there. Is that true?'

'Yes, sir,' Walter whispered.

Reynard rose to his feet and turned his back to Walter. 'I have no intention of trying to justify what you saw in the laboratory, although if my reading of events is accurate I do not have to. You have experienced the machines for yourself.'

Walter nodded his head, almost imperceptibly.

Reynard suddenly swung to face his valet. There was a note of controlled anger in his voice now.

'If this were merely a matter of betrayal of trust it would be bad enough. However, this business has acquired a more sinister dimension. I have been blackmailed, Walter. A person or persons unknown to me wrote intimating knowledge of my ex . . . my activities . . . and demanding an extremely large sum of money. Lord Spearman, thank God, has settled the matter for me. I have tormented myself with the question of who could have supplied this information. I have scrutinised my friends, my patients, in the most suspicious manner. I didn't think to question the loyalty of my own servants.' He dropped his voice. 'And least of all you, Walter.'

Walter felt the need to rest a hand on the desk for support. Reynard didn't seem to notice.

'Now I can't bring myself to believe,' he continued, 'that you had any actual hand in the blackmail plot, but I cannot fail to arrive at the conclusion that you, with your spying and your utter lack of discretion and honour, have been responsible for this information spreading abroad.'

'But sir,' Walter whispered, appalled at the allegation. 'I didn't –'

'Damn it!' Reynard suddenly exploded. 'Do you know how close I came to ruin? Disgrace? Possibly even prison?'

In an instant he had regained his composure. Again he turned away from Walter. He rang the butler's bell and remained facing the wall, his hands clenched behind his back, until Brakes arrived.

'You rang, sir?'

'Brakes, I want Starling out of the house by nightfall. He is to be paid up to the end of the month. No character reference is to be given.'

'Sir?' The old butler wrung his hands in confusion and distress.

Reynard swung to face him. 'Did you or did you not hear me, Mr Brakes?'

'Yes, sir. I shall attend to it immediately, sir.'

'Furthermore, for the short time he is under my roof he is to communicate with none of the staff except yourself, and then you are only to address yourselves to the practicalities of his departure. That will be all.'

Numbly, Walter followed Mr Brakes through the house. He passed through the rooms he now knew so well like a ghost. A chaos of feelings and images tumbled through his mind. He couldn't concentrate on any one of them. Dreamlike memories of the previous night – of all his nights in the laboratory – part-coalesced before breaking up again. Blackmail. The fatal word nagged at him. Vaguely, the question of where on earth he was to go and what he was to do took shape, before vanishing back into the sea of confusion.

At the foot of the stairs leading to the servants' rooms the old butler turned to Walter. Puzzlement, sorrow, distress and disillusionment fought for dominance in the old butler's face. He opened his mouth as if to say something profound and important. Instead all he said was, 'You had better pack your possessions.'

And with that the old man returned below stairs.

It was only when he was packing his few possessions – some items of clothing, his Bible, little else – into his suitcase that the full enormity of the situation descended upon Walter.

He had no family in London, and no friends. He had nowhere to go. Without a reference from his employer he would have little chance of finding a new situation in service.

He had betrayed his employer and benefactor. Worse, he had cut himself off from God. He was damned.

He decided that he had to speak to Dr Reynard. If he could make the master see how completely he understood what was going on in the laboratory, that for him too – as it must be for the master, Walter felt certain – this was more than mere carnality. If he told him that he believed the laboratory was a temple to some new face of God, then surely the master would not cast him aside.

Clutching his suitcase, he descended the staircase to the ground floor. Brakes was in the hallway, waiting for him.

'Walter, where are you going?' the butler asked as he turned towards the far wing of the house and the master's study.

'I have a few personal effects below stairs,' Walter replied. 'May I go and get them?'

Brakes nodded slowly. 'I can't see the harm,' he said. 'The staff have been instructed not to communicate with you. Please do not embarrass any of them by attempting to make them break this injunction.'

Walter rounded the corner so that the butler was no longer in view. Placing his suitcase by the door that led down below stairs, he turned instead and strode quickly towards the master's consulting wing.

As Walter approached the door, it opened, and Philip emerged.

Seeing Walter, he stood before the open doorway as if to block him.

'Philip,' said Walter, 'please help me. I have to see the master.'

'Well, he don't want to see you,' Philip retorted.

'Please,' Walter repeated, his voice beginning to tremble. He moved forward and attempted to side-step the footman. Philip stepped in front of him, legs braced and arms extended slightly. Walter attempted to pass around him and through the door. Philip gripped him by either shoulder and pushed him roughly back down the passage.

'Now don't make me slap you, Walter,' said Philip. 'I wouldn't want to do that.'

There was a note of malice, and of triumph, in his voice. It was reflected in his face, too. Walter's brief ascendancy over Philip was over: this was Philip's revenge for last night.

Casting a last glance past Philip to the closed door of Dr Reynard's study, Walter turned and walked back through the house.

Picking up his case, he went below stairs for what he assumed was the last time. A sudden silence fell in the kitchen as he entered. Meg and Ruby stopped their work and stared. Even Mr Croup the gardener put down the mug of tea he was drinking and watched Walter's passage through the long room.

Mrs Donaldson clapped her hands. 'What's this?' she bellowed. 'The house won't run itself, you know. Everybody back to work.'

She wouldn't meet Walter's eyes.

Mr Brakes was waiting in his little office. He handed Walter an envelope.

'Here are your wages,' he said, 'paid to the end of the month.'

Silently, Walter took the envelope and left. His knuckles tight around the grip of his suitcase, he opened the tradesmen's door and, with a final backward glance, stepped through it, turning to face the wide, cold, expectant city. A sudden gust of wind slammed the door shut behind him.

Book Two

28th November, 1884

It is late, but I cannot sleep. I have risen to try to work, but my concentration has deserted me. For over an hour now I have sought in vain to gather my notes into some coherent form for my forthcoming lecture. I must confess myself in a state of some agitation following the events of the last few days. I must strive to put the whole unfortunate business of blackmail and betrayal behind me.

There is a strange atmosphere in the house: I fear that this morning's drama has affected the staff. I overheard an unfortunate altercation outside my door between my former valet and my footman this morning. My instructions were clear, and yet I could not but regret the brutal manner in which Philip dismissed Walter.

Surely there can be no more base misdemeanour than the betrayal by a servant of his master's most intimate trust.

I find it difficult to set foot in my laboratory. Those infernal machines suddenly seem oppressive to me. They stand there like bizarre gallows, mutely boasting of their nefarious work.

Do I feel ashamed? Should I? Are not shame and guilt merely echoes in the brain of the mindless baying of the mob without? My father certainly thought so. He wrote to me, I recall, on the very subject.

No, what I feel is haunted. I went into the laboratory early this evening intending to order my compounds – more out of a need to busy myself than anything else – and I found I was driven out after less than ten minutes. It was more than the machines. I felt certain I was being watched.

It cannot have been so, of course. I shall never be caught like that again. I find it bitterly ironic that now I know I am alone I cannot shake this conviction that I am being observed, whereas when I was in fact being watched I carried on in blissful ignorance.

Is it Walter I feel, watching me from the gallery? Is it Sabbato among the long drapes by the window? Or is it Spearman, everywhere, drinking poison from that damned flask of his?

I would give much to know where all three are tonight.

I dined this evening at my club, leaving my aunt to dine alone, and feeling less remorse than I ought. After the events of the past few days the house oppresses me; whereas my aunt perceives no shadows there. I pray that that remains the case.

It was strange dressing for dinner without my valet.

Fourteen

The day was wet and blustery. Walter walked blindly from the house, oblivious to the driving rain. Familiar streets spidered out in all directions; Walter chose them at random. He passed Mr Kilby the chemist's shop, the butcher's, the ostler's. He walked for hours. The streets became strange. He crossed the river to a part of London he did not know.

He ate a tasteless meal at a dingy chop-house, and counted his money. Four guineas. If he was frugal he could last a while on that.

His first priority was to find somewhere to spend the night. He stepped out into the relentless drizzle and looked up and down the street. In the time he had taken to eat and ponder his fate, most of the shops had closed their doors and extinguished their lights. A lone gas-lamp at its far end strove inadequately to illuminate the entire thoroughfare, now almost deserted. He struck out towards the light. It stood at a crossroads. The roads were the same in each direction – darkened shops and few people left on the street.

Thin music drifted up the road to his left. Singing, and an out-of-tune piano. A public house. Walter approached it with trepidation: only once or twice, during his time at Billingsgate, had he set foot in such places. His parents had avoided them and Pastor Meek had railed against them.

The name of the house was the Ten Bells (although Walter could only make out three or four on the faded, peeling sign above the door – the rest presumably erased with time). It was a low building with small windows close to its roof. With trepidation in his heart and the voice of the pastor in his head, he pushed open the door and entered. At first the choking, smoky air in the room seemed to him worse than the winter smogs which so often hugged the city. He spluttered and his eyes began to sting almost immediately. He stood at the top of three wooden steps, overlooking a crowded, noisy room. A motley collection of labouring people and vagabonds jostled for space, some standing and others sitting at long, rough wooden tables. Walter descended the steps and edged forward through the crowd towards the bar. He stood at its far end, looking stiffly around him, aware of the way he must stand out against this shabbily dressed crowd. He began to sweat beneath his heavy overcoat, for the room was hot and damp. Great tears of moisture covered the insides of the smoke-yellowed windows, wholly obscuring the view of the street.

A man was playing the piano, and many of the drinkers were singing.

> I was the boy for bewitching 'em,
> Whether good humoured or coy;
> All cried when I was beseeching 'em,
> 'Do what you will with me, joy.'

'You wanting something, mister, or what?' a female voice drawled in his ear. A thin barmaid with limp, bedraggled hair was addressing him.

'Ah, no. I . . . I never partake,' replied Walter.

The barmaid snorted and gave him a contemptuous look. 'What you doing here then?' she sneered. 'Admiring the scenery?'

'I am seeking some advice,' said Walter.

'Advice!' the barmaid snapped. 'The only advice I can give is to get away from my bar. There's people want to be served and you're standing in the way. I'm here to serve drinks. I ain't got time to give out advice. Right, who's next then?'

Walter looked along the bar. Other people were talking to the staff as they drew their ales. He realised his mistake.

'Please,' he said, catching the barmaid's eye. 'I . . . I should like a pint of beer.'

'Beer,' she replied. 'Pint of heavy?'

'Yes,' said Walter, having little idea what it was he was consenting to.

He watched her drawing up the ale, pumping the great wooden handle.

'I am in need of lodgings,' said Walter. 'I was hoping that you might be able to recommend somewhere.'

'Lodgings.' She mused for a second, then, turning her head, shouted, 'George!'

A man pushed his way along the bar.

'This geezer wants a billet for the night.' The barmaid slapped his beer down on the bar.

The little man in front of Walter looked first at her, then at him, then at her again. He was dressed in the manner of a clerk – a brown bowler with a pertly curving rim worn jauntily on his head and a leather-elbowed jacket – albeit a very poor one, for the entire garb looked thin and faded and, small though he was in stature, too short in the sleeves and too tight everywhere. He must have been about thirty, and had a bright, eager face thrusting forward slightly from a wiry body.

Suddenly he thrust out his hand. 'Poskett's the name, squire,' he chirped. 'George Poskett. What can I do for you?'

'I'm looking for lodgings. Something clean and secure, something respectable, but not too expensive.'

'That's asking quite a lot round here, squire. Not too expensive – no problem! But . . . well . . . you gets what you pays for, don't you?'

'Oi! That'll be tuppence!' the barmaid cut in loudly. For a second Walter didn't realise that she was addressing him. He fumbled inside his overcoat.

'I'll get these,' said George Poskett, taking a coin from his pocket and dropping it on the bar. 'Here you are, Poll. Get one in for me an' all, will you?' He reached out and, just for a second, touched the hem of Walter's overcoat. It had been Dr Reynard's

– one of the valet's perks – and barely worn. 'Nice,' George Poskett half-whispered. Then, looking up at Walter: 'We don't get many gen'l'men round these streets. What brings you here?'

Walter flinched from the little man's gaze and his question.

'Sorry, sah,' George Poskett said hastily. 'Not meaning to pry or nothing. A gen'l'man's business is his own, right enough. I would be honoured if you would take a drink with me, sah.'

He picked up his pint, which now stood next to Walter's. Walter did the same.

'Chin chin, wot,' the little man said. Walter raised the glass to his lips, grimacing slightly as the bitter brown liquid slid to the back of his throat.

He gagged.

'No,' said Walter, 'I can't. I'm sorry, but . . . I have to go.'

The man laid a hand gently but firmly on his shoulder. 'As it happens,' he said, 'I do know of a place, only a couple of streets from here. Very respectable 'stablishment – for these parts, leastways – belonging to a Mrs Podger. How much was you thinkin of paying?'

'I could manage a shilling a night,' replied Walter hopefully, having next to no idea how much a room in a respectable establishment ought to cost.

The man drew in a long breath between pursed lips. 'Bessie Podger don't normally go down that low, but . . . what the heck, I've done her a few favours over the years. I'll nip round with you and have a quick word.' He winked at Walter. 'After all, you're one of my drinking mates now. Down the hatch.'

He raised his glass to his lips. Reluctantly, Walter picked up his glass and did likewise.

He was feeling quite drunk by the time George Poskett finally led him to Mrs Podger's rooming house. George hammered on the street door and called out, rather too loudly for the time of night. 'Bess . . . Look alive, gel!'

The door was opened by a woman carrying a candle. Its faint, flickering glow revealed a narrow, dark passage, almost entirely blocked by the woman's body. In the half-light she looked like the biggest woman Walter had ever seen.

'Got a gen'l'man for you here, Bess,' said George. 'Needs a room for the night. I told him he could have it for a shilling.'

'Oh, you did, did you?' grumbled the enormous woman. 'Well, it do so happen I've got a room going, and I don't suppose I'll get no-one else for it this time of night. All right, in you come.'

'Maybe I'll see you in the Bells tomorrow night,' George called after Walter as he vanished within.

The room was small, but clean.

'Thank you,' said Walter to the woman as she turned to leave.

'Privy's at the end of the passage,' she replied, disappearing down the passage.

In his drunkenness, the room began to sway and swim. He undressed, holding the end of the bed for support, then unsteadily groped his way up the mattress and under its thin covers, clinging to the narrow bed as if it were the only certainty left in the world.

He awoke unrefreshed and with a headache. A pale sun shone through the window. Somewhere far off he heard a clock chime . . . ten o'clock. He jumped out of bed, washed hastily, dressed and hurried down the stairs. He never slept this late. There was much to do today. He had to find a means of income and somewhere more permanent to live.

At least the day was dry. He walked from the house to the nearest thoroughfare and boarded an omnibus. He had made a mental list of hiring offices where servants might find work.

He alighted on the Euston Road and, waiting until the team had been spurred back into life and the omnibus moved on, crossed to the other side. Fellowes & Sons, Servants' Hiring Office. Walter pushed the door open and stepped into a large, bare room, at the end of which a thin youth with a pale, acne-ravaged complexion sat amid two large piles of crammed ledgers. He looked up when Walter entered, then continued writing on a piece of paper, biting the nails of his left hand. The clock on the wall behind him ticked hollowly.

'Next,' said a dull voice from the desk.

Walter stood in front of the youth and waited for him to stop writing. After about a minute he looked up.

'Name,' he said.

'Walter Starling.'

He wrote it down.

'Position sought.'

'Pardon?'

'What position are you looking for? What is it you do?'

'I've been an under-footman,' said Walter, 'and recently a valet.'

'Under-footman and valet, eh?' A taut smile passed quickly across the youth's face. 'Who have you worked for?'

'Most recently Dr Reynard of Dorset Street, and before that I was a general servant in the house of Mr James Lipiatt.'

'This doctor bloke – how long was you there?'

Walter didn't answer.

'You deaf or something?' the youth snapped.

'Two months,' said Walter quietly.

'What?' said the youth, screwing his face up.

'Two months,' said Walter, more firmly.

'Two months?' The youth put down his pen. 'I don't suppose there's any point asking you for a character, then?'

Walter blinked at him in confusion.

'A reference,' said the youth impatiently.

'No,' Walter whispered.

'Listen,' said the youth, leaning back in his chair, 'we get a lot of you in here, the young, gormless, pretty ones who went into houses in lowly positions and suddenly gets made right up to valet, and then just as suddenly finds themselves on the street. Personally, I think it's disgusting. We can't take you on.'

He crumpled up the piece of paper he had been writing on and dropped it on to the floor beside him.

'Next.'

Walter incurred the same response – with varying degrees of civility and prurience – at all of the agencies he visited. Even after he begun tampering with the truth – exaggerating his experience and length of service – nowhere was willing to register him on their books without a reference.

He visited eleven offices scattered across London. Eventually he boarded an omnibus going back to Southwark. He dined at the same chop-house as on the previous night and returned to Mrs Podger's dwelling.

His situation was not good. His money would not last long, and the prospect of finding another position looked hopeless. Suddenly he felt terribly alone, in an alien part of London with not a friend to his name.

He had always felt safe and comfortable and content with his own company. He had sought solitude whenever the opportunity had presented itself. Now he was finding it uncomfortable. Something had changed. Alone with himself, it felt as if there was a stranger in the room.

He couldn't bear it. He rose from the bed and donned his overcoat, then slipped from the room, down the stairs and out of the front door.

There was singing coming from Ten Bells.

'Course, we do get a few gents round here from time to time, looking for a change of scenery, like.'

'Well, I'm not really a gentleman,' said Walter, dimly aware that his voice was already beginning to slur.

George Poskett chuckled. 'None of you ever is when you comes round here,' he said with a wink.

Two young women, slightly older than Walter, were standing next to them. They both wore garish make-up, applied far too liberally and in a way that Walter found quite indecent, and dresses which, while somewhat faded, were likewise loud and attention seeking.

'Hello, here's a couple of gels,' he suddenly exclaimed. 'Why don't we buy them a couple of gins? See what happens.'

He winked at Walter. Walter lowered his eyes.

'Fair enough,' said George. 'Not your cup of tea, eh?'

He fished a battered watch from his pocket.

'Corks!' he said. 'Look at the time. I got to sling my hook. I'll walk you back to Bessie's, if you like.'

Drunk again, Walter made his way back and groped his way into his room in darkness, finding the candle by match-light. The candle was new – Mrs Podger had replaced the former burned-out stub – and a deep red colour. It seemed to give off a soothing smell as it burned.

He removed his coat, jacket and waistcoat, and his shoes, and sat on the bed.

There was a tap at the door.

'Come in,' he called.

The door opened and a young man – probably a year younger than Walter – entered the room. He was an inch or so shorter than Walter, with wavy, light-brown hair, a button nose and a delicate mouth. His eyes were large and brown and shy.

Walter looked at him enquiringly.

'Ma sent me up to see if there was anything you wanted,' he said. 'It's not like we gets many gen'l'men round here and . . . well . . . whatever you want, really.'

'No, really, everything is perfectly fine, thank you,' Walter replied.

'Could be better, though,' the boy said quietly. He advanced towards the bed where Walter was sitting and dropped to his knees before him. His hands gently prised Walter's knees apart and stroked his inner thighs through his trousers, his fingertips brushing the underside of Walter's balls. He ran a finger up the underside of Walter's cock, which was rigid and painful behind his fly, and, one by one, undid the buttons. Walter lay back across the bed as the boy massaged his pole through his taut underwear. He felt the boy begin to remove his clothing, item by item. He raised his buttocks to enable his trousers to come off. Soon he was quite naked on the bed.

The boy's shirt was open to reveal a firm, hairless, rosy-nippled chest. Walter reached up and ran his hands over it. The boy smiled and began removing his own clothing.

When both were naked, the boy crawled on to the bed like a cat and began kissing Walter wetly; his face and neck, his chest, his stomach, the neat triangle of hair about his prick. Walter watched the boy, enraptured. There was a gentleness about him, about their coupling, which he had never experienced before. This seemed like a world away from Philip's frenzied attacks or Dr Reynard's bizarre experiments.

Walter gripped the boy's buttocks and steered him around on

156

the bed. On all fours, one knee placed on either side of Walter's head, the boy opened his mouth wide and, extending his tongue, slid his head over the throbbing shaft. The boy's cock swayed slightly over Walter's face. Arching his neck, Walter took the boy inside his mouth, drawing him deep into his throat while feeling his own cock sink deep into the warm, wet cave of the boy's mouth. They sucked and gobbled greedily on one another.

They came together, the boy clenching his thighs about Walter's head and deluging Walter's throat with his sharp seed and Walter thrusting upward with his hips as his cock erupted inside the boy's mouth.

They lay still, spent, their softening cocks leaking their last into one another's mouths. They continued to hold and suck until each became hard again between the other's lips. The boy rolled on to his stomach.

'Fuck me now,' he whispered.

Walter hesitated. The boy took his hand. 'It's all right,' he whispered.

Walter rolled on to the boy's back and hugged him, pressing his lips against his neck and smelling the sweat on his skin. He began running his cock along the boy's buttock cleft, gently at first, then with more vigour, ploughing the crack hard. Then, finding the boy's hole with his fingers, he pushed down into it. Breathing deeply of the boy's milky scent, running his fingers through his hair, across his face, around and between his lips, he fucked him with long, slow strokes, listening to the slap of his belly against the boy's back. Arms stretched, they locked hands, fingers intertwining. Legs stretched, Walter's toes dug in behind the boy's toes. He quaked with his second climax.

He climbed from the boy and lay next to him, staring into his deep brown eyes.

'Let's sleep now,' whispered the boy, hugging Walter to him, one strong arm protectively across his back.

Walter slept deep and dreamlessly, and awoke refreshed. He was alone in the bed. He sighed. He supposed it was too much to have hoped for.

He stretched, got out of bed and washed lazily. He climbed

into his shirt, pulled on his trousers and reached for his jacket. Almost instinctively his hand moved to check the inner pocket where he kept his money. It groped around inside, finding nothing.

Walter stared frantically into the pocket. He searched the rest of the jacket, then threw it down on the bed. He looked in the little cupboard, under the bed, behind the wash stand. He emptied his suitcase and searched through every item.

He ran downstairs into Mrs Podger's parlour. She was sitting down to an enormous breakfast of fried meats.

'I've been robbed!' he bellowed.

Mrs Podger mumbled something behind a mouthful of breakfast.

'I said I've been robbed. Your son –'

'What son?' answered the woman, swallowing. 'I ain't got no son.'

'The man you sent to my room last night –'

'Man I sent?' The behemoth lurched to her feet in anger. 'What the devil do you take me for, sir? I don't run that sort of house . . . and I never will, neither! That's slander, that is. Any more of that and I'll have the law on you. And where's my shilling for yesterday?'

'I don't have it,' said Walter. 'He took all my money.'

'Right, sling your hook, you. You think I'm that green that I can't sniff out someone trying to dodge their back-rent, do you? Come on, pack your bags. I wants you out now, else I'll call the rozzers and you can explain things to them.'

She pushed Walter out of the room and towards the stairs. 'Come on,' she snapped.

Within five minutes, Walter was ejected on to the street, his suitcase in his hand, dizzy from the sudden whirl of events. He had no money left, barring a handful of pennies which had been in a back trouser pocket. All of his pay-off from Dr Reynard's house had been taken. Even his overcoat had gone.

Not knowing what else to do, he hurried to the Ten Bells. The pub was practically deserted. Poll, the barmaid, was washing glasses.

'Where's George?' gasped Walter.

'What?' the barmaid asked abruptly.

'I've got to find George Poskett. I need his help. I've been robbed.'

A sudden, long cackling sound erupted from somewhere to his rear. He turned to see an old, red-faced man sitting in a corner.

'You walked straight into a flatt-trap,' the old man cackled. 'That George Poskett's had you. And I bet it ain't something you'll want to go to the peelers about, neither. George Poskett's clever like that.'

'Where can I find him?' Walter persisted.

'Stow it, Bill,' Poll's warning voice came from the bar. 'You know we don't 'peach to outsiders.'

'Oh, you'll not see George Poskett again,' said the old man to Walter. 'Mark my words.'

Fifteen

B reakfast began as silently in Dr Reynard's house as dinner the night before had, and breakfast before that. The two break-fasters – Reynard and his aunt – once again faced each other across the great expanse of table.

Reynard was bloody-mindedly determined to bridge the gap.

'So tell me, Aunt,' he said, 'are my cousins in good health?'

His aunt looked steadily at him for several moments.

'Richard,' she eventually said, 'what on earth is the matter with your tie?'

'My tie?' he queried.

'Why, it is half undone, Richard.'

Irritably, he fumbled with the garment.

'You cufflink is loose, too.'

'Thank you, Aunt,' Reynard snapped. 'Now, my cousins.'

His aunt commenced a brief, almost cursory inventory of the activities of several of his less interesting relatives.

'All are well then,' he said, having listened with dogged patience. 'Good.'

'I saw Cousin Veronica last week,' said his aunt slowly. 'She said that you had entertained her to dinner.'

'Yes, that is correct,' Reynard replied. 'Shortly before Hallow-e'en, I believe.'

'Though *entertained* was not the word she used. I fear you have some distance to make up before you are once more admitted to our virtuous cousin's favour.'

'I was summoned from the house during dinner. An urgent medical matter.'

'I had to go to a great deal of effort to convince her that you were not a blaggard. I understand that, ignoring the matter of your behaviour throughout the night, the company at dinner was considerably less than desirable.'

Reynard smiled dryly. 'What is desirable, I wonder,' he said, 'to Miss Veronica Reynard? No, I agree, Aunt. My medical colleagues were characteristically high-spirited that night. You know I never give careful thought to these things. I am sorry if the company failed to please our cousin.'

'On the contrary,' said his aunt. 'It sounds as if Cousin Veronica had a most memorable evening. She spoke of scarcely anything else all through our luncheon.'

'You disapprove?'

His aunt smiled. 'Foolish child,' she chided.

Eggs were served and eaten and the plates removed. Fish came and was consumed.

'So do tell me about your work, nephew,' Reynard's aunt implored. 'What miracles have you been working in that surgery of yours?'

'Very little, Aunt,' Reynard replied. 'Most of my work is done in St Luke's parish casual ward nowadays. My private clients I see at the hospital.'

'The hospital ... yes ... Now you must remind me to make a donation. Dear Sir Godfrey is a terrible tease to me about the matter. He really is becoming quite flirtatious.'

'Sir Godfrey?'

'Saddler-Lyon. Your dean, Richard.'

Reynard's mouth dried around the nugget he was chewing. He swallowed it harshly.

'You must excuse me, Aunt,' he said. 'I have work which will not wait.'

'Then I must,' replied his aunt. 'Until the next time.'

She smiled her most charming smile and waved him away.

He never knew with Aunt Julia. It was so difficult to tell when she was merely jousting and when she was digging. Whichever it was, he had no stomach for the game today. Too much had happened; there was too much at stake.

'Oh, and Richard,' said his aunt as he opened the door to leave, 'do have a word with your valet, for heaven's sake. Tell him to pull his socks up.'

'Thank you, Aunt, I will,' said Reynard woodenly, closing the door behind him.

There was only one place Walter could go, and he dreaded going there. Shivering against the cold, he boarded an omnibus heading towards Old Street and paid nearly all of his remaining money to the conductor.

What would he say to him? Should he invent a story? Suddenly a burning desire to confess all came over him; to lay his sins before God; to embrace once more the warm body of the Church; to repent and live again his old life.

Walter had genuinely believed when he entered service that he was entering a better world and escaping the squalor and moral deprivation of his former life. He shuddered when he thought of his years at Billingsgate. There, too, he had been witness to scenes of carnality which had shocked him. Prostitutes, both male and female, were always to be seen hovering about the market's edges. Often they would simply use the towering columns of crates and baskets which stood everywhere as makeshift love-nests. More than once Walter had seen boys braced against the rickety stacks, their trousers around their ankles while some stranger took them, brutally and in haste.

Somehow one expected it there, though, where the lowest echelons of the labouring classes mingled with the legitimate traders to hawk their stolen goods and steal and sell their bodies. It was everything his father had tried, when he was alive, to shield Walter from. It had grieved his mother when he had gone to work there.

Pastor Meek had saved him from all that, and had found him a place in service with a Christian gentleman in a strict moral household. Walter, in his naiveté, had assumed that all gentle-persons behaved as Mr Lipiatt behaved. He had believed, in point of fact, that when he moved to his current position, with a household far higher up the social ladder than that of Mr Lipiatt (who was in trade), he would, if anything, find a clearer sense of moral direction. Instead, he had entered a maelstrom.

How was the world to survive? He now knew with certainty that underneath the righteous exterior of Church and State, Queen and Empire, another world existed; exotic, alluring, secret. It was a world in which good and influential men like his master seemed only too happy to entwine and couple with limbs of Satan; a world inhabited by men who had no regard for their souls. Spearman. Sabbato.

'The vilest sin of all!' Pastor Meek regarded sex with a kind of savagery. He had regularly thrashed the sin of Onanism from his pupils.

He had a solid, rough-hewn wooden box which the boys called the saddle. It sat on four squat legs, the height of a child's waist, crudely rounded and bevelled to accommodate a boy's thighs and stomach as he bent forward over it, breeches and pants around his ankles, in full view of his classmates. The boy would be made to recite the Ten Commandments as the pastor thrashed him with one of his thin, vicious canes, his face always red with exertion and fury.

Beneath their desks some of the class would masturbate as they watched the spectacle. Though invariably in tears, the boy being punished would nearly always get hard, his cock smacking roughly against the coarse wood. This drove Pastor Meek to even greater heights of wrath.

No child – not even one as reticent as Walter – escaped the saddle. He had dreaded his rare communions with its ungiving bulk. More than once he had wet himself with terror as he had waited for the switch to fall.

Now he remembered a particular occasion. One of the older boys – tall, with straight, black hair and a mocking smile – had been making uncharacteristic overtures of friendship towards him. Early one evening the boy had lured him into a storage room where, among stacked desks and writing slates, a group of about five of his fellow pupils – some his own age, two of them older – were standing in a circle around a single desk, their cocks out, masturbating. On the desk lay one of the gingerbread men old

Miss Thirlwell, one of the pastor's most dedicated parishioners, regularly baked for the boys.

'It's a game,' the boy had said to him. 'The last one to come over the gingerbread has to eat it.'

Walter had found himself backing away towards the door. The boy had gripped his arm painfully.

'You can't back out now,' he had said. 'Not now you know.'

He had savagely tugged at Walter's fly-buttons, then thrust his hand inside and pulled Walter's limp prick out, kneading it roughly.

'This had better get hard soon,' he had said, 'or it'll be the worse for you.'

Slowly, watching his classmates tugging at their cocks, he had found himself becoming erect. The boy had released him.

'Go on, then,' he had said, and watched as Walter began moving his foreskin back and forth across the bulb beneath.

Some of his classmates tugged or stroked their balls as they wanked. One had a finger stuck inside his own arse, which he pumped in and out as he stroked himself. One by one they thrust their cocks forward, pumping their seed over the desk and drenching the gingerbread figure in jissom.

Walter was neither first nor last to come. The loser was a boy called Jack, the youngest boy in the school. He had begun to cry when pushed towards the desk by the older boys.

'Eat it,' they had begun to chant. 'Eat it . . . Eat it . . .'

Still crying, his now-limp cock dribbling slightly, the boy had picked up the biscuit and bitten off the slimy head.

'Swallow it,' the boys began to chant.

Gagging, he had swallowed.

It had been too much for him. With a cry he had thrown the gingerbread man to the floor and broken from the circle, running from the room and pulling his pants up as he went. Rearranging their clothes, the other boys had run after him, bellowing abuse.

Walter had hung back. The gingerbread man lay forgotten on the floor. When the room was quiet he had picked it up and slowly eaten it, tasting for the first time the harsh tang of spunk, sweetened by the soft biscuit.

★ ★ ★

He alighted the bus and walked the few streets, past the church, to Pastor Meek's house with its adjoining schoolroom.

He knocked timidly at the front door and was ushered into the study.

Pastor Meek glowered down at him from the high seat of the pulpit-like desk.

'Walter,' he said. 'What brings you to my door in the middle of the day when you ought to be about your labours?'

'Pastor, I . . .' All the words wanted to come out in a rush. All that came was a great sob. Dropping his suitcase, he sank to his knees before the desk.

'Get up,' said the pastor. 'I will have no histrionics here. If you have something to confess, then confess it to me bravely and truthfully. God is listening.'

Walter got to his feet and, as if once more reciting the psalms before his tutor, began to tell the story of his downfall in the house of Dr Reynard. He held nothing back. He told him of the sea of temptation he had found himself in, his unnatural couplings with Philip, his master's abominations in the laboratory and of his own fatal attraction to the place.

Pastor Meek was silent for a long time.

'Lust, deceitfulness, unnatural passions,' he growled, climbing down from his seat. 'Nevertheless, it is good that you have chosen to come to me now, for your soul is surely on the brink of the abyss, boy. Wait here.'

Feeling a strange sense of relief which bordered on light-headedness, Walter waited.

In the schoolroom he could hear the familiar recitations of the class at work. He remembered the lessons well. He heard Pastor Meek's voice, then that of his assistant, Mr Scholes, ushering the children into the little yard. Break-time was early.

Then, to his horror, he heard the familiar sound of the saddle being dragged into the centre of the room. The pastor was going to . . .

Pastor Meek returned to the study. His face was already reddening.

'Sometimes I wonder whether the lengths I go to to produce educated, upright, Christian souls are worth the effort. The Lord knows, I try. Did I not stress to you until my voice was hoarse from the telling the nearness of hell? Did I not arm you with the skills to go out into the world and live a virtuous and worthwhile life? You have seen the moral deprivation, the squalor and the licence which rules in so much of our capital today. There are only two roads to choose between: the one I tried to set you on or that one. Heaven or hell. Come with me.'

Walter felt unsteady on his feet. He felt his bladder slackening, releasing its first few droplets. 'No,' he muttered.

'Do you defy me?' growled the pastor. He reached into his desk and removed one of his whiplash canes.

'No!' shouted Walter. He reached out and grabbed the pastor's hand.

'What! How dare you –'

With his other hand, Walter pushed Meek backward, hard. He stumbled and fell, dropping the cane at Walter's feet. Walter picked it up and strode across to the fallen man. He smiled a grim smile and raised the cane. The figure on the floor flinched, bringing his hands up over his face, and whimpered slightly.

For a moment Walter was sure he was going to cane Meek, just this once, in payment for those wasted canings of his childhood. Far from driving the devil out, the beatings had just made him tougher and stronger.

Instead, he dropped the cane beside the old man, stepped over his huddled form and ran out of the schoolroom and away.

In the yard, Mr Scholes was ringing the bell. Children were beginning to file inside.

Walter ran from the school with no clear idea of where he was going or what he was feeling.

Exhilaration, certainly, but a strangely bitter exhilaration. He had cut himself off from his confessor. He assumed the dry, slightly metallic taste in his mouth must be the taste of vengeance.

Vengeance is mine, saith the Lord.

No, thought Walter, it's mine.

He felt a great clarity of vision, and in that sudden clarity remembered his suitcase. It was still at the pastor's house.

He couldn't go back for it.

He looked around, trying to get his bearings. His options had run out. He walked the streets for hours, getting colder and wetter. Only one plan suggested itself to him. He must return to Dr Reynard's house, somehow get to speak to him, and make his peace. If necessary, he would throw himself on his mercy.

He approached the house from the rear, slipping through the stable gate. Jed, the stable lad, hailed him.

'Aye up, Walter. What you doing out here? I heard –'

'I must see Dr Reynard,' Walter interrupted.

'The master's out,' Jed replied. 'Hours ago. He took the carriage. I think he was operating today. You want to wait?'

'No,' said Walter bleakly. The stable lad's simple offer was absurdly welcome, but he feared discovery by one of the house servants. 'Thank you, Jed.'

Lady Horsnail's curiosity was piqued. Why would a clergyman, particularly one of this fellow's persuasion, be visiting her nephew? She knew he had little time for religion, but she also knew that, bar baiting the occasional Church of England prelate at a social gathering, he strenuously avoided engaging in any sort of debate with the Church, knowing, as she knew only too well, how fruitless an exercise it was.

She had sat him in the drawing room and ordered tea for him. He had sat bolt upright in a chair, sipping at his cup and scowling relentlessly. He had ventured no conversation and, knowing the possible pitfalls, neither had she. Eventually the silence had driven her from the room.

That had been hours ago. Peeping around a crack in the door, she found him still sitting there, upright, motionless and scowling.

The doorbell rang again, and Brakes appeared as if by magic – as the best servants always do – to answer it.

'Lord Spearman,' she heard the old butler say. 'I'm afraid the master is not at home. Were you expected?'

'No,' she heard the peer reply curtly. 'I'll wait.'

She moved to greet him, fixing a cold smile on her face.

'Lord Spearman,' she said, entering the vestibule. 'What a surprise.'

He scowled.

'Lady Horsnail,' he said with the briefest nod of the head. 'An unexpected pleasure.'

'Do come this way, Lord Spearman. My nephew is very popular this evening.'

She led him into the drawing room.

'Who the devil's that?' squawked Spearman, seeing the clergyman sitting stiff as a board in an armchair.

'Ah, Lord Spearman, may I present the Reverend – I'm sorry . . .'

'Meek, madam. And I prefer the term "pastor".'

'Pastor Meek. Of course, how silly of me. May I introduce you to Lord Montague Spearman.'

The pastor nodded curtly.

'You can entertain each other while you await my nephew's return,' she said, beaming at them and gliding from the room.

She closed the door behind her and pressed her ear against it, relishing the painful silence from within and smiling to herself with joyful malice.

For the next hour, Walter loitered close to the house, shivering while he watched the front door. It was dark when the carriage drew up and Reynard climbed out. Walter approached with trepidation. He opened his mouth to speak.

The master closed the carriage door and, sweeping past him, entered the house.

He had seen him – looked straight at him – but there had been no acknowledgement at all. No recognition.

Was it true, what some people said? That, in the eyes of the rich, servants, when not at their duties, do not exist and simply pass beneath their notice?

Reynard was greeted at the door by the butler.

'A hasty business, Brakes,' he said, 'but the operation, I am pleased to say, appears to have been successful. Have I missed dinner?'

The butler briefly informed his master of the matter of the waiting guests.

'Guests,' said Reynard loudly, wrinkling his nose. 'Who in his right mind would come visiting on a night like this?' He removed his coat and tossed it to Brakes, then rubbed vigorously at his chest and shoulders with his hands. 'It's bitter out there,' he said. 'It's going to snow.'

'The guests, sir,' the old butler said. 'Lord Spearman and a clerical gentleman of the evangelistic persuasion by the name of Meek. They are waiting in the drawing room, sir.'

Reynard laughed aloud. 'What, you shut Spearman and some shaker clergyman in a room together?'

'Not I, sir. It was Lady Horsnail.'

Reynard laughed louder still. 'My aunt!' he cried.

'Richard,' Lady Julia Horsnail replied, appearing behind him as if summoned.

'What have you been up to, Aunt Julia?'

'Just a little social experiment, nephew,' she purred. 'To pass the time.'

'Uh, they have been in there for almost an hour, sir,' the butler ventured.

'An hour? Good God, man. We'd better get in there. They might have killed one another.'

He flung the drawing-room door wide open and strode in. 'Gentlemen,' he said, 'please forgive my lateness.'

His aunt followed him, smiling.

'Spearman, old chap.' His friend was pacing up and down in front of the window, glowering at the night. Reynard crossed the room and clapped him on the shoulder. 'And you,' he said, turning to the figure sitting on the lip of an armchair as if it were a spike, 'must be Mr Meek.'

'*Pastor* Meek,' grunted the old man, scowling beneath his pantomime eyebrows.

'Really, Reynard,' Spearman cut in shrewishly, 'I never realised this room was so small. You should knock a wall down.'

'I have come to see you on a matter of the utmost urgency,' growled Meek. 'The utmost urgency.'

'And airless,' said Spearman.

Pastor Meek brought his fist down hard on the arm of the chair. 'The Lord's work is never done, they say, sir,' he said in his low rumble. 'Consequently, I am an extremely busy man. Notwithstanding this fact, I have crossed London on this most inclement of nights to say what I have to say to you, and for the last hour have had to listen to this insufferable buffoon's imbecile prattle and, frankly, highly distasteful comments.' He rose like a thunder-storm from his chair. 'I have come here to talk to you about hell, sir!' he roared.

'Oh, well you should have said so,' snapped Spearman. 'We could have got this over with an hour ago. If it's hell you wanted to talk about, I'm your man, not Dr Reynard. He's a living saint.'

Meek ignored him. 'Today I received a visit from one of my flock,' he said. 'A young man who, until recently, has been employed as your valet.'

'Really, the impertinence –'

Reynard waved Spearman urgently to silence.

'Go on,' he said in a measured voice.

'Send your friends away,' growled Meek.

'I'm not going anywhere,' announced Spearman.

'Very well, he can stay,' said Meek. 'I know of his part in this ... business.' He cast a glance at Lady Horsnail. 'But you must send the woman away.'

She smiled haughtily.

'Leave us, please, Aunt Julia,' said Reynard.

Her face clouded. She looked defiantly into his eyes for a moment then, breaking from their gaze, left the room.

Reynard listened to her departing footfalls.

'Now,' he said in a low voice, 'you may continue.' He cast his gaze back to the door. 'Only quietly, please.'

'As I said,' Meek began, 'I received a visit today from Walter Starling. He told me that he had been in your service and that he had recently been dismissed. And he told me what he saw and did while under your roof.'

'And what was that?' asked Spearman, as if humouring a small child.

'Devilish vices! Infernal machines for the raping of God's holy temple. Unnatural couplings among your servants. Blackmail –'

'Words,' cut in Spearman. 'Hysterical rantings. The boy was obviously mad, or nursing a grudge against Reynard here for his dismissal. Simply made the whole thing up. Presumably to precipitate precisely this sort of ghastly social embarrassment.'

'He told me the precise manner of his dismissal,' said Meek ominously. 'He told me of you, Lord Spearman, procurer of boys, leading them off into the night like some ghoul to torture them on your infernal apparatus. He told me of you, too, Dr Reynard, a snivelling hypocrite hiding his vile lusts behind a lot of half-baked philosophical pseudo-science. Who makes the notes when it's *your* turn to be sodomised, Doctor?'

Even Spearman was shocked into silence.

'He told me more,' Meek rumbled on. 'He told me . . .'

The litany passed over Reynard's head, unheeded. The great infusion of energy he always felt after a major surgical feat had transformed itself into something quite different in the face of this holy tirade. He felt distant, elevated, as if he was watching this scene from far away. It had all the unreality of a stage play to him. He felt more a part of the audience than the cast.

'I must say, you have a remarkable memory for salacious detail, Pastor,' Spearman said when the preacher at last paused for breath. 'I suppose you know where all the dirty bits are in the Bible.'

'Think of your immortal souls!' The man was beginning to rant. 'Repent, while there is still time! If not for yourselves, then for the boy. Think of young Walter. Think what your excesses have brought him to. What I witnessed today was terrible to behold! The boy's mental balance has become disturbed by what he has seen and done in this house. He is lost and friendless on those cold streets. Do you know how many poor, honest folk I have seen ruined by the whims of so-called gentlefolk? I gave that boy the prospect of a decent life. I gave him a chance! You dashed it from his hands.'

Spearman lit a cigarette.

'All right, old man,' he said. 'Here's what we'll do. You will scuttle off back to your little church and get on with scaring the wits out of simpletons each Sunday and taking their money off them, and we will pretend we never met you. And if you breathe one word of this . . . fairy story . . . to anyone whomsoever, I have a lawyer called Montefiore – a lapsed Catholic, like myself –

who will derive great pleasure from taking your church apart brick by brick. Do I make myself perfectly clear?'

'I have said my piece,' growled Meek. 'I do not intend to drag the good name of my church through the sewer in pursuit of your unworthy souls.'

'No, indeed,' said Spearman. 'After all, people might ask where your former pupil acquired his taste for sitting on candles.'

'Please!' cried Reynard.

Reynard's head was suddenly throbbing. He always felt energised, on top of the world, after a successful piece of surgery. Now he had slipped from his Olympian peak. The stage was spinning. Scenery was crashing.

'Please, both of you, leave! I am very fatigued and, I fear, unwell. I must bid you both goodnight.'

'I am going,' said Pastor Meek. 'I shall not return to this hellish house.'

There was a soft knock at the door and Brakes entered carrying a large silver tray of assorted cuts of meat. 'I took the liberty of having a cold collation prepared for you and your guests, sir,' he said.

Walter stood shivering, gazing into the window. Dr Reynard was in the drawing room. Walter tried to make out who he was with. To his dismay he saw that it was Lord Spearman. He would have to wait, and hope that His Lordship would soon take his leave.

There was someone else in the room, marching towards the door. It looked like –

Walter froze, his heart shrivelling. His last hope was gone. He could never go to his master now.

The street door opened and Pastor Meek emerged, wrapping his great black coat around him.

He descended the steps to the street. Walter shrank back into the shadows as he strode past him, staring ahead in fury.

Snow was beginning to fall in flat flakes. The first of the year. They settled on the pastor's shock of thick, stiff, grey hair.

Walter waited for his footsteps to vanish, then slunk away from the house. He had no home and no money; he was cold and he was starving. He crossed the road and turned the corner, then crossed another road, and turned once more. He had no idea where he was going.

He was outside a hotel. The Cavendish, he thought, though the snow was now falling too thickly to make out the sign, half a street's length away. Beyond the railings, below the level of the street, was the long, narrow yard (if so you could call it) of the hotel kitchens. They still had a few lights on.

At least down there he would be sheltered from the snow.

The gate in the railings was locked. Wearily Walter climbed over it and descended the steep steps to the cellar level. He rested his hand on the wall. This was better than he had anticipated – the wall was warm. There must be a furnace on the other side, which might even remain burning all night.

He lay down on the hard flagstone floor and pressed himself against the wall, waiting for sleep to come.

Reynard couldn't sleep. Exhausted though he was, the evening encounter would not relax its grip on his mind.

Spearman had taken an age to leave. 'Well, well, well,' he had mused, watching the pastor depart, 'so that's what the voice of God sounds like. You know, I had quite forgotten. Do you suppose the word of the Almighty is supposed to get louder and more frightening as we grow old? As we draw nearer to the divine presence?'

'Spearman, please –'

'These things matter to me, dear chap.' Spearman was not to be interrupted in mid-flow. 'Good Catholic boy that I am. Now, the thundercloud has departed. We can relax and the evening can unfold in front of us.'

'What are you talking about?' Reynard had snapped.

'I have prepared a surprise for you,' Spearman had said, smiling.

'No. Not tonight. I'm sorry.' Reynard was brusque.

'But I have gone to a great deal of trouble to prepare an entertainment,' Spearman had complained. 'It has cost me a not inconsiderable –'

'Spearman, damn it, man! Get out!' Reynard had finally bellowed.

'That old fool put the wind up you, didn't he?' Spearman had said, donning his hat and cloak and sweeping out of the door.

He was right, of course. Reynard had always been wary of the words of priests. Scared, even. His father – a more militant atheist than Reynard himself – had always considered priests to be malign and powerful men, dangerous liars and fanatics. The enemies of science, of rational thought, and ultimately of human freedom. When he was a child Hugo Reynard had sat at his bedside and told him the story of Galileo Galilei, the genius who had set man firmly in his proper place in the cosmos. He had lullabied the young Richard to sleep with tales of Galileo's treatment at the hands of the Holy Inquisition. The story had both inspired and terrified the young boy. It was one of Reynard's few memories of being with his father.

How would Hugo Reynard have dealt with Pastor Meek? The pastor would never have been allowed over the threshold.

And yet, it seemed, when his father had wanted to express the inexpressible and delve into that most profound of scientific phenomena, the human condition of love, he had turned to Greek myth, magic and superstition for the necessary tools.

For true Thomas, my Ganymede . . .

Walter. Pastor Meek's words haunted him. A fanatic and a bigot, of course, but was not what the old man had said quite true? Walter had been an innocent. A ingenue, sucked inexorably into the whirlpool of his and Spearman's excesses. Not meaning to, he had allowed the boy a glimpse into their forbidden world, and the sight had damned him. Worse, he had cast the poor, damned creature out into the night.

Wasn't that exactly what the God of the Israelites had done to Lucifer? Tempted the angel with his divine majesty, tempted him to fall, and when he had fallen, cast him out of the kingdom of heaven.

He wondered where Walter was now. He hoped that the boy was somewhere warm and dry. He plumped his pillow and tried once more to sleep.

Sixteen

Walter was woken early by a foot roughly prodding him in the back. A man in a long, dirty white apron was standing over him.

'Geddup, you!' the man barked. 'What the hell do you think this is? A bleeding hotel?' He guffawed loudly to himself, then prodded Walter again. 'I'll be back in a minute,' he said, 'and you better be gone.'

The man ascended the steep stone steps to street level, clanging the gate behind him. Walter watched him go, then painfully scrambled to his feet. There was something covering Walter. An old, stained oilskin.

A maid was watching him from inside the hotel kitchen. She smiled nervously, then opened the door. Warmth within beckoned.

'Here,' she said, thrusting a loaf of bread into his hands. 'Now you better hop it. If he catches you here . . .'

She closed the door on him.

Walter ate ravenously, then climbed into the loose brown oilskin and ascended the steps to street level.

Little snow had fallen in the narrow gully between the hotel kitchen and the street, but up here the ground was thick with it. Walter was numb, both from cold and hunger, and still terribly tired.

He felt a great momentum at his back: the momentum of yesterday, from which none of us can escape. It was driving him back into the past, back to the days of his desperate early youth, to the city slums where he had been born. Back to Billingsgate.

It had all the force of logic behind it. Pastor Meek had been right. He had forsaken the road to heaven. He could find work again as a fish-porter. Billingsgate Market. Life had been tolerable there; at least he hadn't starved.

He caught his reflection in a shop window. He looked quite dreadful; dirty and dishevelled, little better than a vagabond. He had been out of Dr Reynard's employment merely a matter of days, and already he was on the brink of ruin.

Wrapping the oilskin tight around him, he trudged through the dirty snow.

Snow made the journey arduous but Walter didn't mind the long trek – he had walked almost this far every day of his school life, often in weather worse than this. In those days he would sing hymns in his head to pass the hours, his feet keeping time on the dusty roads. Now all that came into his head was the bawdy song that the crowd at the Ten Bells had sung, over and over again.

The streets changed as he passed east along Oxford Street and High Holborn, past the Inns of Court, and entered the City up Holborn Hill. Opulent decadence had given way to sober justice and sly enterprise; then began the rapid slide into depravity and neglect. Streets of busy (if decidedly lower-middle class) shops quickly gave way to streets of abandoned shops, the gutters lined with the barrows of costermongers. And even the costermongers took on an air of greater desperation as he travelled east: their wares became fewer and shabbier and their attempts to attract the attention of the passer-by ever more aggressive.

He remembered setting out along these dingy streets day after day before it was light to walk the mile or more to Pastor Meek's school, often pelted with stones by the other, dirty and uneducated, children.

The streets narrowed. Gangs of ragged children began to appear, swarming after anyone who looked remotely prosperous, their hands dipping and fishing in unaware pockets. They ignored Walter.

He paused as he passed the narrow, lightless gash that was Beavan's Court: the street where he and his parents had lived. The tumbling tenement which had been their home was gone. Demolished. Walter felt no regret – there would have been no-one there who knew him, anyway, so rapidly did the dwellers of these slums come and go.

He pressed on towards Billingsgate. He had had a friend there, Peter, about the same age and a porter like himself. Peter Hoplight. The name had delighted Walter. A hoplight was a Greek foot soldier, one of Alexander's army of conquerors, proud and handsome and loyal to their comrades, even unto death.

The market would be shut by the time he got there, but the Mariners would be open, and that was where his last remaining hopes were vested.

Even in the gathering darkness he knew when he was drawing near; even after the market had closed the smell of raw fish was almost overpowering. The dark bulk of the Custom House loomed ahead of him, and beyond it the market. He scanned the street for the familiar lights of the Mariners public house. This was where the porters and costers went after work; much against his will Walter had been taken in there a few times himself.

But there were no lights. Save for one distant, spluttering street lamp, the terrace lay in darkness. Drawing closer he could see that the glass was gone from the windows and the woodwork burned and brittle. Even the stone walls were charred and stained. Walter stared, dismayed, into the burned-out shell.

So much had changed in this turbulent, shiftless part of London. He wandered across to the dead market, passing the empty arches and the high stacks of crates and panniers.

He heard muffled voices and ragged, rhythmic drawings of breath. Passing behind one of the stacks he saw first the broad back of a large man, perhaps in his forties, his trousers loose about his thighs and his bare buttocks exposed.

A younger man – a wild, freckled face, his hair an untidy, carrot-headed crop – stood beyond him, facing Walter, eyes closed, legs wide apart, leaning back against a lamp-post. Gaslight pooled around them. Crates stacked high on either side corralled them. The youth clung precariously to the lamp-post above his head. The man was driving upward into him with short, hard thrusts of his buttocks.

Walter's mind flew back to the laboratory. Even now the memory of his secret night-time observations, so recently the source of his undoing, filled him with a furtive warmth. He found his cock growing hard beneath his clothes. Was there to be no release from the spectre of his lustful thoughts?

Still inside his carrot-headed partner, the man stepped backward, drawing him away from the lamp-post. The youth wrapped his legs around the man's hips and clung tight with hands and feet as, suspended between the iron post and the man's equally hard pole, he allowed himself to be tossed by the jerky motions of his lover's hips.

His grip on the lamp-post slipped and, still clinging to the man with his legs, he slid hard to the ground and lay between the metal pole and the rickety wall of fish-smelling crates. The man leaned forward and continued to fuck the lad hard, holding him by the hips and driving his shoulders into the wet ground and sharp boxes. Walter could see the lad's cock now, untidily adorned with a dense ginger bush but long and hard against his belly.

The man's thrusts were becoming fast and erratic. He released his grip on the young man's buttocks and his cock slipped from inside him. The lad fell fully to the ground. The man flowed over him, seeking the lad's mouth with his cock.

It was too late. His prick spasmed, drenching the boy's face in quick, heavy jets of jissom.

The man's passion subsided. The boy smiled and licked his sticky lips.

'You looking for something, mister?' a voice said softly in the darkness behind Walter.

He turned. He could see nothing.

'I . . . I was looking for a friend,' he said.

'We're all looking for a friend,' said the voice. A figure sidled close to him, touching his arm. 'You got somewhere we can go?'

'No . . . I've nowhere to go.'

'It's all right. I know somewhere. You got money?' The figure was stroking him now.

'No . . . I lost my money.'

The stroking stopped. 'You got no money? What you fucking wasting my time for, then? Fuck off out of here! Go on!'

Walter didn't move.

'Oh, I get it,' the voice said. 'I get what you're about. Well, let me tell you, Maleaver runs this patch and no-one cuts in on him if they knows what's good for 'em.'

There were footsteps approaching. Another voice. 'Everything all right, Jerry?'

'Nothing I can't sort out myself,' Walter's shadowy accuser replied. 'You better get back to your patch.'

'Quiet tonight,' said the new voice. Walter was sure he recognised it.

'Peter,' drawled the other. 'You know what the old man'll do if he catches us together. Now hook it.'

'Peter?' Walter suddenly said. 'Peter Hoplight?'

'Yeah . . .' said the new voice suspiciously.

'It's me – Walter. Walter Starling!'

The new figure drew close and struck a match. It was undoubtedly him – the same mop of curly brown hair, the same impish face, lightly scattered with freckles. It was the most welcome face Walter had ever seen. Awkwardly, he reached forward, placing his hands uncertainly on Peter's shoulders. He tried to speak, but all that came out was a sob.

'All right, mate,' said Peter, just as awkwardly. 'Don't take on so. Here . . .'

He pulled Walter forward in a clumsy embrace. The match went out.

They were standing under the street lamp, gazing at each other, not really knowing what to say. It wasn't as if they had been close friends: Walter had none of those.

'So . . . uh . . . how are you?' Walter asked.

'Fine,' said Peter, a quizzical grin on his face.

'And . . . uh . . . what happened to the Mariners?'

'Burnt out,' his friend replied.

'Shame,' said Walter. 'Shame.'

'You hardly ever set foot in there,' said Peter. 'Why did you

come back here, Walter? I thought you'd got out, and good luck
to you. What's happened?'

'I was hoping I would find you,' said Walter. 'I need to find
work. I was wondering whether you couldn't have a word with
old Mr Noblet. Ask him to take me on again.'

Peter was shaking his head slowly. 'There's no work at the
market any more,' he said. 'Times is bad. Loads laid off. I haven't
worked there getting on for a year now.'

He shuffled slightly, looking down at his feet.

'I'm one of Maleaver's boys now.'

Maleaver. Known as The Fleshman, Walter remembered.
Procurer of boys and young men.

'Oh,' said Walter blandly.

An awkward silence followed.

'So . . . what about you?' Peter asked. 'I heard you'd gone into
service with some gent up Cheapside.'

'Mr Lipiatt, yes. I've . . . moved on since then.'

It must have been something in his voice. Peter once more
placed a firm, gentle hand on each of Walter's shoulders – with
more confidence, this time – and, with a kind expression on his
face, looked him hard in the eye and said, 'Tell me what's
happened, Walter.'

Walter told him of his dismissal (though without mentioning its
actual cause) and of his three subsequent nights.

Peter was quiet and thoughtful.

'So the long and the short of it is you got no gaff and you got
no tin,' he eventually said.

Walter nodded dumbly. Somewhere a church clock boomed
eleven.

'All right,' said Peter, 'you remember Watson's, the old chandlers up by the Basin? Meet me there in an hour. Meantime, I'd
keep out of sight round these streets. They've gone worse this last
year, believe me. Now I got to go and try and earn my blunt for
the night.'

He moved off along the street, watched by Walter. Presently
he stopped to talk to someone, too far away for Walter to make
out their conversation.

Walter himself moved off, wondering how best to occupy

himself for the next hour; how to keep his mind off the cold, the fatigue, the hunger. He wandered up to green Trinity Square, in the moon-shadow of the mighty tower, symbol of the city, prison and palace, huge and hard and cruel. He skirted the edge of its great fortifications. He could see every so often the indistinct irruptions of Maleaver's boys, dotted about the grassy banks, leaning against the mighty walls.

He left the lee of the tower and stood before St Catherine's Dock. He turned and strolled along the deserted jetties, past the cruel cage where hungry men waited every morning in the hope of being taken on for the day by the foreman. Most returned home hungry. Hunger was a way of life in these parts. He wandered past the benighted, creaking skeletons of great ships. The wealth of the Empire flowed through these docks, offloaded by starving men.

He remembered Dr Reynard's unwanted dinner guest, Mr Puddephatt. Perhaps he was right. It all seemed like another world, here where the land and water met, beneath tall, lonely masts and, far above him, the wind-sounded voice of folded, scoffing sails.

In the distance he watched an old woman – a drab – accosting a pedestrian.

'Fancy going somewheres with me, lover?' she wheezed. 'Only cost you thruppence . . .'

The man pushed past her.

'Only thruppence,' she called after him. 'I needs it for my gaff money . . .'

A sudden strong wind caught Walter, causing his oilskin to flap around him like some demented bird. He struggled to bring the shabby garment under control.

Walter made his way to outside the chandlers at the appointed time. Peter arrived some ten minutes later, approaching Walter from behind and startling him. Smiling, he caught Walter's hands as he spun around.

'Come on,' he said, drawing Walter forward.

He led him into a warren of narrow streets north-east of the tower. After several twists and turns, Walter was lost.

'We got to be quiet here,' Peter whispered. He led Walter across a road to where a boy was standing in a doorway. 'The old man about?' he asked in a low voice.

'Nah,' the boy replied. 'He ain't been around for hours.'

'You'll tip me the wink?' Peter said.

'Yeah, course,' the boy replied.

Peter led Walter along a poorly lit hallway with several sharp twists and innumerable doorways.

Peter stopped and opened what Walter assumed to be a cupboard set into the wall, its door barely three feet high. He opened it and crawled inside. Walter waited for him to re-emerge.

'Come on!' Peter's voice was muffled, floating out of the black hole. 'And mind your head.'

Puzzled, Walter crawled after Peter. He found himself crouched under a low ceiling at the top of a short stone staircase. Peter lit a candle and Walter saw in front of him a wide, low, stone room with an earth floor. Eight or ten straw palliasses lay untidily about the floor. A brazier – unlit – stood against the far wall. In spite of its unprepossessing appearance (Walter was certain it was constructed to serve as a coal cellar) the room appeared clean.

He descended the steps. 'Take a pew,' said Peter, indicating one of the makeshift mattresses. 'Christ, have a kip, Walter. You look about done in.'

Walter could only nod. It was true; he was exhausted. He had been walking most of the day and had eaten nothing since his hasty breakfast outside the hotel kitchens.

'Whose bed am I –' Walter began awkwardly.

'Mine, of course.' Peter smiled. 'We normally double up, anyway, being as how it's turned so cold and how we ain't actually got enough beds to go round.'

Walter lay down fully clothed and pulled the thin blanket over him. He watched Peter, standing over him. He seemed restless; nervous.

Walter wondered whether he would climb in next to him. At least they would be warm then.

'Could we light the fire?' he asked suddenly.

Peter shook his head. 'We're not supposed to be here,' he said. 'I ain't supposed to be back for another hour, at least, and you ain't supposed to be here at all.'

'What will happen if we're caught?' Walter asked uneasily.

Peter shook his head briskly. 'Don't you worry about that,' he said. 'Go to sleep.'

Whether he slept or not, Walter was unsure. He was aware of a figure standing over him, but not always sure that it was Peter. Once he sensed the figure reaching down, its hand covering his face.

Peter was shaking him and at the same time trying to drag him to his feet.

'Get up,' he whispered urgently. 'Maleaver's coming.'

Walter struggled to orientate himself. Peter was dragging him into a shallow, narrow alcove at the far end of the room.

'We're dead if he catches us here,' he whispered to Walter, and extinguished the candle.

The tiny door at the top of the steps opened and a hand-lamp appeared through it, followed by a head, followed by an enormous body. The huge, folded figure seemed to uncurl itself as it descended the steps. It stood at their feet, head still bent forward to avoid the ceiling.

Maleaver was without doubt the strangest-looking individual Walter had ever seen. He had thought so when he first clapped eyes on him, and he still thought so now. Well over six feet tall and entirely bald, with a nose like a great hooked beak and a body the shape of a pear, he reminded Walter instantly of some great bird – one of the penguins of distant Antarctica. The shortness of his legs and arms did nothing to dispel the impression. Only his mouth – a gaping great gash – was not that of a bird. It was the mouth of a reptile.

Maleaver looked around, letting his eyes rest on the different palliasses, smacking his smiling lips. A sudden panic hit Walter. The man was drawing near.

A dull sound from the cellar doorway made Maleaver look up. A young head and shoulders appeared through it, saw Maleaver and froze.

'Stebbins, you little ingrate bastard!' Maleaver yelled. 'What are you going back here?'

'T-there's nobody out there, sir,' the boy stammered. 'The snow . . .'

'Damn your eyes, boy,' Maleaver ranted. 'Are you trying to

cheat me? Do you know how much it costs to provide a home for you wretches? To put food in your bellies and clothes on your backs? All I ask in return is a little honest labour.'

'But it's freezing out there . . .'

Maleaver scanned the floor. He spotted a half-brick lying against the wall, picked it up and, with surprising speed and frightening force and accuracy, hurled it at the boy's head. The boy withdrew with a whimper, the brick missing him by an inch.

Maleaver sighed to himself. 'Boys, boys, boys,' he said lightly, '. . . whatever shall I do with you?' And, almost daintily, he picked his way to the entrance and out of the room.

Peter remained silent and motionless for several minutes. At last he let out a long breath. 'We can relax now,' he said. 'He won't be back tonight. We can light the fire now, too,' he added, starting to poke around in the dead brazier.

'What was he doing?' Walter asked. 'Maleaver.'

'Making sure we're all out earning our blunt,' said Peter.

'He sounds awful,' said Walter. 'Why do you stay?'

'Well, it's not heaven,' said Peter. 'But he don't feed us too bad. And he gives us a new set of togs every once in a while, so's we looks all right for the punters.'

A tiny red glow was appearing in the basin of the brazier.

'Might as well get some kip,' said Peter, kicking off his shoes. Quickly he removed his jacket and shirt, trousers, pants, socks, and stood, naked, in front of Walter before diving on to his palliasse and crawling under the blanket.

'Christ, it's cold,' he said. 'It'll be ages before the fire starts warming the room. Hurry up, get in.'

Walter stripped and climbed in alongside him. Their bodies brushed lightly together, eliciting embarrassed giggles from both. Peter placed a hand on Walter's shoulder.

'Come here,' he said. 'Let's get warm.'

Walter shuffled closer and they hugged each other. Peter was thinner than Walter remembered. Although only Walter's age, he looked older now. He was pale and quite hairless save for the neat, dark fuzz on his belly.

Peter kissed Walter lightly on the lips, then more boldly, running his tongue along the edge of Walter's teeth.

Walter could feel Peter's cock swelling, bobbing against his leg. His own prick was growing large beneath the thin coverlet, brushing against Peter's. Peter cupped Walter's balls with one hand, squeezing them lightly, then ran his fingers through Walter's dark-blond bush and his fingernails up the underside of his hard tool, teasing and pulling on his foreskin. He placed his hard prick against Walter's, taking both in one fist, moving his hand slowly up and down the twin shafts, drawing both foreskins back, then pulling them forward again.

Slowly Peter slid down the thin mattress, kissing and nipping at Walter's neck, shoulders, chest. When he reached his nipples he pulled each of them hard with his teeth, then gently lapped around each with his tongue. He ran his tongue down Walter's smooth belly, lingering in his navel, then, disappearing beneath the blanket, plunged it through Walter's pubic forest, round the side of his hard prick and under his balls. He nudged his head between Walter's thighs and nibbled his way back along his perineum to his arse, coating his crack with saliva and nesting his tongue in Walter's tight hole.

There was a sound of low voices and footsteps entering the room. By the dim glow of the fire, Walter could just about make out a group of boys. They separated, each going to a different mattress. One of them – a black boy – stood close to Walter's head and began removing his clothes, still chattering to his mates. He dropped to his haunches and slid under the blanket. Only then did Walter realise what was happening.

'Wotcha,' he said, smiling slightly. 'That Peter under there?'

Walter nodded. The boy was perhaps a little younger than him, his hair a mat of tight black curls, his eyes gentle, his lips full and dark, his skin like ebony.

'I'm Tim'fy,' said the boy.

Walter shivered with pleasure as Peter continued to tongue his arse.

Timothy smiled more broadly. 'Don't mind me,' he said.

He raised the blanket and stared openly down at Walter's hard prick and Peter's head bobbing between his legs. Walter could see that Timothy, too, was growing hard, his long, thick, purple-headed shaft lifting itself from the mattress. Timothy took hold of

185

it and wanked it as he watched. He had no foreskin – Walter had heard of that – and rubbed directly on the exposed, swollen globe.

Peter raised himself on all fours and took Walter's shaft in his warm, wet mouth. His pale, pert, hairless arse stood in the air. Timothy moved behind him and mounted him in the manner in which a dog mounts a bitch. Peter's face creased slightly as the black boy forced his cock into his arse and began a series of short, gentle thrusts. Peter continued to run his head up and down Walter's pole as Timothy's strokes became longer and harder and gathered speed. Walter watched the black boy's eyes narrow and his mouth purse as his arousal increased. He felt himself close to orgasm, and sensed Timothy wasn't far behind him. He clamped his hands around Timothy's head. He felt one of Timothy's own hands cupping his buttocks, then two fingers, then three, snaking their way into his spit-wet arsehole, fucking him rapidly.

He and Timothy seemed to come at almost the same time, filling Peter from both ends at once.

All three lay, contented for a while. Peter kissed Walter deeply, seeding his mouth with his own tangy jissom. Gradually, huddled together on the mattress, sandwiched between Peter and Timothy's warm, breathing bodies, Walter fell asleep.

Richard Reynard was having another bad night. What snatches of sleep he managed to glean were laden with the same dream. It wasn't so much a dream as an obsession; an absolute conviction that came upon him while he slept and propelled him like an alarm back to wakefulness.

The laboratory door was open. He was about to be discovered.

Twice last night the conviction had driven him from his bed, groping his way through the dark house and unlocking the outer door into his consulting wing. Twice, upon examination, he had found the laboratory door securely shut and bolted. And yet, again tonight, he climbed from his bed and padded down the dark stairs in his nightshirt.

The door, when he reached it, was secure.

He rested his hands against its cool surface. It seemed to vibrate with some kind of life. If he listened he could hear the machines chattering like giant insects to one another in the darkness.

The outer door to the wing had been open.

'Unable to sleep, nephew?'

Reynard's heart jumped into his throat.

'I, for one, have never found a sleeping draught which worked,' his aunt finished.

'Aunt Julia!' Reynard gasped. 'Are you trying to kill me? What the deuce are you doing here?'

'I found an old key in a suitcase recently. I reasoned it came from this house, as everything else in the case did, so I set about trying to discover to which door it belonged. It turns out to have been the key to this wing.'

'But it's the middle of the −'

'I was suddenly seized by the most delightful, childish notion. I thought I should love to explore your laboratory by moonlight. Sadly the door was locked, and for that door I have no key.'

'You are to keep away from this wing of the house!' Reynard snapped. He attempted to master himself. 'A laboratory is a dangerous environment, Aunt,' he said. 'Particularly at night.'

'Oh, I can't see the harm, Richard,' his aunt replied. 'At least not now that you are with me. And you did say you had moved most of your equipment to the workhouse, didn't you?'

'I said I had moved most of my surgical equipment to the casual ward, yes. However, I have other equipment in there. I have been conducting a delicate and dangerous experiment in there.' His lips were dry. He tried to wet them. 'The experiment is over now, but the equipment remains, and until it is off these premises I must insist that you obey my injunction. Now goodnight, Aunt.'

He ushered her out into the main body of the house and closed and locked the heavy connecting door.

'Are you going to watch me all the way to my room, Richard?' his aunt teased. 'Oh, very well . . .'

He returned to bed less able to sleep than ever. He wrote a note to Lord Spearman, a terse instruction to have the devices removed from the laboratory.

He knew his aunt only too well. In many ways he was like her. Her behaviour was significant. Both what she had done and what she had not done bothered Reynard. She had made no mention at all of Pastor Meek's visit. She was definitely digging.

187

Seventeen

'All right, my fine beauties, come and get it.'
Walter was woken by a loud, dull, regular clanging and the sound of Maleaver's voice grating around the concrete walls. Someone lit a candle.

Maleaver and another man, just as tall but terribly thin with a long, pale, sunken face, were dragging a huge metal drum down the stone steps. Porridge slopped and spilled over the edges.

More candles were lit. Slurred, sleepy half-conversations began. The room had filled up since last night. All around Walter, figures, often in twos, were peeling away from their beds, yawning, stretching and uncurling; naked, wriggling into clothes, fishing among their few possessions for a bowl or tin cup, crowding about the steaming cauldron.

Maleaver's little eyes danced epicurially among the dressing boys. 'Got to keep you well fed and rosy cheeked,' he cackled. 'Keep my merchandise in good nick.'

'Keep still,' Peter whispered to Walter. 'Keep your face covered. Timothy, keep over him. I'll get you something to eat.'

Without opening his eyes, Timothy rolled over on to his side and slumped against Walter, chest to chest, and appeared to sleep on. Peter sprang to his feet and disappeared into the melee, returning a few moments later with a full bowl, which he slid to Walter, using his own body to screen his friend from Maleaver's gaze. Walter smiled gratefully, raised the bowl to his lips and started to drink. He drained it quickly, then looked at Peter, feeling suddenly ashamed. He had left his friend nothing.

Peter smiled. 'It's all right,' he said. 'There'll be something left in the pot at the end.'

There was no sense of time in the cellar: only darkness and candlelight. It was past midday when Walter emerged, dazzled, into the cold, bright day. The last of yesterday's snow lay on the rooftops, but none was falling now, and all but the gutters were clear of slush.

Walter followed Peter up through the City and into a pub.

'Wait here,' said Peter. 'There's something I got to do.'

With a wink and a smile he left. Walter sat himself in a corner and tried not to be noticed.

After about an hour, Peter reappeared, rushing through the door, breathless. He squeezed himself between Walter and the wall and sat down. There seemed to be some commotion outside.

When it had died down, he spoke. 'Had to earn my tin for Maleaver. I didn't get no trade last night. Nor did loads of the others. On account of the snow. That being the case, Maleaver expects us to go out and rent in the afternoons, but there ain't much trade to be had then.'

'So what did you do?' asked Walter.

'Maleaver collects late afternoon, so we got till then to nick the blunt. There's plenty of rich pockets round these streets. I got this right outside the Bank of England.'

Peter plucked something from his pocket. It was a flat, square, silver box.

'A cigarette case,' said Walter.

'Yeah,' replied Peter, turning the case in his hand. 'Very nice morning's work, that.'

'It looks valuable,' said Walter. 'Perhaps you could sell it. With a little money you might leave –'

'Yeah, and go where?' snorted Peter. 'Come on. Maleaver'll be collecting his dues soon.'

The house appeared empty when they returned to it.

'With all these rooms, why does he make you all sleep in the cellar?' asked Walter.

'The rooms is for the punters. Anyway, he treats us right,' said Peter, somewhat defensively. 'He always says a renter should look his best, cos no-one wants to bed no tramp or sick boy.'

Walter suddenly thought of Lord Spearman in the casual ward, and shuddered slightly.

'So we gets fed, and we gets a roof over our heads. And there's a lot round these parts couldn't say that.'

That was quite true, Walter knew. He only had to look at his own situation.

'What about you, Walter?' said Peter, as if reading his thoughts. 'What are you gonna do?'

'I don't know,' said Walter. 'I had thought to get work at the market again . . . I suppose I could try the docks.'

'Don't be a cod,' scoffed Peter. 'They're laying men off there too. And anyway, what dock foreman would pull you out of the cage over some strong, hard, experienced bloke? No offence, Walter, but you ain't exactly no Hercules.'

Walter smiled grimly. Peter was quite right.

'What about working here with me?' said Peter tentatively. 'As one of Maleaver's boys. It ain't so bad.'

'Would he –'

'Oh, he'd take you on in a minute,' said Peter. 'Pretty, polite, well-mannered boy like you.'

'I'm not sure.'

There were voices outside the cellar door. Boys started to trickle into the cellar through the tiny door. Within moments there were twenty or thirty of them in the room – more than the previous night. Some eyed Walter with curiosity; others with a certain hostility. Walter recognised the boy who had first propositioned him beside the market. The boy scowled at Walter.

'Well, my flowers o' the tower,' Maleaver's voice suddenly called from the entrance, 'it's accounting time once again. And what good fortune have you to share with me today?'

He squeezed himself into the room and descended the steps. Just behind him, as in the morning, was the same tall, pale, thin man.

In response to some unspoken command, the boys formed

themselves into a disorderly line in front of their benefactor. Peter joined the line, pulling Walter alongside him.

As Walter watched, each boy in turn placed a sum of money in Maleaver's open hand, and then pulled the linings of his trouser pockets and, if he was wearing one, those of his jacket too, so that they poked into the air. Each time, Maleaver counted the money in his hand and then passed it to his tall companion.

When Peter's turn came he placed the cigarette case in Maleaver's hand.

Maleaver examined it closely. 'Plate,' he spat. 'You was done, boy. Now, what else?'

'It was a bad night, boss,' Peter replied. 'The snow kept everybody away.'

'David here managed fifteen shillings,' said Maleaver, his voice soft and coaxing. 'Even little James managed ten bob.'

'I . . . Something came up, boss. A golden opportunity, I reckon.' He pulled Walter forward. 'I met an old mate of mine. He's after a job.'

'A job, eh?' said Maleaver, looking Walter up and down. He grabbed his hair and pulled his head back. 'Open your mouth, boy,' he said.

Walter did as he was bid. The room watched in silence.

'Good teeth,' mused Maleaver. He released Walter's hair and gripped his upper arms, his chest muscles and his shoulders. 'Not all that strong, but seems fit enough,' he said. He brought a hand suddenly and roughly down between Walter's legs, squeezing his cock and balls quite hard. Walter let out a gasp.

'Mmm,' said Maleaver. 'He'll do. Turn out your pockets, boy.'

Before Walter had a chance to move, Maleaver was pulling out the pocket linings on his trousers. They were empty.

'Good,' said Maleaver, doing the same to his jacket pockets. 'You don't need nothing of your own no more,' he said, his lips smacking together. 'I'm looking after you now. Which is your kit?'

'I have no kit, sir,' said Walter.

'Mmm,' said Maleaver. 'Well-spoke young cove, ain't you? That'll be worth a bob or two.'

'I told you,' cut in Peter.

A look from Maleaver silenced him. 'Speak when you're spoke to, boy,' he said, in his too-patient tone. 'No kit, eh?' he mused.

'Only that old oilskin, sir, and that's not really mine.'

He pointed to his garment.

'Petherick,' said Maleaver. The tall, thin, pale man stepped forward and picked up the oilskin, and made a rapid survey of its pockets.

'Nothing,' he said.

'Right,' said Maleaver. 'Here's the rules. You're out every night. The boys'll find you a spot and tell you what to charge. Go back somewheres with 'em, if you can, or do it in the street. If you has to, bring 'em back here. Anything the punters says goes. Is that understood?'

Numbly, Walter nodded.

'All you get comes back to me. That way you can't run off. If I find you been keeping anything back from me, I'll kill you. Is *that* understood?'

Walter nodded again.

'Good,' said Maleaver. 'Your clothes'll do, just, but I'll think about getting you a new set. Welcome to our happy family.'

He pushed Walter roughly to one side and stood, palm open, ready to receive his tribute from the next boy in the line.

That night Walter stood in the ruined shadow of the old London wall, shivering. Maleaver didn't let them wear overcoats. A sharp wind was blowing. The shreds of an old theatre poster, still half pasted to the ancient stonework, flapped and cracked in the wind. The noise was a welcome distraction. He tried not to think about what he was doing. He had simply allowed the situation to gain momentum until it had propelled him out here. He had offered no resistance at all, nor even a point of view.

Was this, then, his destiny? To be the servant of other men's sexual desires? Wasn't that just what he had been to Philip?

A man approached from his left. He wore a short, heavy black jacket of the sort favoured by sailors. His small cap and single gold earring also called to mind the sea. He must have been about forty.

'You come,' he said. He wasn't English. Walter stepped nervously forward, obviously not quickly enough. The man reached out and grabbed his arm, pulling him away from the wall.

'I have place,' he said. 'You come.'

Russian, perhaps? Polish?

Walter allowed himself to be led – pulled – through a series of narrow streets to a tumbledown tenement block. They entered the building. The smell within was quite noxious; heavy with stale human odours. Slumbering bodies lined the stairway. They climbed the stairs and entered a first-floor room, lit by a single oil-lamp on the floor. There was no furniture barring two wooden boxes.

The smell was worse here than anywhere. A filthily dressed old woman lay motionless on a scattering of straw in a corner, staring up at him, open mouthed and toothless, an empty gin bottle clutched in her hand. The man cuffed the old woman with his fist and barked something in an alien tongue. The woman crawled unsteadily through the door, which the man kicked shut behind her.

He took off his jacket and shirt. He was stocky and covered from neck to navel in dense black hair. His arms were dark with tattoos. Several days' growth of beard covered his face. He smelt of drink.

'You strip,' he grunted, lowering his trousers and pulling them over his boots. He wore nothing beneath them. His short, fat cock stood out from his furry groin. Naked, but for his heavy sea-boots, he watched Walter undress.

Nervously, Walter removed his clothes and laid them in a neat pile on the floor.

The man reached forward and took hold of Walter's cock and balls with a huge, callused hand. He pulled Walter towards him and began roughly kneading the still-limp member, at the same time gripping his head and pushing Walter's mouth against his own. His tongue delved deep, filling Walter's mouth with the overpowering taste of alcohol.

He raked his coarse black beard across Walter's cheeks, biting his ears hard.

He bent Walter over and turned him around. Walter felt his huge, coarse fingers splayed out over his buttocks, pressing the flesh hard. He felt his two thumbs inserting themselves into his

ROBERT BLACK

sphincter, pulling it apart. Looking around, Walter saw him peering intently into the dark hole.

'You kneel,' said the man.

Walter knelt and the man moved in front of him. He clamped Walter's head between his hands and pulled it on to his fat tool, forcing Walter's lips apart. He was thicker than anything Walter had experienced. He choked. He couldn't breath. The smell of sweat and musk filled his nostrils.

The man came swiftly and noisily. Walter forced himself to swallow his strong jissom. The man stood back and looked at Walter.

'Good,' said the man. 'Now crawl. Crawl like dog.'

Obediently, Walter dropped on to all fours and paced the room.

'Pee,' the man said.

'I beg your pardon?' Walter didn't understand.

'Pee,' the man repeated. 'Pee like dog. Pee on straw.'

Feeling a growing sense of unreality, Walter crawled to the corner of the room and squatted over the straw floor covering.

'Pee,' said the man.

Walter tried, but nothing would come. The man aimed a boot at his side and kicked him hard. A stream of hot, gold liquid began to trickle from Walter's cock, running down his leg and soaking the straw.

'Good,' said the man. 'Now eat.'

'What?'

'Eat straw.' He swung a booted foot at Walter's buttocks and sent him sprawling. 'Eat straw like donkey.'

Walter lowered his head to the wet straw, smelling his own piss. He took a stalk in his mouth and began chewing it half-heartedly. He felt the man's hand come down on the back of his head, pushing his face into the straw.

'Eat!' he roared.

Walter took a mouthful and tried not to gag. He felt a great weight suddenly on his back, and the man's wiry chest hair raking and chafing his skin. He felt that thick penis butting against his cheeks, battering his sphincter, forcing its way inside him. The man took him like a dog, rutting him savagely and digging his

194

steel-cable fingers into his shoulders as he convulsed with his climax.

He stood up, breathing heavily, then reached into his discarded jacket and took out a handful of coins, which he dropped into the straw. Numbly, Walter fished them out. Three shillings.

The man had gathered Walter's clothes in his hands. Now he opened the door and tossed them out on to the landing beyond. Walter crawled, naked, through the door and dressed amid the shadowy, slumbering bodies.

The cold gnawed its way into him as he walked home. He thought of the mornings out on Dr Reynard's cold front step, on his hands and knees, scrubbing. Surely this was better than that? No. This cold had an edge to it. It seemed to burn and sting at the stubble grazes all over his face and neck, the gathering bruises and above all the rim of his anus.

He should return to his spot, he knew. It was early and there was still money to be made. Nevertheless, he trudged back to Maleaver's house and crawled into the cellar.

He didn't care whether or not Maleaver discovered him. He felt abused; worthless. Fully clothed (he could not bear to look at his naked, soiled body), he flung himself on to the thin, shapeless bed and pulled the blanket over him.

He couldn't sleep, of course. The memory of the night repeated itself endlessly in his mind. After several hours, the room began to fill with boys. He was aware of movement next to him in the bed. He felt Peter snuggle down and press himself lightly against his back.

He could contain his emotions no longer. He needed to hold somebody; to feel a welcome embrace where tonight there had only been contempt. Tears in his eyes, sobs welling up in his throat, he turned to face his companion.

It wasn't Peter. It was Timothy.

He could obviously see Walter was crying because he reached out and put an arm around him. 'It gets better,' he said. 'I was like you, my first day. So was Peter, I can tell you.'

He hugged Walter to his chest and let him sob. Gradually he lowered himself down Walter's body until his head was level with Walter's crotch. He unbuttoned Walter's fly, gently took his limp cock between his full lips and sucked, like a baby at a bottle. Walter hugged Timothy's head, feeling himself growing inside the black boy's mouth. Timothy's fingers stroked his balls, gently pulled the loosening sac and prodded his taut perineum. Walter let the sweet sensation overwhelm him, washing away the memory of the night. He pushed his cock deep into Timothy's throat, coming copiously, his eyes still wet with tears.

Walter was awoken once again by Maleaver and his assistant's noisy entry as they dragged their enormous food-drum down the steps. This was a twice-daily ritual: porridge when they awoke and meat broth in the evenings after their master had collected his dues.

Peter still hadn't returned. He missed their late breakfast and was absent all afternoon. Walter moped about the big room, now deserted, except for tall, pale Petherick, who sat on the cellar steps watching him and saying nothing, but smiling faintly. The smile drove Walter from the house.

He was back in time for Maleaver's accounting. Peter arrived, breathless, halfway through the ritual, and pushed into the line.

'That's much better,' said Maleaver as Peter handed him his money. Walter approached the head of the line with trepidation.

Then it was his turn. He handed his three shillings over. Maleaver looked long at the coins in his hand.

'Three shillings,' he said. 'Now, boy, I am prepared to make an allowance, given as how it was your first time last night . . . But if ever you stands in front of me again and insults me with three poxy shillings I'll have the hide off you.'

His fist closed on the coins and swung up, cracking against the side of Walter's head and sending him sprawling. 'Now get out of my sight,' Maleaver said.

Walter crawled to the head of the stairs and through the little door. He could see Peter following him.

'Slow down, Walter,' Peter said, catching him up. 'What's up? Bad night?'

In a quiet, hollow voice Walter recounted the last night to his friend.

Peter nodded slowly. 'You was unlucky. It can be like that

sometimes – I won't pretend anything else – but most of the time it's not like that.' He squeezed Walter's arm. 'Trust me.'

'I was looking for you this morning,' said Walter.

'I had to go on the nick again,' said Peter abruptly. 'No tin.'

'Did you get no custom again?'

Peter shook his head. It was more an involuntary shudder than a shake. 'I'll tell you about it another time,' he said.

'How much money do you think we would need to get us out of here?' said Walter. 'To set us up somewhere for a while.'

'More than we got,' said Peter. He winked and took a shilling from his pocket. 'But we ain't destitute,' he said. 'Come on, I'll buy you a beer – or a coffee, if you like.'

Through the early evening Peter laboured to raise Walter's mood, diligently and unceasingly making light, cheerful conversation. Walter's mind kept returning to the prospect of escape, but whenever he tried to raise it Peter was dismissive and instantly changed the subject.

Peter's efforts were entirely undone by the slow, agonising onset of night. Walter still didn't know if he could face another encounter like that of the night before.

They returned briefly to the cellar just before nightfall.

'I still don't know if I can do this again,' said Walter.

Peter let out a low whistle. He was looking down at their shared bed.

'You got no choice,' he said. 'Look.'

Lying on the bed was a brand-new suit of clothes. A mustard-yellow jacket with jauntily rounded collar and cuffs, matching knickerbockers, shirt and silk cravat.

'He likes you,' Peter said. 'I never got no togs good as them off of him. He means to keep you.'

And so Walter stood in the shadow of the wall for the second night. His new clothes were warmer than his old, he had to concede.

He didn't have long to wait before he was approached. A figure was loitering in shadow, looking at him, but he seemed scared to approach. As he stepped tentatively forward Walter saw that it was a young man, younger than him, dressed in the manner of a poor apprentice clerk. He was small, with dark, straight hair – a pudding-basin cut which fell in fronds over his eyes. Face lowered, he peered up at Walter through the fringe with big, shy, dark eyes.

Walter took a step forward. The lad stepped back.

'It's all right,' said Walter. 'Don't be frightened.'

The lad stepped forward again. Walter gently touched his arm.

'Is this your first time?' he asked.

The lad nodded.

'Come with me,' said Walter. 'Trust me. It will be fine. What's your name?'

'Brian,' said the boy.

'I'm Walter,' Walter replied.

He took the boy by the hand and led him through the streets to Maleaver's house. As they passed along the narrow passageway, Walter could hear that some of the rooms were already occupied. He found an empty one and took Brian inside. The boy sat down on the bed, his arms clamped about his chest.

Smiling, Walter eased his arms apart. 'At least take your coat off,' he said.

The boy allowed Walter to remove his overcoat and jacket.

'You're nice,' whispered Walter. He kissed the boy gently on the cheek, then on the edge of the lips. He began unbuttoning the boy's shirt, but the boy recoiled.

'Relax,' whispered Walter. 'Would you rather I undressed first?'

Brian nodded shyly.

Walter slowly stripped to his underwear, all the time holding the boy's gaze. That had been a favourite trick of Philip's and, sure enough, as he peeled away this final layer the boy's eyes flashed down to his semi-hard cock momentarily. Walter remembered how he used to slyly watch Philip undressing, and how Philip, who always knew, used to mock him for it.

'There now,' he said when he stood, fully naked, in front of Brian, his cock growing to its full length and pointing up at the boy. 'It's just a body: nothing out of the ordinary. Nothing to be frightened of. Just like you.'

He stepped forward and again began unbuttoning Brian's shirt. This time Brian didn't resist. He was looking at Walter's cock, which was bobbing close to his face. He reached out a tentative hand towards it.

'It's all right,' said Walter. 'You can touch it.'

Lightly at first, then with more confidence, Brian ran his fingers around Walter's knob, fingering his foreskin and testing the way it flowed across the bulb beneath, then down the hard shaft, through his blond bush and under his balls.

Walter gradually stripped the boy to his combinations. They bulged at the groin, stretched over a hard prick, unusually large for the boy's age and size. Walter unbuttoned them from neck to navel. The red head of the boy's tool winked over the white cloth. It amused Walter: so innocent yet so large and rude.

When the boy was naked Walter sat next to him on the bed and gently touched his cock. The boy drew back, then appeared to relax. Running his hand in a long, slow, open movement from Brian's tight balls to the red head of his long, thick prick, he kissed the boy on the lips, neck, and chest. The boy had no hair save for the little inflorescences that sprouted under his arms and a neat, furry bush around his prick, and his body still had the last remnants of puppy fat about it.

Walter licked each bollock, then trailed his tongue up the boy's cock. Brian watched in awed fascination. He made a slight noise as Walter's lips engulfed his helmet, drawing the shaft into his throat and sucking him gently to orgasm. As the boy approached his anxious climax, he tried to pull away.

'I'm going to spend –' he croaked.

Walter gripped his buttocks and pulled him close as the head of the boy's prick swelled and spat. He gulped the fluid down.

They lay together for a while, Walter's fingers playing gently over Brian's limp, damp prick, feeling it grow hard again.

'Would you like to fuck me?' he asked.

The same shy nod.

'All right,' said Walter. He spat on his hand and smeared spittle over his hole and the head of Brian's cock then, lying on his back, spread his legs and raised his buttocks. Brian scrambled between his legs and allowed Walter's hand to guide his great cock into his buttock crack.

'Now push,' said Walter as he felt the boy's cock-head nestling in his entrance.

The boy pushed and Walter's arsehole opened wide to receive him. Walter felt himself being drilled deeply by the lad's virgin manhood. Brian leaned over Walter and thrust and withdrew with his buttocks, his belly slapping against Walter's perineum. Walter reclined and looked into Brian's face with charmed amusement. The boy's expression was one of intense, anxious concentration, which increased as his second orgasm overcame him.

Brian shuddered to a standstill and withdrew his cock. For the first time he allowed his face to relax into a toothy, adolescent grin.

Walter reclined in the bed for many minutes after the boy had gone. He gazed out of the tiny window at a pale, indistinct moon.

That had been nice.

Although only a matter of days, it seemed so long since he had lain in a proper bed.

'Boy!' Maleaver was standing over him, looking monstrous in the candlelight. 'You'd better be dead, boy, taking up space in one of my best beds.'

'No, sir,' said Walter, scrambling out of the bed and standing naked in front of his new master. Maleaver reached out and ran a massive, rough hand down his chest and stomach, through his pubic hair and over his semi-limp penis. He squeezed it hard.

'You can stay where you are, boy,' said Maleaver. 'It happens that we sometimes gets gen'l'men who've been here afore coming directly to the house. Such a circumstance has happened tonight. Gen'l'man asking for a boy named Robbie, who sadly ain't with us no more. Now you happen to look a bit like him, so you can be him for the night. Remember that. You're Robbie.'

He turned and left the room. Walter could hear him talking in a wheedling tone to another man, then the door opened again and a stranger entered. He was middle aged, with a strong face and dark, receding hair swept back over his scalp.

'Well, Robbie,' the man said. 'We meet again.'

Walter smiled uncertainly. The man sat himself in the room's only chair and held Walter in a long, expectant gaze.

200

'Come now,' he said after a moment, 'on the floor with you.'

Walter tensed, fearing a repeat of the previous night, but nevertheless obeyed the instruction. He sat at the foot of the bed awaiting his next instruction.

'Well,' said the man. 'Let us see how you play with yourself.'

Dutifully Walter lay back on the floor and took hold of his prick, stroking it to hardness. The man perched on the end of the chair and stroked his chin slowly, watching him intently.

Every so often he would issue Walter with an instruction. 'Change hands.'

Walter changed hands, enjoying the less familiar sensation and the man's scrutiny of his most intimate self.

'Raise your legs,' the man said. 'Let me see your hole.'

Still masturbating, Walter lifted his legs and parted them to reveal his dark rosette.

'Now put a finger inside yourself.'

Walter obeyed, feeling the slight nick of the nail, as he pushed the digit as far in as it would go.

'Two,' the man said. Then, 'Three.'

Soon Walter had all four fingers inside his anus, pumping them in time to his cock strokes.

'Now your thumb,' the man said.

It was too much. Walter couldn't get it in. The man sprang forward from his chair and swatted Walter's hand from his hole.

'Like this,' he said. He licked his fingers and thumb, then, bunching them together, pushed them hard into Walter's crack. His nails snagged at Walter's sphincter and inner walls as he drove his hand forward. Walter felt himself opening wider than he had ever been opened before. The man's knuckles passed inside him. He began to fear that he would tear. Soon the man had his whole hand inside Walter. He began working it around in there, pumping like a piston engine. With his other hand he pulled his cock free of his trousers and began flogging it.

Walter felt the fist withdraw. The man licked his hand all over, sniffing deeply and savouring the tastes and aromas which now coated it. He shuddered with some deep passion.

His initial composure had completely vanished. With a sort of moan he grabbed Walter's legs and slung them over his shoulders, lifting his buttocks from the floor. Rapidly he inserted his cock where his fist had been. He fucked Walter with an angry urgency, driving him into the foot of the bed and coming within moments. He pulled out quietly, adjusted his dress with haste and left without a word.

When he had departed, Walter also dressed and stepped out of the door.

'Where d'you think you're going?'

Maleaver.

'I got 'em banked up tonight,' he said. 'Get back in that bed.'

Eighteen

Reynard had taken to answering his correspondence over breakfast in bed in the mornings. It enabled him to avoid his aunt.

There was a letter from Lord Spearman.

My dear Reynard,

I fear that my behaviour during our recent encounter with our holy enemy may have caused you some distress. Please let me assure you that, in spite of my flippant manner, the stance I took was the right one. There is only one way, in my not inconsiderable experience, to deal with such people. I have no doubt your late father would have dealt with him yet more directly.

Nevertheless, I regret the pain the pastor's words and my necessary response seemed to cause you. You must not take the madman's words to heart. Perhaps we are in some indirect way responsible for the downfall of your valet, but what's done is done, and cannot now be undone. Even if we could find him now, which we could not, if the pastor is to be believed, his wits have fled, and it is my guess that he would not regard us as friends.

Moreover, if a man were to be held responsible for all the ills which arise, quite unintended, from the smallest of his deeds, then we should all of us be dancing on a rope at Newgate.

Please trust my judgement in this matter, as you did on the recent previous unfortunate occasion. I promise you that the matter of Pastor Meek does not merit any further consideration.

My friend, I fear that you have been exhausted by the trials of the last week. You have almost certainly been working too hard as well. I therefore have a suggestion to make to you. My steam yacht is berthed at Folkestone, ready to sail. I had intended to pass the rest of the winter in the house in France, but sadly commitments here in London demand my further incarceration within her freezing walls. Much of the house has been closed for some time, but that could easily be fixed. Why do I not send a wire and instruct old Antoine to open up a few rooms for you? He and Marie will look after you well, and the solitude will provide a perfect antidote to the demands of London society, even out of season, of which you so despair.

Sadly I should not be able to join you before the new year, but a spell on your own could only do you good.

I shall await your thoughts on this matter.

Your friend,

Montague Spearman

PS. I shall of course, in accordance with your wishes, send some men around to remove certain equipment from your laboratory. If you do not wish to have any part in the proceedings (as perhaps you should not) leave a key to the outer door with your stable lad and put the matter from your mind.

The dean of surgery at St Mary's had also sent him a letter, demanding his attendance at his very earliest convenience. He pondered Spearman's letter as he rode to the interview.

The dean was angry.

'It's no good playing at being a doctor, Reynard,' he said. 'The most noble profession there is demands one hundred per cent commitment. Most of the time it demands more. Where have you been, man? You have missed two lectures, and Dr Farjean has undertaken no less than three operations you were scheduled to carry out. Heaven knows, man, we have granted you ample time for your crusade among the poor, but my understanding is that you have been seen at the St Luke's parish poor ward almost as infrequently as you have been seen here.'

Reynard was silent.

'Well . . . Have you nothing to say for yourself?'

'What would you have me say, Sir Godfrey?'

The dean let out a gasp of exasperation.

'Reynard, I want your assurance that you intend to fulfil your obligations to this hospital.'

Still Reynard said nothing.

'For God's sake, pull yourself together, man,' the dean barked. 'Look at you. Your wardrobe is a disgrace. I am embarrassed to be seen in your presence. You should sack your valet on the spot.'

Reynard got to his feet. His voice was cold and mechanical. 'I cannot give you the assurance you require,' he said. 'The governors will have my letter of resignation in the morning. Now, if there is nothing else, Sir Godfrey . . .'

The dean looked at him with astonishment. When he spoke, his voice was quiet and threatening. 'Be careful, Reynard,' he said. 'Your behaviour is drawing attention to itself. People are talking. Rumour, however unfounded, spreads like plague. Be careful, young man. You're riding for a fall.'

Reynard's aunt cornered him by the main staircase.

'There is a small domestic matter which I should like to bring to your attention,' she said. 'I had been hoping to have the opportunity to peruse the library. You know how the beacon of literature guides me through my many sleepless nights. Unfortunately, I have found it is locked, and Brakes does not seem to know the whereabouts of the key. I fear my daily enquiries have made the poor man quite agitated.'

'The key is lost,' Reynard snapped. 'I mislaid it some time ago.'

'But surely there must be a spare.'

'Apparently not,' said Reynard. He had given the spare key to Walter.

'And the key you mislaid, might it not be somewhere in your wardrobe, in some forgotten pocket? Perhaps your valet could –'

'Aunt, did you come here to spy on me?'

'Richard,' replied his aunt, 'I came because you invited me.'

'And are people talking about me? Your friend Sir Godfrey Sadder-Lyon seemed to think so.'

205

'Would it worry you if they were?' asked his aunt. She sighed. 'So much like your father,' she said.

'So you never tire of saying, Aunt,' he snapped. 'Alas, I knew practically nothing of him beyond his handwriting. Spearman's people were more like my family when I was a child.'

'Dear Helene . . .' mused his aunt. 'How I miss her. How she despaired of that son of hers.'

'He was my friend,' said Reynard emphatically. 'I had no others in that lonely school. You – my family – were hundreds of miles away. Apart from Father's letters and your occasional visits . . . Do you know how often I saw my parents during those years?'

'Your father was sick.'

'And my mother?'

His aunt was silent.

'At least Father wrote to me. I treasured his letters. I so longed to know him.'

'He was a strange man, Richard,' his aunt said. 'Many people saw only one side of him – the brilliant, headstrong surgeon who became a broken imbecile at the end. But he was a complex man, full of contradictions. I don't think any of us really knew him. He was a sphinx of a man, with all manner of riddles at his heart.'

Reynard smiled sadly. 'Ah, well,' he said. 'Perhaps, then, I am no less fortunate in this matter than anyone else.'

He turned to leave. 'I must take leave of you, Aunt,' he said. 'Other matters demand my attention.'

'Richard . . .'

He turned in the doorway.

'Do not doubt that your mother loved you,' said his aunt, 'for she loved you dearly. She too suffered in her final years. She blamed herself for the onset of your father's affliction. She tormented herself. Her greatest fear was that she would pass some of his madness on to you. But she never ceased to love you, Richard, any more than your father did.'

'Thank you, Aunt,' said Reynard, moved. 'I appreciate your telling me that.'

'Please do not feel afraid or ashamed to come to me if you are in need of help,' his aunt said as he left.

Reynard wrote two letters, one to the hospital governors in the terms he had outlined to the dean of surgery, and the other to the dean himself, explaining – or inventing – his situation more fully.

In his paper drawer he found his journal, and Spearman's gift to him, the memoir of the Duc du Guerrand.

The book had become a sort of grim almanac for Reynard. He could not resist a further excursion into its pages.

'I had received notice of the pale intentions of the townsfolk, and had ample time to prepare to receive their delegation, which was to consist of the sergeant-at-arms, the mayor and, of course, a priest. It could scarcely have been better for my purposes, for the sons of both the mayor and the sergeant were among my playthings.

'Immediately, upon their arrival, I had my guests seized and conveyed to the lower dungeon, where they were bound and gagged and left in darkness. The upper dungeon I had flooded with the light of burning torches, and it was there I had installed the two young men. The two great stone cells, one above the other, were linked, floor and ceiling, by a circular iron grating set into the heavy stone slabs. Naked, I stood upon the grille while the lads, also naked, knelt at my feet. As I had taught them, one drew my buttocks apart and pressed his face into the crevice, his tongue delving deep into my arsehole, while the other took my great cock in his mouth, running his lips up and down the hard shaft, tickling the knob with the roof of his mouth.

'Unknowing, the innocents played about my privates while their kinsfolk – and the church – looked on, helpless. I imagined what must be going through the minds of those proud fathers – their sense of civic duty crumbling, giving way to fear, then to paternal outrage as I took their sons. And what then? Did their cocks grow hard in their codpieces as they watched? I knew for certain the priest would be rigid with holy lust.

'I took the mayor's lad – a strapping young man, his body hardened by work in the fields – and kissed him deeply, tasting my own ordure on his tongue, then, setting him on all fours on the grating, I took him from behind with hard, savage strokes. I could see his fingers clinging to the iron lattice set into the floor, knuckles white.

'It was now the turn of the sergeant's boy – a skinny thing, womanly in his ways and doubtless a disappointment to his martial father – to service my arse with his tongue, which he did with relish, running it up and down the hairy crack in hot, slow, wet licks. Craning my neck I could see him frigging himself frantically, squeezing and pulling upon his pretty little prick.

'I climaxed, knocking the mayor's boy on to his belly on the grid with the force of my final, battering-ram thrust. More for effect than anything else, I bellowed a curse to God the Father as my orgasm shook my frame.

'Below, in the darkness, unable to move, unable to speak, the proud fathers could only gaze upon that pool of light overhead and pray to the empty heavens as I took their sons, each in turn, for the rest of the afternoon.

'I have crossed the rubicon. It is war now.'

Reynard replaced the book, shut the drawer and locked it. He left his study and donned his coat. He would at least try to prove worthy of the esteem in which he was held at the casual ward. While there was still time.

Walter slept with five men that night. He was still in the bed at dawn. The house was quiet now. He curled up and went to sleep. He slept through the midday breakfast and didn't wake until the sun was getting smoky and low.

He entered the already crowded cellar. The atmosphere was different down there today. A boy stood with his head close to the door, listening. The other boys were huddled together in earnest conversation.

'It's the same one as took Robbie and Steven,' someone said. There was a general murmur of agreement.

'What's happening?' Walter asked Timothy.

'Ain't you heard?' said Timothy. 'Peter was nearly done in last night. They reckon it was the bogeyman.'

'Now hang on a minute,' another voice said. Walter recognised the scowling boy, whose name he now knew to be Jerry. 'We don't know what happened to Steven, for a start.'

'We know what happened to Robbie, though,' said another. There was more murmuring.

'He's coming,' the boy at the door whispered loudly. Immediately the crowd broke up into its constituent parts. The lookout withdrew into the room. A moment later Maleaver entered.

Walter had made nearly two guineas the night before. He had slipped six shillings into his shoe before leaving the bedroom – his first contribution to his and Peter's escape fund. He handed the rest to Maleaver with something akin to pride.

'Better, Robbie,' the man purred. 'Much, much better.' His lips smacked and slavered as he spoke.

The drum of evening broth was dragged down the stairs and Maleaver departed, leaving the lads to eat and argue. Immediately the debate resumed. Peter was in the thick of it.

'What is this about?' asked Walter. 'Who on earth is the bogeyman?'

'We calls him that,' said Timothy. 'We reckon there's someone out there who's down on renters. There was a boy here called Robbie – looked a bit like you, he did. He was found one morning by the tower, dead. Naked he was, and cut up so's his own mother wouldn't recognise him. Cuts all over him, there was. His face was practically ripped off, his throat was cut, and his . . .' His voice dropped to a near-whisper. 'His cock was cut off and shoved down his throat. And then, a couple of weeks later, another boy, name of Steven, he just ups and vanishes. Not a word to no-one. And everyone knew he was happy here. And now Peter reckons . . . well, listen.'

Peter was telling the tale again. 'So he's tied me to the bed, and he gets this huge knife out and starts running it all over me. Across my chest, round my nipples, and down to my prick, which is starting to go soft again. So he sticks the point of the knife in my ball-bag and says summink like, "If that don't get hard again, I'll have to cut it off." And then he starts making nicks all over me with the knife. Then he starts carving around one of my nipples, and choking me with his other hand. Well, thank Christ, one of the cords weren't tied properly, and I manages to get my hand free. Well he's leaning over me and I just lashes out in the dark, and I think I got him in the eye with my fingers, cos he jumps back, swearing, and crawls out of the room on his hands and knees. So I manages to untie myself, and dresses, and runs like bloody hell out of there.'

'So what was he like?' someone shouted.

'It was dark,' said Peter. 'He never lit no lamp in that place. But I tell you summink – he was a toff. A tall, scrawny toff. And I think he was on laudanum. He kept swigging out of this flask he had in his pocket.'

Walter felt himself turn cold. He spilled broth from his bowl on to the floor. 'Did he just say the man was drinking from a flask?' he croaked.

'I wasn't listening,' replied Timothy between mouthfuls. 'I heard it all earlier. Don't you want your wittals?'

His face ripped off. His throat cut. His ... cock ... cut off and pushed down his throat.

Robbie. Maleaver kept calling him Robbie. The name of the dead boy.

That night, standing by the wall, Walter tried in vain to tell himself not to jump to conclusions. There was no real proof that the man Peter had encountered was Lord Spearman. And even if it were – and the activities Peter had described sounded only too characteristic of the peer – that did not necessarily make him this bogeyman character. And yet the coincidences frightened Walter. He had tried to talk to Peter, to extract more information from him, but Maleaver had ushered them out on to the street and watched them depart in opposite directions.

But suppose it *was* Spearman? Walter would not have put it past him to kill someone. His first thought was of dread at the prospect of meeting him and being taken to some out-of-the-way, rented room where he was totally at the madman's mercy.

His second thought was for his former employer. Was Dr Reynard in danger from his so-called friend? Walter had observed the power the peer appeared to wield over his former master. Was there a chance that Spearman would entice him down this hellish, murderous road?

The theatre poster to his rear, flapping in the wind, was no longer a comforting distraction. Its insistent death rattle got on his nerves. For some reason he thought of the dying Tom in his room of crucifixes.

He turned to the poster, intending to rip the sodden paper shreds from the wall.

He froze. The poster was faded and indistinct, and he hadn't bothered to read it before. The Infernal Cabaret. The shredded face of Sabbato, eyes still somehow burning, stared out at him.

A footstep behind him. He swung around, uttering a little cry as he did so.

It was the boy. The boy from last night. Relief overcame Walter. He rushed forward and clasped the boy's hands.

Over the next week, Walter struggled to come to a resolution about what to do. He badgered Peter constantly about leaving; stealing sufficient money if necessary.

'How much do you think we should need?' Walter quizzed.

'Too much,' Peter replied.

The bogeyman played on Walter's nerves constantly. Should he share his suspicions about the killer's identity? He was making an allegation of the gravest kind – accusing a peer of the realm of murder – and he had no proof whatsoever. He had suffered once for an unacceptable indiscretion and – his natural reticence had come surging back to the fore – would never make that mistake again.

He tried to talk to Peter. He would, in the strictest confidence, have shared his awful suspicions with his friend, but Peter resolutely refused to discuss it with him, changing the subject or even leaving the room.

Another question hammered insistently at his conscience. Should he, or should he not, warn Dr Reynard? If so, how could he, reduced to selling his body on the street, now face the man he had betrayed? Besides, there were practical considerations to be overcome. There were no nights off in Maleaver's family. Walter soon saw how Maleaver treated his flowers if they strayed from his patch. A boy, Alfie, spontaneously absented himself for a night. When he returned, Petherick stripped him naked in front of the assembled boys and he and Maleaver set about him with flat wooden paddles – flat so as not to break the skin, Walter was told – until Alfie was nothing more than a shivering, sobbing heap on the stone floor.

No-one spoke of the bogeyman when Maleaver or Petherick were around. One loose-tongued boy was loudly expressing his opinions on the subject when Maleaver appeared through the cellar door.

'Go on with what you were saying,' said Maleaver sweetly, drawing close to the boy.

'I was just . . . what I was saying, boss,' he stammered, 'was, if this bogeyman's a toff, then the law won't lift a finger against him.'

The room had fallen silent.

'I see,' said Maleaver. 'An interesting opinion. Would you like to hear mine?'

The silence stretched almost to breaking.

Suddenly Maleaver's leg shot out and kicked the boy's feet out from under him. He crumpled to the floor. Maleaver kicked.

'There is no bogeyman!' he shrieked as he kicked. 'Understand? All of you! There is no bogeyman! And the next one of you brats I hear talking about him, I swear I'll make you wish I was him.'

Maleaver, it seemed, didn't like talk of the bogeyman. It was demoralising and bad for business.

Nineteen

Walter found he got used to the work. He was only too eager to welcome a customer, seeing that it was not Lord Spearman, and to take them back to the relative safety of Maleaver's house. 'Do they never have places to go?' Maleaver asked Walter querulously one night. 'I'll have to put your bleeding name on that headboard.'

Much of the actual sex passed in a sort of numb dream for Walter, although some of it he found he enjoyed. The tastes of his customers varied. Most wanted to fuck him; some to be fucked; one insisted on dressing in his wife's wedding dress. One wanted Walter to read his dead concubine's love letters to him while he masturbated, coming over Walter's face.

It was only the time spent waiting by the wall which Walter hated and dreaded. The cold tortured him; the shadows menaced him, and every sound became a malevolent footfall, the swish of a cloak, the unsheathing of a knife.

Maleaver held Walter back after breakfast one noontime.

'Robbie,' he said, 'how would you like a little change of scenery? Trip up west.'

Trip up west. He thought of Dr Reynard.

'I . . . should like that, sir . . . boss.'

'Good,' said Maleaver. 'Very fine gent wants a couple of boys. He's entertaining a guest – some young military cove what they

213

expects very great things of . . .' Maleaver leered and tapped the side of his great beak nose. 'Ol' Maleaver knows things, see?' he chortled.

'Might I inquire as to the identity of the gentleman?' asked Walter, suddenly nervous.

'No names, no pack drill!' Maleaver snapped.

'The address, then?'

'Forty-seven Eaton Place. It's Brompton way, close to Beaufort Square.'

Walter was relieved. Lord Spearman lived nowhere near there.

'You're to be there at eight o'clock sharp,' said Maleaver. 'Choose another lad to go with you.'

'If I am to take another lad, I should choose Peter, boss,' said Walter.

'Not him,' Maleaver snapped. 'Choose another. You can take Charlie. He looks fairly posh. Girly, like. Take Charlie.'

He prodded Walter on the shoulder. 'An' payment's agreed in advance, so I know how much you're to bring me back. It's a deal of money, but don't you think of creaming a bit off the top.'

'I wouldn't dream of doing such a thing, boss,' Walter lied.

'I knows you wouldn't' said Maleaver, tousling Walter's hair. Walter shuddered. 'You're a little gent, Robbie. A proper little gent, you are.'

Charlie did indeed look 'girly, like'. He was slender and statuesque, with a fine complexion, elegantly shaped cheekbones and a delicate yet sensual mouth. A fringe of auburn hair flopped over one dark eye. He walked like a woman, dressed in clothes far too tight to be decent, and wore jewellery and rouge.

'My mother used to dress me this way,' he declared to Walter as they rode west in a hackney. 'She was bringing me up to be a whore.'

Forty-seven Eaton Place was a grand house, far larger than Dr Reynard's. Charlie let out a low whistle.

They were admitted to a drawing room where they waited for nearly half an hour. Charlie paced the room, picking up ornaments. At last a servant came and showed them up several flights of stairs to a quiet landing near the top of the house, and into a small sitting room. Two men were within, drinking wine. One was in his fifties, with grey hair and a kindly face. There was something of the cleric about him. The other was clearly the military man Maleaver had referred to. He wore the uniform of an officer and was in his mid-thirties with a stern face, an imposing handlebar moustache, piercing, unblinking eyes and a look of unchanging disapprobation.

The two were drinking wine and discussing the Sudan question. The military gentleman favoured stern action. The clerical-looking gentleman agreed. For some minutes they ignored Walter and Charlie, then finally the elder of the two waved them on to a sofa.

'Do take some wine,' he said, in a tone which would brook no refusal. The boys allowed him to pour them a measure each.

Walter winced as he sipped. The wine had a brackish, bitter taste.

'Drink it up, boy,' said the military gentleman. 'It's a tincture.'

'Laudanum,' whispered Charlie.

'Now,' said the older gentleman, 'go through that door. You will see a tallboy to your left. Put on what you find in there.'

'Whatever you say, your grace,' said Charlie.

Your grace . . . So the man was a bishop! A look from Charlie silenced Walter's unspoken question.

They did as they were told. Beyond the door was a small, private schoolroom with just four desks, including the teacher's, and a blackboard. In the cupboard hung half a dozen choristers' cassocks.

The two boys stripped and climbed into the garments. Charlie's compact, well-formed cock was already standing out from his belly. Walter was still limp.

He felt strange. His skin was beginning to tingle. He felt his heart was beating too fast. The commonplace shapes of the room were acquiring a vividness and a strangeness that disturbed him slightly. He felt ridiculous dressed as a choirboy.

The two men entered.

'This was where I received my basic education,' the bishop said to his friend. 'To read and to write and to praise God.' He turned to the two renters with a smile. 'I like to pass on what I learned.'

He reached out and ran his hands down the front of both boys' cassocks, bunching them tight around their cocks and balls and squeezing hard. Charlie's erection was clearly defined through the thin material. The bishop sunk to his knees as if in prayer and sunk his mouth over the shrouded pole. Charlie closed his eyes and gripped the man's grey head.

The military gentleman looked on, licking his lips.

After a moment, the bishop stood up. 'Bend over the desk, please,' he said.

Charlie did as he was bid. The man opened a drawer and removed a thin, flexible cane. Walter caught his breath, memories of his own schooldays flooding over him.

'Raise your cassock,' said the man. He was running a stick of red chalk along the cane's edge.

Charlie hauled the white robe up around his waist. His firm buttocks stood high in the air. The bishop raised his arm and brought the switch down hard. It cracked across the twin, fleshy orbs, leaving a livid chalk stripe where it connected. Charlie let out a long gasp.

The bishop's arm rose and fell and the whistle and crack of the cane settled into a slow rhythm, punctuated by Charlie's muted cries. A familiar mixture of fear and excitement filled Walter. He badly wanted to urinate. He clenched his bladder tight and felt himself growing hard.

Charlie's arse was turning purple. It was striped with powdery-red gashes. He was in tears.

'You,' the bishop said to Walter. 'Bend over the desk, please.' He chalked the cane once more.

Walter took Charlie's place and hoisted his cassock above his waist. The sense of déjà vu – perhaps enhanced by the laudanum – was overpowering. He felt he was bent over his old friend the saddle once more, facing the wrath of Pastor Meek.

The first stroke descended, firing his flesh. The loving reprimand of the cane's sharp bite against his cheeks, the reassurance of solid, hard wood against his legs and belly, the old familiar way in which his hardening penis bumped up against the rough surface of the wood . . . together the sea of sensation transported Walter.

He began to recite.

'And God spoke . . . spake . . . these words, saying, I am the Lord thy God, which have brought thee out of the land of Egypt, out of the house of bondage. Thou shalt have no other gods before me.'

He was back in school, reciting the Ten Commandments as the pastor's penitential cane thrashed him.

'Thou shalt not make . . . make unto thee any graven image . . .'

'Perfect,' cooed the bishop. 'Divine.'

Walter mouthed his way through the holy litany as Pastor Meek brought the cane down, again and again, hard against his burning buttocks. Turning his head he recognised the look on the bishop's face: something between fury, intense concentration and divine rapture, his eyes unfocused, his tongue protruding slightly between his clenched teeth. The pastor had always worn such an expression. What had the old man been thinking and feeling? All those thrashings . . .

His cock almost fully hard, Walter felt a familiar, urgent burning. A trickle, then a flow, of hot, golden liquid poured from his cock, soaking the cassock, as it ran in rivulets down his legs and over the desk.

'Oh, sublime,' said the bishop as Walter wet himself.

The military gentleman suddenly stepped forward.

'Out of the way,' he barked. 'Let me show you how we do it in the army.'

He snatched the cane from his friend and pushed him aside.

'Really, Kitchener . . .' said the bishop.

The soldier wasn't listening. He swung the cane wildly at Walter's arse and legs, growling as he did so. Walter could sense the familiar red welts already beginning to rise.

The cane snapped and clattered to the floor. The soldier stood, breathless, behind Walter.

'Get up,' he said. Slowly, Walter obeyed. Too slowly. The man grabbed a handful of his hair, hauled him to his feet and dragged him, tripping on the hem of his long cassock, across the room.

There was another door. The soldier kicked it open and dragged him through it.

Walter's scrambled senses lurched. He felt a creeping air of unreality. They were in a child's nursery. A playroom. The walls were decorated with ducks and rabbits. A vast paraphernalia of dust-covered toys covered the floor. In the middle of the room was a painted wooden rocking-horse, spring-mounted on a stand, with running-boards for a child's feet below either flank.

The soldier threw Walter over the horse.

'Mount!' he barked.

Walter vaulted the wooden body. The toy was much too small for him.

'Ride!' the soldier commanded.

Walter gripped the leather reins and began rocking the beast.

'Faster!'

He raised his buttocks from the beast's back and leaned forward. The horse's stand began to shake.

Walter felt the soldier pulling up his cassock, once more baring his scourged buttocks. The man's uniform was undone and a small, hard cock stood to attention in front of him. He gripped Walter by the hips and pulled him backward down on to his angry tool. Walter felt it sink between his sore cheeks and felt the rough caress of braid and buttons buffeting against his raw skin.

Every backward movement of the horse was met with a bayonet stab from the soldier's prick. Looking back through the open door, Walter could see Charlie, once more bent over the desk with his cassock pulled over his head. The bishop's rampant cock was drilling his arse. He watched the old man pull out of Charlie and pump a fountain of jissom over his back. The man sunk to his knees. 'May God forgive me . . .' he whispered.

There was no such plea on the soldier's lips as, snarling savagely, he discharged his load into Walter's arsehole.

The evening was already assuming the aspect of a dream to Walter as they walked home, passing a wine bottle between them. It was wine tinctured with opium and helped numb the pain of the thrashing they had received. Laudanum dribbled from his mouth, staining his clothes. He clung on to Charlie, and Charlie on to him.

They were lost, and Walter was quite disorientated. The road was starting to tilt and lurch. His stomach was starting to roll. He gripped the railings of a large town house, not unlike the one they had just left. The pavement sparkled and blurred, rushed towards him then dropped away again. His stomach heaved, and he fired a salvo of vomit to the ground.

'Oh, God,' he slurred.

'Oh, shit,' said Charlie. 'Here.' He took out a white handker-chief and began ineffectually dabbing Walter's face, swaying as he did so.

Walter was aware of sudden light to their left, and of voices. The grand front door of the house had opened and people were spilling out. A woman was bidding effusive farewells.

'So wonderful to have seen you again . . . You must call more often . . . So charming . . . You and the dear doctor . . .'

He recognised the voice. What was her name? Mrs Maitland, his master's one-time dinner guest, stood in the doorway, sur-rounded by her giggling daughters. The object of their adulation was a tall man who now stood on the step with his back to Walter.

Walter knew who he was before he began to turn.

Lord Spearman swung around and descended the steps.

He stopped in front of Walter, regarding him across a carpet of vomit. Vomit still dripped from Walter's face. Momentarily, his eyebrows raised themselves in sardonic greeting. He recognised Walter.

'Yes . . . Yes, goodnight, Mrs Maitland.'

His master's voice. He was descending the step.

'What's this, Spearman?' he asked, drawing next to his friend and fixing his gaze on Walter.

Walter dropped his eyes. For a long moment Spearman was silent. 'A couple of street whores, by the look of them. They stink of laudanum. This one has just charmingly vomited on the pavement. Come, Reynard.' He stepped around Walter and a grinning, fawning Charlie. 'We should walk home. The night is fine . . .'

Dr Reynard followed his friend down the street, casting a single glance behind him, catching Walter's eye, then turning away.

What had Walter seen in his eyes? Was that recognition, or just morbid fascination?

He had known in that instant that he would never speak to his master again. In any event, his master would never believe anything he had to say. Not now. He had seen what he had become: a street whore in a hideously garish suit, badged with love-bites and reeking of laudanum and vomit.

They walked home though the long, unreal night. Actually seeing Lord Spearman again had shaken Walter badly. The look of certain recognition in his eyes alarmed Walter more than the lack of recognition in his master's. He felt he had been marked in that instant. Marked by the bogeyman.

Twenty

T he laboratory was silent and empty at last. The heavy drapes
were gone from the huge windows and, on this clear, cold
night, the moonlight shone in.

'I always loved this wing of the house,' said Reynard's aunt. 'So
beautiful by moonlight.'

Reynard smiled. All had been arranged and carried out as
Spearman had promised. Tonight, after leaving Mrs Maitland's
house, they had finalised their plans.

His aunt was looking at him now in the silver light, a puzzled
expression on her face.

'You had an agreeable dinner tonight,' she said. There was a
perplexity and a sadness in her voice, which sat ill with the words.

Did she know what he was doing?

It didn't matter now, in any event.

'Richard,' she said in that same strange, high voice, 'what is
going on?'

'Aunt Julia,' he said, slightly too loudly, 'I am going away.'

She looked quizzically at him.

'Lord Spearman has invited me to spend some time at the
chateau. Aunt, I am away to Picardie.'

'This is rather sudden,' she said.

'More sudden than you think,' he replied. 'I shall be taking the
eight o'clock train to Folkestone tomorrow, where Spearman's

yacht is berthed. We sail at noon. And you needn't worry, Aunt. Lord Spearman himself will not be there. At least, not until the new year.'

'You are planning to stay that long?'

'Oh, perhaps longer, Aunt,' he cried.

His aunt's brow clouded for a moment, then cleared.

'Then again,' she said, 'Christmas at the chateau. It quite takes me back to when I was a young woman. Your friend's mother, Helene, and I were great friends, you know. Yes, I think some time at Abbeville might do us both a world of good.'

For a moment he was speechless. Then he began to laugh. 'Oh, no,' he said. 'Not this time. I knew you would try to stop me. That is why I have said nothing to you about this.'

'"I would try to . . ." You sound like a child, Richard,' his aunt snapped. 'Pull yourself together. I do believe you're drunk.'

'Slightly drunk, certainly, Aunt Julia. I am celebrating my imminent departure. My imminent departure alone, Aunt. Without you.'

'I don't trust Spearman,' said his aunt bluntly. 'He has a devious and malignant mind.'

'I told you, Aunt, he will not be accompanying me. Apart from the staff, I shall have the chateau to myself.'

'I take it I may stay on here in your absence?' his aunt asked sulkily.

'Of course,' Reynard replied.

'Then there is nothing more to say, except *bon voyage* . . . and be careful. And to bid you goodnight.'

She turned and glided from the still, moonlit room.

Lady Julia Horsnail stood long into the night, gazing by the light of a lamp on the portrait of her brother which dominated the staircase. This was going to be difficult. Her nephew was fighting her.

She was worried about him, now more than ever. She had been prepared – even anxious – to dismiss the gossip which had begun to circulate about her nephew. She was not prepared, however, to dismiss her own instincts. What had begun as a mere curiosity at the back of her restless mind, the faintest inkling that all was not well in her nephew's house, had grown into something far more acute. Her fears had accumulated with each passing day.

The rumours were still mere ripples; nothing tangible, just sidelong comments about her nephew's increasingly eccentric behaviour (no-one saying it, but everyone covertly looking for signs that he was going the way of his father), and about the fact that he seemed restless and irritated in company and was spending a great deal of his time away from his work and in the company of *that* Lord Spearman. Julia Horsnail was aware, however, of how easily ripples could become great waves.

She had seen enough to know that the rumours were quite true, and knew enough to begin to be able to glimpse the truth behind them. She prayed she might be mistaken, knowing that she was not.

Too many omens. History repeating itself.

Why had Richard not told her that he had dismissed his valet? She had alluded to the fellow often enough.

The same valet she had seen sneaking into the laboratory the night before his dismissal. The same valet the mad Pastor Meek had come to the house to talk about.

Why was it always the valet?

She raised the lamp and stared at the portrait of her brother.

'You wicked, stubborn old fool,' she whispered. 'What have you condemned us all to?'

The cry of gulls followed Reynard along the quay. He loved the sound of gulls, shouting their freedom to the wind.

He had been woken by Brakes when it was still dark. His coach had been waiting. The rest of the house had slumbered on in ignorance.

He located Spearman's steam yacht and bounded up the gangplank.

An elderly man, small and weather-beaten, in a sailor's jacket and captain's cap, saluted him as he boarded.

'Dr Reynard, sir,' the man said in a thick foreign accent. 'A pleasure to welcome you aboard.'

'Captain! Excellent!' Reynard exclaimed. 'You may cast off whenever you wish.'

'We are ready to sail now, sir,' the captain said. 'I will show you to your quarters.'

He led Reynard through a low door in the deck and down a wooden staircase.

'The state room, sir,' he said, opening a set of narrow double doors. 'The dining room is beyond. Your room is to the left.'

'Thank you, captain, you may go,' said Reynard. 'I shall ring if I need anything. I should be grateful if you would set sail at once.'

'Yes, sir,' said the captain, turning to leave.

Reynard watched his legs disappear up the steps, then closed the doors and looked about the luxurious room. Among comfortable sofas and lush plants little cupids peeked and hid. Naked, ceramic homunculi, frozen in play.

'Charming, are they not, nephew?'

Reynard spun around. His aunt was emerging from a door next to the dining room.

'Aunt!' Reynard was breathless with fury. Outside he heard the order to raise the gangway given. 'You can't do this to me! You can't . . .'

His aunt eyed him steadily. 'For heaven's sake, breathe properly, Richard,' she said. 'You will give yourself a seizure.'

He felt the craft lurch away from its mooring and begin to turn.

'I shall have you thrown off,' said Reynard hoarsely.

'Then you had better have a word with Carlo. Get him to lower the gang again. Or will you just have me dropped over the side?'

Reynard located a decanter and poured himself a glass of water, which he downed in a single draught.

'Don't be foolish, Aunt,' he said. 'I shall simply ask that the vessel return to its berth so that you may be put ashore. Now, who is this Carlo?'

'Oh, he's the captain,' his aunt replied. 'He's been with the family since dear Helene was a little girl. Did you never meet Captain Carlo during your visits? He and I are old friends.'

Reynard slumped into a seat. 'You confound me once again, Aunt,' he sighed.

'Do not distress yourself, nephew. The chateau is large and

empty. We shall be able to hide from each other quite easily, if that is what you wish.'

'I do not wish to creep about hiding from you, Aunt,' said Reynard irritably.

His aunt smiled sweetly. 'Then do not do so,' she replied.

Reynard remained on deck almost throughout the journey. His aunt reclined below, reading. After some three hours Carlo knocked on the door of the state room and entered.

'Why do you stay all the time down here, Madame Julia?' he asked.

She smiled at being so addressed. 'I am avoiding my nephew,' she said. 'He is rather annoyed with me.'

'Always you are wicked, Madame Julia,' he said. 'As a girl, you and the *madame* . . .'

'It has been a long time, Carlo,' Lady Julia said. 'Tell me, is your friend still with you? Your mate. Gaspard? I have not seen him aboard.'

'*Ah, non,*' sighed Carlo. 'He is gone, many years. All of the old crew are gone. This new crew –' he spat dryly at the carpet '– they are not sailors. Criminals. Idle men the young master find around the ports. Half of them are missing already. And the ones who remain – so much work I have to do with them . . .'

At that moment they heard voices from the deck, clamouring for the captain's attention. They both smiled.

'I'll come up,' said Lady Julia. 'I wouldn't want to miss the approach.'

She followed the old man on to the deck. Ahead of her, her nephew watched the Channel waters chop and break against the prow of the boat. Every so often he would close his eyes and, smiling, draw a long, deep breath of wet salt air.

The French coast was in sight. Presently, Lady Julia stepped from the shelter of the doorway and joined her nephew, slipping her arm around his.

'We shall see the chateau soon,' she said. 'Once we have rounded the next headland. I haven't approached it across the water in twenty years, and yet this memory is as strong for me as if it were yesterday.'

She looked briefly at her nephew. What was going through his mind? Was he really so innocent? Like his father, he had a dangerously naive view of human nature. Of all the Reynards, only Lady Julia really appreciated the wiles of the English social animal. Subtle, unfailingly instinctive, and utterly without mercy.

The park was in view now; the rolling green acres, ending in low cliffs and dunes. And there, perched on a gentle hill, overlooking its domain, the house.

She stiffened. A flood of memories washed through her mind, but they brought her little pleasure. There were too many apprehensions carried along with the flood.

Too many omens.

'There she is!' shouted Reynard over the roar of the sea.

Walter counted the money he had put aside. Just over £2. It would have to do. Over the last week he had resolved to act. All he had to do now was to force Peter, somehow, to come with him. Walter was determined not to spend another night on the streets.

The meal finished, the boys sallied out to their respective posts. Walter stayed beneath the ancient wall for less than five minutes. Peter's spot was close to the Custom House.

He found him easily. 'Peter,' he said, 'we have to talk.'

'What you doing here?' Peter hissed. 'You know Maleaver walks his turf at night. If he catches you here –'

'Then we must be quick,' said Walter. 'Come with me now.'

'Where?'

'I don't know,' said Walter. 'Away. It doesn't matter.'

'Are you mad?' Peter shouted. 'It's the middle of bleeding winter! We'd freeze to death.'

'Trust me,' said Walter. 'We must leave! I think I know who the bogeyman is, and I think he knows me! I saw him last week!'

'Oh, course!' Peter snorted. 'I was forgetting last week. That bleeding trip up west's turned your head. You thinking of going back up there? Getting some cushy position again, like none of this ever happened? Cos if you are, forget it. You're one of Maleaver's boys now. You just talks a bit posher than the rest of us, that's all. But you're still just a renter, like what the rest of us is. And the sooner you learn to accept that, the happier you'll be. Now naff off, I'm trying to earn my tin.'

'I am going tonight,' said Walter quietly, 'whether you come or not.'

'Don't be daft, Walter! Maleaver likes you. There'll be more trips up west for you if you plays your cards right –'

'Peter, look at you! You could do better than this! Freezing on the streets, selling your body to anyone for a few shillings, not knowing whether or not you're going to get your throat cut –'

'Walter, I can't come with you,' said Peter bitterly. 'For pity's sake, what would I do? I ain't got your education . . . I can't even write my own name! Don't you think I'd've left here afore now if I could? Maybe I'm just scared, but . . . I got respect here, Walter. I got food in my belly, an' family around me. I never had much in the way of family. Out there I got nothing. This is where I belong, don't you see?'

Walter ran his hand through Peter's curls and kissed him gently on the lips. 'Look after yourself,' he said.

'You too,' Peter called hoarsely after him as he left.

The night-fog had closed in. Walter could barely see a footfall in front of him. He struck out west through the City, rootless once again.

Sounds sprang at him, carried on the fog. He was certain on several occasions that he was being followed; that sly footsteps which walked when he walked and stopped when he stopped were dogging him.

He reached a square. He could see the outline of a coach through the mist. He hoped it was a hackney. He just wanted to get clear of these blighted streets.

'I say,' he called, his voice tremulous with relief, hurrying towards it.

He heard sudden, quick footsteps behind him, then a sharp, sickening blow to the back of the head which sent him reeling to the pavement. A figure loomed over him, a hand reaching down towards his face. There was a thick wad of cloth in the hand. It smelt strange and bitter. It closed over his mouth and nose, and he knew no more.

Twenty-One

The first week passed painlessly and pleasantly at the chateau. Reynard strolled the park or walked the long beaches by day, gazing out at the water and shedding his anxieties like stones sent skimming across the waves. He was eating well and sleeping soundly, refreshed by the sea air. His dreams were odd, but this he attributed to the uncharacteristically large amount of foreign food he was ingesting. They should fade as his stomach became acclimatised.

It was strange that if anything the dreams were becoming stronger and more real. He was sure that he was spending semen during his sleep.

Not that that troubled him. Nothing seemed to trouble him here. He had difficulty, when awake, remembering the substance of the dreams, but they left him with a vivid sense of well-being and a growing lethargy, pleasing and unexpected, which crept across him as the days advanced.

Presently he gave up walking the beaches and contented himself with getting up late and sitting in a chair on a high balcony overlooking the long green sweep to the sea.

His aunt, by contrast, seemed to have gone into shadow. She said little and rarely left the house, crouching in rooms or prowling the passages. She spent much time talking to the servants. Antoine, Spearman's man, was particularly delighted by her unexpected arrival, and in his company, or his wife's, she seemed to blossom briefly and regain some of her customary animation, but the rest of the time she seemed to shrivel in the winter sun.

When their paths crossed she said little. Reynard found the encounters easy: in his current state of serenity little perturbed him.

'You should take the air more, Aunt,' he said, encountering her in the main hall late one evening. 'I find it remarkably efficacious.'

'I fear I have not the stamina, Richard,' she said. She sounded tired. 'I must find my amusements indoors. I was hoping to spend some time in the excellent library. Alas, like yours, it is locked. What do men keep in locked libraries? Or locked laboratories, for that matter.'

'Good night, Aunt,' Reynard said, smiling.

Lady Horsnail watched her nephew retire. It was only just past nine o'clock. She too was feeling desperately tired. She had been sleeping soundly here for practically the first time in her life. She was sleeping far too much, finding it difficult to drag herself from her bed in the mornings and feeling perpetually tired through the day.

She was finding it impossible to remain alert. She had come here determined to guard her nephew – against what she still did not know – but it was proving impossible. Her questioning of Antoine and Marie revealed little of substance beyond their devotion to their young employer and to his dear mother's memory. Nevertheless, her conversations with them had fuelled her unease. The staff was tiny – just the old couple and their two sons. Most of the house was shut up. The master, it seemed, had not been there in over a year. 'The house is so quiet now, madame,' old Antoine had said sadly. 'So different from the way it used to be. Marie . . .' Suddenly he had sounded hesitant, looking swiftly around him as if to check that no-one was listening. 'Marie thinks that the house is haunted. She has become afraid to go beyond the great staircase. All those big, empty rooms.'

'And what do you think, Antoine?' she had asked.

'I do not know, madame,' he had said. 'We have been here many, many years. I think perhaps the memories are just too strong for her.'

Sometimes they were too strong for Lady Julia, too. She walked the quiet, closed-off corridors, the elegant landings and dignified state rooms, while her memories whispered among themselves. Sometimes the recollections were so potent they acquired almost physical presence. She swore she could hear someone picking out a tune on the pianoforte in the music room. By the time she got there the sound had vanished and she walked into an empty room. A door closing at the end of a long passage . . . a swift footstep in the ballroom . . .

There was never anyone there.

If only she were not so tired all the time that she could no longer trust her own senses. If only the memories were not so confused.

The library . . . Something about the library. She wanted to get in there. She didn't know why, but she felt an urgent need to penetrate its locked door.

Or was she thinking of Richard's library in London? She was no longer sure. Something was wrong here, undoubtedly, but sometimes she could barely remember the reason for her coming.

Outside his window, the sea turned and slumbered. Reynard curled up in bed and waited for the dream to come.

Shadows seemed to peel themselves from the walls, moving in the darkness, becoming solid. The air was thick and perfumed. Where had the bedclothes . . . ? Something soft seemed to flow across his skin: a veil being drawn up his legs and belly, up his chest, over his face. Beyond the veil, indistinct, wraithlike figures danced and twined, naked, darting and recombining like shoals of fish. He felt the soft caress of hands – many hands, gauze-softened hands – upon his thighs and buttocks, his chest and his face. Faces – man faces, boy faces – minnowed about his belly, lapping, nibbling, more distinct now, lips brushing his manhood, kissing and whispering secrets.

An undersea swell, a current, drawing him rigid, drawing him down. Teeth, nipping at his flesh. Legs, chest, nipples. His fingers tested, every one, teeth nipping at his nails, his cuticles, his knuckles. Hungry mouths gorging on the hair of his armpits and chest, the hair that curled luxuriantly about his penis, biting down on his scrotum, his balls, his hard, thick shaft, his foreskin, ragged at the masthead. Tongues like eels fought and dived in the black cavity of his mouth and rimmed his anus. A dark, insistent undertow took hold of his penis, dragging it through the depths, crushing with oceanic force, a whirlpool, sucking him down. Storm ravaged, he spent.

A figurehead, a gaunt, sunken effigy, a drowned idol, watched his ruin with lidless eyes through which sea-worms swam.

The deep-sea night closed, calm about the wreck of his manhood.

He was definitely remembering more. Wraiths? Sea-ghosts? Mer-boys? He smiled faintly. It had felt so real.

The half-memory kept him warm through the day.

The other figure, the stranger, seemed to be watching him out of the dark. For some reason Reynard thought of Sabbato.

He laughed aloud. That fraud. To Reynard, staring from his balcony out over the late-afternoon sea, the cheap world of secret, side-show sex seemed a cosmos away.

His reverie was interrupted by his aunt.

'Richard,' she said, 'we have to speak urgently.'

'What is it, Aunt?' he whined. 'I was half asleep.'

'You have been half asleep almost from the moment we arrived here,' said his aunt. 'So have I. This cannot be a natural state.'

'It is the air, Aunt. So clean. The smell of the sea, the smell of wild plants . . .'

'The air inside the house is not so pleasant,' said his aunt darkly.

'I find the house remarkably agreeable,' said Reynard, 'and the countryside even more so. There is a matter I have been intending to bring to your attention for some time, and now is as good a time as any. Aunt, I have decided to stay here permanently. I shall sell the house in London and buy a property in the area.'

'I had suspected that you had something like this in mind,' said his aunt. 'But to sell your father's house –'

'That is precisely the problem,' cut in Reynard. 'It *is* my father's house. I feel his presence there all the time, Aunt.'

'I feel it even here,' his aunt muttered.

Reynard yawned again. 'If you have nothing else to say to me, Aunt.'

'Indeed, I have a great deal to say to you,' she replied. 'Richard, I am convinced that we are being drugged.'

'Drugged?' Reynard laughed aloud. 'To what end?'

'I can only speculate, but in my case, at least, I should not be surprised if my death were intended.'

'Murder?' This was absurd. 'Who on earth − or in France, at least − would wish to murder you? Antoine?'

'No,' said his aunt. 'Of course not. I have questioned Antoine and Marie, and their sons, and I am sure all four are above suspicion.'

'Who, then?' laughed Reynard. 'Do you think I smuggled Spearman across the channel in my portmanteau, and that he is hiding about the house somewhere? Well, I can tell you that is not so. I received a wire from him only this morning. I must say, he seems to have taken the news of your uninvited presence in good part. He bid you stay as long as you wish.'

'How very unlike him,' said Reynard's aunt acidly. 'No, I do not believe that Lord Spearman is lurking about this house, but I believe someone is.'

'Preposterous!'

'Why? It would be perfectly feasible for some person or persons to be at liberty within these walls without our knowledge.'

'And the staff's too?'

Reynard was losing patience.

'I believe so,' his aunt said.

'Preposterous!' Reynard said again.

And yet wasn't he half certain that he had been visited at night on any number of occasions?

'I do not know how the drug is being administered,' his aunt laboured on. 'In our food or drink, I suppose, or perhaps via the air. I have heard of such things. Vapours from the east that can turn a man's mind, or even kill him. Have you not noticed the strange scents − very subtle perfumes, I grant you − which linger about certain of the rooms and passageways, particularly in the evenings?'

'No, Aunt, I have not,' Reynard lied.

'I came here determined to satisfy my own fears,' his aunt

232

continued. 'To get to the bottom of whatever it is you are mixed up in.'

'Your concern is very touching,' sneered Reynard, 'but quite misdirected. Disturbingly irrational, really. Were I a doctor of the mind I should say that you were afflicted by some form of morbid melancholia.'

'In any event,' said his aunt, ignoring his words, 'I have changed my mind. I now think we should leave for England at once.'

'I understand your wiles, Aunt,' said Reynard. 'You said that you suspected my intentions to depart England permanently: I see you have hit upon a typically devious plan to persuade me not to do so.'

'Child, you misjudge me grievously,' his aunt protested. 'I fear for you. I so fear that you might suffer the fate of your father —'

'My father again!' snapped Reynard. 'Even here!'

Even here.

'Richard, I urge you to come with me tonight.' His aunt sounded quite agitated.

'Impossible,' said Reynard. 'For one thing, Spearman's yacht has returned to England.'

'Then we shall travel by other means, but we must leave!'

'You may leave whenever you wish, Aunt,' Reynard replied, airily. 'I shall be staying.'

His aunt scowled. 'I shall not leave without you,' she declared.

'Then we shall continue to enjoy one another's company for some time to come,' Reynard declared flatly.

His aunt began to pace about the balcony.

'I anticipated this response,' she said, 'and have acted accordingly. I have eaten and drunk nothing all day, and have taken a long walk to the village and back. My mind is somewhat clearer. I must beg you to be on your guard, Richard, and urge you to do as I do. Do not trust anything you are given in this house —'

'But Marie prepares our meals, and Antoine serves them. I thought you said —'

'Some sleight of hand . . . Some prestidigitation . . . I do not know what is going on in this house, nephew, but I am certain I am right.'

Sleight of hand. Sabbato again.

His aunt was irritating him, like a damned French mosquito.

'I have brought some provisions from the village,' his aunt said, her voice suddenly low. 'Bread and cheese, and bottled water. I suggest we touch nothing else.'

'I have already ordered dinner, Aunt,' Reynard said angrily. 'And then I had thought to drive into Abbeville. I was undecided, but you have quite convinced me that it is the right thing to do. In fact, I believe I shall forego dinner – just to please you, Aunt – and go into Abbeville immediately. I feel in need of some rational male company!'

He rose from his chair, stretched himself and stomped back into the house.

The evening was pleasant. As the chateau and his aunt receded over the horizon, Reynard's languid good cheer returned. One of Antoine's lads, about twenty, cheerful, homely and big boned with a dark, untidy mop of black hair atop his head, drove him into the town in an open trap. Reynard conversed with Pierre in laughing, broken French as they drove.

He teased the big, shy lad, probing him with questions about his love life and the habits and appetites of the local peasant girls – or boys. He had read about the sexual vitality and uninhibited sensuality of those who grew to young manhood so close to the earthy vibrancy of the farm and countryside. Pierre grinned all over his freckled, dirty, sun-beaten face, and lowered his head, too bashful to answer.

Reynard watched the twilit countryside roll past. It was quite dark by the time they reached the outskirts of town.

Reynard laid a hand on Pierre's shoulder. 'Pull up just here,' he said. 'I shall walk the rest of the way.'

Pierre drew the trap to a halt beneath a tree.

'I shall see you in the main square at nine o'clock,' said Reynard. '*A neuf heures.*'

He stepped down and patted the horse on the rump. He felt a hand on his shoulder, and swung around. Pierre had climbed down and was standing behind him. As he watched, the lad loosened his breeches and pulled them down around his muscular thighs. His cock, thick and heavy, hooded with a loose foreskin and wreathed in thick black hair, swung between his legs, fattening and lengthening and standing out from his belly as Reynard watched.

Pierre was still grinning. Reynard stumbled forward and clamped his mouth in a rough, wet kiss. His hand fumbled at Pierre's hard cock, rudely massaging its uneven surface, snatching at his hefty balls and drawing the foreskin back and forth in long strokes.

Reynard knelt in front of Pierre and took him greedily in his mouth. Pierre groaned in Gallic as Reynard sucked. He leaned back against the tree's great trunk and gripped Reynard's head, probing his face with his big farm-boy hands, pushing his fingers clumsily into Reynard's mouth alongside his long, thick prick. Reynard could taste the dirt and sweat of the day on them mingling with the juices the lad was leaking.

The boy came heavily, his cock slipping from Reynard's mouth with the bucking of his hips and pitching a great white wad of jissom over his face in three or four hard bursts.

Reynard licked his salty, slimy lips. The lad turned around and leaned against a tree, and said something in quick French. He was offering Reynard his arsehole.

Reynard lowered the lad's britches to his ankles and the boy stepped out of them and stood with his legs braced and his feet apart.

Quickly glancing around him to ensure that the road was deserted, Reynard loosened the front of his trousers and took out his painfully hard prick. He dribbled spittle into his hand and rubbed it about his cock-head and then around the entrance of Pierre's hole. He sneaked a wet finger inside, and Pierre chuckled.

Pulling the boy's cheeks apart he pushed forward with his slimy-wet cock, which slipped and slid in the crack before settling in his entrance, parting the tight ring and the tight tunnel walls beyond.

He fucked Pierre slowly and easily and in long strokes, feeling the breeze ripple his hair and the lad's arsehole gripping and sucking him. The faint slap of his belly against the lad's buttocks blended with the calls and sighs of evening. Only when his climax was almost on him, taking him by surprise, did he begin thrusting fast and earnestly, gripping the lad's haystack shoulders and tensing his whole body against Pierre's great peasant back.

Reynard relaxed and smiled, his softening cock still buried in Pierre. Like a scene from Mr Constable, they stood together beneath the tree, the trap-horse lazily munching the grass at their feet.

With a grin, Pierre hauled himself back into the driver's seat and shook the reins. Reynard watched him canter off, then strolled into the little town. He passed an hour at a small bistro and drank several glasses of Marsala, watching the easy evening flow of the townsfolk.

His aunt's suspicions had long since melted from his mind.

Strolling through the narrow, pretty streets to his rendezvous with the carriage, he was soon lost. It was enjoyable to be lost here. He found himself in an unfamiliar square of small, simple houses. A single, ancient tree grew out of the middle of the uneven square. Its great roots had caused the intricate stone flags to twist and buckle. Carefully he crossed the square, drawing close to the mighty trunk.

There was a poster on the tree. A theatre poster. Two eyes.

He froze, tense and rigid. Sabbato stared out at him from the poster. The Infernal Cabaret. Performing in Abbeville through the winter.

He turned and hurried from the square, passing under a low arch. There, on the side of the arch, was a second poster, identical to the first. He hurried on, beginning to run now, out into a familiar, broad street.

The posters were everywhere. Why had he not noticed them earlier? Had his mind been that addled?

He stepped into the path of an old man shuffling by on the pavement.

'Excuse me,' he said, forgetting where he was, 'where is the Theatre Robert Houdin?'

The old man looked at him, puzzled, for a moment, then pointed up the road and shuffled on.

Reynard hurried up the road until he reached the small, quaint-looking theatre. Sabbato's face was plastered about the walls.

There were people going in – a performance was about to start. Reynard joined the queue and slowly moved inside.

There seemed to be nothing unusual about the interior of the theatre. Reynard sat among the expectant audience – all ordinary townsfolk and *paysans* – and listened to the little pit orchestra tuning up, waiting for the curtain to rise.

They did so to the accompaniment of a series of bright flashes and puffs of smoke. The orchestra produced a long, stirring chord, and the show began.

It was all magic and acrobatics. Cleverly done, Reynard conceded, but containing – beyond the familiar Diabolical trappings and dressing of the show – no hint of the spectacle he had seen and been a part of in London.

The show ended, and Reynard made to leave with the rest of the audience. Approaching the foyer, he slyly applied his weight to a door to his left. It opened, and he slipped inside, closing it behind him.

The room he was in was little more than a cupboard. He pressed his ear to the door and listened to the theatregoers depart. He waited a further half-hour, then quietly emerged into the dark theatre.

He re-entered the auditorium. The house lights were extinguished, and a dim glow was visible behind the curtain. Reynard crept down the aisle towards the stage.

He climbed into the empty orchestra pit and stood at the lip of the stage. Minutely he raised the edge of the curtain. A dusky-red light filled the stage. Indistinct figures moved about in the smoky gloom.

There was a rattling, swishing sound above him. With horror Reynard realised that the curtains were opening. The fiery luminescence bathed him. A figure stepped forward, silhouetted by the light. He leaned towards Reynard until his face was close. It was Sabbato.

Reynard felt the urge to run, but stood his ground.

'Dr Reynard,' the magician whispered in his thick Italian brogue. 'Sooner than expected, but doubly welcome for that.'

'What are you doing here?' Reynard growled. 'What were you doing up at the chateau?'

Sabbato raised an eyebrow in what might have been amused bewilderment. Then he smiled. 'We knew you would come,' he said, stepping back. 'Come, join us on stage.'

Reynard was about to speak – to renew his accusations – when he felt his arms suddenly pinned to his sides. Unseen hands – barely glimpsed figures – lifted him and set him on his knees on the stage. In front of him stood an immense crucible set on a metal tripod, from which white smoke billowed. He felt a fist tugging at his hair, pulling his head over the thick column of smoke. His eyes stung; his throat burned with a sickly sourness.

His mind was beginning to cloud, and still they held him there . . .

He toppled, choking, to the floor. His skin tingled all over. His eyes could barely focus. Through a haze he saw Sabbato towering over him, and behind him the stark outline of a metal frame, from which chains hung low, ending in vicious hooks.

'No . . .' he tried to protest, but no words came out. The red, foggy glow seemed to enter him. A whirlpool of dark-clad bodies raged and eddied around him. His clothes were pulled from him, piece by piece. He felt his shirt tearing. He attempted to rise, to crawl from this storm of bodies. Hands pushed and punched him, knuckles cracked off his balls, and a foot caught him in the back and sent him sprawling back to the stage.

Sabbato stood over him, holding a long pole with a small loop of wire protruding from either end. The instrument was frighteningly familiar. The magician swung the pole down and lassoed Reynard's cock and balls. The noose tightened painfully. Many hands gripped the pole and pulled. The boards rough on his bare back, Reynard was dragged by his prick and balls, floundering, to the centre of the stage.

The other end of the pole was attached to a hook which hung on a rope from high above. Reynard cried out as he felt the rope tauten and rise, pulling up the pole, hauling him from the floor by his genitals. His back arched, his hands and feet barely touching the stage, his shoulders and his groin on fire, Reynard hung like some bizarre, paralysed crab.

His strangled cock grew hard. Dark and livid above his belly, it seemed darker and more distended than he had ever seen it.

They came at him in ones and twos, in groups, naked now, their faces wrapped in thin black silk, drawn tight so that their features blurred and distorted. He felt his teetering legs being forced apart, the pressure of a man's hips against his inner thighs and a cock forcing its way between his cheeks. The noose tugged at his cock and balls. His vision blurred as a man stood over his face. He was staring up into a hairy perineum and dark arse cleft, and a pair of heavy, hairy balls. The man bent forward – Reynard was sure he was smiling beneath his mask – and rubbed a hard, thick, circumcised cock across his face. It was leaking clear juices. The man anointed Reynard's face with his lubricants, then forced his lips apart with his swollen cock-head.

They fucked him viciously, the two masked men jabbing forward together so that Reynard was crushed between the twin onslaughts, the one choking, the other burning. They spent themselves quickly inside him, only to be replaced by another pair of frenzied lovers, then another pair. The rest of the group crowded in around him, their cocks exposed; wanking, pissing and drenching his skin.

Like the hot liquids, the pain from his genitals washed over Reynard in waves, warming him. He was nothing but a plaything in the hands of these masked strangers. The zinc tang of semen burned Reynard's throat and he could feel a constant stream of hot jissom trickling down his crack and dripping off his legs as the company took him.

He could feel a great burning in his cock, as if he hadn't pissed for days. It stood like an over-ripe fruit, swollen with dark sugars, about to burst. He felt his burning balls tighten and constrict, his stomach muscles cramp, and his saturated cock brim over, spilling great runnels of jissom slowly down itself, into his pubes and on to his belly.

Instantly, the constriction around Reynard's genitals loosened and he fell like a sack back to the stage. He lay there on the hard boards, his head swimming, his body warm and wet, all thoughts of resistance banished. Let him be initiated into their atrocious rites . . .

They were on him, a hungry shoal, in an instant. He felt his legs parted once more and fingers probed his crack and pushed

239

themselves roughly into his hole. He felt an arsehole jam itself across his face, its rich, bitter scent filling his nostrils, only to be replaced by a thick cock, then another, fighting for space in his mouth. To his left he saw a naked body slithering across the floor towards him and felt it pressing into his side. A long cock pushed itself under his arm, its head grinding against his bicep, burying itself in the hair of his armpit. Another wriggled in from the right and did the same. A cock entered his arsehole, and a finger alongside it.

The twin pricks in his throat came within a second of one another, swelling and spitting. His mouth overflowed with jissom. It ran down his cheeks and chin. Jissom squelched in his arsehole as penetration followed penetration. Jissom hung like stalactites from the hair of his armpits.

His head was next to the burning crucible. He tasted once more its sharp, sickly odour, and the ceiling plunged. Still being fucked, Reynard passed out.

He came to on a concrete floor in a long room dominated by a rail from which hundreds of garments hung. A costume store, evidently.

He shook his head to try to clear it.

A book lay starkly on the floor in front of him. He picked it up. It was the memoir of the notorious Duc du Guerrand. He threw it to the floor, then picked it up again and opened it. He looked at the last illustration of the book. A naked man, dangling over a pit from which flames belched, his penis erect, and three boys, wraithlike and insubstantial, wrapping themselves around him, tugging at his limbs and member, and drawing him down into the fire.

I am gone too far to care, if care I ever did. If these be the lick of hell's flames, I find them pleasantly warming. Its pleasure gates open before me, and I enter willingly.

He selected an unremarkable suit of clothes from the rail and dressed hastily.

The door was locked.

'Master Reynard!' A broad French whisper from the other side of the door.

Thank God. 'Pierre,' Reynard called back. 'Can you force the door?'

'I try,' said the French boy. 'Go back.'

Reynard moved away from the door, which seconds later groaned and collapsed inward on its hinges under the weight of the lad's broad shoulder. Pierre staggered into the room.

'Quickly,' Reynard said. 'Can you find the way out of here?'

'I think so,' said Pierre.

They were backstage. The theatre seemed deserted. Ropes, pulleys, and towering ghost-flats hung around them.

'This way,' said Pierre, pushing through the forest of hanging ropes and weights.

Reynard followed him along a twisting corridor to an open outer door. He pushed past Pierre and dived through the door.

'Are you all right, Master Reynard?' asked Pierre.

Reynard was looking around him. They were at the back of the theatre. Next to the wall was a water trough for horses. Reynard knelt and plunged his head into the cold water, then lifted it out and shook it.

'That's better,' said Reynard. His head felt clearer now. 'Where is the trap?'

Pierre motioned across the road, to where the horse, in harness, was tethered to a tree. Reynard ran towards it. Pierre followed.

'I saw you go in there,' said Pierre. 'I waited. When you did not come out again . . .'

'Thank you,' said Reynard. 'We must return to the house. My aunt was right. I fear she might be in great danger.'

Lady Julia Horsnail spent the evening on the balcony of the chateau, looking out over the darkening park and reassembling her wits. Her thoughts, so fogged and pained over the past week, were gradually becoming clear. She ate some of the bread and cheese she had bought in the village to fortify herself for action. She was determined to act that night.

She now knew why the library had nagged at her so much. It wasn't the library so much as what lay beyond it. She had been a regular visitor to the chateau as a young woman, particularly following the early death of dear Helene's husband, Montague

Spearman's father. She had always considered the young Spearman an unlovely child, furtive and dishonest, and contemptuous of his adoring mother. During one particular visit she had mislaid her journal and a case of highly important personal correspondence. An exhaustive search of the house had brought them to light in a tiny room off the library – a cupboard, really, doubtless built as a store-room, and thought disused. The child Montague Spearman, it seemed, had turned this room into his den. Later his mother Helene had indulgently described it as his Aladdin's cave. Lady Julia had considered it merely a thief's hideaway. In addition to her missing effects, the room contained a robber's hoard of diaries, letters, two lockets with personal portraits inside and a cornucopia of materials belonging to his parents and to a dozen other people who had at one time or another been guests at the chateau.

Spearman was still a malevolent child at heart. She was confident that his unpleasant childhood habits and rituals would have survived into adulthood, and that his childhood hideaway would still be in use. There, if anywhere, she would find some clue to the peer's intentions.

The question of how to enter the locked library had confounded her all week. Now she thought she had the answer. Reaching back to the very furthest extent of her recollection, she brought struggling forward the image of a door. There was another door to the library, leading from a side landing on the upper floor on to the narrow gallery which ran around its lofty walls, affording access to the highest shelves of books. The door had fallen into disuse many years before, as she recalled. She also recalled that it had never seemed to be locked.

She entered the house and lit a lamp. The house was dark and deathly quiet. She approached the main staircase, looking around to ensure she was not being watched. Once again she detected the faintest of exotic odours in the air. Her nephew might be correct – it might just be the scent of foreign plant life – but Lady Julia would not allow herself to be pacified by this thought. She might have only a little time before her mind became confused once more.

She thought of old Marie, and her conviction that the house was haunted. In some ways this comforted Lady Julia more than her own notion that an all-too-real, living presence was hiding among the dark, empty rooms and corridors.

In the silence every sound she made reverberated eerily. Her breathing and her soft footsteps came back at her down the long passageways.

If her memory served her . . . There, at the end of a long landing, was the little door. She tried the handle. It was locked. No, it was merely stiff from years of disuse. She pushed against it with her whole weight and slowly, loudly, the door creaked open.

The squeal of the hinges bounced around the walls. Lady Julia stood very still, listening. If anyone was lurking in this shadowy labyrinth they would surely have heard that.

Holding her lamp ahead of her, she stepped through the door and on to the gallery beyond. She pictured in her mind the mighty, elegant walls of books, now lost in the darkness beyond her feeble light. She picked her way around the gallery until she came to the spiral staircase which led into the library below. She descended, and began feeling her way along the walls, searching for the door.

She found it without difficulty and turned the handle. It was locked. It was really locked this time. The key . . .

Spearman had always had the key. He had refused to hand it over to his mother, and gentle Helene had given way.

Spearman had had a hiding place for the key. She had watched the boy closely, following the recovery of her possessions, and had seen him hide the key in a book. Of course. It had been *The Prince*. Machiavelli. Spearman had always been a bright child, she recalled. That, in part, was what made him so frightening.

She had read Machiavelli – in secret – herself as a child.

She ran the lamp along the shelves. The books, as she recalled, were divided by century. Machiavelli. Early sixteenth century.

She moved slowly along the shelves, back through time. Balzac, Tennyson, Wordsworth and Coleridge. Back through Beaumar-chais and Blake. The volume of books declined with the centuries. Goethe, Goldsmith, Samuel Johnson, Pope, Congreve, Bunyan.

She found Machiavelli and opened the book. The key clattered to the polished wooden floor. She groped around for it, found it, and returned to the door. It turned easily. The lock was well used.

She opened the door and stepped inside. Piles of correspondence, books, newspapers and photographs were stacked everywhere. Hanging on one wall was a small portrait of her brother, Hugo Reynard. She recognised it – it had hung for years in her brother's house in Dorset Street.

She picked up a pile of photographs and looked through them. Quite obscene pictures of young men, naked, tumescent, coupling with one another.

He worst fears were being confirmed.

She began picking through the mountainous trove. Many of the letters were written by, or addressed to, people she knew. She had to resist the urge to read them.

She must concentrate. Was the air in here becoming tainted?

She searched for an hour before she found anything. She opened a small cupboard set against one wall and a stack of books, all identical, fell out. She picked one up, and closed her eyes slowly, drawing in a great, choking, sobbing breath. Her greatest nightmare was true. The Duc du Guerrand had returned to have his revenge; to destroy them all.

Pierre drove the poor horse to the limit of the animal's exertion. When they arrived at the chateau Reynard didn't wait for the trap to come to a standstill. He jumped down, rushed to the main doors of the chateau, and threw them open.

'Aunt Julia!' he shouted.

He crossed the dark hall, receiving no answer. He stumbled through the dark rooms they customarily used and found them empty.

Antoine appeared behind him in his nightshirt.

'Is anything the matter, *monsieur*?' he asked.

'Where is my aunt?' Reynard demanded.

'She has not rung for me all evening,' the old servant replied.

'Get some lights on, Antoine,' Reynard said and, pushing past the servant, rushed back into the hallway. 'Aunt Julia!' he called again.

There was a noise behind him. Turning, he saw the library doors swing inward. There was a small light within.

'Richard,' his aunt said in a ghostly voice.

She had turned and withdrawn into the darkness of the library. Reynard followed her bobbing lamp.

'Aunt . . .'

She was standing in a doorway, looking into a tiny room beyond, a room cluttered with junk and paperwork.

By the light of the lamp he could see his father's picture staring from the wall.

'I haven't seen that picture for years,' he said. 'What's it doing here?'

'I imagine Lord Spearman stole it on one of his visits to your house,' his aunt said softly. 'The material contained in this room betrays an alarming interest in your father. Did you know that the two of them used to correspond regularly?'

'Father and Spearman?' Reynard was surprised, and a little uneasy at this revelation. 'No,' he said, 'I did not know that.'

'I should have put a stop to it,' said his aunt. 'I who was so solicitous in overseeing the letters your father sent you. The truth is, I did not care for Spearman as a child, any more than I do for the man, and I cared not what he was exposed to, or became of him. I have helped to breed a monster, Richard!'

Reynard stepped forward into the room. His feet kicked a heap of books lying on the floor in front of a small cupboard. The Duc du Guerrand's memoir. Dozens of copies.

From his pocket Reynard drew the copy which had been left for him at the theatre.

'So I am too late,' said his aunt. 'Are we all doomed? Are we all to be driven mad like your poor father?'

'Aunt, you are making no sense,' said Richard. 'What are you saying about Father? What exactly was the nature of his madness? You know, no two people – not even the doctors I have questioned upon the matter – have ever given me the same answer to that question.'

'Your father, as you know, was a man of huge intelligence and immense will, a radical free thinker who was unafraid to put his principles into practice. What you probably do not know is that he was also a man of immense personal passions.'

'Passions . . .'

'Unnatural passions, Richard. Some years after he married your mother, though still before you were born, he commenced an . . . affair of the heart . . . with a young male servant. His valet, in fact. I discovered it early on and, for better or worse, aided him in secretly furthering his amorous ends, for I believed fervently that one should follow one's own heart. Unfortunately your father had a fatal blind spot in his reasoning. Once he had convinced himself that something was right he could not conceive of the need for discretion. In fact, he often went out of his way to avow his beliefs and opinions. This tendency grew markedly worse as the affair went on. He began to display the sort of disaffection and restlessness in society that myself and others have witnessed in you, Richard. He grew obsessive about the wretched servant – he made no effort to conceal from his friends and acquaintances the fact that, in his own words, mark you, every moment spent away from the boy was a moment in hell. Well, naturally, scandal seemed just around the corner. Tongues were starting to wag. There was even a threat of criminal prosecution. I took action – myself and your father's solicitor, with your poor mother's consent. You were sent away to school in Geneva. You were still quite young –'

'I was five,' Reynard interrupted.

'Your parents, meanwhile,' continued his aunt, 'went on an extended trip abroad. Illness was circulated as an explanation, and it was not an entirely false one, for your father had indeed sickened in the mind as a result of the double life he was leading, and your mother was scarcely any better. When they returned to London they were made to live quietly. Your father retired from many of his medical duties, again claiming ill health, and gradually things returned to a semblance of normality. The servant, of course, was dismissed.'

'There you are wrong, Aunt,' said Reynard. 'There, I think, my father confounded you. Tom was never dismissed, merely demoted to the position of footman. He was still there when I returned to England to take over Father's affairs in his last years, when he truly was mad. I made him Father's valet again.'

'Richard!' His aunt was shocked. 'What that must have done to your poor father's confused wits . . .'

'I don't think it did the servant much good either. If only I had known, Aunt . . .'

'It was my decision to keep you ignorant of the whole matter, and perhaps it was a bad one –'

'You censored my father's letters to me.'

'You were a child,' his aunt pleaded.

'But when I grew up . . .'

'Things were much worse by then. How old were you when your mother died?'

'Eleven,' said Reynard.

'Your father had lived quietly for the previous six years,' said his aunt. 'Although, in the light of what you now tell me, I can only assume his affair continued. Besides, much of his time was spent taking care of your mother when her health began to decline. Your father was solicitous to her in the extreme. In his way he truly loved her. After she died, he changed. At first he seemed merely to be regaining his old self-confidence, but then his behaviour started to become erratic again. And then . . .' She took the book from his hand and tossed it on the pile with its fellows. 'But the rest you know, of course. I see Lord Spearman has seen to that.'

'No, Aunt, I do not know,' snapped Reynard. 'Spearman gave me a copy of that book some time ago. What has it to do with my father?'

'Oh, Richard,' his aunt wailed, 'this book is your father's invention. He wrote it. He was, if you wish, the Duc du Guerrand. He was consumed by bitterness and regret. His reason quite deserted him. And worst of all, he published it.' She moved the pile with her foot. 'I thought I had succeeded in recovering all the copies. It seems not. In any event, your father was quite raving by this stage, and wholly incapable of managing his affairs.'

'So you had him declared mad.'

'He *was* mad, Richard! If only you could have seen him!'

'By the time I saw him he was a broken old man,' said Reynard. 'Practically an imbecile.'

'I so feared for you, child,' said his aunt. 'The Reynards have a history of . . . instability.'

'Am I then mad?' demanded Richard. 'I have read the book. I have even participated in similar rituals.'

His aunt drew a sharp breath.

'Yes, Aunt, I too! I am afflicted by the same malady as my poor father!' shouted Reynard.

'And Lord Spearman?'

'He saw it. He opened my eyes to it. In a strange way I suppose I am indebted to him for that.'

'He has manipulated you, Richard,' said his aunt. 'For what ends, I do not know – perhaps merely as a diversion. I would not put it past him.'

'Nor I, Aunt. Spearman *is* playing a game with me, and I intend to confront him the moment we reach London.'

'We are going at last?'

'Pierre will drive us to Abbeville at first light. From there we can take the train to Calais and board the earliest scheduled crossing. I have been foolish and selfish, Aunt, and I fear there are those to whom it is too late to make amends for my actions.' He was suddenly thinking of his own valet, Walter. He looked down again at the pile of books. His father's books. 'And there are those with whom there needs to be a reckoning.'

Twenty-Two

'H ello.'
Walter blinked and tried to clear his head. The figure speaking to him was no more than an indistinct outline.

He was lying on a soft, comfortable bed. A fragrance of fresh flowers filled the room.

'I'm John,' said the blur. 'How d'you feel?'

'Where am I?' asked Walter.

The blur was becoming more distinct now, and features were beginning to form. It was a lad of about Walter's age, slender, pretty and frail looking, with a mop of loose blond curls on his head. 'You're at Mrs Warren's house,' the lad said.

'Mrs – How did I get here?'

The last thing Walter could remember was the blow to his head and the figure reaching down. His head was still sore.

The boy looked terribly familiar. 'Do I know you?' Walter asked.

'We have met before,' the boy replied. 'Only then it was me that was in bed sick and you that was helping tend me.'

Walter recognised the boy now. John. Of course. The lad from the casual ward. The lad had lain poisoned in – Walter was sure – this very room.

'How did I get here?' he asked again.

John lowered his head. 'The baron brought you here.'

249

'The baron?' The title meant nothing to Walter.

'Lord Spearman,' John whispered.

Panic overwhelmed Walter. His head reeled. Dizzily, he tried to rise from the bed, but slumped back, his vision blurring once more.

'John!'

Mrs Warren's voice was calling from beyond the door. Sheepishly, John turned and left the room.

For the next three days, Walter was too sick to rise and too frightened to rest. John brought him food and emptied his chamber-pot but no-one else came near him. He occasionally glimpsed Mrs Warren, hovering at the end of the corridor. She looked pale and drawn, and in no sense her former, glamorous self. Once or twice he saw Richard, the little black boy. He too seemed subdued and anxious; frightened, even.

There was one new presence in the house: he was immensely tall and broad, with a hard, Asiatic face. Bald-headed and tattooed, he had a huge gold ring dangling from one ear. He spoke no English, it seemed, and made no attempt to communicate with Walter, merely stalking the passage like a guard dog.

It quickly became clear to Walter that he was a prisoner in the room.

'He's a sailor,' said John. 'A Lascar. He hardly speaks any English.'

'What is going on here?' Walter demanded. 'Where are all the renters?'

'Spearman's in charge now,' John told him. 'He bought Mrs Warren out. He's sent them all away. Closed the place down.'

'What does he want with me?' Walter pleaded.

John merely shook his head. He would not meet Walter's eyes.

Walter attempted once more to rise from the bed. 'I must get a message to Dr Reynard,' he said. 'Please, you must help me!'

John looked at him doubtfully.

'His address is seven Dorset Street,' Walter persisted. 'Tell him where I am. Tell him Spearman is holding me here. Tell Spearman is dangerous. Mad.'

Walter had to wait until the following day for John's return. He spent his time pacing the room and peering through the keyhole at the motionless bulk of the Lascar. He checked the window. It was small – probably too small for egress – and nailed shut.

'Dr Reynard sends his compliments,' said John on his return. 'He knows you are here, and asks you to be patient. Lord Spearman will deliver you to him presently.'

John departed in haste, leaving Walter to puzzle over the message. Was John telling the truth? Was Reynard in Spearman's confidence? Why didn't he come for him? Was this Walter's punishment for his betrayal of his master's trust? Heaven knew, he had paid for that.

He couldn't sleep. The house was noisy. A man's voice, indistinct, was shouting. Later a rhythmic banging came from one of the distant rooms.

It must have been past two in the morning when his door creaked open. Walter sat bolt upright in bed. A figure entered the room and moved towards the window.

'What do you want?' challenged Walter in a quavering voice.

A sniff.

Walter could see the figure in the moonlight now. It was John. He was naked, and he was crying. He moved towards the bed and crawled beneath the covers, pressing himself against Walter. He clung to him as he sobbed. A little awkwardly, Walter put his arms around him.

'I'm sorry,' John whispered through his tears. 'I'm sorry, Walter.'

Walter kissed him gently on the mouth, sweetly silencing him. He kissed his tear-damp cheeks and his weeping eyes. He moved his mouth softly and wetly down John's skinny body. The lad winced as Walter kissed his shoulder. His flesh felt puffy and bruised. Walter stopped and raised his head.

'No,' whispered John, drawing his face back down. As lightly as he could, Walter's lips continued their loving journey. He gently kissed the ragged operation scar on John's chest, his mouth yielding to the rise and fall of the boy's slightly sobbing breaths.

Turning on the bed, he kissed John's groin, nuzzling the blond curls which sprouted there, and nibbled his tight balls. He closed his mouth over his neat, upright cock. With his lips he drew John's foreskin up over his cock-head then released it and let it fall back before pushing it down and stretching it back over the bulb beneath.

He felt John move slightly, then felt the light brush of the lad's lips against his cock-head. The lips expanded and opened, flowing over Walter's swollen helmet. He felt the warm, dark, damp cavity of John's mouth close around him. Silently, tenderly, they sucked one another.

Soon John's tentative fluids began to seep into Walter's mouth. He began responding to Walter's sensitive lips with little shufflings of his hips, which grew firmer and faster as his arousal advanced. He gripped Walter's blond head and began to drive his cock deep into his throat with quickening thrusts. His breathing became rapid and uneven, his movements jerky. He came with a little cry, biting down on Walter's cock and flooding the back of his throat.

John released Walter's still-hard cock from his mouth and crawled out from underneath him. He lay on his back at the head of the bed and raised his legs, folding them into his chest. Then he spread his buttock cheeks with his fingers, pulling apart the rim of his anus. Walter's cock was still wet with John's saliva. He scrambled up the boy and placed it along the line of his arse crack, finding his open hole and pushing inside it. He felt it tighten, soft and firm, around the hard shaft. He fucked John gently at first, with slow, even strokes, then harder, gathering speed, as his passion began to flood over him. Gasping, he came inside John.

Walter felt strangely at ease. He listened to John's shallow breathing. The sleep which had evaded him for days now washed over him.

He awoke to find John was crying softly again. By daylight Walter could see the full extent of the bruises on his upper body. He reached out and touched John's swollen arm.

'Who did this to you?' Walter asked.

'Him,' said John bitterly. 'Oh, but . . . I'm so sorry, Walter . . .'

'I don't understand,' said Walter.

'I lied to you yesterday,' said John. 'I didn't take your note to Dr Reynard's house. I was told what message to give you.'

'By whom?'

'Him. Spearman.'

He'd done this to John. He'd done worse things in Reynard's

laboratory. Was he, then, capable of the unspeakable crimes of the bogeyman? wondered Walter. And what had he in mind for him?

It was several more days before Lord Spearman visited Walter's prison, accompanied by Mrs Warren. He stood in the doorway and stared, saying nothing, while she hovered behind him. He looked more dreadful than Walter had ever seen him look: his mouth drawn back to reveal his teeth, his fingers fidgeting with one another. His eyes looked sunken. They had a livid redness about the lids.

At last he stepped forward, smiling a ghastly smile.

'Walter!' he said in a voice overloaded with warmth. 'My dear fellow, how are you feeling?'

'Mrs Warren.' Walter cast a begging eye on the mistress of the house. She would not meet his gaze.

'Leave us!' Spearman snapped at her. Wordlessly, she did as she was told.

When she was gone, Spearman sprang forward and stood in front of Walter, crouching slightly. He poked him with tentative fingers, occasionally bringing his face close to Walter's neck and inhaling deeply, staring all the time.

Walter stood rigid.

'What do you want with me?' he said.

'You believe in God, do you not, Walter?' the peer asked.

Walter was silent. He wasn't sure any more.

'*I* believe in God,' said Spearman. 'I didn't used to, but I do now. You know, it's strange, even as a boy – a good, Catholic boy, going to church every Sunday – I never actually believed in God. I feared him. How could I not? I saw his power everywhere! But I never actually believed in him. But I do now. You know why? I have witnessed a miracle! The hand of God has moved across my life. He has delivered unto me the final piece of the mosaic I am constructing.'

He raised his eyebrows, questioningly and enticingly.

'You, Walter. You're the final piece,' he said. 'It will be perfect now. The old man was wrong! The Almighty does exist!'

He groped inside his jacket and pulled out his flask. He unstoppered it and took a quick, deep drink. The liquid spilled over his lip and down his chin.

'How did you find me?' Walter asked.

'Fate!' Spearman exclaimed. 'I saw you on the street with one of Maleaver's tarts. I . . . know his patch. It was easy.'

'But what do you want with me?' Walter asked again.

'Merely to reunite you with your master,' said Spearman. 'Rest now.'

He placed his face in front of Walter's so that their noses were lightly touching, and blew him a kiss.

'I shall not keep you waiting long,' he whispered.

Within an hour Walter's revulsion at the encounter had given way to fear and outright desperation. He tried to force the window open but the nails held it fast. He picked up the small bedside table and swung it at the glass. The pane shattered. Walter threw the table down and clambered on to the sill. Glass cut his hands and his legs as he hauled himself through the tight aperture.

He was almost free. He swung one leg over the sill, then stopped. Two hands clutched at his belt. The Lascar stood behind him, pulling him back.

'No!' Walter bellowed in a sudden rush of tearful rage.

Lord Spearman was standing in the doorway. The Lascar deposited Walter on his feet in front of the peer. Spearman reached forward and grabbed one of Walter's wrists, lifted Walter's hand to his lips and slowly, gently, ran his tongue along the bleeding palm. He closed his eyes and smiled a satisfied smile.

Then he flashed a glance at the Lascar before returning his craving, lecherous gaze to Walter.

'Tie him to the bed,' he hissed, smiling. 'Only leave one hand free. I have a present for him.'

He pulled a flat package from his cloak. It was wrapped in gold-leaf paper and tied with ribbon.

'Open it when I have gone,' he cooed.

The Lascar pushed Walter back on to the bed. Spearman opened a cupboard set into the wall.

'One of the advantages of an establishment such as this,' he said. 'All the rooms come with their own ropes. No home should be without them.'

He tossed several short lengths of rope to the Lascar and watched with something approaching glee as Walter's legs were separated and bound to the bedframe. This done, his left arm was similarly tied.

Spearman tossed the package on the bed next to him.

'Destiny,' he whispered and, followed by his servant, departed down the passage.

Walter turned awkwardly and looked at the package. He dreaded what horror might be inside it, and yet a part of him wanted to know.

Fatal curiosity. Lord Spearman preyed on it. It was how he had snared his master, Walter was sure.

Using his one free hand and his teeth, Walter tore at the fine packaging and spat it to the floor. Inside was a book. He turned it over and frowned with puzzlement. *Ganymede*.

Why that book?

It was a more recent copy than the one in Dr Reynard's house. He turned to the fly-sheet and his confusion deepened. On it there was an inscription, handwritten in ink. It said, *For loyal Walter, my Ganymede, my master, my pupil, my angel, my doom*. It was signed Richard Reynard.

Walter understood none of this. It wasn't his master's hand, he was sure – he had seen his writing often enough to know – and certainly not his signature. The fact that Walter's predicament was becoming more inexplicable by the moment angered him. That and his helplessness; tied like a pig about to be slaughtered. He pushed the book to the floor. He tugged at the ropes and fumbled at the knots with his free hand, but they were complex and tight. The cord cut deeply into his wrist and ankles. The pain just added to the cold rage which was steadily displacing his fear. Suddenly he resented his constant buffeting before the winds of mischance and the whims of wicked men. Not long ago, shorn of all other hope, he would have prayed, abjectly and earnestly. Now all he wanted to do was think and try to anticipate Lord Spearman's intentions. And try to envisage any opportunity of escape.

How could one read the mind of a madman? Spearman clearly was mad. Walter had never seen him like this before, snapping in an instant between lustful rage and cloying, repulsive love-talk. The beast in him, as Pastor Meek would have said, had finally taken over.

They must come for him at some point. At the first opportunity, he would run. Walter could come up with no better plan. He tried to change his position to ease his discomfort. The plump pillow cosseted his head.

Walter's vigil carried him deep into the night. The house grew noisy again. Footsteps, voices, the same hammering sound as the previous night. And then something else. A distant scream. Another, then another.

Then silence. An awful silence which stretched the night paper-thin. How long it lasted, Walter could only guess. It ended as suddenly as it began with footsteps, hasty and urgent, getting nearer. The door to his room burst open and his tormentors rushed in. Spearman was holding a lamp which bobbed and swayed erratically. His face in the lamplight had a drawn desperation about it which Walter had never seen before.

'Do it,' he hissed to the Lascar.

The giant moved to the bed. Walter tensed. This might be his only chance. If he was now to be untied . . .

But the Lascar made no attempt to untie him. He had a thick wad of cloth in his hand, which he brought down hard over Walter's face, enclosing his nose and mouth. The familiar reek and tang of chemicals filled his throat and stung his eyes. The room began to swim and the light of the lamp faded to nothing.

Twenty-Three

The journey had been tiring, the crossing rough. Reynard and his aunt's unexpected return to the house threw poor Brakes into consternation. Nothing was prepared.

'I'm sorry, Brakes,' Reynard said. 'There was no time to wire you.'

The servants bustled around. Lady Julia ordered tea.

'For one, only,' Reynard said. 'I have business to attend to.'

His aunt had given him a warning stare. 'Richard,' she said, 'I pray you, rest. You are tired, as am I. And our enemy is cunning. We shall need all our wits about us if we are to come up against Lord Spearman.'

'He is working to some sort of plan,' Reynard replied. 'Of that I am sure. God alone knows what he intends – or what he will do next – but he is dangerous and, I now believe, insane. He must be stopped immediately.' He smiled. 'Besides, Aunt, it is I who have been telling you to relax for the entire week. You were quite right not to listen to me. Instruct the staff. I want no-one to know of my return.'

He marched through the cold, blustery streets to Spearman's house. An expansive holly wreath hung on the front door.

'Dr Reynard!' Spearman's butler seemed surprised to see him.

'Announce me to your master, Hoskins,' Reynard instructed.

'That will not be possible, sir,' the butler replied. 'His Lordship is absent.'

'Then I shall wait,' Reynard replied.

'We have scarcely seen anything of him for some time, sir.' The butler sounded anxious. 'He has come and gone a few times. Sir, he did not seem himself.'

'In what way?' Reynard demanded.

'He seemed in a highly agitated state, sir. By the look of him I should say he hadn't been sleeping at all. His bed has been empty for a week or more.'

Reynard moved to enter the house.

'Sir . . . the master instructed me to receive no-one,' the butler said apologetically.

'All right, Hoskins,' Reynard said. 'Listen carefully. I want you to do something for me. I believe your master is ill. Perhaps I can help him, but I fear he will not see me. I want you to send word to me as soon as your master appears again. Should he leave again, try to determine his destination. And – mark you – this is to be done without your master's knowledge. He is not to know that I was here.'

The butler looked troubled.

'Trust me, Hoskins,' Reynard said. 'It is for his own good.'

The butler nodded his troubled assent, and Reynard departed.

The next move would be Spearman's, and Reynard could not begin to guess what it might be. All he could do now was wait.

Days passed without word.

Reynard spent much of the time going through his father's effects and possessions, struggling to understand the man of whom, it seemed, he had known so little. He looked again at the inscription at the front of *Ganymede*. A love token from his father to his valet.

He found himself thinking a great deal about Walter. A hapless victim in this game that he and Spearman had been playing. A servant. Disposable.

His father had not thrown Tom out. In defiance of the wishes of those who wielded power over him, Hugo Reynard had protected his servant. Reynard had simply cast Walter into the street.

He would never find him now.

At least, Reynard consoled himself, Walter was free of Spearman's machinations.

The waiting was preying on his nerves. He felt the need to occupy himself. He decided to try to find Walter, if he possibly could.

He set out early one morning, armed with a list provided by Brakes, to visit the numerous servants' hiring offices dotted about town. Few were in any way helpful, though in one or two the clerks did recall someone vaguely answering the boy's description. None had registered Walter, or had any forwarding address.

He even visited Pastor Meek's church. He recalled, as he approached the unprepossessing edifice, how he had first encountered Walter coming out from prayer. How he had approached him in – he now saw – a quite unorthodox manner. What must the boy have felt? And was he, the respectable Dr Reynard, the boy's employer, even then snaring the lad with the sly barbs of some unvoiced desire?

Was he that different from Spearman?

A woman – maid, housekeeper, preacher's wife; Reynard was unsure – answered the door to him. The pastor, it seemed, was suffering from fatigue and, by way of rest and meditation, had departed on a gruelling walking tour in the Alps.

Reynard returned home, confounded. No message from Hoskins awaited him. He sat long in his study, thinking about the last time he had heard Walter's voice, through this very door, pleading with Philip to be allowed to speak with him. He had sat here at his desk, and done nothing.

His aunt discovered him that night, standing in the moonlit laboratory.

'I heard you questioning Brakes this morning,' she said. 'I saw the list he gave you. You have been searching for your former valet.'

Reynard said nothing.

'You were not successful,' his aunt ventured.

'No,' he replied hoarsely.

'I fear that I am in part responsible for his fate,' said his aunt. 'That night, when I saw him in here . . .'

'The fault was not yours, Aunt,' said Reynard hollowly. 'Unwittingly I turned this place into a trap and Walter stumbled into it.'

'An experiment, you said –'

'A paltry justification for . . .' His voice tailed off. 'If it was an experiment,' he said, 'then I was experimenting on my own soul. Testing it to breaking point, to see if it existed.'

'And . . .'

'I fear I have lost it, Aunt. But that seems a trivial thing compared to what I did to Walter. I must find him.'

'Richard.' His aunt sounded tentative. 'I shall not ask you to reveal anything you wish to keep to yourself, nor shall I try to counsel you to do anything other than follow your heart, for in spite of everything I still believe that this is the true route to human fulfilment. I am no stranger to that road myself. When I divorced my husband London was briefly awash with vicious gossip and inaccurate speculation. I know how hard, how unforgiving, this road can be, Richard. Your father blazed down it and it destroyed him. All I am saying is . . . be careful, nephew. Be sure you know your own heart.'

'I know nothing, Aunt,' said Reynard quietly. 'Only that I have done him a great wrong. One that tears at my heart. I think about it – about him – a great deal. Beyond that, who knows?'

They were interrupted by the sound of swift-running feet, and Brakes's voice, calling breathlessly.

'Dr Reynard!'

This scene had an odd familiarity about it. Richard, the young black boy from Mrs Warren's house, burst through the door of the laboratory.

'Dr Reynard, come quick! It John, sir. Something happen to him.'

'What has happened?' asked Reynard authoritatively, trying to instil some calm into the boy.

'The baron, sir. He do something . . .'

'Richard, what is happening?' his aunt asked. Reynard was already striding about the room, filling his medical bag.

'Spearman,' he said bluntly. 'Now, young man, tell me whatever you know.'

'I no see, sir,' said the boy. 'Mrs no let me. But there blood!'

'My God,' muttered Reynard. 'What has the madman done now?'

Brakes ran through the door, in a state of near collapse.

'I'm sorry, sir,' He gasped. 'I tried –'

'Yes, all right, Brakes,' said Reynard, pushing past him. With young Richard bounding ahead of him, he donned an overcoat and strode through the house and out into the street.

A hansom was waiting in the street for Reynard. The streets were deserted and they made good time.

He entered the house to find Mrs Warren in tears.

'What has happened?' he asked.

Silently Mrs Warren led him to a door and pushed it open. The room was dominated by a crude wooden frame, from which hung several lengths of chain. Richard knew the principle behind it only too well. On the end of each chain was a hook, and from the hooks John, naked and bloody, hung, lolling and senseless.

'My God,' Reynard muttered. The lunatic had tried to reproduce Sabbato's ritual, with ghastly results.

Hooks pierced John's arms and shoulders, back and chest. The chains were uneven. Some of the hooks had torn away from the flesh, ripping great gashes, now gorged with bright blood.

'Help me get him down!' barked Reynard.

With difficulty they lowered the boy from the frame, then carefully Reynard removed the hooks. John whimpered in pain.

'Get some linen,' Reynard ordered. 'I don't have enough bandages.'

By the time he had bound the boy's wounds, Reynard was covered in blood.

'What in God's name had been going on here?' he demanded. 'Where is that mad dog Spearman?'

'Oh, sir,' Mrs Warren was wracked with remorse. 'I ought to have known it would end like this, sir. I was only doing what I thought best.'

'Calm down,' said Reynard. 'Tell me where he is.'

'Fled, sir,' she replied. 'Him and that big servant of his and . . . oh, sir . . .'

'Spit it out, woman,' Reynard said impatiently.

'Sir, they took your manservant with them. Walter, sir.'

'Walter? What was he doing here?'

'He came here nearly two weeks ago,' said Mrs Warren. 'I wanted to call you but Lord Spearman –'

'Where did they go?' Reynard demanded.

'I'm not sure, sir,' Mrs Warren replied. 'Although a few days ago he was talking about visiting you. He and Walter. Maybe he just wanted to set my mind at rest –'

'He thinks I'm in France,' said Reynard.

'His yacht is berthed on the Thames,' Mrs Warren replied.

Reynard sprang to his feet. 'You must attend to John,' he said. 'Don't worry, he will recover. Wrap him up as warm as you can and take him to St Mary's Hospital. And summon the police.'

'The police, sir?' Mrs Warren drew back.

'You have seen what Spearman is capable of –'

She nodded. 'Very well, sir,' she said. 'The police it is.'

'Tell them that I have gone in pursuit of the culprit,' said Reynard. 'He has a private mooring on the Thames close to Westminster Bridge. I hope we may apprehend him there.'

Outside the house he hailed a cab and instructed the driver. 'A sovereign if you don't spare the horse!' he shouted as they rattled away.

Walter first became aware of a disconcerting motion beneath his feet. The floor was moving. He was propped in a position even more uncomfortable than his bed confinement. He was upright, his arms spread to left and right and his feet bound together. He was attached to a wooden structure: a vertical spur, to which his ankles were tied, running up his legs and chest and over his head, and a horizontal beam to which his arms were lashed.

He was naked, and tied, the wrong way round, to a cross.

Lord Spearman stood in front of him, twitching and staring. 'Do you like it?' he cackled. 'It's what your God calls upon you to do, is it not? Take up your cross and follow him?'

'What do you want with me?' demanded Walter. His voice was

firm. The measured anger which had taken hold of him at the house had not abated.

'Have you heard of the Anabaptists? No? They were a religious community who flourished in Germany, in Munster, in the sixteenth century. They professed a creed of free love. Men and women might express themselves sexually in any manner of their choosing, free from censure, free from shame. And you know what your people did? The Christians? Stormed the town and butchered the people.' He tapped the cross to which Walter was tied with his fingernails. 'The Christians.'

He began pacing around the room, one arm behind his back, the other gesticulating learnedly.

'And then there were the Cathars, peaceful ascetics, wiped out in southern France. They, unlike the Anabaptists, were *too* pure. You see, it's impossible to get it right with you Christians. Your heretic burnings, your Holy Inquisition. Walter, yours is a religion built on pain. Nourished by it!'

He pulled a table into the centre of the room. A white cloth covered a variety of small, indistinct objects.

'I just want you to understand,' he said quietly, 'about the things I'm going to do.'

The floor moved again. They were on a boat.

'Where are you taking me?' shouted Walter. A note of panic crept into his voice. He strove to master it.

'My dear boy,' said Spearman, 'we are going on a little trip. I am going to reunite you with your master, the dashing Dr Reynard.'

'What makes you think he would wish to see me?' Walter asked. 'He dismissed me from his service.'

'Boy,' said Spearman, 'you cannot know – indeed, he scarce suspects it himself – the power you have over him. But *I* know. And through you I have power over Richard Reynard.'

'You already have wealth and power to far outstrip Dr Reynard,' Walter exclaimed. 'Why do you need to injure him?'

Spearman came close, clutching the upright of the cross and placing his face close to Walter's. His breath reeked of whatever was in his flask. Dried runnels of the stuff clung to his unshaven chin.

'Injure him?' Lord Spearman sounded incredulous. 'I want to free him! For years, even when we were children together at school — I a little older than he — I watched his titanic internal struggle. The struggle of his learned beliefs, duties and principles to keep his wild spirit and almost self-immolating sense of his own mental independence in check. Indirectly I watched the same struggle consume his father. I saw more of that than poor Richard did — he was kept shielded from the lunacy and the scandal. All I have ever wanted to do was to save my dear friend from the same fate which destroyed his father. To free his mind, to temper his spirit in fire. I wanted him to blaze as bright as I! I wanted to set us among the Gods with our excesses, our sublime piquancies of pleasure!'

Walter was blunt. 'Do you love him?'

Spearman stepped back, obviously surprised by the question. 'Yes . . . Yes, I suppose I do. Not that one could ever admit to such a thing, of course. Terrible scandal, actually *loving* another chap. Whatever next?'

He stood, rigid, for a moment, staring at a wall. His face seemed to be twitching, minutely and rapidly convulsing. He snatched his flask from his pocket and greedily took a drink.

'Where is Dr Reynard?' Walter asked.

For a moment his tormentor ignored him.

'France,' he finally said. 'He is being prepared. He is waiting for you. History's great crime will be absolved at last. The curse of the Reynards will be lifted. Oh, rest assured, Walter, you will be reunited with your master soon, and a truly mystic union it shall be.'

He took another drink.

'But first I must prepare you,' he said. 'First I must carry out certain . . . procedures on you . . . your lovely body . . .'

He ran a hand down Walter's back and over his buttocks. Walter closed his eyes and gritted his teeth.

There were footsteps outside the door, and a knock.

'Yes, what is it?' demanded Spearman.

'May I come in?' said a foreign voice.

'Carlo . . . What do you want? I told you I was not to be disturbed.'

'Stormy weather in the Channel, sir,' the voice said.

264

'Don't bother me with that,' snapped Spearman. 'And don't disturb me again. Keep to your own parts of the boat from now on. Is that clear, Carlo?'

'Yes, sir,' the voice said, and the footsteps resumed.

Too late it occurred to Walter that perhaps some form of help lay beyond the door. Too late he opened his mouth and yelled.

The yell was cut off in a second as Spearman jammed his fist in Walter's mouth. Outside the footsteps seemed to hesitate, but only for a moment.

Walter bit down hard on Spearman's hand. Spearman hissed with pleasure.

'Learning not to turn the other cheek?' he whispered. 'That's very good.'

He returned to the little table he had moved forward.

'As I am sure you are aware,' he said, 'your friends in the Inquisition had a habit of showing their prisoners the instruments of torture before commencing to use them. The idea was to give them a chance to meditate on their fate. A chance to confess.'

He pulled back the white cloth and Walter let out a tiny, voiceless scream. On the table lay a hammer and a pile of long, thick, iron nails.

'Well, Walter,' he hissed. 'Have you anything to confess?'

Whipping a large handkerchief from his pocket, he moved behind Walter and thrust it into his mouth. Walter choked and gagged on the cloth.

'What do you feel when you see those nails?' Spearman hissed. 'How real is your fear? You cannot imagine the pain . . . They say that fear can make men hard.'

Spearman reached down roughly and gripped Walter's cock, squeezing it hard, stretching it and twisting it. He gripped his balls and gave them a sudden, hard squeeze. His unshaven face raked across Walter's neck and cheek. His teeth clamped cruelly down on Walter's ear. Pain fired through Walter's head. He struggled against the wooden beams, but the ropes just bit deeper. Spearman pressed himself against Walter. The buttons of his jacket raked against Walter's bare back. Spearman tugged at the front of his trousers, and Walter felt his long, hard cock against his bare buttock cleft, ploughing dryly up and down the crack. Rough, agitated fingers clawed and probed Walter's hole, the fingernails biting at his soft inner flesh.

With a grunt, Spearman jammed his cock up into Walter, rutting him hard and slamming his stomach against the rough wood of the cross. His hand reached around Walter and tugged again at his limp cock. To Walter's horror it began to engorge.

'You're growing hard,' Spearman whispered, his lips brushing Walter's ear. 'I told you. Is it fear? Is it passion? Soon you will realise there is no difference. This is the holiest act of all, Walter.'

He drove his cock high into Walter. Walter felt his heels briefly leaving the floor with each upward thrust. Spearman's fist roughly pulled Walter's foreskin up and down over his swollen knob.

By the door the Lascar was watching and masturbating, his trousers loose, his prick hard in his hand. He shuffled across the cabin and stood in front of Walter, watching and grunting, grabbing Walter's hair and jerking his head back as his knob spewed a white spray over his chest and belly. The slimy pool trickled down into Walter's pubes. Spearman's pumping hand became slippery with it, smearing the fluid into Walter's pole. It ran down over his balls and along his perineum until its last drops were caught by Spearman's thrusting cock and fed inside his hole.

Spearman's hands clutched at Walter's face, forcing the handkerchief deep into Walter's throat. Walter began to choke.

Spearman began to babble hotly at Walter's ear. Walter could make little sense of the noise. Something about God . . . something about Reynard . . . fucking . . . fucking . . .

With a high moan – almost a wail – Spearman came inside him, flooding his battered tunnel. Spearman clung to him for several moments as his orgasm receded, then stepped away and hastily adjusted his clothing. Bound and gagged, Walter hung, exhausted, from his pillory.

There were animated voices on deck.

'I believe we are ready to cast off,' Spearman said. 'I must go for awhile.' He stroked Walter's cheek. 'I shall not leave you long, my sweet,' he cooed. 'Soon we shall be far from this island of shame and suffering. A better world awaits us.'

With the Lascar at his heels, he sashayed out through the door.

Twenty-Four

Rain lashed the uneven streets. The hansom cab bounced through sluices of water, horse snorting and sweating, Reynard rattling around like a die in a cup, about to be thrown.

There were lights aboard Spearman's yacht. Figures moved across the light. There was movement on deck. They must be making ready to leave.

'Stop here,' said Reynard when they were still some yards from the boat. He tossed a coin to the cabman and crossed the road to the waterfront. Keeping his head low he skirted the line of vessels, gathering speed as he neared Spearman's yacht. The gangway had been raised. She was pulling away from her berth.

Almost before he realised what he was doing, Reynard stepped over the low chain that ran along the wharf, and jumped. He collided with the side of the boat. His hands gripped the deck-rail and his feet kicked against empty air. His hands were still slimy with blood – which was now thinned and washed into rivulets by the rain. His grip was loosening. He was slipping.

With a groan he heaved himself upward and over the rail and fell on to the soaking deck. He crawled behind some crates and surveyed the scene before him. The Thames was choppy. Sailors loped across the deck. Reynard crept forward, trying to remain behind cover, scurrying between boxes and hatches. He could see no sign yet of Walter.

He approached the prow of the boat and the steps down to the luxurious state room. At the top of the steps stood a huge sailor, an Asiatic, sallow-skinned and shaven-headed. He looked every inch a guard. Walter must be down there.

He had no clear plan; his only thought was to reach his former servant. What plan could he make, cut off from aid or escape, surrounded by water and his enemies? He remembered something his aunt told him, which Carlo, the captain, had told her. The crew, it seemed, had been hand-picked by Spearman from the lowest and most crime-infested dockyard taverns on the entire Mediterranean seaboard.

For the first time it occurred to Reynard that this adventure might well end in his death.

He crouched behind some huge coils of rope and watched the door. The rain and the sea soaked him. Most of the sailors soon disappeared below decks. The guard didn't move. Reynard waited.

The boat was cutting through the river at speed. They had already left the bridges and the City far behind. The river widened as they moved through Limehouse Reach and around the Isle of Dogs.

He heard Spearman's voice somewhere in the depths of the vessel, raised in fury, and the captain, Carlo, shouting back at him. A hatchway burst open and the peer stormed on to the deck, followed by the captain. Carlo was shouting in Italian now. Spearman was covering his ears like a child.

'Silence!' he shrieked at last. 'I own this vessel! I could have you thrown to the fishes!'

A tense silence descended between the two men. For Reynard it became a roar, as the realisation crept across him that Carlo was staring directly at him. For a moment their eyes met and held one another, then the captain looked away.

'Storm gonna be bad,' he grunted at his employer, then turned and stomped away aft.

Spearman began pacing around the deck, muttering to himself. He drank frequently and heavily from his flask and occasionally aimed a savage kick at whatever piece of sea tackle he found in his path.

He stopped within a few feet of Reynard's hiding place and stood, staring out across the river. Reynard tensed his body and clenched his fists, testing their strength. Surely now he would be discovered. What chance had he against the giant at the door?

Presently Spearman moved away. He stood at the vessel's prow – exactly where Reynard himself had stood only a week ago – and continued gazing out at the black, haunted waters.

It was hours before he or the guard moved again. Reynard was caught between them as if in a trap. He dared not move a muscle now. He barely dared breathe. He was wet through to the skin, and dog tired. The river had opened out and dissolved into a restless sea and there was no land in sight. He doubted his capacity to do anything to help Walter even if he found him alive.

At last Spearman turned and strode back across the deck, barking a command to the huge sailor as he did so. The sailor turned and followed him back into the shadows of the ship's aft end.

This might be the only chance Reynard got. He slipped along the deck to the steps and furtively descended.

It took all his doctor's nerve, when he entered the state room, to keep his wits about him. Walter lolled, naked, hanging, the wrong way round, from a wooden cross that rose out of the floor. Reynard rushed across the room.

'Walter,' he said in a low voice. 'Can you hear me?'

A mumbled reply. There was a wad of cloth stuck in his mouth. Reynard pulled out the handkerchief and dropped it to the floor.

'Walter,' he said again.

'I'm all right,' said Walter in a quiet, firm voice. 'Where's Spearman?'

Reynard started pulling at the ropes which bound him. The knots were tight and complex.

'He might be back at any moment,' said Reynard. 'We haven't much time.'

'What can we do?' said Walter. 'We must be miles from land by now.'

'There are lifeboats,' said Reynard.

'Can't you feel how rough it is out there?' said Walter.

'I cannot think of a better option,' said Reynard, still struggling

269

with the ropes. 'I believe Spearman is quite capable of killing us both.'

Walter appeared to shudder. He was blinking back tears.

Reynard ran his hand through the boy's hair. 'If he's hurt you –' he said.

He felt a sudden surge of guilt, revulsion and shame at the thought of his own complicity in this whole affair. The scene in the state room reminded him too much of what he had participated in nightly in his own laboratory, he and Spearman.

'I'm all right,' said Walter again, attempting to steel his voice.

Reynard let his hand linger in Walter's hair for a second before returning to the problem of the ropes.

'No,' said Walter suddenly. 'Leave me here.'

'What?' Reynard carried on working.

'Stop!' hissed Walter. 'Listen to me!'

Reynard stopped and stood, almost quizzically, before his former servant.

'If we were to use the lifeboats this far out, we would surely perish. We must wait until we're closer to land.'

'We are still many hours away from the French coast,' said Reynard. 'Spearman will surely return his attention to you before we near land.' He glanced uneasily at the table containing the hammer and nails.

'That is why you must leave me here,' said Walter. 'So that when he returns he will not suspect you are here. You must hide in one of those side rooms. Spearman is not using this suite, except to keep me imprisoned. He is quartered towards the rear of the boat, I believe.'

'Walter,' said Reynard, 'I must warn you that if Spearman should return here with his henchmen my efforts to protect you will probably prove insufficient. Spearman will have you in his power to do as he pleases.'

'Please, master,' said Walter. 'It's our only chance.'

'I'm not your master any more, Walter,' said Reynard. 'If anything, you are mine. I shall do as you say.'

He placed a hand on the boy's shoulder, leaned forward and kissed him lightly on the forehead.

'Put the handkerchief back in my mouth,' said Walter.

Closing his eyes for a moment, shamed by dreadful necessity, Reynard did as he was bid. Then, scanning the room, he made for the nearest door.

This had been his room during the earlier crossing. Reynard removed his overcoat and tossed it on the comfortable bed, ignoring the appeal of the soft mattress and warm coverings. He was desperately tired. He perched himself on the edge of a chair next to the door. He left the door open a crack and gazed out at Walter. The boy smiled weakly at him, then closed his eyes and brought his head to rest against the cross. He looked almost serene; almost happy.

Walter felt a warm, purposeful calm he had never felt before. The last vestiges of fear had left him as Spearman and the Lascar had entered and abused his body. Now that the master was here – Richard Reynard would always be his master – he felt a sense of completeness. In the strong touch of his master's hand, wrongs had been righted and bonds had been sealed. Even if they were to perish on this nightmare voyage, they would perish together, in common cause.

Resting his head, closing his eyes, Walter drifted into sleep.

Reynard felt himself falling and jolted awake. The heaving of the boat had nearly tipped him from his chair. He cursed himself for having fallen asleep. Spearman was beyond the door, talking to Walter.

'I have given you time to contemplate your fate,' he said in a voice of terrible sweetness. 'Have you anything to confess? Hmm? Anything at all to say to me?'

Walter said nothing.

Spearman picked up the hammer and one of the nails.

'Do not think God will help you,' he said. 'He who watched and did nothing when they drove the nails through the flesh of his own son. When the pain of this is over, you will arise, reborn, in another place. A better place, free from shame, free from pain. All has been prepared.'

271

He placed the point of a nail against the back of Walter's hand and raised the hammer.

With a bellow, Reynard lunged through the door and threw himself on his former friend, flinging him against a bulkhead. Spearman turned and swung the hammer. The yacht rolled violently and the hammer skimmed past Reynard's head. Reynard followed it, slamming Spearman's hand against the wooden bulkhead. Spearman dropped the hammer with a thud.

'Help me!' yelled Spearman. Reynard struck him across the face with his fist, and the peer reeled to the floor.

'Look out behind you!' shouted Walter.

Reynard felt two vicelike hands gripping him. He was flung across the room, colliding with a chair. The Oriental giant and another sailor loomed over him. The sailor swung his foot into Reynard's stomach. Reynard doubled up in pain.

'Enough!' shouted Spearman. He sidled close to Reynard and peered at him as if at some rare, exotic insect.

'What are you doing here?' he demanded. 'You're supposed to be in France. Sabbato is supposed to be preparing you –'

'Your scheme failed,' snarled Reynard. 'At last I have seen through your lies and manipulations.'

'And much good it has done you,' sneered Spearman. 'You sought to play chess with a master. You never had a hope. You have been dancing to my tunes all along, Reynard, and now you lie like a dog at my feet.'

'You will not get away with this, Spearman,' said Reynard. 'The police have been informed about what you did to John. They know that you are making away on this boat.'

'The police,' said Spearman in mocking awe. 'My, how you have changed, Reynard. What has become of the cowering hypocrite who came snivelling to me when his degenerate lifestyle exposed him to the threat of blackmail!'

'You were the blackmailer,' said Reynard.

'Of course I was the blackmailer!' cried Spearman. 'I knew you would come to me. You gave yourself into my power quite voluntarily. From that point you were a plaything in my hands.'

'And John. Did you also administer to him the poison which led me back to Mrs Warren's house?'

'How very clever of you to have worked all this out, Reynard,' Spearman sneered. 'And so quickly. Did your aunt help you?'

Reynard attempted to clamber to his feet. 'The police, Spearman,' he said again.

'We shall soon be in France,' Spearman sang. 'Do you really think they will come for me there? A man with my connections? A peer of the realm? Think of the scandal! And think how many others might be brought down! They will breathe a sigh of relief that I have chosen to put myself out of the way.'

He gazed long into Reynard's eyes. Reynard gazed back, and saw nothing that he recognised.

'Hold him,' Spearman said to the giant sailor. 'Bring him forward.'

Once again Reynard found himself as powerless as a rag doll in that iron grip.

'You,' Spearman said to the other sailor, 'fetch more ropes.'

The sailor was only gone for a moment. On Spearman's orders, Reynard was dragged to the cross, and his arms spread.

'Bind him,' said the peer.

Ropes were strung around Reynard's wrists, cutting into his flesh and strapping him to the cross. His ankles were similarly bound. Master and servant faced each other, tied together, over the cross's wooden arms.

Spearman paced around them, rubbing and ringing his hands. He did not seem to notice the lurching of the ship.

'At least let Walter go,' said Reynard. 'You have me in your power. What further good can he do you?'

'You understand nothing!' cried Reynard. 'The boy is the perfection of my plan. No – more – he is a gift of fate. You hear that, Reynard? Fate delivered him to me. I cannot separate the two of you! The gods themselves could not separate the two of you. You are his destiny, and he yours. You walk the path your father walked –'

'How dare you even mention my father,' growled Reynard.

'Your father . . . Yes, let me tell you about your father,' said Spearman with a leering smile. 'I first met your father when I attended your mother's funeral with you. I was thirteen at the time. While your aunt employed all of her powers of artifice and

273

distraction to keep you away from him, I spoke with him a great deal. Thereafter he and I corresponded regularly for many years. You have often told me what an inspiration he was to you. Let me tell you, he was no less of an inspiration to me!'

'How dare you speak of –'

Spearman struck him across the head with his fist. Reynard's forehead cracked on the cross.

'He spoke to me of those things which he could not discuss with you,' Spearman continued. 'They censored his letters to you, you know. That witch of an aunt of yours and others. But to me he wrote freely and fully. He loved you dearly, Reynard, and wanted so much for you to know him, but they would not let him reveal himself. He gave you what he could – his knowledge, his good advice – but he could not give you his real self. You were his pupil but I was his confessor! And now I shall heal the breach between you – I shall restore to you your inheritance. That is my mission!'

'You are insane!' shouted Reynard.

Spearman didn't appear to hear him. His voice was acquiring a sort of chilling rapture. 'It is right that you should come together in this way.' He picked up one of the iron nails from the table and ran the point around the back of Reynard's neck. 'A truly alchemical wedding . . .'

The door opened.

'*Monsieur* –'

Carlo stood in the doorway, his mouth open in shocked silence.

'Well?' snapped Spearman.

It only took a moment for the captain to regain his composure.

'The men,' he said. 'They are taking the lifeboats. The storm –'

'You must stop them!' shouted Spearman.

'They are not true sailors,' said Carlo. 'They are cowards. Their courage has gone.'

Swearing, Spearman marched from the bucking cabin. His giant apprentice followed. Carlo cast a final glance – a look of concern mingled with disgust – at the pair bound to the cross, and followed his master up on to the deck.

'Sir . . . Dr Reynard . . .' said Walter when they were alone.

'I'm all right,' said Reynard.

'Do you think Spearman means to kill us?' asked Walter.

'I think that whatever he says, whatever he believes, our lives are indeed in danger.'

'I've never seen him this bad before,' said Walter. 'He keeps drinking from that flask of his.'

'That flask,' said Reynard grimly.

'Laudanum,' ventured Walter.

Reynard shook his head. 'No, not laudanum,' he said. 'Although he does indeed use the drug quite regularly. No, that flask contains something far worse. Chloride of mercury. I prescribed it to him some years ago, when he had the pox. The infection nearly killed him – you saw what the marks did to his face. Chloride of mercury is at best a dangerous cure, and only prescribed in the most pressing cases. I no longer supply him with the compound. I have tried to warn him. It can affect the mind.'

'He drinks it all the time,' said Walter.

Reynard smiled grimly. 'Believe it or not,' he said, 'Spearman is terrified of the pox.'

There were footsteps descending the wooden stairs. The door opened again and Carlo entered. He walked straight to the cross and began deftly undoing their bonds.

'Dress,' he said gruffly. 'I need all hands if the ship is not to be lost.'

He turned and hurried from the room. Walter released his grip on the cross and sank to the floor. His limbs were useless. Stiffly and feebly, he struggled to dress.

The deck was awash with water. Giant waves broke against the sides of the ship. Warm rain cascaded from the heavens. Carlo was single-handedly furling the last of her sails. Torn canvas flapped from the vessel's masts. The low, black French coast stood like a vast wall of shadow, rising and falling with the waves, just off the boat's prow.

Spearman was staring out to sea. Eight sailors tossed and dived upon the waves in one of the ship's lifeboats.

Walter clung weakly to the side of the door. Reynard struggled across the deck to join the captain.

'What must we do?' he shouted over the gale.

Carlo was staring past him.

'Mother of Christ . . .' he muttered

Reynard swung around. Spearman was holding Walter close to him, his knife pointed to the boy's throat. His henchman was trying to lower the remaining lifeboat.

'Carlo!' Spearman shouted. 'Help him!'

Reynard started forward.

'Stay where you are!' Spearman snarled. 'Carlo!'

The captain struggled across the sloping deck. Between them, he and the giant lowered the boat into the water. The giant pushed a rope-ladder over the side of the yacht.

'Do not be a fool,' said Carlo. 'You will die, for sure.'

Spearman didn't reply. His eyes, all fear and madness, flashed between Carlo and Reynard. He tossed Walter to the giant and descended the ladder. The giant hung Walter effortlessly over his shoulder and began to follow. Walter struggled feebly and in vain.

When they had vanished from sight over the hull of the yacht, Reynard rushed across the deck. The giant was already rowing hard, hauling the boat away from the yacht with huge sweeps of the long oars.

Reynard turned to see Carlo rushing towards the stern of the vessel and disappearing below the deck. Without a further thought, Reynard kicked off his shoes, ripped off his jacket and shirt and dived over the deck-rail.

The night was warm. The water was bitter by contrast. He felt it smothering him; trying to drag him down. He surfaced and struck out for the boat, crawling up the rising face of a huge wave and descending its further slope within touching distance of an oar. He struggled towards the side of the boat.

Spearman was shouting. The giant had risen from his place and was wielding one of the great oars like an axe. He swung it high above his head and brought it arcing down. Reynard kicked away from the boat and the oar cleaved at the water.

A wave caught him, filling his eyes and mouth with sharp salt-water. His stomach heaved; his lungs closed. He struggled and went under.

★ ★ ★

Walter saw the oar descend, saw Reynard vanish beneath the waves, closed his eyes and prayed. Walls of black water towered about the little boat. *Yea, though I walk through the valley of the shadow . . .*

The hours of constraint had rendered his limbs useless. Only now was any strength returning to his muscles.

The Lascar was still standing, scanning the water, the oar held above his head. Walter saw Reynard's head break the surface of the sea. He looked desperately tired, struggling against the ferocious swell. The oar descended again. Again Reynard vanished beneath the surface.

A loud crack cut through the howl of the wind. The Lascar straightened, arcing his face towards the sky, his eyes wide and his mouth open. He remained frozen for a long moment then dropped the oar into the boat and toppled forward, like a felled tree, over the side and into the water.

Yards away, Carlo was standing on the deck of the yacht, bathed in a pale light from the doorway. He was holding a pistol.

A pair of hands gripped the side of the boat and Reynard heaved himself aboard, panting.

Carlo was shouting something from the yacht. He threw something over the side, towards the rolling boat.

Spearman was struggling to fit the oar back into its rowlock. He gripped both oars and heaved against the thrashing water.

'Don't be a fool, Spearman!' shouted Reynard. 'We must return to the yacht!'

Spearman ignored him.

'It takes two to row one of these things!' Reynard shouted.

He was right. The oars were massive. Even the Lascar had struggled to propel the boat through this maelstrom.

Carlo was shouting again. The yacht was further away now. A lifebelt bobbed some distance from the boat.

'We must go!' Reynard shouted to Walter. He turned once more to his former friend. 'Spearman, please!'

Spearman growled something indistinct and continued his futile rowing.

'Come on!' Reynard shouted to Walter. Walter looked at the

lifebelt. It was further away now. Walter had never swum in his life. His limbs were still largely useless.

Reynard jumped over the side of the boat and beckoned to him.

'I'll hold you!' he shouted. 'You'll be all right!'

Closing his eyes he crawled over the side of the boat and into the water.

'Lie back!' shouted Reynard. 'Don't struggle!'

Walter was incapable of struggling. Reynard placed a hand under his chin and drew him slowly backwards through the water. They seemed lost in an endless, churning cauldron.

At last Walter felt the hard nudge of the lifebelt against his head. He raised his arms and closed them around the hard red and white ring. Reynard was clinging on next to him. A rope led to the yacht; Carlo heaved them through the water.

The voice of Spearman rang on the wind. 'It is accomplished!' He was still hauling at the oars. 'I'll be waiting for you in hell, Reynard!' he bellowed.

The wind seemed to be laughing – a high, mad laugh, carried from behind Walter mingling with the peer's voice. Walter looked up at the bucking, riding yacht. Its masts towered above them, furled sails flapping and hammering.

He was sure there was someone up there, up among the topmost rigging of the tallest mast. A figure seemed to be somehow standing there, leaning out over the chaos of the sea, a ragged cape flapping around him, pointing out across the water. Laughing.

It was the figure of Sabbato, Walter was sure.

A wave splashed across his eyes. He was wrong. It was just the voice of the wind, just a tangle of torn canvas and loose rope wrapping itself around the mast.

Walter craned his neck and peered back out to sea. There was no sign of Spearman's boat.

The yacht loomed over them now. Carlo was above them, shouting. Reynard let go of the lifebelt. 'Hold on tight,' he said to Walter. 'Pull him up!' he called to Carlo.

Walter felt himself rising from the waves. His clothes were heavy with saltwater. He bumped the ship's hull as he rose through the air. Carlo's feet appeared before him, and he collapsed on to the deck.

He rolled to the side and peered downward. Reynard was hauling himself doggedly up the rope-ladder. Soon he crouched beside Walter. Carlo tossed each of them an oilskin.

'Can we save the ship?' panted Reynard.

'It is too late,' shouted Carlo. 'Soon we are aground.'

Almost as he spoke there was a rending, wrenching sound from below them. The yacht shuddered and lurched to one side, motionless. The deck was sloping badly. A wave hit the hull, drenching the deck, and the boat lurched again.

'Under here!' Carlo shouted. He was indicating a long bench which ran along the deck wall close to the prow. He was hauling coils of rope from beneath it and throwing them over the side. Pulling Walter by the hand, Reynard crawled towards the captain. Walter felt himself being pushed into the long, narrow space. He felt the press of Reynard's body as he crawled in beside him.

'What about you!' Reynard shouted to Carlo.

'I am all right!' the captain shouted. 'Stay under there!' He turned and made his treacherous way towards the rear of the ship.

Walter felt his master's arms close about him. He wrapped himself around Reynard and squeezed him tightly. The ship continued to creak and roar and spasm under the impact of the sea. Would she break up? Walter had read of such things.

He buried his face in Reynard's shoulder and hugged. His master hugged him back.

Twenty-Five

The search lasted most of the day, though Walter took no part in it.

They had remained in their poor shelter until the sky had lightened and the sea spent its fury, and Carlo had come picking his way across the deck, now perilously steep.

'We are close to the shore,' he had said. 'God has spared our lives.'

With the aid of the lifebelts, the land had been easily reached. A carter passing along the coast road had driven them several miles to a massive, beautiful house – Spearman's, it seemed – where the old servants had fussed around them. Reynard had immediately set about organising a search of the coast for any survivors.

He had conveyed Walter to an elegant bedroom and insisted that he take to bed and remain there. It was dark by the time he returned.

'We found the wreck of a boat, and two bodies. Two of the sailors,' he said.

'And Lord Spearman?' Walter asked.

Reynard shook his head. 'We found nothing,' he said.

He slumped on the edge of the bed, his head hanging.

'You came for me,' whispered Walter.

'I did you a great injustice,' Reynard said. 'I had to try to undo the harm I had done. God help us all.'

A sudden urge took hold of Walter to feel again his master's strong, reassuring arms about him. He rolled on to his side and gripped Reynard about the waist. Reynard smiled gently and slid down the bed until he was next to Walter. They held each other for long minutes, their bodies pressed together. Reynard kissed Walter; he smothered Walter's cheeks, his forehead, his nose and mouth and chin with urgent, wet kisses.

He paused, gazing tenderly at Walter. He ran a strong, gentle hand down his neck and shoulder, down his arm, his hip, pushing the blankets aside. Walter lay, naked, dappled in moonlight, before the gaze of his master. His prick throbbed with hard expectancy. Reynard reached down and gently stroked its length with his fingertips. Walter felt he would burst at the touch.

Reynard lowered his head. He extended his tongue and touched the knob that peeped out from Walter's foreskin. He played with the neat ruff of skin for a moment before folding his lips around the swollen bulb, taking Walter deep into his throat. His warm, wet mouth bathed the aching pole. His hands massaged Walter's chest, squeezing his slender pectorals, circling and pinching his nipples and tousling the sparse golden hair of his armpits.

The past rolled over Walter like a wave. The brief lovers, the paying men, the machines ... All the time, somewhere at the back of his mind, Walter had been looking to this moment, this stellar possibility. It was not faith; it was not God; it was this pinprick of hope which had sustained him through the valley.

Suddenly his head was flooded with light. He gripped Reynard's thick brown hair and pushed his hips forward into his face. His balls tightened and his cock erupted inside Reynard's mouth.

Reynard held him tight about the buttocks as he shook with his orgasm. He continued to suck Walter's cock long after it had begun to soften, then trailed his jissom-soaked tongue down Walter's sparsely furred balls and perineum, gently, firmly, parting his legs. His jissom-slick tongue nuzzled into Walter's arse cleft. Walter raised his buttocks as Reynard licked and soaked his hole. He felt the warm, firm graze of Reynard's strong, hair-dappled chest upon his legs, his stomach, his own slender breastbone. He arched up into the great bole of Reynard's ribcage, his tight stomach-lattice. Reynard gripped him strongly under the arms, holding him tightly to him. His cock nudged along Walter's wet cleft and pushed through the puckered eye into his arse. Walter thrust his buttocks high as gradually his master opened him up with his thick, long prick. Reynard began a long, slow sickle motion with his hips, slowly withdrawing his adamantine shaft, then plunging it home again.

'Harder,' said Walter. 'Fuck me so hard I –'

So hard he forgot all the others. Bludgeon out the memory. Let all the past be subsumed in this sublime act of consecration.

Reynard seemed to understand. He dug his toes into the mattress and propelled himself forward, lifting Walter's buttocks from the bed and driving him back against the pillows, forcing his tight passage open with his hard prick. He was practically standing now, leaning down on Walter, whose legs hung down his strong back and who was propping himself on his neck and shoulders. Reynard drove down into Walter. Their eyes met. Reynard's face seemed to mirror the anguished desire which filled Walter – the suffering, almost, in his need for his master. They were battling across the chaotic, torrid landscape of the months, swimming through a sea of naked, writhing memories, to reach each other. Reynard almost seemed to be weeping and whimpering in exquisite agony, his high, fast breaths following every hard down-stroke of his cock.

He cried aloud as he came. His knees buckled and he sank down on top of Walter. Still pumping its white fountain, his cock slid from Walter's arse, splashing his perineum and balls.

Master and servant lay together in easy silence, their chests – the one so slender and smooth, the other broad and hard and hairy – rising and falling in time with one another.

Reynard awoke from a dreamless sleep some time later. It was still dark. He was aware almost at once of a warm, wet tightness around his half-hard cock. Looking down he saw the silhouette of Walter's golden head, rising and falling keenly on his shaft.

He placed his hands about Walter's head and held him as he sucked, shivering with pleasure at the slight nicking of his teeth against the distended cock-head, feeling his tongue lapping at the shaft, which was butting up against the hard, ridged dam of his palate. He could see Walter wanking his own hard cock as he sucked.

The guilt, the remorse, the grief – all had been washed from him when he fucked Walter. Now he bathed in the raw fact of their coupling, he and this marvellous boy; in the raw sensation of Walter slurping and supping with the greed of a child on his painful prick. His second orgasm was longer, easier than the first, sweeping over him in great, shuddering waves. Walter was coming too, splashing his legs with hot jissom, biting down hard on his convulsing, disgorging cock.

They settled once again in each other's arms. Walter could see Reynard, silhouetted in moonlight, gazing out of the tall windows at the speckled night.

'What are you looking for?' asked Walter.

'A star,' Reynard replied.

'A star?'

'*Where is he that is born King of the Jews? For we have seen his star in the east, and are come to worship him.* Isn't that how it goes?'

Walter suddenly understood. 'It's tonight,' he said.

Reynard placed a gentle finger upon Walter's lips. 'Tonight is *our* sacred night,' he whispered. Through the darkness Walter could sense he was smiling.

Walter lay awake late into the night, listening to his master's slumbering breath, feeling its damp warmth on his neck. Reynard held him close as he slept.

It was a fine, clear night. The clouds had blown away. The calm which had settled in the wake of the storm still lolled and lingered.

Walter found himself reflecting without pain on the past months, on the strange road he had travelled. He thought of Peter, on the cold streets of Billingsgate. This night, of all nights, he hoped he was indoors, with someone who, at least for the next honeyed hour or so, cared for him. He thought of John, and was glad that he would have nothing more to fear from Lord Spearman.

He even thought of Philip, whose violent, crass lusts had baptised him and had been the unwitting *agent provocateur* of his fate. He bore the footman no ill will. It all seemed so long ago now.

Outside, a hunting owl hooted. London was a world away, a lifetime away. Walter lay back in his master's arms and listened to the sighing darkness. He had never known such a calm, blessedly silent night.

12th January, 1885

The days are long and easy here. We spend our days, Walter and I, walking the empty beaches or strolling in the park. Every day I learn more about him, and about myself.

We have been given leave by Spearman's family to stay here for as long as we please. They have taken me to their heart now, as they did so often when I was a child. Antoine and Marie are distraught at the loss of their master, and spend their days in mourning. We are attended by their sons, Pierre and Etienne. I am grateful that none here will ever know the truth about their adored master, their beloved son.

The house lies easy now. I find it incredible that once this place seemed haunted and oppressive. Was Sabbato ever here? In truth I do not know. Is he here now?

I went into Abbeville last week. The Infernal Cabaret has left town, bound for who knows where.

Some questions remain unanswered, and I suspect will always remain so. Perhaps this is for the best.

I am informed by my aunt, who is now entirely in my confidence, that Mrs Warren has left England, and is engaged in setting up a new house in Paris. She has my good wishes, but I fear I shall not be paying her a visit.

My aunt is conducting my affairs in London. She has moved into the family home in Dorset Street. As for me, I am determined to carry out my intention to remain here. I shall not return to London. I find a contentment here which always eluded me at home. I believe Walter feels it too. There is an ease about his manner, and a confidence in him, which I have never before seen. I can envisage no earthly desire beyond his love and companionship.

Several days ago I received from my aunt a large parcel of documents taken from my study. Among the paperwork was this journal. I had formed the intention never again to open its pages; still less to write on them. But every experiment ought to be properly reported, the conclusion written up in good order.

After today I shall write no more. I shall consign this journal to a safe place, and bring it out again only if I feel the pull of pride and arrogance and wayward will threatening to disorder my mind once more: then I shall read it and, I pray, be cautioned.

Or perhaps I shall do what my father did. Publish, and damn the consequences.

From thought to thought, from mountain to mountain,
Love leads me on; since every marked path
I find contrary to a tranquil life.
Where'er a river or fountain adorns a lonely slope,
Or 'twixt two hills a shady vale is hid,
There the disturbed soul can calm itself;
And, as love bids,
Either laughs or weeps or fears or is assured.
And the face, which follows the soul where'er it leads
Is tormented and serene by turns,
And stays little time in any one state.
Whence, on seeing it, a man learned in such a life
Would say: this one burns, and is unsure of his condition.

Petrarch

IDOL NEW BOOKS

Also published:

THE KING'S MEN
Christian Fall

Ned Medcombe, spoilt son of an Oxfordshire landowner, has always remembered his first love: the beautiful, golden-haired Lewis. But seventeenth-century England forbids such a love and Ned is content to indulge his domineering passions with the willing members of the local community, including the submissive parish cleric. Until the Civil War changes his world, and he is forced to pursue his desires as a soldier in Cromwell's army – while his long-lost lover fights as one of the King's men.

ISBN 0 352 33207 7

THE VELVET WEB
Christopher Summerisle

The year is 1889. Daniel McGaw arrives at Calverdale, a centre of academic excellence buried deep in the English countryside. But this is like no other college. As Daniel explores, he discovers secret passages in the grounds and forbidden texts in the library. The young male students, isolated from the outside world, share a darkly bizarre brotherhood based on the most extreme forms of erotic expression. It isn't long before Daniel is initiated into the rites that bind together the youths of Calverdale in a web of desire.

ISBN 0 352 33208 5

CHAINS OF DECEIT
Paul C. Alexander

Journalist Nathan Dexter's life is turned around when he meets a young student called Scott – someone who offers him the relationship for which he's been searching. Then Nathan's best friend goes missing, and Nathan uncovers evidence that he has become the victim of a slavery ring which is rumoured to be operating out of London's leather scene. To rescue their friend and expose the perverted slave trade, Nathan and Scott must go undercover, risking detection and betrayal at every turn.

ISBN 0 352 33206 9

HALL OF MIRRORS
Robert Black

Tom Jarrett operates the Big Wheel at Gamlin's Fair. When young runaway Jason Bradley tries to rob him, events are set in motion which draw the two together in a tangled web of mutual mistrust and growing fascination. Each carries a burden of old guilt and tragic unspoken history; each is running from something. But the fair is a place of magic and mystery where normal rules don't apply, and Jason is soon on a journey of self-discovery, unbridled sexuality and growing love.

ISBN 0 352 33209 3

THE SLAVE TRADE
James Masters

Barely eighteen and innocent of the desires of men, Marc is the sole survivor of a noble British family. When his home village falls to the invading Romans, he is forced to flee for his life. He first finds sanctuary with Karl, a barbarian from far-off Germanica, whose words seem kind but whose eyes conceal a dark and brooding menace. And then they are captured by Gaius, a general in Caesar's all-conquering army, in whose camp they learn the true meaning – and pleasures – of slavery.

ISBN 0 352 33228 X

DARK RIDER
Jack Gordon

While the rulers of a remote Scottish island play bizarre games of sexual dominance with the Argentinian Angelo, his friend Robert – consumed with jealous longing for his coffee-skinned companion – assuages his desires with the willing locals.

ISBN 0 352 33243 3

CONQUISTADOR
Jeff Hunter

It is the dying days of the Aztec empire. Axaten and Quetzel are members of the Stable, servants of the Sun Prince chosen for their bravery and beauty. But it is not just an honour and a duty to join this society, it is also the ultimate sexual achievement. Until the arrival of Juan, a young Spanish conquistador, sets the men of the Stable on an adventure of bondage, lust and deception.

ISBN 0 352 33244 1

WE NEED YOUR HELP . . .

to plan the future of Idol books –

Yours are the only opinions that matter. Idol is a new and exciting venture: the first British series of books devoted to homoerotic fiction for men.

We're going to do our best to provide the sexiest, best-written books you can buy. And we'd like you to help in these early stages. Tell us what you want to read. There's a freepost address for your filled-in questionnaires, so you won't even need to buy a stamp.

THE IDOL QUESTIONNAIRE

SECTION ONE: ABOUT YOU

1.1   Sex (*we presume you are male, but just in case*)
      Are you?
      Male   ☐
      Female   ☐

1.2   Age
      under 21   ☐   21–30   ☐
      31–40   ☐   41–50   ☐
      51–60   ☐   over 60   ☐

1.3   At what age did you leave full-time education?
      still in education   ☐   16 or younger   ☐
      17–19   ☐   20 or older   ☐

1.4   Occupation _____

1.5   Annual household income _____

1.6 We are perfectly happy for you to remain anonymous; but if you would like us to send you a free booklist of Idol books, please insert your name and address

_____

_____

_____

_____

SECTION TWO: ABOUT BUYING IDOL BOOKS

2.1 Where did you get this copy of *Dr Reynard's Experiment*?

Bought at chain book shop ☐
Bought at independent book shop ☐
Bought at supermarket ☐
Bought at book exchange or used book shop ☐
I borrowed it/found it ☐
My partner bought it ☐

2.2 How did you find out about Idol books?

I saw them in a shop ☐
I saw them advertised in a magazine ☐
I read about them in _____
Other _____

2.3 Please tick the following statements you agree with:

I would be less embarrassed about buying Idol books if the cover pictures were less explicit ☐
I think that in general the pictures on Idol books are about right ☐
I think Idol cover pictures should be as explicit as possible ☐

2.4 Would you read an Idol book in a public place – on a train for instance?

Yes ☐ No ☐

SECTION THREE: ABOUT THIS IDOL BOOK

3.1 Do you think the sex content in this book is:

Too much ☐ About right ☐
Not enough ☐

3.2 Do you think the writing style in this book is:
      Too unreal/escapist   ☐   About right   ☐
      Too down to earth   ☐

3.3 Do you think the story in this book is:
      Too complicated   ☐   About right   ☐
      Too boring/simple   ☐

3.4 Do you think the cover of this book is:
      Too explicit   ☐   About right   ☐
      Not explicit enough   ☐

Here's a space for any other comments:

SECTION FOUR: ABOUT OTHER IDOL BOOKS

4.1 How many Idol books have you read?

4.2 If more than one, which one did you prefer?

_____

4.3 Why?

SECTION FIVE: ABOUT YOUR IDEAL EROTIC NOVEL

We want to publish the books you want to read – so this is your chance to tell us exactly what your ideal erotic novel would be like.

5.1 Using a scale of 1 to 5 (1 = no interest at all, 5 = your ideal), please rate the following possible settings for an erotic novel:

      Roman / Ancient World   ☐
      Medieval / barbarian / sword 'n' sorcery   ☐
      Renaissance / Elizabethan / Restoration   ☐
      Victorian / Edwardian   ☐
      1920s & 1930s   ☐
      Present day   ☐
      Future / Science Fiction   ☐

5.2 Using the same scale of 1 to 5, please rate the following themes you may find in an erotic novel:

Bondage / fetishism ☐
Romantic love ☐
SM / corporal punishment ☐
Bisexuality ☐
Group sex ☐
Watersports ☐
Rent / sex for money ☐

5.3 Using the same scale of 1 to 5, please rate the following styles in which an erotic novel could be written:

Gritty realism, down to earth ☐
Set in real life but ignoring its more unpleasant aspects ☐
Escapist fantasy, but just about believable ☐
Complete escapism, totally unrealistic ☐

5.4 In a book that features power differentials or sexual initiation, would you prefer the writing to be from the viewpoint of the dominant / experienced or submissive / inexperienced characters:

Dominant / Experienced ☐
Submissive / Inexperienced ☐
Both ☐

5.5 We'd like to include characters close to your ideal lover. What characteristics would your ideal lover have? Tick as many as you want:

Dominant	☐	Caring	☐
Slim	☐	Rugged	☐
Extroverted	☐	Romantic	☐
Bisexual	☐	Old	☐
Working Class	☐	Intellectual	☐
Introverted	☐	Professional	☐
Submissive	☐	Pervy	☐
Cruel	☐	Ordinary	☐
Young	☐	Muscular	☐
Naïve	☐		

Anything else? _____

5.6 Is there one particular setting or subject matter that your ideal erotic novel would contain:

_____

5.7 As you'll have seen, we include safe-sex guidelines in every book. However, while our policy is always to show safe sex in stories with contemporary settings, we don't insist on safe-sex practices in stories with historical settings because it would be anachronistic. What, if anything, would you change about this policy?

_____

_____

SECTION SIX: LAST WORDS

6.1 What do you like best about Idol books?

_____

6.2 What do you most dislike about Idol books?

_____

6.3 In what way, if any, would you like to change Idol covers?

_____

6.4 Here's a space for any other comments:

_____

_____

_____

_____

Thanks for completing this questionnaire. Now either tear it out, or photocopy it, then put it in an envelope and send it to:

> **Idol**
> **FREEPOST**
> **London**
> **W10 5BR**

You don't need a stamp if you're in the UK, but you'll need one if you're posting from overseas.